Rachael Stewart adores conjuring up stories, from heartwarmingly romantic to wildly erotic. She's been writing since she could put pen to paper—as the stacks of scrawled-on pages in her loft will attest to. A Welsh lass at heart, she now lives in Yorkshire, with her very own hero and three awesome kids—and if she's not tapping out a story she's wrapped up in one or enjoying the great outdoors. Reach her on Facebook, Twitter @rach_b52, or at rachaelstewartauthor.com.

Being an author has always been **Therese Beharrie**'s dream. But it was only when the corporate world loomed during her final year at university that she realised how soon she wanted that dream to become a reality. So she got serious about her writing, and now she writes the kind of books she wants to see in the world, featuring people who look like her, for a living. When she's not writing she's spending time with her husband and dogs in Cape Town, South Africa. She admits that this is a perfect life, and is grateful for it.

Also by Rachael Stewart

Tempted by the Tycoon's Proposal

Billion-Dollar Matches collection

The Princess and the Rebel Billionaire
by Sophie Pembroke
Surprise Reunion with His Cinderella

And look out for the next book
Caribbean Nights with the Tycoon by Andrea Bolter
Available August 2021

Also by Therese Beharrie

Island Fling with the Tycoon
Her Twin Baby Secret
Marrying His Runaway Heiress
His Princess by Christmas

Discover more at millsandboon.co.uk.

SURPRISE REUNION WITH HIS CINDERELLA

RACHAEL STEWART

AWAKENED BY THE CEO'S KISS

THERESE BEHARRIE

MILLS & BOON

First Published in Great Britain 2021
by Mills & Boon, an imprint of HarperCollins*Publishers* Ltd,
1 London Bridge Street, London, SE1 9GF

www.harpercollins.co.uk

HarperCollins*Publishers*
1st Floor, Watermarque Building,
Ringsend Road, Dublin 4, Ireland

Special thanks and acknowledgement are given to Rachael Stewart
for her contribution to the Billion-Dollar Matches miniseries.

ISBN: 978-0-263-29984-7

07/21

MIX
Paper from
responsible sources
FSC C007454

This book is produced from independently certified FSC™ paper
to ensure responsible forest management.
For more information visit www.harpercollins.co.uk/green.

Printed and bound in Spain
by CPI, Barcelona

SURPRISE REUNION WITH HIS CINDERELLA

RACHAEL STEWART

MILLS & BOON

For you, Aunty Carolyn.

For always believing in me
and reading every book I've ever written, even when they were in my handwritten scrawl many moons ago!

Love always,

Rachael xx

PROLOGUE

JASMINE WRUNG HER hands together. 'I'm not sure this is a good idea, Freddie.'

'It needs to be done.'

'But now?'

Nervously she bit into her lip and reached for his hand, tugging him away from the doors that led into the manor's great hall.

The noise from the other side ebbed and flowed with music and chatter, the clinking of glasses, the sound of laughter. The Highgrove Boxing Day party was in full swing. Friends, relatives and staff all gathering to enjoy the centuries-old tradition of handing out gifts and enjoying the festivities.

'It's your parents' big day.' She tried again. 'They love this party.'

'*I* love this party.'

Freddie turned to look down at her, his foppish dark hair curling over his forehead and softening the sharp cut of his tux. Didn't matter that she'd known him for ever, her breath still caught as she took his handsome face, his dreamy blue eyes all alive with his excitement.

She loved him. Loved him too much to refuse him, but *this*?

She toyed with her sleeves, their bell shape the reason the dress had caught her eye in the charity shop window. Its medieval style fitted her petite frame perfectly, enhancing her subtle curves and gaining Freddie's wholehearted approval in the process. But now...now it just felt cheap and out of place.

'Everyone is here,' she whispered, her voice starting to fail her.

'Isn't that the point?' He combed his fingers through her hair, pressed his forehead to hers. 'Come on, Red. Isn't it time you got some fire to match your blazing hair?'

Was it? She chewed the corner of her mouth and tried to lose herself in his gaze, to let it work its magic. To warm her heart, ease her fear…

'I'm sick of them denying us, Red. I'm sick of the staff whispering about us. I'm sick of being made to feel like we're doing something wrong, like we should be ashamed. Doing it this way, they will have no choice but to acknowledge our relationship, to accept it. And we can look to the future, *our* future.'

A shiver trickled down her spine. Her mother was one of the staff. She too would witness what was about to happen. And she didn't want to make trouble for her. She'd been the Highgrove housekeeper for seventeen years. They'd employed her when others had passed her over for being a single mum with a one-year-old to provide for, so in a way Jasmine owed them too.

But Freddie was right, they'd tried to gain acceptance quietly and no one had taken them seriously. What choice did they have?

'I love you, Red.'

Her heart soared with his emphatic declaration, her love for him swamping all else as a smile broke through. 'I love you too, Freddie.'

'And it's time the world knew it, yes?'

She nodded and he lifted her left hand to his lips, kissed the tip of the diamond ring she should be used to wearing after six months. But tonight it felt heavy, weighed down by what they were about to do.

'I can't wait,' he whispered over the stone, his eyes catching hers as she took a courage-seeking breath.

She wished she could have his confidence, but then it was always this way. Freddie was the adventurous one, forever pushing her to come out of her shell. Though she wouldn't be able to hide behind him once they broke through those doors, hand in hand.

'Hey, you want to be Mrs Freddie Highgrove, right?'

He straightened, his eyes still hooked on hers, and she felt the colour bloom in her cheeks, the excited flutter in her heart—*Mrs Freddie Highgrove.*

'More than anything.'

He took both her hands in his and squeezed softly. 'Then trust me…'

CHAPTER ONE

JASMINE WALKER STARED out at the tropical paradise beyond the floating white drapes that framed her serene, picture-perfect view, and clutched both hands to her fluttering stomach.

It was just nerves.

Nerves she should be able to deal with.

It wasn't as though her livelihood was on the line.

It wasn't as though she was heading into a critical investors' meeting.

And it wasn't as though she was standing before the stern face of Highgrove senior, having just been caught stealing from Maggie's tray of freshly baked goods. Or worse, standing outside the doors to their great hall preparing for Freddie to announce their engagement.

So why couldn't she get a handle on this?

And why on earth was she even thinking of the Highgroves now, and a ten-year-old memory at that?

She swallowed, closed her eyes and forced her hands to relax. She breathed in the soft fragrance of her room. Subtle and deceptively simple, its floral notes were designed to instil a sense of calm, something she could certainly do with now as her body tripped over itself.

You know why you're thinking of them—thinking of him—so quit kidding yourself...

She opened her eyes, and saw the answer in everything around her, everything she heard. The suite with its mix of wood, soft cream furnishings and colourful creole art. The private terrace with its king-sized thatched cabana and the infinity pool that dropped off into the endless turquoise sea beyond. The lulling sound of the waves and the native wildlife.

It was a secluded oasis designed for romance and relaxation. For lovers. For honeymooners…

Of all the places the M dating agency to the rich and famous could have sent her on this crazy, outrageous weeklong blind date, they had chosen here.

The Seychelles.

The one place Freddie Highgrove, her childhood friend, her teenage heartthrob, her one and only love, had promised to take her. And not just for a holiday, but for their honeymoon.

A bittersweet smile touched her lips and she dropped onto the plush mattress behind her, lay back and stared up at the netted roof to her four-poster bed.

Freddie. She breathed in his name and let it out with all the guilt, the remorse, the sadness. It was a lifetime ago, but she felt it all like yesterday. He was the reason every one of her relationships failed.

No one could stack up to the wild intensity of the naïve passion they'd shared.

The day their relationship had crossed over from friends to lovers had marked the start of a whirlwind affair that had seen Freddie proposing on her eighteenth birthday. The memory was so perfect and yet not, because it had heralded the beginning of the end.

She hadn't been good enough, and that version of her—the insecure, shy little wallflower—had run. She had loved Freddie too much to bear the rejection of his family or, worse, to see him rejecting them.

It was time to let that version of her go.

Only…she wasn't so sure that being matched by M was the answer.

Decisions made on nights out with your rowdy and far more adventurous girlfriends had a tendency to go a little pear-shaped. And of all those decisions, this was the most expensive and riskiest to date.

It was insane. One hundred thousand pounds and then some, insane.

As though her friends, Sadie and Izzy, could sense her rising doubts, her phone buzzed beside her. Sadie, the main instigator of this whole trip, had dropped a message into their group chat.

You there yet? Have you met him? What's he like? Please tell me he's hot. Like seriously hot!

She smiled, in spite of the continued butterflies and tapped in her reply.

Yes. No. Now, shh!

Sadie's response was instant, her fingers like lightning thanks to all the practice.

Then text in a timely fashion and I won't need to nag!

Jasmine shook her head.

Yes, Mum.

Then:

Have fun. xxxxx And don't do anything I wouldn't do!

'Yeah, right!' Jasmine laughed. 'From you, that means do everything and anything, Sades!'

She tossed her phone aside and shook her head all the more. *This* was the kind of crazy thing Sadie would do. Not her.

'Not sensible, boring, workaholic, need-to-get-a-life Jasmine.'

She shuddered as she remembered those exact words spilling from Sadie's lips and Izzy's vigorous nod of agreement. But her friends were right. She did need to get a life outside work.

But now she was here…and so was he. Her 'perfect match' according to M. And of the hundreds and thousands of possible destinations, they were in the Seychelles.

She'd asked for somewhere hot. She'd asked for somewhere without too much digital interference—she should have specified no mobile phone signal on top of it and then she wouldn't have to cope with friend inference either.

Truth was, she'd wanted a holiday, a break from it all, but *the Seychelles…*

She swallowed again, pushing the resurfacing Freddie from her mind and her heart.

It was no good being stuck in the past. This was about the future, *her* future. And if M said they had her match, then she owed it to them and to her bank balance to make the most of it.

Plus, Sadie and Izzy would never let her live it down if she bailed.

Her mobile buzzed with a new message and she sat up, taking it with her. It was Izzy.

Hope you had a good journey! Now enjoy and keep us posted! xx PS Sades, back off! ;-*

Jasmine grinned and started to type a response but a rap at the door sent her stomach somersaulting and her fingers stilled over her phone screen.

Another rap. 'Miss Walker, it's Monique, I'm here to take you to dinner.'

Oh, God. She shot up off the bed, wiped her hot and

clammy hands on the little black dress she'd chosen and sucked in another breath. If she kept taking breaths like this she'd faint from an overdose of oxygen.

'Miss Walker, are you there? Your perfect match awaits!'

Perfect match. Another gulp and she clutched a hand to the locket that she wore, the locket that contained a photo of her late mother. *She who dares, wins,* came her mother's voice.

'Coming,' she blurted.

Taking one last scan of her serene room, her safe haven for the week, she told herself how perfect it was. That no matter who her date was, this week was a holiday and she hadn't had one of those in a long time.

She walked to the door, pulling it open to see the petite woman who had shown her to her room earlier. She was lovely. Deep brown skin, warm conker-brown eyes and a big smile.

'Thank you for coming to get me.'

'It's my pleasure. If you'd like to follow me... Tonight you are dining at the lighthouse.'

She offered her a smile over her shoulder, and Jasmine tried to return it, trapping the squeak-like hum that threatened to erupt.

She tried to focus instead on what she was seeing, the raw wooden floor, the soothing cream walls, the colourful artwork and the various plants, all much the same as her suite. Monique herself was the picture of sunshine, her button-down dress a lemon-yellow, her hair pulled back from her face by a floral band, and her white slip-on shoes flat and quiet as she walked. Jasmine's gold heels, on the other hand, click-clacked with a deafening resonance, her dress feeling too clingy and cloying.

Or was it more that her senses were in tingling overdrive as she fretted over the person she was about to meet?

It had taken M months to find him—*months!* She'd almost forgotten she'd signed up for the service when the email had pinged to say they had her match… Okay, so she'd *tried* to forget but, still, here she was…with him.

Just him.

On an entire island that was theirs for the duration. Rosalie Island. It even sounded romantic. The only other people here were the Golden Key resort staff, on hand to cater to their every whim…

At least her match had been properly vetted. A properly vetted man couldn't turn out to be some axe-wielding serial killer. A possibility she'd thrown at Sadie and Izzy who'd both just rolled their eyes and blamed the crazy notion on her overactive imagination. They had then reminded her of the ridiculous sum each client had to pay up front and suggested that at least he would be a very *rich* axe murder who didn't need to feast off her wealth.

But who exactly *was* her perfect match? She certainly didn't know, and there was a part of her curious to find out.

Only one man had ever come close to perfect…

'Freddie. Freddie. Freddie.'

Both Sadie and Izzy were in her head again, rolling their eyes dramatically.

'Forget about Freddie!'

And they were right. She could not—*would* not—compare her match to him like she had every other partner she'd been involved with over the years. She had to stop.

The love one felt as a teenager, that first love—the lust, the heat, the newness of it all—made it intense. It had the power to sweep you off your feet. But she was an adult now, she didn't need a fairy tale.

And waiting for her at the lighthouse was a man who could potentially be 'the one'.

But therein lay the rub.

She had zero expectation that they'd found him.

In fact, Jasmine Walker was convinced 'the one' just wasn't out there…

Or he was…but she ruined her chance with that particular man a long, long time ago.

What are you doing?

Freddie Highgrove let his gaze drift from the pretty white brick lighthouse to the impressive vista beyond. With the sun hanging low in the sky it cast everything it touched in a warm amber glow. The endless sea, the luscious vegetation, the white sand beach with its rolling granite boulders breaking into the water. It was all so very easy on the eye and he tried to feel nothing. Nothing at all.

But the grip he had over his chilled glass mimicked the tight hold around his heart and both told him otherwise.

There was only one woman he'd ever intended to travel here with.

Jasmine Walker. The one that had got away. The one that had *run* away, even.

The moment the pilot of the private jet arranged by the M dating agency had announced their destination, he should have ordered them to stay grounded and let him make his exit. Quick, sharp, painless.

Instead, he was waiting on the arrival of said date with a bitter taste in his mouth and no amount of the island's chilled finest could see it off.

It was his own sorry fault too. Not M's.

When Madison Morgan, the owner and very much the heart of M, had asked *'When I say romance, what location do you think of first?'* he should have ducked it. Not said the first thing that had come into his dim-witted brain.

He gave a brutal laugh, the sound as harsh as it had been when she'd posed the question.

The Seychelles.

He could have said Paris, Rome—anywhere else—but no.

And why? Because of her. Jasmine.

Ten years and he couldn't rid himself of the woman. And she hadn't even been a woman then, not really. They'd been teenagers counting on a future so rosy it made him feel sick to think of it now. Sick and foolish.

He rubbed his freshly shaven jaw and tilted his head back to the setting sun. Now there wasn't a romantic bone left in his body, he had no interest. No interest in a date of M's choosing, or a marriage of convenience designed to elevate his illustrious family's reputation.

So, what on earth was he doing here?

His lips quirked. He knew what he was doing, all right. He was delaying the inevitable, putting off his Scottish parents' wish that he marry into the English aristocracy by convincing them he was finding his own 'rich' and 'suitably entitled' wife.

He ran a finger through the collar of his black polo shirt, the fabric, though breathable, felt too thick and heavy as he wished he was anywhere but here. Anywhere but about to sit down with some unsuspecting woman who through no fault of her own could never be the one for him. Regardless of what M may think.

Truth was, what heart he'd possessed had left with Jasmine ten years ago. And try as they might, his parents were going to be sorely disappointed if they were depending on his marriage to enhance their place in the world. As for grandkids, more lairds-in-waiting, it wasn't happening.

Ten years ago—*yes*. It was all he'd wanted. Marriage. Kids. A family home filled with love and warmth. He would have taken that over his family's wealth and status any day. But Jasmine had bailed on him.

Fifteen years of friendship. A year as lovers. A ring on

her finger. And it hadn't been enough to make her stay and fight.

His hand pulsed around his glass and he threw back the chilled liquid, not tasting a drop. He wouldn't be that fool again.

'Mr Highgrove?'

He turned at Monique's voice, forcing a smile, and—

No.

He had to be seeing things.

It wasn't.

It couldn't be.

'May I present Miss—'

'Jas!' It choked out of him. This had to be some kind of sick and twisted joke.

The Jasmine lookalike gasped, her hand flying to her mouth, her eyes—those eyes that had haunted his dreams, his nightmares too—wide. *'Freddie?'*

Monique frowned. 'You two…' she looked at Jasmine, looked at him '…know each other?'

He couldn't respond. He felt like every grain of sand on the beach had made its way into his lungs, his chest, his body. He couldn't breathe.

Monique cleared her throat. 'It seems I needn't introduce you after all.' She clasped her hands together, her eyes dancing in the golden light. 'How clever M has been on this occasion! Do please take a seat, Miss Walker.' She gestured to Jasmine's chair like the tension weighing heavy in the air didn't exist. How could she not feel it? He couldn't even move for it and neither could Jasmine. Her mouth was still agape, her pallor obvious in spite of her make-up and the warm glow of the evening.

'I shall pour the champagne,' Monique said as Jasmine stayed stock-still.

'No.'

Both women jumped and Monique's eyes narrowed on him. The 'no' had come from him… *Oh, this wasn't good.*

'Excuse me, sir?'

'What I mean is…' He softened his voice, working hard to relax his posture, but his heart was pounding, his pulse beating wild at the sight of Jasmine. His first glimpse in ten years, and it wasn't just a glimpse, *she* was his date! 'I will pour it.'

'Of course.' If Monique still considered his behaviour odd, she made no show of it as she beamed. 'I will leave you to get reacquainted and bring your starters out when they are ready.'

She walked away, her whispered words carrying on the breeze. 'Well, well, well, this has to be a first.'

A first he could have done without...

'Take a seat, Jas.' He waved his empty hand at her chair before pulling out his own. 'I won't bite.'

He couldn't look at her as he said it, though. He was in shock. Utter shock.

'Did you set this up?' she whispered.

A laugh erupted through his chest, his eyes soaring to hers. 'Are you serious?'

She was. He could see it in the accusatory glint to her brilliant green eyes, her glossy pink lips pursed.

This couldn't be real.

Only it was…

'Do you honestly think that of all the women in the world I would choose to bring you here?'

As intended, his words stung. He watched with forced satisfaction as her eyes flared and her throat bobbed. That beautiful slender throat in that petite little frame that had hardly grown in the time they'd been apart.

Compared to his six feet one, was she still only five feet three?

He remembered the day he'd measured her, pressed up

against the wall of the kitchen in Highgrove Manor. Her refusing to believe that he was almost a foot taller than her, him proving a point, while enjoying every inch of her body trapped against his.

He breathed past the sudden rush of tension, the lustful hit the silly little memory sparked, and dragged his eyes from the alluring green of hers.

'No, Jas.' Like it needed stating in clearer terms. 'I did not set this up.'

He reached for the champagne and poured two glasses, the gentle fizz of the drink as it bubbled up in the glass more pronounced for the silence now stretching between them.

And still she hadn't moved.

He rested the bottle back in the ice and looked at her. Her blazing red hair was cut into a long, smooth bob that smacked of both sophistication and maturity. The black dress she wore clung to her curves and ended just above her knee with the smallest of front slits, and a pair of gold heels that gave her an added inch or two.

Classic. Smart. Disturbingly stunning.

And aside from her obvious shock, there was a confidence about her, an unfamiliar poise that made him shift in his seat.

'I take it from the persistent shock on your face that you didn't set this up either?'

'How could I possibly…?' She shook her head, her arms folding around her middle in a protective gesture that dug beneath his skin, wounding as much as it angered. It wasn't him that had broken her heart. It wasn't her that needed the protection.

And neither do you...you're older and wiser and know better.

'No.' She wet her lips. 'I didn't set this up.'

'In that case, why don't you sit, and we'll offer up a toast to this cruel twist of fate.'

She eyed him, wary and silent. Long, drawn-out moments when he thought she might turn and run—*again*.

But finally she stepped towards him, her scent carrying on a sudden breeze, and his chest spasmed.

How can she still smell the same?

He raised a hand to his face, a barrier to her scent as he masked it with his own and watched her lower herself into the chair opposite. He didn't want to feast on the sight of her up close, of the flames from the firepit in the centre of the viewing platform flickering in her eyes, dancing over her skin and making her hair even more vibrant.

He sought distraction in the drinks he'd poured and took up hers, offering it to her. He realised his mistake the second her delicate fingers brushed against his. Their eyes collided and for the briefest of moments time fell away. They were in the Highgrove guest house, the fire roaring, a diamond ring fresh on her finger, champagne in hand.

He gritted his teeth and retreated back into his chair, taking his drink with him.

'To us.' He raised his glass to her, the vulnerability in her eyes holding him captive, and inwardly winced. He could practically feel her reaching inside his soul and stamping all over it anew.

'To…' She swallowed and wet her cupid's-bow lips. 'To us.'

CHAPTER TWO

THE CHAMPAGNE STUCK in Jasmine's throat as she lost herself in the sight of him.

Freddie. *Her* Freddie. The man whose heart she had broken, shattering her own in the process.

She'd been convinced he was a figment of her imagination. With the sun setting at his back, she'd tried to convince herself it wasn't him. That it couldn't be.

But it had been a sixth sense, a growing awareness that the man standing there, waiting for her, his smile as frozen as his body, was him.

She cleared her throat, swallowed with a gulp that she prayed wasn't audible and lost herself in the dark glittering gaze that was so familiar and yet not. Those blue eyes that had once sparkled with such humour, such love, such passion…now they were almost black, the flames from the firepit playing in their brooding depths.

She shuddered as the flutter in her stomach returned tenfold and she covered it with her palm.

'Cold, Jas?'

She shook her head, words refusing to form.

'I don't think I've ever known you to be lost for words, not in my presence at any rate.' His eyes narrowed on her. 'There was a time when you had plenty to say.'

His soft-spoken observation was all the more powerful for the past it recalled and the frostiness in the air that no amount of paradise could warm.

'It's just…it's a shock. It's been…' She broke off. She had the awful feeling her champagne was about to make a reappearance.

'Ten years,' he supplied for her. 'Ten years in December.'

She lowered her lashes, raised her glass to her lips and took a larger sip. If a small amount was threatening to return, maybe a larger amount would weigh itself down. And she needed the Dutch courage.

She felt eighteen again. Insecure. Out of place. Unworthy.

But she was none of those things any more. And, boy, did she need the timely reminder.

'How have you been, Freddie?' She forced her eyes back to his as she acknowledged just how much he'd changed too.

He wasn't the tall, athletic man of his youth. He was broad, sculpted, his voice deeper. His black hair, no longer foppishly long, was trimmed, tailored to fit his new persona—sharp, empowered, all man—and she shivered anew. He demanded attention, dominated her vision, made her feel things she'd long given up hope of feeling again.

He leaned back in his seat and rested his elbow on the arm of his chair as he ran his index finger over his lips. She tried not to watch, tried not to take in the fullness of that bottom lip, or feel the tingling sensation it sent through her body.

'I'm good. Very good.' His mouth lifted to the side, not quite a smile, his stare intense as he watched her. 'No need to ask how you are, I can see that well enough for myself.'

'Still…' Her hand trembled over her stomach and she lifted it to her hair, sweeping it back behind her ear as she raised her chin to him. 'It would be polite to ask.'

'Polite?' He surprised her with another laugh and leaned forward in his seat. Planting his elbows on the table, he steepled his fingers and rested his chin on them, his eyes pinning her in place.

'So, Jasmine…' He was too close now, much too close. His aftershave—expensive, masculine, woody—reached her and her nostrils flared, panic lifting the hairs at her nape. 'How the devil are you?'

The question reverberated down her spine as her heart tried to clamber up and out of her throat. She didn't like how he said it, his Scottish high-born inflection colliding with an American twang and making him so far removed from the boy she once knew.

But then he wasn't the boy trying to be a man any more, the boy so willing to reject his family for her, offering to run away and make a new life with her.

No.

He had his own wealth now, his own life across the Pond, and everything about him spoke of that new existence, of that independence and liberation. But his eyes… His eyes still showed the broken heart she'd left him with and it was that which held her tongue-tied.

Did he still hate her after all this time?

She hated herself enough for walking away. But she couldn't bear facing his hatred too.

'I think this is a mistake.' She started to rise. 'I'm sorry you've paid good money for this…*this*…'

Her hand flapped about, words failing her.

'Date?' He looked up at her, his eyes glinting, his mouth twitching. Was he laughing at her?

'Yes.' She tried to detach herself from the cocktail of emotion fogging up her brain. 'I'll contact M and see if something can be done.'

'Why?'

'Because you can't want to spend this week with me.'

'Why?'

She blew out a flustered breath, felt her cheeks heat with a combination of shame, panic, hurt, even anger that he would make her put words to it. 'You know why.'

She stepped away from the table.

'Running away again, Jas?'

She stilled. It was a low blow. But there was something

in his voice that made her pulse trip over itself, and not entirely with anger.

She wanted to stay. She wanted to show him that she wasn't the same person that left him ten years ago. She wanted to show him the person she had become. Confident. Successful. Worthy.

It no longer mattered what the Highgroves thought of her. Freddie included.

Yeah, like you really mean that...

'No.' She ignored the inner scorn. 'If you really must know, Freddie, I'm trying to salvage what we can of this week. Maybe M has another date in reserve for you, someone she can send out to accompany you so the week's not a total waste of your time and money, and I'll leave.'

Someone more accustomed to champagne and fine dining and the demands of a family as high-born as his own. Because it didn't matter that she had become a woman of standing. In their eyes she would never be worthy. She would always be the help's daughter.

'And what if I said I don't want someone else?'

Her eyes lifted to his. Her heart stuttered in her chest. He couldn't mean it.

But try as she might, she couldn't read his expression.

He looked serious, but his posture was far too relaxed to be genuine as he leaned back in his chair.

Or at least that was how she'd like to interpret it.

'Don't look so shocked.'

She shook her head, her laugh high-pitched as she eyed the view instead. The sun was almost gone, a sliver of bright amber radiating out across the waves, the sky, its soft hue so golden and warm. But she was cold. Chilled to the bone. 'You can't want to spend this week with me,' she repeated.

'On that you're very much mistaken.'

She met his gaze, confusion and apprehension making her frown. She couldn't deny the bubble of excitement, too, that against her better judgement she was getting carried away with the meaning behind his words.

'To be completely honest, Jas, now that you're here, I can't imagine anyone else I'd rather spend this week with.'

And, again, what on earth are you doing?

Maybe this question would hound him all week, because common sense, or rather his heart, told him to re-insert an ocean between them as soon as possible.

But then he hadn't been thinking clearly when he'd blurted it out. His only goal had been to avoid the alternative: her leaving and someone coming in her place.

Or, worse, her staying and him being replaced.

It was madness.

Ten years they'd gone without seeing one another. She could have married, had a thousand boyfriends, lovers, whatever and he shouldn't care. But now that she was here, in front of him, the idea of her being with anyone else…

And it was just a week. One week.

Seven days with the woman his parents had so cruelly rejected was an interesting twist of fate.

Seven days with the woman who had so cruelly rejected him in turn was even more twisted.

But where he had once been weak, he was now strong and here before him was the opportunity to lay the ghosts of the past to rest and finally get her out of his system. Move on. It was a sound plan. And he always liked to have a plan.

'What do you say, Jas?'

'What do I say to what?'

The line between her brows deepened and she caught the corner of her lip in her teeth just like she used to when she was on edge. It made his chest ache even as he shut the emotion down for what it was—ridiculously sentimental.

'One week together. We can catch up, and then we can go our separate ways again.'

'You can't be serious?'

He raised his hand palm up and shrugged. 'I don't see why not.'

She continued to flounder, quiet and contemplative, and he forced himself to act as though he wasn't perturbed in the slightest. Not even a bit.

'After all, we always wanted to visit the Seychelles.'

Her eyes glistened, and his skin prickled, his chest quick to tighten. Was she going to cry?

He started to straighten, blinked once, and weak Jasmine was gone, replaced by a pale, stone-faced replica. He settled back once more. Better. This was better. *This* version he could cope with.

'That was a long time ago, Freddie.'

'Indeed. We've both grown up a lot since then...' He let his eyes travel over her, memories heating up his body, tightening up his core. Her chest lifted under his appraisal, the pulse in her throat fluttering as her cheeks coloured. They still had it. The spark. It arced between them just as readily as it had back then. 'It could even be quite...enjoyable.'

'Enjoyable?' She choked over it. Her eyes wild. Her laugh sudden. 'Are you crazy?'

'No, I'm not crazy, Jas.' He stared back at her, determined, hungry. 'I'm a man used to taking the opportunities life throws my way.'

'And you see me—*this*—as an opportunity?'

'Definitely.' His lips quirked. He wanted to laugh at her outright horror. Provoking her was something he could definitely enjoy. The potent mix of anger and lust had him feeling more alive than he had in years.

And now that he was over his shock, he couldn't think of a better way to spend the next seven days. A little reacquaintance, testing the chemistry that so obviously still fizzed and pulsed between them...

'Seven days getting to know one another again, each other's likes, dislikes…'

He let the suggestion hang in the air, ran his index finger beneath his lip and watched her eyes flit to the move, the heat so obvious in their depths. She was shaking her head, but the rest of her…

'You can't seriously hope to just pick up where we left off?' She lifted a hand to the gold locket she wore, clutched it to her chest. 'We were practically kids, Freddie, kids with naïve expectations of how life could be.'

'True. And now we're adults. Our eyes wide open to the wonders of the world and its harsh reality. In all honesty, I have no time or need for a relationship. Pleasure, on the other hand…'

Her sucked-in breath made him want to laugh all the more, laugh and kill off the rising heat deep within his gut. He was playing with fire and if he wasn't careful, he'd be the one burned. That was if she didn't take flight first…

'We hired M to find us a love match, Freddie, a *relationship*! *You paid* for that. Not for a week of…of…' She gesticulated, looking so deliciously flustered he had the urge to grab one flapping hand and tug her onto his lap, to seal her parted lips with his.

Would she still taste the same?

'Sex, Jas. You can say it.'

She clamped her mouth shut, clutched the locket tighter. He wondered whether it housed a photo. And if so, whose…?

'May I remind you…' he lifted his eyes back to hers, halting his thoughts, which were getting too personal '…you also paid for a love match.'

Her nose flared with her breath. 'Only because my friends wouldn't leave me well alone.'

Now he laughed, until it hit him that her confession

relieved him far too much. 'In that case, it's definitely a win-win.'

She pressed her lips together and her eyes started to dance. Her shock and panic were dissipating, replaced with something that looked far more like amusement. 'You really are serious?'

'Always.'

Her lips started to curve up, her head shake became softer, one of wonder and possibility.

'And let's be honest, Jas, the way I see it, M hasn't really failed. Seems Madison Morgan is actually rather skilled.'

'But don't you want to see who else she has out there for you? Don't you—?'

'What I want...' He grimaced as her eyes widened and he realised his exasperation at life, his parents and their expectations had erupted with his interjection. He tried again. 'What I want is a week away from my interfering family. A week to forget the world exists outside these islands. A week to forget our past and just have fun, enjoy ourselves.'

He watched her frown ease, her hand lowering to her side as her eyes softened with what looked too much like compassion and he had to look away. He didn't want to *feel* around her, not in that way. He'd handed her the reins to his heart long ago, and he wouldn't do that again.

'Let's be clear,' he stated, wanting to avoid any potential misunderstanding. 'I had no intention of coming here for love, Jas. I was foolish enough to fall in love once and that was enough. This week was about putting my parents and their matchmaking schemes on the back burner for a while. Buying myself some time, so to speak.'

Her throat bobbed, realisation dawning and dousing the flush to her skin. 'Still so desperate to marry you off to a lady of status and means, are they?'

There was a tease to her voice, her words, but he wasn't blind to the fact she was trying to cover up a pain of old.

'Won't they always?'

Her lips parted, her shoulders lifting as she went to say something and stopped, her body deflating with her breath .

'What?' She was quiet. Too quiet, and he wanted to know. 'Jas?'

Maybe, for all she claimed to have been coaxed into signing up to M, deep down she did want to find herself a man. And since he'd so clearly stated that man wasn't him, he'd ultimately ruined her week.

He hated that it had the power to hurt him. That ten years on she could get to him as easily as she had then. And yet he didn't even know her now.

Not quite true...

He knew plenty from the internet. How she'd become a rising star in the world of tech. How her app had made her millions. How it had made her clients successful too. She was an industry icon with the kind of money that made M's price tag a drop in the ocean.

But money and power told him nothing of the woman beneath the accolades…and he wanted that knowledge. He wanted to get to know the woman she was now. And that need should have had him running, but instead he was pushing for more.

So much for keeping away from the personal…

'Unless, of course, you'd prefer I leave so that M can send you their next candidate?'

'No.' She came alive, dropping back into her seat and burying her head in her hands.

She shook her head, her glossy red bob hypnotic in the light of the fire.

'But this is crazy, surreal even. I mean…' She raised her head, her eyes spearing him. 'It's you, Freddie! You!'

'It is.' His smooth voice belied the chaos within, the swarm of emotions that he couldn't get a handle on.

'I still can't believe this is really happening.'

He took a sip from his glass, waited until he knew his voice was steady. 'You'd better believe it, Red.'

Red.

His nickname for her. He shouldn't have used it. Shouldn't have, but he'd done it anyway, the name flowing off his tongue as easily as breathing and causing the colour to creep into her cheeks, spreading beneath the freckles that he remembered so well. Freckles that covered her creamy skin, top to toe. Would there be more now?

'Don't,' she breathed.

'Don't want?'

'Don't look at me like that.' She reached for her drink, took a gulp.

'Look at you like what?' He feigned innocence but he could feel the hunger so blatant through his body that it was sure to be blazing in his eyes too.

'Like…' Another swallow. 'Like you possess that X-ray vision you so often spoke of.'

He chuckled, the sound so throaty and thick he hardly recognised it as his own.

'If I remember rightly, you often wore the same expression…'

Her eyes raked over his chest, their green depths dark and luscious and oh, so vivid as she appraised him.

'You're doing it now,' he murmured.

Her eyes collided with his. 'I blame you.'

'You hungry?'

Her lips parted, her cheeks flushing all the more. 'Freddie, I don't think this is a good idea.'

'Best not tell the chef…' His eyes flitted to the right, to where a smiling Monique was approaching. 'It would be a shame to tell Monique to turn around.'

'To tell…' She turned to follow his line of sight and instantly snapped back to him. 'You could have said!'

'I was having too much fun.'

CHAPTER THREE

SHE WAS TREADING a dangerous path. That much was obvious.

But could she walk away from him now?

No.

She knew the risks of what she was agreeing to. A week with him, like this. And with that look in his eye, she *knew* that he would want more from her than she could safely give.

Because he would never want her love, and she wasn't convinced she could give in to the lust heating the very air they breathed without falling deep.

But, then, who was to say she would love the man he was now? The man who still blamed her, hated her even, for what she'd done. The man who'd just declared he had no interest in love and labelled his younger self as foolish for having done so. This man's blue eyes didn't sparkle with easy teasing, or warm with love, or dance with happiness. There was an edge to his humour, a reservation to his remarks.

No, this man looked and behaved much more like his father. Cold and severe.

This man would hurt her as readily as he would take his first bite of the delicious meal being placed before them. She didn't doubt it for a second, so why was she still sitting here like some willing lamb off to the slaughter?

It was an impossible situation and as she eyed the exquisitely arranged dish and smiled up at Monique blankly, pretending to listen to what the woman was saying about the food, all she could really hear was the inner rant telling her to end it before it ended her. Extreme, but…

'Thank you, Monique,' Freddie said when Jasmine couldn't manage a word. 'This looks delicious.'

His eyes flicked to her and she smiled wider. 'Yes.' *Breathe!* 'Thank you.'

'Bon appétit.' Monique bowed her head and turned away, her muted footsteps loud in the sudden silence.

He picked up his cutlery and tucked in. All the while she watched him, his hum of appreciation filling her ears as she appreciated him. The masculine cut to his jaw as he moved the food around, his clean-shaven skin enhancing the dimple in his right cheek, the bob to his throat as he swallowed…

'You should try it,' he encouraged, so calm, so in control. 'It's delicious.'

She didn't think she'd be able to swallow anything past the swell of desire persisting irrespective of her fears, determined to torment her. And then it hit her: the spark she always attributed to being young and naïve, the power and intensity of one's first love—it wasn't down to that at all. It was him. Freddie.

He was the one who inspired those feelings in her, those feelings that no one else had come close to triggering. Not even Tim, her closest thing to an ex, and she'd almost married him.

'I meant what I said, Jasmine. I want us to make the most of this week. We're both cut off from the world and there's something to be said for having that kind of privacy, don't you agree?'

She considered his words, considered the way she felt inside. Reawakened. Hot. Wanton. As for her heart… She swallowed. Ten years she'd been haunted by their breakup. She'd not only lost her best friend, she'd lost the love of her life. Now they had a chance to make new memories, happier ones. A seven-day reset on ten years of pain.

She took up her glass, felt his eyes trace the movement as she sipped at her drink, forcing down the wedge in her throat, the panic and the thrill.

'Yes.' It was soft, barely audible. 'I agree.'

'So, let's make a pact.' He lifted his glass out to her, drawing her eyes to his, their magnetic sparkle sucking her in. Did it matter that it wasn't the same kind of sparkle? That there was an edge she couldn't dismiss? No. In fact, it helped keep this within the realms of reality, it would stop her getting carried away. 'We lay the ghosts of the past to rest and at the end of this week we go our separate ways. We move on.'

He made it sound so simple, but…

'Okay.' It caught in her throat, her tummy twisting in warning, but she smiled over it, gave a very definite nod.

His grin was worth every second of discomfort. The haunted look of Freddie that fateful Boxing Day ten years ago, when she'd walked away from him on the doorstep, was replaced for a split second by Freddie now. Pleased. Satisfied. Wanting her.

'You're on.' Smooth. Confident. Better. 'One week to forget it all. One week to just be.'

'Agreed.' His jaw pulsed, his eyes flashed, and he raised his glass to her. 'One week to just be.'

She clinked her glass to his and lost herself further in the intensity of his gaze. She took a sip of the champagne that sealed the deal and his eyes trailed lower. Following the journey of the chilled liquid as it glided down her throat, settling somewhere amongst the dizzying dance kicking off down low.

This was insane but she wasn't about to stop it.

For the first time in too long she was living for the now. Not for her business, not for her mum or her friends. Not even him.

Just her.

He couldn't take his eyes off her.

He was constantly noting what had changed, what was

the same. Her accent had mellowed, much like his own, the curse of conversing with anyone outside Scotland, or even Edinburgh for that matter.

Her oval face was sharper, her cheekbones more pronounced. He watched as she played with her food and wondered whether she ate properly at all. Did she look after herself? What had changed over the years to bring about such change?

And the truth was, he didn't just wonder, he worried.

But he shouldn't be worrying. He was here for a week with a beautiful woman, and she was that, no more…if he were to adhere to their pact and forget the past.

M truly had outdone themselves. He'd given them a list as long as his arm, a challenge he'd never expected them to meet. And he certainly hadn't expected them to throw his past back in his face.

He was intrigued. What was it about Jasmine now that made her his 'perfect match' according to M?

'Do you not like it?' He gestured to her plate, to the barely touched prawn tartare and its equally delicious kiwi guacamole.

Her eyes flittered to his, her cheeks flushing and making her eyes appear greener, brighter.

'It's lovely.'

She covered her lips with her fingers, their dusty pink tips perfectly manicured, not bitten as they had been all those years ago. This Jasmine was more refined and yet still possessed the blushes and the edgy mannerisms of her youth.

'I'm just…' She frowned even as her lips curved up. 'This whole thing…it's crazy, unbelievable…'

'You're saying the shock of it has stolen your appetite?'

'I'm saying I'm distracted by it.' She picked up her glass of wine, a chilled Sémillon chosen to complement the dish, and smiled softly. 'You have to admit, it's a little surreal.'

'You've said that already.'

Her smile grew as she swallowed a considerable gulp. 'And I'm still coming to terms with it.'

'Well, let's pick it apart.'

She frowned. 'Pick it apart?'

'Yes, work out what we said to M to make us so perfect for one another.'

He didn't like saying 'perfect' out loud, it gave the idea merit, the idea of a relationship again merit…

Never going to happen.

'Okay,' she drawled.

'You start.'

'Me?' She arched those perfectly shaped brows at him—again, another change. He wondered how often she had her appearance tended to these days. She never used to be quite so careful with such things. 'Why me?'

'It's polite to let the woman go first.'

She laughed, the sound rippling through him with its familiarity, its authenticity. She was relaxing into this meal and he was glad of it, even as he felt his own defences lower.

'I can't even remember half the stuff I said to Madison now.'

'No?' It was his turn to arch his brows. 'I don't believe you.'

She pursed her lips, the fire flickering gold in her green eyes and making him want to lean in closer. 'You just want me to feed your ego.'

'Ah…' He cleared his throat as the sound caught, stuck by the lust he couldn't dampen. 'Guilty as charged. I indeed have an ego that likes the occasional stroking.'

'Like it ever really needed it.'

History passed between them again, a charged stillness where the air crackled and the years evaporated. They were young and easy again, teasing one another, having fun.

Until they weren't.

'Okay.' Discreetly, he shook off the chill. 'I'll start. We're both from Edinburgh.'

She laughed again, the sound just as tantalising, just as addictive, and he wanted to coax out more—more smiles, more lightness.

'We're the same age,' she fired back.

'You're older.'

'Hardly.' She shifted in her seat, sat straighter. 'There's two months between us!'

And there was that laugh again. It made his body warm from the inside out, an experience he rarely, if ever, felt these days. Her laugh tapered off as her lashes lowered to where his fingers toyed with the base of his wine glass. 'I wanted someone skilled with their hands.'

The husky edge to her voice set his blood on fire and he gave a soft chuckle. 'How forward.'

Her eyes snapped to his. 'Not like that.'

His lips twitched. 'No?'

'No! I meant...you know, creative, arty. I like the thought that goes into bending over a canvas or a potter's wheel—'

'Or a workbench?'

'You still carve?'

A smile touched his lips. 'When I can. Not that I have much time for it these days. Still paint?'

She mimicked his smile. 'When I can. Like you, life has a habit of getting in the way.'

'Other hobbies?'

'I hike on the weekends, run in the week.'

'Me too.'

'You hike?' She looked surprised and quite rightly so.

'Less of the hiking, more of the running. I spend so much time sitting at a laptop or in meetings, getting fresh air when I can escape is important to me.'

'Me too.'

'You hated running when we were kids. You'd never come with me.'

She laughed. 'That's because back then you'd run on a Sunday morning when Maggie was doing her big baking session, and getting first dibs on her shortbread was far more important.'

'Aah, yes, so true.'

'Plus, it gave me some peace and quiet to read.'

He grinned. 'Still a romance lover?'

'Of course.'

'Still after your own happy ever after?'

Her hand stilled as she reached for her wine glass, her eyes hesitant. 'Isn't that why we're here?'

'No,' he bit out, his defences rebuilding so fast he felt something akin to whiplash. 'I've told you why I'm here. I have no intention of marrying and you claim you're here because of your friends, but there was a time…' He eyed her left hand, the finger that had once borne not only his ring but another man's. 'What happened between you and Tim?'

She straightened up, forgetting her wine entirely as she swallowed and eyed him carefully. 'Tim? How did you…?'

The warning bells chimed. He'd given far too much away. Revealing that he knew of her life after him revealed that he'd cared enough to find out. It was stupid, but he could hardly take it back. Seeing her announcement on social media, the happy couple with the hand bearing the ring on show, had been a turning point for him. A reason to look to the future and to accept that she would never be a part of it.

'I used to keep tabs on you.'

'You kept *tabs* on me?'

'What?' He shrugged. 'You never looked me up in this day and age where everyone's business is everybody's thanks to the wonder that is social media?'

'But you're not even on…' She broke off, her cheeks

flushing anew. 'Okay, so, yes, I did search for you. But other than the great strides you've made with your charity, your business, which I know has nothing to do with your family and everything to do with you, you're a mystery.'

'My sister more than makes up for my lack of presence in the media—social or otherwise. She's been adept at courting the media ever since she could talk.'

Her smile was slow but filled with affection now. It caught at him even as he acknowledged it wasn't directed at him but his sister.

'How is Ally?'

'Now *that* you must know already.'

She picked up her cutlery, tasted a morsel. 'I'm sure the media don't give the whole truth, though.'

'In this case, they've not gone far wrong. She's well, she's happy and she keeps them away from me, which is just the way I like it.'

Her smile was one of understanding. 'I read she was expecting her second child.'

'She is.'

'So, how does it feel, being an uncle?'

His chest warmed, masking the pang that lay beneath. He was happy for his sister, the marriage she'd been steered towards had been good for her—she'd found love and happiness and in turn had made their parents happy too. 'Much the same. Though it's had me coming home more.'

She seemed to struggle with the portion of food she had taken, swallowing and chasing it down with more wine. 'It has?'

'Yes.' He nodded, trying to understand her reaction. 'I always intended to return eventually.'

'Permanently?' It virtually squeaked out of her.

'Yes. I couldn't stay away for ever. My parents are getting older, the estate still needs managing and though Rupert does an excellent job, he too is getting on.'

'So…the prodigal son returns?'

'Something like that.'

She considered him for a long moment. 'Well, there's another tick in M's box.'

'How so?'

'Edinburgh. It's not just where we're from…' She placed her cutlery together on her plate, signifying she was done, and sat back in her seat, taking her wine with her. 'I take it you mentioned your intention to set up more of a base there in your talk with Madison?'

He frowned, thinking back over his conversation. 'I did. But I thought… Are you saying you live in Edinburgh now? I thought you moved away.'

'I did. I left to study at Warwick University, then moved to London, but my heart was always in Edinburgh. When Mum got sick…'

She stopped, her eyes glistening as she looked away and her hand went to her locket—her mum, that was who was inside it, he should have guessed. And now he felt like an insensitive buffoon for leading them down this path.

'I was sorry to learn of your mum's passing, Jas,' he said softly, hoping that she would believe him and take the apology for what it was, sincere and heartfelt, regardless of their history. 'I wanted to pay my respects and come to the funeral, but…well, by then you had Tim and had obviously moved on. I didn't want to tread on anyone's toes, or…' He waved a hand as words failed him.

'You should have come.'

Her ardent declaration surprised him. 'Why?'

'Mum would have liked it, she always thought highly of you.'

'That wasn't the impression she ever gave me.' He frowned. 'Or you.'

'She just wanted her only child to be happy. She wanted to protect me.'

'And she didn't feel I could do that? I would have done everything in my power to make you happy. Protected you, doted on you, loved you.' He could feel his voice vibrate with vehemence, but this was ancient history, he shouldn't care as deeply as he so obviously did. It shook him up just as much as it so obviously did her. Her eyes were wide, her body still.

'I know you would have,' she said quietly. 'But it wasn't about you, it was about the situation we were in.'

'It was about my family.' He threw it at her, condemning her, because it didn't matter that her reasons had centred on *his* family. At the end of the day *she* was the one who had walked. She was the one who hadn't had faith in him to make it work.

Ten years it had been, and he remembered it like yesterday. The moment he'd turned to her in the great hall, the glass of champagne clutched so tightly in his hand he'd been surprised it hadn't snapped.

'I can't do this, Freddie,' she had pleaded, avoiding the eyes of his disapproving parents beside him, her hand squeezing his as she'd tried to tug him out of centre stage.

'At least one of you is talking sense, son,' his father had said, uncaring of their audience as his mother had given a high-pitched laugh.

'Yes, dear, you can be so fantastical at times.'

'Fantastical,' he had thrown back at them. 'I'm being nothing of the sort. We're in love and we're getting married, whether you like it or not.'

'Quieten down,' his father had warned through gritted teeth, forcing a smile as he'd waved down their growing audience. 'Do you really want to turn this family into a laughingstock?'

His mother had turned to his father then, her hand gentle on his chest. 'Easy, Alan…'

'Freddie.' Jasmine had tugged on his hand. 'Freddie!'

He'd seen Jasmine's mother amongst the stunned audience, her face ashen, her panicked, fearful eyes on her daughter. How could she not have known that he would love Jasmine for the rest of his days?

He'd smiled then, determined to show them all as he'd raised his glass to the room. 'Ladies and gentlemen, may I introduce you to—' Her hand had slipped from his, killing off his words. She was running away, pushing through the people, her body and head shaking.

'Jas!' He'd run after her, through the double doors, the hall, out into the night.

He'd caught up with her on the stone entrance steps. Fairy lights had adorned the trees and the topiary cones, the festive warmth all the more jarring for her—she'd been ghostlike, her harried breath billowing in the frosty night air as she'd spun to face him.

'Just let me go, Freddie,' she'd begged. 'This will never work. You belong here, I don't. Listen to your parents, they're right.'

'No, Red.' He'd tried to reach for her, but she'd backed away, tugging his ring from her finger, and when he'd refused to take it, she'd placed it on the ground between them.

'I won't give up on us,' he'd told her.

'You have to.' She'd stared up at him, green eyes wide. 'I can't do this, it's over.'

'I think you'd best leave her.' Jasmine's mother had appeared, her hand soft on his shoulder, and he'd gaped at her, his head shaking.

'But I love her.'

'I can't love you, Freddie,' Jas had thrown at him. 'I can't.'

'But you do!'

She hadn't answered, only turned away and run, her mother hot on her tail. She hadn't given him a chance to talk her round, to hold her, to reassure her.

'Freddie?' Jasmine reached across the table, jarring him back to the present and the stinging sensation in his tightly clenched fist as she covered it with her palm. 'It doesn't help, raking over old ground.'

'No, it doesn't.' He unclenched his hand and pulled it away from her, flexing his fingers to ease the damage his nails had done, not to mention her touch… 'Your mother was the final straw, though. She took you away, she helped convince you I wasn't good enough.'

'No.' She shook her head, her lonely hand going to her wine glass instead, and he wondered if it was her way of hiding how his physical withdrawal hurt. He hoped so.

'All my mother did was tell me everything I already knew. That your family were powerful, influential, and they had their hopes pinned on a high-profile marriage and no matter how much I loved you, I would never be good enough in their eyes. In the eyes of their peers. And that, eventually, it would wear me down.'

'And I would have picked you right back up again.' Why was he even fighting this out now? It didn't matter. It didn't change anything.

'It wasn't that simple, and you know it. You love your family and I couldn't bear to come between you.'

'That was for me to decide, not you.' And there he went again, fighting her on something that should be ancient history. Only now they were together again, airing an age-old argument they'd never had the opportunity to have.

She dragged in a breath, the mood at the table turning dark, haunted by the past, shaken up by the future and the possibility of seven days without the outside world interfering.

'I don't want to argue about this.' She set her wine glass down again, crossed her arms.

'Neither do I.'

'You were the one who said to forget the past, to focus

on this week and forget everything else. And yet here we are, focusing on the past.'

Movement off to the right caught his eye. Monique was returning and he sent her a smile before looking back to Jasmine.

'You're right.' She was. And yet still the questions burned through him, demanding answers, demanding closure after so many years. 'Saved by the next course.'

She turned to smile at Monique, her eyes lighting up her face and sucking the very breath from him.

He should have taken the option to jump when she'd given it. Because one thing was for sure, he wasn't as over the past as he'd like to be and what that meant for the next seven days, he didn't know…

But there was no avoiding it. He wasn't running like she once had.

CHAPTER FOUR

'SO, YOU LIVE in Edinburgh now?'

Freddie waited for Monique to leave before asking the question and the bubble of relief Jasmine had felt at moving on from the past burst. Because Edinburgh was their past. And her future.

His, too, it now seemed.

She nodded as her stomach turned over and she looked at her plate. The arrangement of food seemed too pretty to eat, she only wished she had the appetite to fully appreciate it.

Living in the same city. No ocean separating them. It was too close. Much too close.

She scooped up some potato confit and popped it in her mouth, her eyes returning to his, and she realised he was waiting for her to expand on the nod. She swallowed, the smooth, creamy potato going down like a boulder.

'I lived with Mum quite a bit towards the end,' she admitted, pain mixing in with the unease. 'And afterwards, when Tim and I split up, I moved back permanently.'

He was concentrating on his plate, dicing up his food. 'He was one of your lecturers at university, wasn't he?'

She dropped her cutlery with a clatter and his eyes lifted to hers with a frown.

'Sorry, I didn't mean it in a negative way.'

'Then why say it at all?' she threw at him. She'd hated that judgement back then and she hated it all the more coming from him now.

'I was…making conversation.'

'Would you like me to quiz you on your exes?'

'Hey, I'm sorry.' He lowered his cutlery and gave her

his full attention. 'I didn't mean to upset you. I was just stating a fact.'

'Yes, well, it wasn't like that.' She couldn't calm her voice, or her pulse that raced with the frustrating need to explain herself—she didn't owe him an explanation, yet there she was giving it anyway. 'We didn't date until I graduated. He—he was involved in the launch of my company. He believed in me, gave me the confidence to go after my dreams, helped me secure funding. He was a good man.'

'He was twice your age.' His jaw twitched and she got the impression he was as annoyed with himself for saying it as she was hearing it.

'*And?* We cared for one another, we shared the same interests, and he was passionate about my business venture.'

'As well he should be…' His eyes softened, his mood changing so swiftly she was caught off guard. 'It was a great idea, Jas. Aspirational. Innovative. It had such potential and, of course, it succeeded. I mean, look at you now. I don't know much about your business in recent years, but it's clearly doing well if you can afford the services of M.'

Her chest bloomed with pride, her mouth twitching into a smile she wasn't quite ready to give.

'Yes, it's doing well.'

'So, what happened with Tim?'

'*Seriously*, Freddie?'

'What?' His eyes widened into hers. 'You can't blame me for being curious. The last I knew you were engaged and I…' He shrugged. 'I stopped looking.'

He stopped looking...

She let the confession swirl around her brain, around her heart, her quick-fire anger dissipating in an instant.

'Why were you looking?'

'You really need to ask me that?'

'Okay, why did you *stop* looking?'

'And I repeat, you really need to ask me that?'

He looked away and reached for his glass, but she could see the haunted look in his eyes, could see his answer even if he wouldn't put words to it.

'Tim and I broke up because…'

She stopped. How could she tell him the truth? That on her sick bed her mother had told her not to go through with the marriage, told her it wasn't true love, not like the love that she had shared with Freddie. That if Jasmine searched her heart well enough, she'd know it too. That she was sorry she hadn't backed them all those years ago…

No, she couldn't tell him that.

He sipped at his wine, watched her over the rim of the glass. 'You broke up because…?'

'Because he felt I was married to my job.' It was close enough to the truth.

His lips quirked, his eyes suddenly shone. 'Now, on that I'll raise my glass to you, because there we are one and the same.'

'You too?'

'Haven't I already said I don't have time for a relationship? It wasn't some throwaway remark, it's something that's been proved many times over by the women I date. They get needy, I cut the ties.'

'How very caring of you.'

'Quit the judgement, Jas. I'm always honest and open, maybe brutal at times, but it's as much for their benefit as it is mine.'

'And you're happy living like that?'

'What? Single?'

'Alone?' It sounded sad coming from her lips. It *felt* sad. It didn't matter that she too had proved over the years that her job came first. That anything serious demanded time she couldn't give. Or was it more that she hadn't *wanted* to give that time? That her mother had been right to think true love would have encouraged her to find that balance?

That Freddie would have.

'It's the only way I know how to be.'

His honest declaration sliced through her thoughts, chilling her through. Freddie, alone. It wasn't him. Not the Freddie she'd grown up with, surrounded by his family, her. She wet her lips, started to say something but he got there first.

'So, you broke off the engagement?'

She bristled. She didn't want the focus back on her, but she didn't want the rush of guilt either, the feeling that she was the reason he now stood alone…

'It must have been hard,' he pressed. 'You were together a while.'

'Tim knew it was coming,' she rolled on, trying to shrug it off. 'We'd grown comfortable with one another. We still loved each other, but it was the kind you share with a best friend, not a husband.'

'We were best friends once.'

Her heart pulsed in her chest. 'We were lovers too, Freddie.'

A small smile touched his lips. 'I'll take that as a compliment.'

A compliment?

She frowned as his smile lifted off to one side, his brows rising, and his meaning hit home: he was more of a lover than Tim had ever been.

'All right, Casanova…' she laughed in spite of herself '…get back in your box.'

He laughed too, his eyes drifting to the ocean.

A silence descended, more marked for the laughter that had preceded it. He was lost in the view—and the past, she was sure—and she dreaded whatever was coming next. She searched for something to fill the quiet, anything to get there first…

'So, has there been anyone since?'

She started as he struck at the same nerve, his eyes coming back to her.

'Are we really doing this? Going over our exes?'

He shrugged. 'Why not?'

Because it was the last thing she wanted to discuss.

She didn't want to know about the women that had warmed his bed over the years.

There were sure to be many. A man who looked like Freddie, with his confident and charming aura, would never be short of a willing companion.

'Because it's in the past, remember?'

'I'm just curious. Past aside, it's hard to date in general, but when you have money, it's a different challenge altogether. Wouldn't you agree?'

'Aw, don't tell me little Freddie Highgrove is worried women want him for his money rather than his dashing good looks…' She was trying to deflect, to tease, but instead she'd given more away than she'd intended.

'So, you still think I'm dashing?' His dark smile was dangerous to her libido and she tried not to look at him—tried and failed.

'That wasn't what I meant…' But the blush to her cheeks was confirmation enough and she cursed the colour of her hair for making her so transparent.

'You have to admit money is a problem,' he pressed. 'It's part of the reason M is so successful.'

'True.'

'So, has there?'

She shook her head, exasperated. '*No*, Freddie, as it happens, there's been no one I would call serious. Not since Tim.'

'No one at all?' She didn't like the surprise and disbelief in his wide and far too alluring blue eyes.

'Not everyone needs someone to fill their bed, Freddie. Judging by your reaction, you're not one of those people.'

'Having your bed warmed, as you so put it, is different from a serious relationship, and I'm all for the former.'

She wasn't sure which irked her more. The acknowledgement that Freddie's bed had been well and truly warmed over the years, or his affirmation to stay single. One told her she was jealous, the other told her that a small part of her hoped for an impossible future together.

Both were utterly ridiculous.

She stabbed at her food with gusto, her eyes burning into the plate. Why should it bother her? Any of it? He'd stopped being hers long ago. She shouldn't care. And she hardly had time for a real relationship herself. Didn't the breakdown of her engagement with Tim prove that?

But the fire still blazing inside simply mocked her, his dry chuckle provoking it.

She glared at him. 'What's so funny?'

'You.'

Her breath gusted out of her. There were no words. None at all.

'I may not live the life of a monk…' he took up his cutlery, releasing her from his far too astute and disturbing gaze '…but I never pretend to be after more.'

'Well, bully for you!' She forgot about her food, her appetite going on, off, on, off with their conversation. 'Did you tell Madison you were only looking for a bit of fun?'

His lips twitched with contained laughter as he met her eye for a beat. 'I was honest enough. Now eat. You look like you could do with it.'

His eyes flicked over her again, and this time it wasn't with the raw hunger she'd spied there previously, or with teasing, or anger, it was…concern.

She prickled. 'Don't you start.'

'What?'

'Telling me to eat. My friends get at me enough, I don't need it from you too.'

He gave a small shrug. 'There must be something in it if they're saying it.'

'I've already told you, I run, I exercise, and I am busy. I eat as and when I can. Satisfied?'

She knew she was overreacting, her anger coming from the confusing mess inside. The last thing she needed was for him to send her mixed messages. The one that said they could enjoy seven days and go their separate ways again was fine. It was simple, clear, she knew where she stood.

The one looking at her with concern softening his gaze and making her tummy flutter was not fine.

This one suggested he cared. It confused things, and confusion could only open her heart up to trouble.

'Fair enough.' He didn't quite meet her eyes this time. 'I guess you no longer have easy access to Maggie's baked goodies either.'

She got the distinct impression he hadn't wanted to say it, but it had come out anyway. There was a sadness, a distance to both his voice and eyes.

'No.' She studied his face, desperate to understand where his head had suddenly gone. 'How is Maggie? Does she still cook for your parents?'

'She does.' He took a bite of his food, chewed it. 'She's as much a part of Highgrove as the building itself.'

'She certainly made the place smell heavenly and if I'm honest…' his eyes lifted to hers and she almost kept the rest locked inside, but '…I miss her hugs as much as her shortbread.'

He gave her a small smile. 'I think she'd say the same about you.'

'Except I'm a lousy cook, so cuddles would be her lot.'

The smile was still there, but his eyes were lost in his thoughts, and she opened her mouth to ask for them, but he cleared his throat and looked back at his plate, the moment and the pleasant memories evaporating.

'Anyway, tell me more about your app. What sparked the idea?'

It took a while for her brain to catch up with his rapid switch in focus but her company, her app, were things she could talk about in her sleep and she followed his lead, her smile coming with her words. 'It was actually Mum that gave me the idea.'

Not just Mum, but herself and Freddie too—their inequality due to their start in life—but she wasn't about to tread over that ground again. She hurried on, 'I realised that Mum had an eye for business but not for technology. And, of course, every business needs a web presence in this day and age, and it can be quite a barrier to entry.'

'Indeed.' He was listening intently, and she found she liked it. Liked it a little too much. 'It's a necessary evil in some cases.'

'And it's not just about getting the web presence, but maintaining and updating it, keeping it simple to use. Then there's the financial aspects, billing, accounts and so on. I built an app that would give people like my mum access to all this in one place. Not only does it manage the operational side of things, it gives them a face on the web, a means of advertising their services to garner new clients as well as advertising for vacancies too.'

'Work Made Simple—it's a catchy name too.'

He really had read up on her…

'Again, Mum.' She smiled all the more as she remembered that particular brainstorming session.

'My parents missed her when she left, you know.'

She took a shaky breath, her fingers fluttering over her locket. 'I'm sorry for that.'

'Why are you sorry?'

'Why do you think?'

'It wasn't your…well, all right, but we all had a hand in it.'

She swallowed. So much for steering clear of their past again.

'Anyway, Mum built up a business that contracted out skilled housekeepers, maids, she even had a few butlers on her books by the time…the time…' Her voice cracked and she tried to hurry on, eager not to break down, eager not to feel the pain. 'And then one of those butlers took over the business. It's still doing well now. He's my longest-running client.'

'That's good.' He held her gaze, and she couldn't breathe for the compassion she could see in his. 'I meant what I said, Jas. She was a good woman. I'm sorry I wasn't there.'

She tried to wave down his sympathy, tried to swallow back the tears and the pain tightening up her throat. And then his hand was there, taking hers, which she was still waving between them.

His fingers, warm and reassuring, pulsed around hers. 'I am sorry.'

She gave him weak smile. 'I know.'

She took a slow breath as she pulled her fingers away from his grasp, the physical connection too tempting to maintain, and took up her cutlery. 'Now we should definitely eat, or this will be stone cold.'

'Of course.' His voice was husky, his eyes still on her. She had the sense there was more he wanted to say, more he wanted to do even, but then he followed her lead.

They kept to safer topics for the rest of the meal, both of them skirting around the past that was never far from rearing up again. The food was delicious, the wines chosen to accompany each of the five courses perfect too. But the more she drank, the more she could feel herself getting lost in his eyes, the more she *wanted* to get lost in those eyes.

'You okay, Jas?'

'Hmm?'

'You're sporting that glow.'

She shook her head, felt the lighthouse spin around her. 'That glow?'

He reached out, his palm soft and warm on her cheek. *Wow, so nice.*

'The one you used to get when you'd had one too many Bacardi Breezers.'

Oh, no. He was right. She wasn't used to drinking. And they'd had a glass with every course, plus the champagne, and that made…that made how many glasses?

'Come on, I'll walk you back to your room.'

'How do you know where my room is?'

'I was given the grand tour before your arrival.'

'Oh…'

He stood and walked around the table, offering his hand to her. She eyed it, wary and wanting to take it all the same. It had felt nice, too nice, to have him hold her hand earlier. The same again when he'd touched her cheek, offering comfort. And now…

She looked up into his face, her smile weak with the runaway thoughts inside her. She slipped her hand into his and lowered her lashes, trying to hide the way the contact made her feel. There was no hiding the flush to her cheeks, though, and she prayed he'd put it all down to the alcohol.

'Thank you.'

She let go as soon as she was standing, her cautious side still capable of taking the driving seat as she sought to put some distance between them. But it was no use. As they walked, they seemed to get closer and closer. She wasn't sure who was to blame. But as his scent wrapped around her, she felt her entire body thrum with awareness of his.

They reached the head of the steps down to the main house and then she felt his palm soft on her lower back, the light contact working right the way through her.

She didn't dare look up at him, just kept moving, focused

on putting one foot in front of the other as he kept his palm there, a connection she didn't want to break.

Her heart pounded in her ears, her breaths coming too fast and too loud. Surely he knew what he was doing to her? Surely he knew how much she wanted to turn into him and kiss him? Kiss him with an abandon she hadn't felt in…in for ever.

She barely noticed the beauty of the garden at night, the swaying palms, the flying fruit bats, the lizards in the undergrowth. She was wholly wrapped up in him and the realisation that she didn't want to go into her room alone.

'Well, we're here.'

'Hmm?'

He gestured to her door, his smile bemused, and she blushed—of course, they were here, she could see that for herself, only…

She looked up at him, her mouth feeling too dry to speak.

'Freddie…' It was barely audible and she wet her lips to try again, watched as his eyes fell to the movement, darkening with the same fire she could feel building inside.

'Yes, Red.'

A thrill rippled down her spine. 'I don't know what I want to say.'

She knew what she wanted to do, though, and her palms pressed into his chest, almost of their own volition.

'Red…' His muscles contracted beneath her touch, his warmth teasing into her as he bowed his head and she closed her eyes… *Oh, yes.*

But he bypassed her lips and as she opened her eyes, his cheek brushed ever so slightly against her heated flesh.

'It is good to see you again,' he whispered beside her ear as her breath caught. 'Sweet dreams.'

And then he was gone, the moment with it.

Had she imagined it? Had it all been in her head that he'd wanted to kiss her? Was he *teasing* her?

She watched him walk away, pleaded silently with him for one backward glance, just one…

Nothing.

Nothing at all.

And her heart felt it as fresh as it had ten years ago, only then it had been her doing the walking.

Was this to be her punishment now? To have him within reach for a week but his heart unattainable? Her own, on the other hand…

She clenched her fists together and turned away. She'd just have to make sure she remembered the score, remind herself of it at every opportunity. Freddie would never be hers again, no matter what her reawakened heart was trying to say otherwise.

And it was as it should be.

It had been hard enough to move on ten years ago. To fall in love now when he was so set against marriage, relationships even…

And she had a life in Edinburgh, a successful business that kept her occupied twenty-four seven. She didn't have time for a real relationship either, *Freddie dearest*.

She pushed open her bedroom door, ignoring the voices of Sadie and Izzy in her head, reminding her of why she'd needed M in the first place: to get a life.

A life was one thing. A life with Freddie was something else entirely, and he'd made it very clear it was not, neither would it ever be, an option.

And that was fine with her. She swung her door closed with finality. One hundred percent tickety-boo!

CHAPTER FIVE

'OH, NO, YOU'VE got to be kidding!'

Freddie looked up at the sound of Jasmine's groan and tried to ignore the way his heart lurched at her arrival. And the way the sight of her slight frame still nagged at him. Or was it just that he was so much broader and muscular now that she only *appeared* to be worryingly slender?

'What's wrong?'

Behind her fashionably large shades, she eyed the bicycles he was crouched over.

'Are we *really* doing this today?'

He straightened, chuckling even as he acknowledged how she'd shaken up his trusted composure, his entire life, by turning up here. 'Haven't you looked over the itinerary M prepared?'

'I did. I just...forgot.'

He rubbed the back of his head as he fought the way his body warmed, every degree nothing to do with the midday sun high in the clear blue sky and everything to do with her. 'Are you saying you don't want to cycle?'

'No—no, it's fine.'

She pressed her fingers to her temples and his eyes dipped to take in more of her. She'd swept some gloss over her pink lips. The freckles dusting her nose, her chest, her arms were more prominent in daylight. Her hair too gleamed as it swung freely over her shoulders. The emerald-green vest top she wore was tucked loosely into a pair of cropped white shorts that left too much of her legs on show, their toned and lightly freckled lengths teasing at him.

She blew out a breath and his eyes shot back to her face.

'Feeling a little delicate?'

She raised her chin, her eyes glaring at him, he was sure, and he cursed the tinted barrier between him and her green eyes. He'd missed them. Until last night, he hadn't realised just how much he'd missed them.

'Don't rib me.'

His mouth lifted to one side and he raised his hand, fighting back the urge to laugh. 'I wouldn't dare. It explains why I missed you at breakfast, though.'

Not that he'd *missed* her missed her, because that would be foolish.

Her brow wrinkled with her frown and she pocketed her hands, looking back towards the bright yellow bicycles.

'I wasn't hungry. And it was a long day of travelling yesterday. And sleep wasn't exactly…' She chewed the corner of her mouth and he wondered where her thoughts had gone. Were they with his somewhere in very non-platonic territory?

Or was she simply nervous? She always used to distract him with her mouth when she was nervous. Much like she had last night. Biting it, chewing it, drawing his attention…*eyes up!*

'Sleep wasn't really forthcoming.'

'Too much wine?' he managed to ask through the tightness in his throat.

'I said don't rib me!'

Her frown deepened and he had to bite back his grin. He did feel for her, especially as she'd paled over his mention of wine.

'Apologies.'

She pressed her palms to her cheeks and sucked in another breath, blew it out slowly.

'Right… I can do this,' she murmured against her hands, turning to scan the deserted pathway and gardens.

Almost every colour of the rainbow was covered in the island's vibrant vegetation and fauna, but there wasn't another human in sight. Her eyes came back to him—slow, unsure—her hands falling to her sides. 'Do we not have a guide for this little escapade? I really don't fancy getting lost in the wilderness.'

He laughed now. He couldn't help it, and it felt good. Different. Lighter without the shock hanging over them. 'You know this island is tiny, right?'

'And you know I can get lost in a shopping centre, right?'

He shook his head, his grin uncontainable. 'You can't still be as bad as all that?'

'Wanna bet?'

He laughed more. 'In that case, I'll lead the way, though…' He looked at her feet, at the dusty pink-tipped toes in the gold leather flip-flops, and felt a ridiculous tightening in his core. Was there anything about her that didn't seem alluring and dainty, calling to his protective instincts as surely as a wounded puppy would? 'You might want to change your footwear.'

She followed his line of sight, fluttered her toes. 'You've got a point. Just give me a wee minute.'

She turned and hurried back in the direction of her room, her behind far too tantalising in the flimsy shorts, and he wished he'd asked M to send them skiing. Not only to avoid the Seychelles but to gain extra layers, lots and lots of extra padding, anything to stop him lusting over her like some lovesick teen.

Like the lovesick teen he'd once been…

He threw his attention into making sure the bikes were solid, safe. Checked and checked again that the two cool bags Monique had given him, containing a picnic lunch, were still snug inside the baskets on the front of the bicycles. And waited.

True to her word, she was quick, swapping her sandals for a pair of trainers and a white cap.

'I'm all yours.'

No sooner had she said it than she coloured, her cheeks clashing with the colour of her hair, and he cleared his throat and tugged his sunglasses out of the chest pocket of his linen shirt. He shoved them on, gaining the same layer of protection to stop her reading him like an open book.

'You have sunscreen on?'

She planted her fists on her hips and tapped her foot. 'Yes, as it happens. Do *you*?'

He chuckled. 'Sorry, force of habit.'

The force of habit that always had him looking out for her, looking after her…but he wasn't so sure this Jas would ever need looking after. Oh, she suffered with the blushes still, but there was a fight to her, a confidence. And he liked it and hated that he liked it.

He kicked the stand up on her bicycle and the thing lurched forward.

'Easy, tiger.' She gave a laugh-cum-snort and he pretended not to notice the curious look she sent him.

'Climb on, the seat should be about right. If not…'

She gripped the handlebars, preparing to hook her leg over. 'This should be fun.'

She clearly didn't mean it.

'Not a fan of cycling?'

'I haven't been on a bike, not one of the non-static variety, since I was in my teens.'

Since they'd been together...

The thought came unbidden, the memories too. Of bike trails and picnics and exploring the grounds of Highgrove and further afield. Happy times. Easy.

He shot it all down and reached out to grip the centre of the bike handlebars, holding it steady for her. The move brought her close, so close that her scent drifted up to him, the power of it all the more forceful without the shock of last night.

Was it her perfume, her shampoo…?

He didn't know, but it was soft, floral with a hint of coconut, and his body stirred to life.

'You know what they say…' He cringed at the hoarseness to his voice. 'You never forget.'

She grumbled something incoherent but very definitely curse-like and he grinned, forgetting his discomfort. 'I can arrange for a buggy if you'd rather explore the island that way?'

'What, and give you the satisfaction of thinking I'm chicken?' She turned to him then, her smile so bright he was imprisoned by it, immobilised, and thanked the heavens that he still had his sunglasses on. 'No way.'

She hooked her leg over, her body forcing his away a little as she planted her feet either side of the bike, went up on tiptoe and nudged the seat with her bum. 'It's good, you can let go now.'

'You sure?'

She pursed her lips and raised her eyebrows above the rim of her shades.

'Okay.' He lifted his hands, palms out in surrender, and stepped back. 'Off you go then.'

She looked down, kicked a pedal into position, sending it too far, tried again and had it. She pushed off with a wobbly, 'I've got thi-i-i-s.'

He chuckled after her shaky form, too entertained to be ill at ease now.

'You sure you're okay?' he called after her, his grin unstoppable.

The front wheel was going this way and that, her movements stilted and awkward and so very funny.

'I'm fi-i-i-ne.' It undulated out of her as she kept her eyes fixed ahead, her balance steadily returning. 'Are you go-going to lead the way before I get us lo-o-st?'

'We're still on the premises, Red!'

'And?'

He laughed, his head shaking as he took hold of his own bike and kicked the stand up. He rode after her, realising the sooner he was in front of her, the sooner he wouldn't need to look at her because the sight of Jasmine riding a bike with all the balance of a toddler was as appealing as seeing her do something as sexy as a lap dance in next to nothing.

Not that she'd ever done such a thing for him, not that she would ever do such a thing in the future, but now that idea was firmly planted in his brain, he was struggling to think straight.

'You there, Freddie?'

He nodded himself out of his stupor. 'Undertaking on your left.'

'You what, on my…' Her bike veered left just as he came up alongside her and they juddered to a stop. He planted his feet and steadied his bike with his thighs, reaching out to grip her by the waist as he did so.

'Good Lord, Red! Please tell me you know your left from your right.'

Her cheeks flushed as she harrumphed up at him. '*Of course* I know my left from my right, I'm a world-class programmer!'

Not that he could see the relevance of that.

'You just…you just distracted me,' she blustered, her body swelling in his grasp with her sucked-in breath, and he knew he was no longer listening. He was too busy feeling her soft warmth beneath his palms, her breasts pushed up against him and those lips… She'd trapped her bottom lip in her teeth and it was calling to him, nagging at him to tease it from her bite and nip it with his own.

He swallowed back a groan, felt his control seeping through his fingers into her, gifting it to her like he had ten years ago…

'You can let me go now, Freddie.'

She sounded as breathless as he felt and he snapped his hands away, pushed off with his feet and led the way.

He should have looked over his shoulder to check she was following okay, but he couldn't trust himself not to throw the bike down and pull her into his arms. Kiss her like his body so desperately wanted him too.

And if it was just his body demanding it, he'd do just that. It wouldn't matter that it was a brief fling, a bit of fun, he would enjoy it and move on.

But she'd only been back in his life a night…one night, and already those feelings of old were returning. The need to be with her, the joy he found in her smile, in her laugh. All those feelings that pulsed too close to his heart, his heart that had barely survived her ten years ago.

How would he fare now? Ten years older. Ten years wiser. With a multitude of women since and none of them capable of sparking anything close to what she could.

'All right, all right, Freddie!' she called after him. 'You didn't tell me this was some kind of race.'

He grimaced and eased his speed, softly applying the brakes. His fight or flight instinct was clearly kicking in. He looked behind him to see her pedalling faster, steadier, her grin wide. Despite her admonishment, she was having fun. It shone around her in the sun, like an aura that called to him, sucking him in.

Fight or flight?

Right now, he knew which he would choose, and it wasn't the safe and sensible option.

'We *could* have a race.'

She laughed. 'Are you serious?'

'Absolutely.'

'Ever the competitive one, you haven't changed at all.'

'Neither have you.' The soft observation came out automatically and he knew it wasn't quite true. She had changed. And so had he. They'd both grown up, experienced the world, succeeded as far as their corporate dreams were concerned. As for their hearts…

Well, they wouldn't be here now if they'd succeeded there.

And now they were together again…

He shot the thought down as quickly as it sparked.

There would be no second chance.

This wasn't some fairy tale romance, this was reality. And the reality was he had no space in his life for a relationship, not any more. And even if he did, he couldn't trust her to stand by him in the face of his family, he couldn't trust her with his heart again, but he could let go for a week. They could have this time together. Make it as wild and as adventurous as they liked.

'First one to the gatehouse!' she called out, pedalling faster and overtaking him, flashing him an electric grin.

'You're on.'

This truly was paradise and, for whatever reason, they'd been gifted this time together and he wasn't going to waste it getting caught up in feelings he'd long ago shut down.

He was going to make the most of every last wild and adventurous second.

CHAPTER SIX

'I HAVE TO SAY, when I saw the bikes I did think less luxury holiday and more military boot camp,' Jasmine teased as she pressed her hand to her very full stomach and sighed. 'I was wrong.'

'Don't forget, we have a full body massage awaiting us this afternoon. You can see it as earning that little bit of luxury.'

She laughed softly. 'True. And I'm going to need the cycle back just to work off all that food.'

They were lying on a red-chequered picnic blanket under the shade of the gently swaying palms above and the pillowy softness of the white sand beneath. Impressive granite boulders of all shapes and sizes punctuated the coastline, creating a perfect secluded cove.

They truly were in their own private paradise, and what she would give to make things different between them. To rewind ten years…

A sharp squawk from the circling white birds above jarred her out of her reverie and Freddie caught her flinch, his mouth quirking to one side in a gesture that she was swiftly getting used to, her attraction to it much less so.

'Noisy, aren't they?' he said, his eyes on the birds.

'Very. Just like the seagulls back home…though I have to say these are slimmer, more angular.'

'I can't imagine these have ready access to fish and chips.'

She grinned. 'True. And I guess we are intruding on their paradise, they have every right to tell us to do one.'

'What, so they can get at the leftovers from our feast? See, not so different, after all.'

She laughed again and rolled her head to the side, eyeing the spread only half-finished between them. Crusty ciabatta, cheeses, pâtés, pickles and preserves, freshly prepared fruit, homemade nougat and fudge…

He chuckled, his head turning to the side too, his grin touching both corners of his mouth now and flashing his perfect white teeth, the cheeky dimple on the right that reminded her so much of the boy he'd been.

Her heart did a little skip and her eyes flicked to his. They were as blue as his shirt, as endless as the sea and the clear sky above. Their depths ever more captivating and ever more dangerous to her misbehaving body that wanted so desperately to act on his suggestion at dinner the previous night. His suggestion that they '*enjoy*' themselves, indulge in a week of pleasure…

She shivered with the recollection, bit her lip to stop the whimper that wanted to erupt.

He was much less severe today. His smiles were easier, his body less tense. The change as marked as night to day. But maybe that was it, maybe having the sun shining down on him had lifted the serious aura and made him more like Freddie…*her* Freddie.

And that wasn't a good thing. Freddie looking like his father, reminding her of his father, made it easier to keep some distance between them. But that distance had shrunk with the ease of the day, the fun on the trails, the beauty of their surroundings.

And now as she looked at him she wanted nothing more than to close the physical gap and kiss those lips that looked, oh, so familiar and yet not.

'Jas?'

Scratch the less severe. He looked pensive now. As pensive as she felt, his voice soft and laced with…*lust*?

But she didn't want to get her hopes up, not after last night when he'd left her hanging almost literally.

She looked at the sky, hiding from him. 'Hmm?'

He rolled onto his side, edging that little bit closer, and she kept her eyes up, her palms on her fluttering tummy. This could be it, the moment he would kiss her, the moment they would embark on their six-day fling…

'Do you want some more coconut water?'

She twisted to look at him, her eyes narrowing. 'No. No, I don't want more coconut water.'

I want you.

'Fair enough.' He grinned. Was he doing it on purpose? Drawing it out? Teasing her? Just like he had last night… 'Mind if I finish it?'

'No.' Crumbs, was she going to have to jump him? 'You knock yourself out.'

Her eyes flitted to his hand as he lifted the flask and poured out the remainder, her attention on his fingers, on those tanned lengths that she wanted roaming all over her skin. Old memories merged with new fantasies. He'd been a skilled lover before, thoughtful, attentive, what would he be like now? With all the experience, the added strength to his frame, those shoulders so broad and dominating, she could lose herself against him.

His chuckle pulled her sharply back into reality and she realised she was staring, her lips parted, an expression that could only be interpreted as longing on her face.

'You *sure* you don't want some?'

Eyes on the heavens again, she felt her cheeks burn. 'No, no, I'm good.'

He was still watching her, though. Even as he arched his head back, downing the drink and exposing the long, muscular length of his neck that looked, oh, so very appetising…and now she sounded like some blood-starved vampire!

Eyes to the heavens, Jas.

'That's so good.' He groaned. 'I'm sure it doesn't taste that way back home.'

'Where's home for you now?' she blurted out, desperate for some conversation to beat back her interfering libido. 'Until you return to Edinburgh, that is?'

He lay back on the blanket, his hands behind his head, and she breathed a little easier, even as the chill of disappointment ran through her.

'New York.'

'Will you miss it when you leave?'

He was quiet and she sneaked a peek. Deep in thought, his brows pinched together, he was really thinking about it. 'I don't have time to miss things.'

It was a strange way to put it. But then…didn't she get that? Hadn't Tim accused her of being married to her job, always being on edge when she wasn't at her laptop, tapping out a new programme, identifying opportunities, acting on them. Didn't her friends accuse her of it now?

A man was supposed to change that, but if she was honest with herself, would it really? Maybe she and Freddie had more in common now than ever. And maybe she should be taking his lead and accepting that a relationship, as ideal as it was on paper, just wasn't practical when all was said and done. Not when her heart now belonged to her business. Her business and Freddie from the past…

'If only we could find a way to create more of it.'

'Time?' He grinned at her. 'Your programming skills up to inventing a time machine yet?'

She laughed, a sense of ease building with the realisation that they weren't so different. That Freddie was right to keep it about the week, about the newfound ease they had found, and enjoy it. Not to get hung up on the future…

'I'll be back in New York often enough anyway,' he continued. 'My business and my charity HQ are there, that won't change.'

She thought of all he'd achieved over the last ten years. The amount of effort it must have taken to make something of himself, having broken away from his family. He hadn't taken his family's wealth and survived off it, he'd done his own thing, created his own investment company and his own charity from the ground up. He was as married to his work as she was and as her chest swelled with pride for him, she also acknowledged that he wasn't hers to be proud of any longer.

Her heart was less inclined to agree… But then it was okay to be proud of him, she could still respect him, admire him, *like* him even.

She could still…want him.

She took a steadying breath as her heart raced with her thoughts and silence stretched between them, broken only by the waves and the wildlife serenading them. A striking red bird fluttered down to peck at a fallen palm leaf an arm's reach away and she smiled.

The pace of life was so very different here, as was the kaleidoscope of colour. Cycling along the shady forest paths, spying all the wildlife going about their daily routines unfazed by the gentle whirring of their bicycle wheels, had been incredible. And they'd seen birds of all shapes and sizes, vibrant frogs, geckos…

'I almost feel like we're on a movie set,' she murmured.

A movie set where the man, at any moment, would seduce his willing companion…though there was nothing to say the woman couldn't make the first move.

'It's not called paradise for nothing.'

She sneaked a look at him, the way the muscles in his arm flexed as he rested his head on his hands.

'True,' she agreed softly. 'It's perfect.'

'As we always knew it would be.'

He looked at her, his eyes piercing straight through to the sudden pang in her chest, and she looked at the sky again, pulling her sunglasses back down. Thank heavens for oversized shades. She needed the shield just as much now as she had that morning when she'd finally accepted she couldn't hide out in her suite any longer and that she'd have to face him: Freddie. Her perfect match.

She could slap herself silly.

Of course, Madison Morgan and M had chosen Freddie. She'd virtually *asked* for him. His dark hair, his blue eyes, his Scottish roots, his sense of honour, duty, loyalty. His passion for others. His care. His charity efforts.

And had he done the same?

Subconsciously, had he listed all the attributes he'd once loved in her?

M wasn't one-sided, the match depended on the answers he'd given too. And if that was the case, then it didn't matter how married to their work they were, on paper they were as perfect now as—

'You've really made something of yourself, Jas.'

His husky compliment startled her into a choked 'Beg your pardon?'

'You really have.' He grinned in the face of her surprise. 'It's impressive.'

Her heart bloomed under his praise, his smile, pushing out the shock and the uneasy realisation that she cared about his opinion so very much.

'I could say the same about you.'

His brows pinched together. 'Really?'

'Of course,' she said, putting words to what she'd been thinking not minutes before. 'Your charity work is incredible. The strides you've made helping disadvantaged children pursue their dreams...it's something to be commended.'

He shrugged, the movement so dismissive, so small. Did he really not see it that way? And had he been doing the same as her for the past few minutes, thinking over the last ten years and what the other had been doing?

'It's *wonderful*, Freddie.' She said it softly but no less insistently. 'Truly wonderful.'

'I'm not sure I quite see it like that.'

She rose up onto her elbow, stared at him in disbelief. 'How would you see it?'

'My motives aren't so altruistic.' His eyes flicked to her, the slight and very out of place blush to his cheeks telling her he meant it. 'I'd love to say I did it entirely out of the goodness of my heart, but… I don't know, it's not that straightforward.'

'In what way?'

He was quiet for so long, lost in his thoughts, and she wondered if he would answer at all, but eventually he spoke.

'Sometimes I feel like I'm trying to right a wrong.'

She frowned. 'Why would you think that?'

'Because it's like I'm trying to offset my easy start in life. Offset it by ensuring those who don't have it so easy get the same chances.'

'*And?* That's admirable. It's not something you have to do, it's not your fault, it's not you righting a wrong that *you* have done. You're levelling the playing field of life and *that* is out of the goodness of your heart.'

'Maybe…'

'There's no maybe about it, Freddie.' She needed him to see the good he was doing, she needed him to be proud of it, pleased even.

But there was a strange look in his eyes as they came back to her. 'I can't say I'd be doing it if it wasn't for you.'

'Me?' Her surprise made it more of a gasp.

He nodded, his eyes darkening in their intensity. 'I'm sorry for how my parents treated you, I'm sorry they made you feel like you weren't worthy, I'm sorry they drove you away—'

'No, don't do that. Don't apologise for them.' She shook her head. 'It was me…it was me that left in the end. I just… I just couldn't bear it…'

Her heart was spiralling in her chest, her thoughts so jumbled she couldn't string them into a good enough sentence. The past just wouldn't stay in the past. And the truth was he was perfect just the way he was. The man that loved his family, was loyal to them. To break him away from them ten years ago would have broken that loyalty. It would have broken him.

'It doesn't matter what drove you to set up the charity, Freddie, what matters is that you did.' Her voice vibrated with the pain of old and her desperate need to convey her faith in the man he was now. 'You've helped so many people and have so many success stories under your belt. Your charity has produced sports stars, celebrities, artists, mathematicians, soon-to-be astronauts…'

His mouth twitched. 'You really have been reading up on me.'

Her laugh was soft. She didn't care that she was laying her heart bare just a little, confessing to the fact that she'd never let him go. It was more important that he listened to what she said, absorbed it, acknowledged it for what it was—the truth.

'Those kids stand in the limelight and praise you and your charity for helping them achieve their potential. You must know it in yourself. You must be proud.'

His eyes sparkled, but the shadow of doubt was still there, nagging at her heartstrings, tugging at her breath.

'Carry on like that and I'll be entering my room by the sliding doors at the rear just to get my head inside.'

She knew he was trying to lighten the mood, to take the focus off his accomplishments—to all intents and purposes dismiss them—and she wasn't having it. She touched her hand to his cheek, felt his warmth tease into her palm, felt his jaw flex, his body tense as she encouraged him to hold her eye.

It was the first time she'd touched him so intimately in ten years, ten *long* years, and it made her realise she wanted so much from him. Not just physically but emotionally. It should have scared her off. It should have had her running, but she wouldn't run again, not from him.

'You should be proud of it, Freddie.' She smoothed the pad of her thumb over his cheekbone, marvelling at the chiselled line, the hint of softness and strength. 'You should be pleased with all you've achieved and are continuing to achieve.'

'It's not that I'm not pleased, Red,' he said gruffly. 'And it's not that I'm not proud of the charity and all we've been able to accomplish. It's the lack of fulfilment. It's never enough.'

'But you're driven because you care, that doesn't just go away. There will always be people that need your help and that of the charity.'

'True. But it's the sense that something's missing, like an itch you just can't scratch.'

His eyes strayed over her face, the world around them seemed to slow down, even the noises around them faded.

'Ignore me,' he said softly. 'I'm making no sense.'

'No…' She wet her lips. 'I get it.'

And she did. She knew exactly what he was talking about.

He came up onto his elbow with her. 'You feel it too?'

'The sense that you're still searching for something to make you feel whole?'

He nodded and she returned the gesture, unable to speak, unable to breathe. The air shifted around them, the world falling away completely. He looked at her lips, a small smile playing about his own.

'Crazy, hey?' he murmured. 'Here we are in paradise, money no object, and still we feel unfulfilled.'

Her smile wavered. It wasn't so crazy, not when she thought about it. Not when she acknowledged that the last time she'd felt anywhere near content had been when she'd been in his arms.

But life had been simpler in so many ways then. She'd had Mum, she'd had time for him, she'd had a life…not that she could see a way back to that. Mum was gone now and she had responsibilities, people to help, a company to run…

She could feel him getting closer, or was she leaning in? Her eyes fell to his lips, the appealing fullness to the bottom one, the arch in the centre of the top one…

Yes, Freddie, please, Freddie...

He reached out and anticipation coursed through her, fizzing up her bloodstream, warming her body. His palm smoothed against her cheek, cupped her neck and she tilted her head back, her eyes closing. The first brush of his lips was electric, the sweet sensation all the more powerful for its brevity. A whimper caught in her throat and she leaned closer, seeking more. Another light brush, too delicate, not enough. She parted her lips, angled her head…

'Freddie…' It sighed out of her and she eased closer, let her tongue glide softly against his. *Oh, yes.* And then he was gone, his mouth replaced by his finger as he sealed her lips shut and her breath hitched anew.

'Shh,' he said softly as her eyes flicked open. 'There's a tortoise right behind you.'

Wait, what?

A gulp of air, of disappointment, of humiliation at her wanton state when he was so…*unaffected*?

And then she turned her head and saw just what he was referring to. A giant tortoise was right beside them, bigger than any she had ever seen before.

How had she not sensed it approach?

How? She mentally mocked. *You really need to ask yourself that?*

'He's an Aldabra tortoise.' Freddie was so close she could feel his breath sweep over the delicate skin of her nape, provoking her nerve-endings and the lust still beating fresh in her veins. 'And I'd say he's nearly as big as you.'

'He's incredible.' And he was. But he wasn't the reason she sounded so breathless. No, that was all Freddie.

Undaunted by their presence, the tortoise paused less than an arm's reach away, his neck straining as he reached ever so slowly for a leaf to munch on.

It was remarkable to watch up close. Like they'd jumped into a TV documentary and any second now the narrator would pipe up: *'And here we see the giant Aldabra tortoise of the Seychelles in its natural habitat and two unsuspecting tourists caught by surprise mid-clinch...'*

The amusing commentary and awe-inspiring sight should have beaten back the emotion swelling inside her, beaten it back and taken over.

Only it didn't...

She wanted Freddie, she wanted his kiss, his body, him...and no amount of paradisal wonder was going to distract her.

No amount of fear over where this was heading either.

CHAPTER SEVEN

Saved by a tortoise…

It was a new one for him.

But he'd most definitely been saved.

Because that kiss had been a nanosecond away from being way out of his control. Her trapped whimper, her eager response…and he'd been exposed. Raw under her heartfelt praise, lost in the shared sense of dissatisfaction, the acceptance that something was missing for both of them and the merest hint that this could be it.

This could be what they both needed.

Even now, hours later, it hounded him, and he'd been massaged until every limb felt loose. Jasmine too. The masseur and masseuse skilfully ensured every knot was banished as they'd lain beside one another on their separate beds in a cabana high on the granite clifftop. No privacy for more talk, more intimacy.

And it had been a glorious hour, perfect in every way. But no sooner had they stood, their matching bath robes back in place, and he'd looked at her, the high colour in her cheeks, the dreamlike state of those green eyes that he remembered so well, and he was coiled tight again.

They'd walked back to their separate wings in a comfortable silence, but he hadn't missed the way she'd looked at him from beneath her lashes, the smile playing about her lips giving away her thoughts. He'd come so close to pulling her to him and kissing away all sense.

But fear had kept him distant, fear over how much he wanted her.

He wasn't stupid, he'd been able to stay detached from women over the years because he'd never felt an inkling of what he'd felt for Jas. He'd stood alone and had been happy to do so. It had given him the focus he'd needed, the drive to succeed, to keep succeeding.

But this thing with her…it was swelling out of his control. She saw him for who he was, she saw beneath the cool façade, the businessman, the charity organiser. He'd *let* her see beneath it all, confessed his deepest worry, his honest motivation.

He cursed, his fists flexing at his sides.

He needed to keep it within his control if he was to keep his heart out of it, but as he looked towards the beach that was to be the setting for their evening meal and took in the romantic ambience of the scene, he knew he was in trouble.

Monique and her team had excelled themselves. With the sun dipping into the ocean, the scene was already cosy enough, but that was merely a backdrop to what they'd created.

He'd expected a table and chairs, some candles. Instead, there were oversized red cushions, plumped up next to the thick trunk of an aged palm and arranged into a U-shape big enough for the two of them to lounge on. Two copper oil torches were staked into the sand, their fiery glow complemented by tea lights scattered around the ground, their flames protected from the sea breeze by glass domes. A low table housed a copper bowl filled with ice, a bottle of water and champagne already nestled inside. Another table had a selection of glasses and appetisers ready to be devoured.

It was soft, inviting and above all romantic. The perfect scene in which to let go.

No more restraint.

His gut rolled as his flight instinct tried to kick in, telling him to run the other way because the lure of a second chance was getting stronger every second he spent in her company. The idea that maybe he didn't have to go it alone.

He blamed M for being far too good at what they did.

Tantalising him with hope, with the belief that this was a second chance. Some quirk of fate with the help of a very clever matchmaking team had brought them back together to make it possible.

But he couldn't believe in it.

He'd been that foolish once to believe in her, in an 'us', and it had ruined him, torn him apart, and it had taken years to let her go.

Correction, it had taken the sight of a ring on her finger to let her go.

But now that ring was long gone.

As was the physical distance between them.

They were very much together, in surroundings geared for a passionate love affair, and he was slowly losing the ability to distinguish between reality and a short-lived fantasy.

He'd been confident, cocky even, to suggest they let go for the time they were here. Put the past in the past and have a wild ride for seven days. Then go back to life as it had been.

Like it would be so easy, so simple.

He'd cursed his younger self for being a fool. What did it make him now as a man whose heartstrings were so readily tugged?

A blasted idiot. A sucker for punishment. An even more desperate fool. And how on earth could he possibly balance a future that was already rammed with his work, his charity pursuits and what would eventually be his inheritance—his title, the land, the Highgrove estate—and all that would demand of him, with the possibility of more?

He could never give Jasmine the attention she would deserve, justifiably demand even. He would be as bad as his father, as bad as—

'Freddie?'

He spun on the spot and lost the ability to breathe. There

she was. All he'd been missing for the last ten years as obvious as the feelings clambering back to the surface.

She looked incredible. Her burgundy knee-length dress, hanging from slender straps, twisted across her front, the style and silken surface accentuating every luscious curve. She wore the same locket as the night before and her skin shimmered with whatever product she had applied. As for her hair, it blazed in the setting sun, its kinky undone look softening the angles of her face and making the colour of her eyes all the more striking. The make-up she wore gave them a subtle cat-like slant and he wasn't sure if it was that or the true train of her thoughts that had her looking quite…predatory.

Heat spread through his core as her cheeks flushed pink and she nipped her lip, her fingers lifting to her locket.

She was *nervous*, not predatory. And he was all the things he'd accused himself of being—an idiot, a sucker, a fool!

'Jasmine.' He smiled, hid all of his panic, all of his worry behind it, because the one thing he knew for sure: there was no stopping this. In a week's time, when this was over, he would be free to worry about it as much as he liked…

He offered his hand and she slipped her fingers in his. 'You look amazing, Red.'

Her smile was small, her eyes trailing over him. *Now* she looked predatory and it stoked the fire that hadn't quite gone out.

'So do you…' And then she looked at the cushions, the candles, her free hand waving over the entire set-up as she sighed softly. 'And so does this.'

'You going to talk about it being like a movie set again?'

She laughed, walking with him as he led her to the cushions. 'Well, it is.'

'I prefer dreamlike.'

He released her hand as she lowered herself down, her

hands sinking into the pillowy softness either side of her as she leaned back and looked up at him. 'Why?'

Because dreamlike meant that he would wake up safe, unaffected, his life wouldn't have changed, his heart wouldn't...

He said nothing. In truth, breathing was proving difficult enough as he took in the sight of her reclined back, her legs curled to the side, a small slit in the dress revealing a tantalising glimpse of thigh, her creamy skin striking against the red of the pillows, her dress, her hair...

He wished he had a camera to capture the moment, to capture it and keep it...*and that was way too sentimental!*

'What is it?' She cocked her head to the side. 'Why are you looking at me like that?'

He tried to swallow past the dryness in his mouth and shook his head. 'You are stunning, it feels like this backdrop was made for you, made for your unique beauty, your smile, your eyes, your hair.'

Her brows pinched together. 'Have you been drinking already?'

He knew what he sounded like. He knew it because he felt it. Punch drunk. But not from alcohol. From her. All her. His Jasmine. His Red.

Only she wasn't his any more. She had ceased being his ten years ago and by her own choosing. He should be keeping that in mind, using it to protect himself now. Along with the knowledge that by their agreement she *was his*, for six more days, and every cloud...

'Can I not compliment my date when the mood takes me?'

She relaxed back, her smile enchanting. 'Well, when you put it like that...'

'Champagne?'

He needed something to do with his freed hands before he hunched down beside her and pulled her to him and whispered all the sweet nothings that were searing his brain, his heart. Each too loving, too real, and far from temporary.

'Please.'

He lifted the champagne out of the ice, throwing his concentration into unwrapping the foil.

'So-o-o,' she drawled, 'why a dream?'

He studied the metal holding the cork in place, started to unravel it as he gave her enough of the truth. 'Because a dream feels so very real, despite the fact it's temporary, that when you wake up it's over and there's no going back.'

He looked at her, his eyes delivering the message he needed to not only believe in himself but needed her to understand too. He gripped the cork and twisted the bottle. It released, its pop filling the silence that felt far too heavy thanks to his explanation. Silently, he cursed. He didn't want to ruin the moment. He wanted them focusing on what they had now.

'We can enjoy it while we're in it, though.' He smiled and placed the detritus on the table next to the glasses and took up a flute. 'I propose a toast...'

He filled the glass and offered it to her, forcing himself to hold her eye with confidence and positivity. She took it from him, her smile and eyes both curious.

'Another toast—are you incapable of drinking fizz without one?'

He knew she was referring to his toast the previous evening. How had he phrased it, a toast to their cruel twist of fate? He forced back the rising tide within him and poured a glass for himself. 'Are you objecting to another?'

'Not at all.'

'Good.' He placed the bottle back in its bed of ice and lifted his glass to her. 'To our dream.'

Her lashes fluttered, her eyes shone with...with sadness, and he felt winded.

'Our dream…' she whispered, shaking her hair out a little as she lifted her chin. 'And then we move on.'

'And then we move on,' he repeated.

Because moving on was the right thing to do. He clinked his glass to hers, threw back a gulp…but if it was so right, why did it feel so wrong?

She lowered her gaze, releasing him from its pull as she stroked the cushion beside her. 'Are you going to join me?'

He sat where her hand had been. Hunched forward, his elbows on his knees, his gaze lost in the bubbles rising in his glass, the gold of the drink enhanced by the flickering light of the lanterns and the tea lights.

'Do you wish it had been someone else M had matched you with?' She leaned towards him, her arm brushing against his, the directness of her question so unlike the Red of their youth. Younger Red would have shied away from it and he would have had to press and press until she'd had no choice but to give up the question that was on her mind. Not this Red, though. Not the one that had gained in confidence over the years and built a company from the ground up, a mover and shaker in the tech world, an entrepreneur with both brains and looks and who still had the very kind heart that he'd fallen for.

'I mean, I *know* you came without the true intent of finding love,' she carried on, unaware of the emotional rollercoaster underway inside him. Or maybe she was aware and pressed on anyway. 'But now that you know M is so good at what they do, wouldn't you have liked to meet the person they would have picked if I'd not been on their books?'

'No.' He didn't need to think about it. He turned to look at her, really look at her. 'It doesn't matter what my intent had been when I came here, I am happy to see you Jas. I'm more than happy. M couldn't have called it any better.'

A smile flickered on her lips. 'Your parents will have a hissy fit.'

He grimaced. 'Please, can we not talk about them?'

'You were the one that said this week away was to pacify them, convince them that you were hunting for an appropriate bride. If they find out that M threw me in your path…' She turned away, sipped at her champagne. 'What will you tell them?'

'The truth.'

Her head snapped round, her eyes wide. 'Are you serious?'

'Of course I am. I didn't care what they thought then, and I couldn't care less now.'

Her eyes blazed. 'Don't say that, Freddie. You *do* care, you *always* cared. And so you should. They're your mum and dad, they only want what's best for you.'

'And what *I* want is what's best for me. I told you that then, and I'm telling you again now.'

He watched her drag in a shaky breath, watched the emotions passing rapidly over her face, and he couldn't bear it any more. Having her so close and not…

He reached forward, his hand sinking into her hair as he held her close.

'And what I want right now, is you, Red.' He looked into her eyes and leaned in, any sign, any rejection and he would have stopped. 'I want you.'

She tilted her head back, her lips parting softly. 'You do?'

'I do.'

And then he was there, capturing her mouth with his, the contact lighting up his core. She tasted of champagne. Champagne and something else. Something that was all her. He groaned as he lost himself in it, heard her own little whimper through the blood pounding in his ears. She forked a hand through his hair and clung to him, deepening the kiss.

It was everything and not enough at once, the heat consuming him, driving him to want so much more, regardless of their surroundings and the champagne flutes still clutched in their hands.

He broke away, pressed his forehead to hers as he sucked in a breath.

'I want you, Red.' He was repeating himself, but he couldn't stop the words from tumbling out. 'Tell me that you want me too?'

'More than anything.' He saw the assurance in her eyes, heard it in her breathless words. He closed his eyes, let it sink in, felt its warmth surround his heart, fill his head. 'Tonight? Come back to my room after dinner?'

She nodded, bit into her lip.

'You will?'

'Yes, Freddie.'

He pulled back before he went too far, before his body took over and he took all that she was offering in her gaze. Because although they were cocooned by the line of palms and luscious vegetation, their sounds masked by the wildlife, he knew Monique and her team would be along to check on them shortly.

'Appetiser?' He reached out for the loaded tray and offered it to her, knowing full well nothing would beat the taste of her.

She picked one up, her eyes fixed on him and full of spark. 'I know what I'd rather be tasting…'

She parted her lips and slipped the delicacy inside, drawing the entire movement out, and he gritted his teeth against the lustful heat that threatened to have him throwing both the tray and his caution to the wind.

'You've become impatient in your old age.'

She swallowed, her smile one of absolute tease. 'Says you.'

He grinned. Red of old wouldn't have flirted with him

so brazenly either, but he found the confidence of her now even more tantalising than the veiled flirtation of before.

And it should have had the alarm bells ringing ever louder, ever clearer, only they were dull, drowned out by the thud of lust in his bloodstream and the all-consuming rush for her.

Jas. Jasmine. Red.

All her.

Now he wished Monique and her discreet staff would hurry up and disappear again because he wasn't so sure he wanted to wait until they got back to his room…

Red, lying back on the cushions, bare to the moon and his gaze, was far too tantalising an image to resist.

CHAPTER EIGHT

JASMINE *THOUGHT* THE food was delicious. It had to be. A place as exclusive as this wouldn't dare serve anything less, but…

She hardly tasted it. Everything about her was attuned to him. His scent, his presence, the sight of his throat bobbing as he swallowed, the muscles in his forearms flexing each time he reached across her…like he was doing right now.

He took up the bottle of dessert wine and offered to top up her glass.

She nodded, her voice disappearing with the moisture in her mouth. She wanted to kiss him again and the way his eyes kept connecting with hers it was clear she wasn't alone in her desire. His eyes were as dark as the night, projecting such fire, and her insides were molten with it, her limbs taut with growing need.

She sipped at the glass he'd refilled, but really she wanted to be sipping from his lips. The taste he'd given, the sampling of his mouth against hers had been far too brief and far too wicked. The slight graze of his tongue against hers, the way his body had trembled and her own had come alive… Now all she could do was press her thighs together to nurse the budding ache and wish away the rest of the food so she could feast on him.

'Are you no longer hungry?'

She gave a small smile, a shake of the head. If she'd still been high on their kiss, confident with it, she'd tell him exactly what she was hungry for.

'Not even for the last strawberry?' He picked it up and raised it between them.

Her smile grew. She didn't care how clichéd it was, whether he'd meant the offering innocently or not, she was using it to take what she truly wanted. Him.

She placed her glass down and leaned into him on one palm, her free hand coming up to gently clasp his wrist. She pulled him closer, held his eyes as she did so.

'Now, that's an offer I can't refuse.'

She surrounded the plump ripe fruit with her lips, purposefully brushing them against the tips of his fingers. She savoured the sensation, caught how his eyes flared and his lips parted. Her smile was one of both satisfaction and tease as she bit off a piece and devoured it. Freddie plus strawberry...a *true* taste explosion.

'Nice?' It rasped out of him, filled with the very lust she was struggling to keep at bay.

'Very.'

His grin was slow, his eyes heated as they watched her mouth. 'Would you like the rest of it?'

Her stomach clenched tightly as she nodded. There was only one way to get the rest... She surrounded his fingers with her lips and dragged her teeth along them, taking the sweet, ripe fruit with her. She pressed a kiss to his fingertips as her mouth closed around it.

'I think Monique and her team are long gone for the evening.' He was so very close now, his scent wrapping around her, engulfing her, drawing her in. 'What do you think?'

All she was thinking was how much she wanted him to kiss her...how much she wanted to kiss him...

She swallowed and subtly licked her lips. 'Yes, I think they're leaving us to it.'

He reached out, his fingers soft in her hair, caressing the sensitive skin of her scalp, and she smiled, her head rolling back into his touch. 'You always knew just how to touch me.'

She didn't care about the many wondrous and varied

ways he could take that statement, because every debauched one of them was true.

'Is that so?'

She hummed her agreement as he encouraged her closer.

'Care to elaborate?' he whispered against her mouth, anticipation making her entire body tremble.

She gave a soft laugh. 'The way you would toy with my hair…the way you would kiss my neck, my collarbone, my…' her breath hitched a little '…breasts.'

He inhaled sharply, his nose flaring. Her boldness had surprised him—*good.*

'What else?' he rasped.

She reached out to fork her hands through his hair. It was time to show him more of that boldness, more of the woman she was now.

'The way your fingers would play over my skin while your teeth would nip.' She brushed her nose very lightly against his, let her lashes fall. 'The way you kissed my lips like you wanted to reach every part of me, like you wanted to possess me, brand me…claim me.'

He growled low in his throat and tugged her to him, his lips crushing hers. Hard and demanding. Making up for the last ten years of absence and she was delirious on it. The force of it, the desperate pressure of his mouth, of hers.

She shifted her body closer, dragged him back with her as she dropped to the cushions, forcing him to cover her.

He shook his head, broke the kiss. 'I'll crush you…'

He tried to take his weight onto his elbows, and she tugged him back against her. 'You won't.' She wanted to feel all of him, top to toe. His hot, hard heat covering her own. 'I want you, *all* of you.'

'You have no idea how it feels to hear you say that.' Both his body and his words shook with his sincerity and hope fluttered alive deep inside her, the hope for a future, the kind of hope that could destroy her if she let it in.

She tried to stamp it out, to laugh it off. 'You've been working on your platitudes.'

'I've had years to perfect them.'

An icy shard pierced her heart, a stab of jealousy towards the faceless women over the years. She clutched at it like a life raft, used it keep her afloat and hope at bay. Threw her focus into his mouth, his body, his touch.

He traced hot kisses from her mouth to her ear, flicking her lobe with his tongue, scraping it with his teeth. 'How I missed you, Red.'

His words teased along her ear canal straight to her heart, straight to the hope she was trying so hard to suppress. That they could find a way to make it work, to be together and have all they had achieved…

She gripped his head closer, bit into her lip as his teeth nipped the sensitive pulse point at her throat, and she arched into him.

'I missed you too.' It rasped out of her, broken up by her desire, choked up by her fear. She hooked her legs around his, holding him to her. She never wanted to let him go.

He groaned as his straining erection pulsed against the very heart of her, delivering pressure to the small cluster of nerves begging for his touch, and she moved against him, desperate, her own cry telling him she needed more. His mouth was back on hers, fierce, eager. She rolled her hips, and he pressed against her, a rhythm that she dictated, working her desire to fever pitch and taking him right along with her.

He sucked in a ragged breath, lifted his head to look down into her eyes, his own filled with something akin to wonder. He looked so incredibly sexy. All mussed up by her hands, his cheeks streaked with colour.

'I want to taste all of you, Red. I want to remember every inch of you.' He rested his elbow into the pillow, gazing down at her as he stroked her hair back from her face. 'I want to learn what's changed and what has stayed the same.'

He lowered his hand to the locket around her neck, a sudden shadow falling over his features, and an overwhelming sadness clawed at her throat. No. She didn't want his focus there. On the past. On Mum. She didn't want to remember how he hadn't been there. How she hadn't been able to go to him. To lean on him. And, oh, how she'd wanted to.

'*Kiss me*, Freddie.' Her desperate plea called his attention back to her face. A second's hesitation and then he was there, kissing her with the same desperation she felt inside. The desperation to be rid of the past, the pain, to be consumed by the present.

She clawed at his shirt, raking it up his back, tugging until their kiss prevented it from going any further and he leaned back. She ripped it off, threw it aside before bringing her palms back against him. His chest contracted under her touch and she marvelled at his heat, his strength, both her fingers and eyes taking in every ridge as she clamped her bottom lip in her teeth. And then he was there, nudging her head back, replacing her teeth with his, a sharp tug. Punishing. Carnal.

'You're driving me crazy, Red.'

She raked her nails down his back in answer, arching her body and feeling his heat scorch her breasts through the light fabric of her dress. She wanted it gone, she wanted no more barriers between them, and even as she thought it, she knew it wasn't just the physical barriers she wanted gone. It was the wall around his heart—she wanted it to crumble just like her own, against all of her better judgement. She whimpered, both pleasure and pain forcing the noise to the surface, and he broke away from her lips, dragged kisses along her angled jaw, her arching neck and down further, his fingers easing beneath one skinny strap of her dress.

He slipped it over her shoulder, down her arm, the slowness of the move at odds with the dizzying caress of his tongue, his teeth. Goosebumps erupted over her skin, her nipples straining against her dress, no bra to impede the friction as he ran it lower. She held her breath, heat rushing to every extremity, and choked on a whimper as he exposed one tingling peak. She lowered her gaze, watched as he dropped a kiss to the curve of her breast, the edge of her nipple and then…

She hissed in a breath, bucked as his mouth surrounded her, taking her in deep. She clawed at his hair, cried to the heavens. He was ravenous, his tongue flicking over her, his teeth grazing, a crazy combination that had her writhing and begging and desperate for more.

Her cries clashed with those of the wildlife, the waves, his deep and hungry growl. He slipped his fingers beneath the other strap, faster this time as he lowered the fabric to her waist and reared up. His eyes, dark and carnal, seared her skin as they travelled her length.

She wanted to beg him, plead with him not to stop… She wriggled her hips, closed her thighs around his, telling him with her body what she wanted.

'Please, Freddie!'

'It's been ten years, Red, I'm not rushing this. Seeing you like this, your hair splayed out like a halo, your skin so creamy soft against the red of the pillows.' He dragged in a breath, his body straining above her. 'Let me have this.'

He fisted his hand in the skirt of her dress and gently tugged. 'Let me see you.'

'What if someone comes?'

'They won't. The beach is ours for the evening.'

'How can you know?'

'Trust me, I know.'

He was so certain, so sure, and she did trust him. She trusted him more than she knew was safe. But the time for reservations was long gone. She lifted her lower body, granting him permission to take her dress away, and then she was laid bare. Not just physically, her lace thong concealing nothing, but mentally. Her desires, her wants, her heart…it was all there in her face. There would be time for regrets later, much later…

She bit into her lip, wanted to cover her eyes like it would in some way help, but instead she clamped them shut.

'Red?' His voice was a husky plea. 'Look at me.'

Slowly, she did as he asked, felt the colour burning her cheeks in the face of his impassioned smile. 'You are beautiful, let me worship you like your body deserves.'

She knew he'd misread her hesitation and was thankful for it. She didn't want her emotions getting in the way of this. She wanted to forget them, and he had the power to take them away. Temporarily at least.

She reached out and stroked his cheek, nodded her willingness and brought his head down to hers, kissed him with all the passion still swirling inside. She tried to angle her breasts into his chest, desperate for more friction, and he pulled back.

'Patience.' He brought his hand between them to trace circles over her skin, teasing at her puckered nipples, her navel, the tip of her thong.

'Freddie…' Her body pulsed into him and his fingers answered her plea, dipping inside the lace, parting her to circle over where she ached the most. Her eyes flared open, caught his looking back at her intently, drinking in her every response.

He almost looked like he loved her. She could almost believe that he loved her. And her heart bloomed in her chest, the warmth spreading out from her core with the spiralling tension. She tried to reach between them, to take him in her hand, to give him the same pleasure he was so readily giving her, and he shook his head.

'No, Red.'

It was gruff, determined, and she hesitated, her frown telling him how she felt as she panted with her mounting climax. She wouldn't last much longer, and she wanted him with her. She wanted him inside her, but…

'I have no protection here,' he whispered, sensing her continued hesitation. He kissed her deeply, his fingers keeping up their dizzying caress.

'But I can still…' she said against his lips.

'There's no rush, we have all night, and right now I have other ideas and every one of them involves pleasuring you.'

Her entire body shuddered with the promise of it all, the wave of heat so strong it pushed her to the precipice.

'Freddie, I can't—I can't…' She clutched his body to her, her nails clawing into the taut muscles of his back, and she cried out into the night. She was gone, wave after wave racking her body as pleasure akin to that which he had delivered so many years before consumed her. And even then it hadn't felt as all-consuming as this.

He wrapped his arm beneath her, held her against him tightly until the rocking of her body dissipated and she was spent. He kissed her. So deeply and so thoroughly she thought she might expire from lack of oxygen.

But expiring like this…with Freddie so hard and desperate for her…was a fate she would readily face. Because she truly was in paradise, and paradise was where she wanted to stay…as long as he was by her side.

The bedroom spun, his heart pounded, and he knew panic was setting in. Because outside he'd given her his all, had felt her come apart under his touch, his kiss, and he was already addicted to it. The need to pleasure her, to please her, to make her cry out his name, again and again. To cling to him and not let go.

And now she was in his bed, naked and waiting. The

locket, glinting in the low light of the room as it nestled between her breasts, exactly where he wanted to be.

Only he wasn't. And why?

Because he was losing it. His control. His grip on reality. On what this was, and what it very much wasn't.

His entire body pulsed with his need for her. Ten years and he hadn't wanted a woman as much as he did her. And he feared that giving in to it would not only strip him of his restraint but his last barrier against her, that this would tip him over from what was safe, what was manageable, into so much more.

But it had been his idea that they do this. Let go for a week and walk away satisfied, the past laid to rest, the future no different.

He'd been a fool, a blind fool. He hadn't seen their connection for what it was, unstoppable, overpowering, impossible to resist. Barely twenty-four hours in, and he was as caught in her unique web as he'd ever been, unable to escape.

'Are you going to stand there all night?' She rolled onto her side, her palm smoothing over the space next to her, the space he should be filling.

'No.' He stalked towards her, breathed deep to get a handle on the heat within and lay down beside her. Took in her entirety stretched out beside him, her skin blushing from where he'd touched her, caressed her, kissed her… He reached out, his fingers gentle on her hip as he caressed the diamond-shaped scar there. Take it slow…just take it slow. 'I remember when you got this.'

She hooked her hands around his neck. 'Well, you should do, since you rescued me.'

'Hardly.'

'I could have been devoured by the Highgrove dogs if not for you.'

He grimaced as he pulled her naked body up against

his own, breathed in the fresh scent of her hair and let the memory take over, soothe his core, calm his pulse. 'Well, if you will go scaling walls in desperation to see your lover...'

She nudged her body against him. 'Well, if you will live in heavily guarded fortresses...'

Now he laughed, the sound hearty and earnest and erupting far more frequently than he was used to. His easy grin too. He couldn't remember the last time his cheeks had ached from it, like they did now.

He buried his head into her neck and she laughed, wriggling as the move tickled her sweet spot.

'I missed that sound too.' It was out before he could stop it. The sentiment, the meaning, and she stilled, her fingers soft in his hair.

'Make love to me, then.' She urged his head up to look into his eyes. 'Make me forget those ten years apart existed.'

If only...

He wanted nothing more than to do the same. To forget. To pretend that they'd moved seamlessly from their teenage love affair to now, where they were much older, much wiser and better prepared for reality. Only...

He needed those ten years, he needed the fateful night she'd left him, to remember this wasn't suddenly going to work out. They had different lives to lead, responsibilities that filled not only their weekday hours but their evenings and weekends too. He wasn't blind to the fact that she worked as hard as he did. Even if her failed relationship with Tim hadn't made that clear, her friends encouraging her on this crazy M date told him plenty.

He kissed her, pushing out the voice of reason as he shucked the rest of his clothes, not once leaving her lips as she helped him.

'You know,' she murmured against his mouth, 'it's lucky no one saw you carrying me back to your room like this.'

'I think if they had they wouldn't have let on.'

'Oh, goodness, I hope not.' She leaned back, looked up at him, wide-eyed. 'Do you think…?'

'Shh…' He bowed his head, pressed his lips to hers. 'If they had, they would only have been pleased that their efforts were paying off.'

She laughed and he treasured the sound all the more.

'You are so beautiful, Red.'

'You need to stop with the platitudes, or else it'll be me struggling to get my head back into my room later.'

He kissed her. 'Why would you need your room again?'

She laughed all the more, rubbing her nose against his. 'Are you inviting me to stay in your room for the rest of our stay?'

'That depends. Are you accepting?'

She hooked her hands behind his neck and looked up into his eyes. A long drawn-out moment when he doubted everything and hoped for everything all the same.

'Yes.'

He didn't dwell on how her agreement made him feel. 'Good.'

He kissed her again, purposefully losing his mind in her as he reached out blindly for the protection in his bedside drawer. Wishing it could protect him from so much more. He kept kissing her as he rolled it over himself, closed his eyes to push out the look in hers. There was so much going on there, so much emotion, so much…*love*?

But it couldn't be. They couldn't go there. Not again.

'Freddie?' She pushed her hands through his hair, broke their kiss until he opened his eyes. 'What is it? What are you thinking?'

'Nothing, Red.' He shook his head, positioned himself between her legs as she wrapped them around him. 'Nothing's more important than this.'

Now he held her eye, stared down into her endless

greens and asked the question that needed to be voiced, even though he knew the answer well enough, could see it in her eyes, feel it in the way she tried to encourage him against her. 'Are you sure you want this?'

She stared up at him. 'How can you doubt it?'

He didn't doubt it for a second, but he wanted to hear her say it. Didn't matter that she already had, he wanted to hear it from her lips again.

'I want you, Freddie.' She kept her eyes open and pressed a kiss to his lips. 'If I'm honest, you're the only man I've ever truly wanted.'

She sounded so sincere, so much braver than him, and his heart pulsed in his chest, fire coursing through his veins as a long-forgotten possessive streak sprang to life and he couldn't hold back any more. He sank himself inside her, his eyes locked on hers, and she clenched around him, taking his all.

His chest tightened. It was too much, the sense of coming home, of being where he belonged. He shut his eyes, moved inside her, tried to override it all with lust.

Sex was simple. It was just sex. They were where they wanted to be, where they needed to be at that moment.

She clawed at his hair, whimpered and rocked, his name leaving her with every panted breath, and he couldn't keep his eyes closed any more. He had to drink her in. Her flushed cheeks, her glazed eyes, her every endearment pushing him higher and higher.

'Red, Red, my Red!' It burst from him in a growl as ecstasy claimed him, sheer bliss shuddering through every limb and she tightened around him, her cry drowning out his own.

Her body pulsed, her legs and arms locking him against her. He collapsed, shaken to the very core, his breaths ragged and merging with hers.

Silence descended, their breathing slowed, her grip

around him relaxing as her fingertips stroked against his skin, teasing at the goosebumps fresh in the aftermath.

'Wow… Freddie,' she murmured into his throat. 'That was something else.'

He couldn't even look at her, fear of what she would see holding him back. He kept his head over her shoulder, his forehead pressed into the pillow, their combined scent filling up his senses.

How could he get enough of her?

One deep breath.

There were five nights remaining. Could he really have his fill and let her go?

Another breath.

Could he really continue this and leave in one piece?

'Freddie?'

He didn't move.

'Freddie?'

Slowly, he lifted his head, tried to make himself immune, but her eyes…they shone, the golden light of his bedside lamp dancing in their emerald warmth and sucking him in.

He took another breath, rolled onto his back and looked to the ceiling as he pulled her to him. *Chicken.*

'Yes?' he said over the mental gibe.

'Do you think—?' She broke off, her fingers trailing over his chest as she disappeared into her thoughts, but the damage was done, he had to know the rest.

'Do I think…?' He looked down at the top of her head, her blazing red hair all tangled by his hand, and lifted a finger to her chin, titled her head back to look at him.

It was a bad move. Her hesitant green eyes tugged at him, chewed him up inside, but curiosity overrode caution.

And then she blinked, shook her head as she lowered her gaze. 'Doesn't matter.'

His gut twisted—a crazy mix of disappointment and relief.

Whatever she'd been about to say had run deep. Deep with the kind of feelings he was trying hard to avoid. He covered her fingers on his chest, stilling her caress and shutting down the inner torrent. 'We should get some sleep, it will be a busy day tomorrow.'

'It will?'

'You really didn't read the folder M prepared, did you?'

'I did, I just— I keep forgetting.'

'You never used to be this forgetful.'

She gave a small shrug, snuggled in closer to his side. 'You never used to be this distracting.'

And just like that the mood lifted. 'I don't know if I should be flattered or let the younger me be offended.'

'Flattered, definitely flattered.' She pressed a kiss to his pec, her fingers circling over his chest once more. 'So, remind me, what's the plan for tomorrow?'

'We're kayaking in the morning, followed by an evening of cooking the creole way.'

'Couples kayaking and cooking. M really know how to keep you together as much as possible.'

'Is that you saying you're tired of my company already?'

'No. Never.'

His lips curved up, her ardent confession warming him through…until he remembered why that was a very bad sign.

A very bad sign indeed.

CHAPTER NINE

KAYAKING WAS MORE than an adventure activity, it was a scenic delight, the transparent kayaks making not only above sea level a sight to behold, but also below. And with Freddie right behind her, sharing the same kayak, it was a good job too, because she wasn't just distracted by Freddie, she was hooked on him. Dangerously, irresistibly so.

No amount of entertaining chatter from their tour guide and instructor could hold her attention. Each time she turned her head and caught him in her peripheral vision, her body reacted with a fresh wave of heat. Just a glimpse of his skilled hands at the paddles or the broad, muscular expanse of his chest in the tight-fitting blue rash guard that he wore set her off.

And that was before she even got to his grin, or his cerulean eyes, not to mention the sound of his voice, so close… They all just served as a reminder that he was a lover like no other…

A lover like no other? Really, Jas—poetry?

She wanted to roll her eyes, give herself a slap, anything to wake herself up from this Freddie-induced stupor.

'Leaving me to do all the hard work, hey?'

There went his voice again, making her smile and freak out in one, because he was the reason she'd stopped paddling. He was the reason her hands had gone limp around the paddles as she threw her all into getting a grip on her heart.

Her heart that was getting too carried away with every second that passed.

'As it happens…' she angled her head to *almost* eye him, forced a grin as she kept her voice light and breezy '…I'm giving you the opportunity to wow me with your strength and prowess.'

He chuckled, her body getting high on the deep, reverberating sound as she clamped her thighs together and fixed her grin in place.

'I thought I did that last night.'

'Freddie!' She startled, her eyes darting to their guide, Philippe, who wasn't that far ahead in his own kayak.

'You weren't half as bashful last night.'

A laugh erupted from her, her body dizzy with the recollection, dizzy with him.

'Just speaking the truth, Red.'

'We stop here!' Philippe called back, preventing any response she could have thought to give, not that any clear thought existed above the racing of her pulse.

She tugged her eyes from Freddie to see Philippe waving to a section of beach that encapsulated all she had come to love about the island. The luscious greenery sprouting between the granite boulders, the perfect white sand disappearing into the vibrant turquoise sea. Stunning didn't even come close.

'Now I'll show you something really special,' Philippe said as they tugged their kayaks up the beach and straightened.

Philippe's grin was wide, his deep brown eyes sparkling against his bronzed skin as he slung a bag across his back and turned away. He was heading back inland, into a dense stretch of rainforest that she and Freddie had only skirted around on their bikes the day before. It hadn't looked passable with its steep incline and the low-growing plants at the base of the palms. Was he taking them on a hike? In the *midday sun*?

At least with the bikes they had generated a refreshing breeze to keep their skin dry. After being in the sea and on the kayaks her salt-caked skin felt more in need of a shower than a hike.

'Come. Come.' He gestured and Freddie overtook her, grabbing her hand as he went and shooting sparks of delight right through her.

'Slowcoach.'

'I'm coming,' she returned, a smile teasing at her lips as she shook her head at the back of his.

Yes, Freddie was all man now, but over the last three days, the excitement, the spark of his youth had started to return. The same carefree spark he'd possessed before their relationship had evolved and his parents had learned of it...

Less of the past, Jas! She shoved away the melancholy descending with the thought. *Remember you're living for the now.*

She raced after him, struggling as her feet sank into the sand.

'We'll lose him if we're not careful,' Freddie murmured as Philippe disappeared into the thick vegetation.

'I seriously hope we're not hiking.'

'Don't worry, it's not far,' came Philippe's disembodied voice. 'It's just along this trail.'

Freddie shoved the low-hanging fronds from a palm aside to pull her through and Jasmine frowned at the sight ahead.

What trail?

All she could see were plants, new growth mixing with old as the fallen palm fronds lay dry and crisp along the ground, colour sprouting up in between.

'Come. Come.' Philippe called again, clambering up the sharp incline straight ahead, most of his body disappearing into the trees, and that was when she heard it, the sound of rushing water.

They hurried after him, the excited trill of the wild birds building with the rush of the water.

'Et voilà!' Philippe declared, his arms outstretched in a clearing that took her breath away.

She stilled, Freddie too.

'Wow.' She stared, open-mouthed. It looked like a mirage. A tiny oasis dominated by the palms all around, cut off from the world as the waterfall above their heads fed a small blue lagoon. It was like seeing paradise for the first time all over again. 'I hadn't expected this.'

'You and me both,' Freddie said, squeezing her hand, his one-sided smile just as awestruck.

'You like?' Philippe asked, turning to beam at them.

'Very much so,' she said.

'You can swim here, the water is a little cold, but fresh and good. Deep too, so be careful.' He dumped the bag he'd been carrying on the rock beneath his feet. 'There are refreshments and towels in the bag, and I will go get a coconut.'

He was already off, traipsing back into the forest.

She smiled at Freddie. 'Do you think he's literally going to pick a coconut?'

'I'd say so.'

She shook her head, looking from him to the vision before them, and felt the slick layer of sweat and salt on her skin. It was cooler here, the shade from the towering palms protecting them from the sweltering midday sun, but the water…it looked so inviting. *And* necessary.

Freddie was already stripping off his rash guard. 'Last one in's a rotten egg!'

'How old are…?' Her chastisement died on her lips as she lost herself in the ripple of his exposed abs, his pecs, his wide grin… She cleared her throat. 'Do I need to remind you we're not five any more?'

'And?'

She laughed.

'Are you sure it's safe in there? What if there's some

river snake or…or…' She waved her hand about her helplessly, but his grin didn't waver.

'Philippe would have warned us. Come on, aren't you hot? Or are you chicken? A *very hot* chicken.'

She laughed more. 'I'm not chicken. Hot or otherwise!'

He lifted his brows at her, fisted his hands on his hips, drawing her eyes lower, and she gulped. 'I'm not… I'm just…cautious.'

'You look like you could do with a dip just as much as me.'

His eyes travelled over her, and her skin prickled beneath the layer of sweat that had her rash guard clinging ever more to her skin. But it wasn't the sun working its fiery magic, it was all Freddie and those eyes that seemed to tease and ignite in one.

'Don't worry, I've got you, Red.'

His voice and his words snagged at her heart and she bit into her lip.

'You nervous?'

'Why?'

'You're biting your lip.' He shrugged. 'It was always one of your things. That and chewing the corner of your mouth whenever you were nervous. Nervous or…'

He let the rest hang in the air unsaid and her heart bloomed along with the warmth building inside. Was there anything he didn't remember about her? And if he remembered so much, surely that meant something, that *she still meant* something, or at least she could still mean something if he let her.

And now she was thinking in riddles.

'I'm a little nervous.' Not of the water and what might lurk beneath the rocks any more, but of him and the way her heart was beating out of her control.

'Come on, Red, live a little.'

She was living a whole lot and that was the problem.

She nodded, not trusting her voice as she peeled her top over her head and tossed it to the ground beside his. Her hair clung to her neck and she shook it out before dipping to remove her shorts and adding them to the pile. Freddie hadn't moved an inch.

She sent him a look from beneath her lashes as she straightened and tiptoed to the water's edge, passing him by.

'Are you letting me win?' she said over her shoulder, and caught the way his heated gaze raked over her bikini-clad body, leaving her effectively stripped bare, her skin sensitised and eager for his touch.

'You'll forgive me if watching you strip distracted me somewhat.'

She shook her head, a smile teasing at her lips as she tried to brush off his compliment as a flippant remark, nothing more.

'Are you still a sore loser, Freddie?' She didn't wait for his response. Burying her worries for her heart, her sanity and what lay beneath the water, she jumped...and mentally cursed. It *was* cold.

But it was just what she needed, in more ways than one.

Breaking the surface, she let out a whoop, kicking her legs to tread water. She cleared her eyes, swept her hair back from her face and turned to see him still standing on the rocks.

'What was it you said—"I've got you, Red"?' she called out, grinning.

'Always.'

And with that he took a running leap, breaking the water a metre away and showering her as his promise hit home. *Always.* She kicked harder, told herself to quit it. But how could he say it and not really mean it?

And you shouldn't want—no, need—him to mean it!

'You did that on purpose!' she scolded when his head surfaced.

He turned to her, flicking his hair back off his forehead as he made for her.

'What?' His eyes danced, his closing proximity making her pulse race.

'Showering me with water!'

And making my heart swell with love for you.

She swallowed back the realisation.

Love.

Was she in love with him? Her face seemed to prickle with pins and needles, the warmth draining from it, and she forced a smile, needing to mask it as he got closer and closer.

No, it couldn't be. Not again. Not so soon. Falling, yes, not *fallen*.

He grinned. 'But you're already wet.'

She gulped at the naughty gleam in his eye, the double entendre very much intended, and she shoved water at him, backing away.

'And there I was thinking you're all grown up with your successful business, your charity…' She glared at him, trying to be playful and ignore the panicked beating of her heart. 'But really you're still a child.'

'I hope not.'

'You hope not?'

'Else I'd be worried about the nature of my thoughts right this second.'

She shook her head, her laugh heady in spite of the undercurrent within her. She swam back faster… The chase was always fun, wasn't it?

'You know you can't outswim me.'

'Wanna bet?'

Excitement bubbled up inside her and she let it, let herself feel like the teen she'd once been when he'd first looked at her like that.

'One delicious coconut!'

They quit their speedy strokes, their attention shifting to the rocks where Philippe now stood with said coconut held above his head. 'I'll leave it here for you and return in an hour or so. Would you like me to prepare it?'

'I reckon we can manage.'

She looked at Freddie in surprise and he shrugged. 'It can't be that hard surely?'

'Okay.'

Though she got the impression it had more to do with Freddie wanting them to be alone sooner than it did with his skill at preparing a coconut.

And she shouldn't be so dizzyingly excited by it.

She really shouldn't.

'*You* can crack a coconut?'

Jasmine waited until Philippe had left to ask the question and Freddie got the distinct impression it was a distraction technique. A way to question his ability while avoiding the heat fizzing between them and it made him grin all the more because he knew she felt it. He could see it in the way her eyes blazed, the way the colour crept into her cheeks, and he exulted that she was as powerless to stop it as he was.

He closed the distance between them. 'Yes.'

'Really?' Her eyes laughed at him, the water beading on her dark lashes making them all the more captivating as she backed away.

'Yes.' Another stroke forward. 'I've done it before.'

She nodded. 'Yeah, right, in between business meetings Stateside, you enjoy cracking open a coconut.'

'No, in fact, I—' He broke off as he realised what he'd been about to say.

'You?' She stilled, her brows nudging skywards, a smile dancing around her lips, and he wanted her smile to stay.

That was why he didn't want to admit what he'd been about to.

'Nothing.'

'Come on, Freddie, just say it.'

He looked away, guilt weighing heavily in his gut. But he had no reason to feel guilty, they hadn't been together in for ever, and…well, time moved on.

Not so much your heart, though.

He ignored the inner gibe and clung to the sense that told him it was nothing for Jasmine to get upset over and in turn nothing for him to worry over either. And his heart had no place in this anyway.

'We sailed around the Caribbean for Dad's sixtieth, plenty of time for coconut hacking.'

'I see…' She frowned, the water rippling around her as she trod water. 'So why the hesitation?'

'I didn't want to dampen the moment by mentioning them.'

'Look, Freddie, they are your mum and dad, it's okay to talk about them. They only ever had your best interests at heart.'

He scoffed. 'I think it was more the case they had their own interests at heart.'

She shook her head. 'Seriously, Freddie, we were young back then, too young! Even you must see that now, with hindsight?'

Did he? Too young for marriage, perhaps. But surely it should have been their own decision to make, their own mistake to rectify.

'So, the Caribbean?' He knew she was trying to change the subject, clear the sudden cloud. 'Sounds lovely.'

'It was.'

Her frown returned. 'But?'

'But?'

'You don't look like it was lovely. In fact, you're acting kind of awkward still…'

'We were there with the Darlingtons.' His words came out with his breath, feeling very much like a confession.

Now she really frowned. 'The Darlingtons?'

'You know, Lord and Lady Darlington? Distant relations to the royal family, Darlingtons?'

'Oh, *those* Darlingtons. Don't they have a daughter about our…?' Her voice trailed off.

He saw the moment realisation hit, saw it in the way she looked away and the invisible cord that had been pulling them together in the water snapped.

'Is she the one your parents have in mind for you?'

He nodded, his jaw tense as he wished away this conversation entirely.

'Lady Sara Palmer-Darlington.' She nodded over her name. 'She's very beautiful. Isn't she the face of the designer Danielle? Not to mention her charity efforts and connections. Your parents must be beside themselves at the match.'

Her voice was strained and he wanted to reach for her, even though she was the one that had pushed them into this conversation.

He attempted a shrug. 'They can't seem to help themselves.'

'And you, can you help yourself, Freddie?' It blurted out of her and she bit her lip, the colour gone from her face, her eyes spiking with tears, and he cursed the whole situation, the way it made her feel, the way it made *him* feel. Guilty, and unreasonably so.

She turned and swam away and he followed, anger firing in his blood. 'There was a time when you told me I should listen to them, that they were right. Now you're, what? Telling me to fight back, to tell them that we live in an age where social status no longer matters when it comes to marriage and that I should be free to choose my own way?'

He sensed her flinch rather than saw it and knew he'd hit his mark.

'Shame you didn't feel that way ten years ago, Red.'

She stilled before the waterfall, her feet finding the rocky bottom at the edge of the lagoon, and she stepped forward, raising her head to the assault of the water.

And he hated it. He hated that she was shutting herself off from him. He hated that the past kept coming between them. He hated that he couldn't simply reach out and pull her into his arms, reassure her that she was the only woman he'd ever wanted to marry.

And why? Why tell her all that? She didn't deserve to hear those assurances from his lips. She was the one that had left, that had given up on them.

He stood behind her, his hands fisted at his sides.

'I was a child then.'

Her voice was a whisper disappearing in the rush of the water, but he heard it.

'You weren't a child. We were eighteen. We were—'

'We were too young for you to turn your back on your family.'

He shook his head, even though she couldn't see him. 'For all you say you left because they didn't approve, because *they* thought we were too young, it seems to me that you thought it too. It was *you* who left because deep down *you agreed*.'

She didn't even react and he pressed on, unable to stop.

'They would have come round eventually, Jas, they wouldn't have had a choice. I wouldn't have given them one.'

'And by then you would have been a changed man.'

'What do you mean?'

She spun into him, her head shaking as she gazed up at

him imploringly. 'It doesn't matter. Just leave it, I shouldn't have— I didn't—'

'I want to know what you mean.' He was chilled to the bone and he wasn't letting this go. Not now.

Her eyes trembled as she stared at him, quiet, and then, 'You were already changing, don't you see? There were times when I'd catch you looking so anxious, so worried about us and the future, and the more your parents pushed back, the more determined you were. But…but…'

She waved a shaky hand up and down his chest, her eyes lowering. 'It was tearing you apart, it was destroying you, taking away your happiness, the light in your eyes, the easy humour, the joy.'

'I was worried about the future, yes. I was worried about providing for us while still pursuing my degree if the worst happened and my family cut us off completely. I was worried you would be forced to give up your studies, your dreams. So, yes, Jas, I was worried, but—'

'Can't you see I didn't want that for you?' she interjected, her voice shaking with sincerity as tears joined the water already running down her face and he couldn't breathe for the pain of seeing hers. 'I'd see the worry in your face, and I'd try to tell myself it didn't matter, that as long as we loved one another we could get through it.'

'And we would have,' he blurted, his own hurt making his words harsh, 'if you'd only given us a chance.'

'But at what cost?'

She looked so fragile and pale before him now, her head tilted back, her hair dark with the water running through it.

'A cost I would have been willing to pay, Red.'

Her nose flared with her breath, her lashes fluttered. 'I wasn't.'

He stared at her, words failing him, movement too.

'Mum and me…' She took a deeper breath, her shoulders rolling back as she mustered her strength. 'There had always been just Mum and me, you know that. But you, you had a family, you were surrounded by love. I couldn't ask you to walk away from that and risk damaging you for ever.'

His smile was sad, cold with the truth of it. 'And yet I did it anyway.'

'You did, didn't you?' Her mouth quivered, her arms wrapping around her middle. 'I was shocked when Mum told me you'd left Oxford and got yourself into Harvard.'

'I was angry.'

'But Oxford was your dream.'

'No, *you* were my dream.'

Her eyes widened, glistening anew. 'I'm sorry, Freddie. I just couldn't take the risk. I couldn't take the risk that one day you would turn around and regret it. And Mum... well, you were always so feisty and quick to act, she worried that your parents backing you into a corner gave you all the more reason to stand your ground—'

He went to object, his anger building with her honesty, but she wasn't stopping. It was rushing out of her, her eyes ablaze with it.

'—to stand and fight, and that—that it might not have been about love at all, and that one day when life settled down again and the fight was over you'd regret it and then where would you be? It would be awful and devastating and... I don't know...'

Finally, she trailed off, her hands gripping her upper arms, her eyes not leaving his.

'You should have known me better than that.' His voice was raw with the pain of it, the anger, the disbelief.

'But I did know you, Freddie, I knew how loyal and loving you were, and those traits tied you to me just as much as they tied you to your family.'

Her words were chipping away at the age-old hurt, shining a new light on an old understanding. His family life versus hers. It hadn't just been about social standing, a divide they couldn't overcome, it had been about the bonds of love, of family, of her worry for him.

'I couldn't bear it, your parents' disapproval, my mother's concern,' she stressed into the quiet. 'I couldn't bear you giving up everything for me. I loved you too much to risk your regret, to have you blame me with time, hate me even.'

'I could *never* have hated you.'

'That's not quite true.'

'It is.'

'You hated me when I left.'

Her eyes blazed up at him, her sincerity wrapping around his heart, teasing at the mess of emotion inside.

'I wanted to hate you, Jas.' He took a shaky breath. 'It would have been so much easier if I could have hated you.'

They fell quiet, the rush of the water, the wildlife falling away too as they both absorbed the power of his confession, the meaning of it.

'I—I tried to find you after you left Oxford,' she said softly. 'I was worried, but you were nowhere to be found.'

His brows drew together, surprise making his question choke out of him. 'You did?'

'Yes. I left to protect you from making that decision, and then you went and did it anyway and I wanted to find you, I wanted… I knew you wouldn't want to see me, but…'

'I travelled. I took some time out to reimagine my future after you took ours away. I couldn't stand being in Scotland, I couldn't stand being in the UK. I wanted to get as far away as I could.'

'Far away from me.'

He swallowed, ignored the clawing sensation in his gut. 'Not just you, my family too. At first I blamed you for not having faith in me, for taking that choice away. Then I blamed them for making you feel it wasn't a choice in the first place.'

'And now? Now that you've achieved all you have without me—?'

'Now that you've achieved all you have without me, you mean.'

She took a breath, gave a small nod, her words quiet. 'If I'm completely honest, I'm not sure our relationship could have survived trying to pursue our careers, coping with our families' disapproval and all the growing up we had left to do. I don't want to hurt you, and I'm still sorry that I left, but—but can you honestly say you think we would have stayed together had I not left?'

He couldn't speak. His gut ached, his heart too. And not because he thought she was wrong…

He reached out, his palm soft on her cheek as her words sank in, struck a chord with such resonance he felt choked by it.

She covered his hand against her cheek and he closed his eyes to shut out the pain he could see in hers. She was right. So very right.

He opened his eyes slowly, took in all that was exquisite in her glistening green gaze.

'As much as it pains me to admit it…' he cupped her other cheek, held her in his hands '…you're right. Not in the way that you left… I can't…' He swallowed, fending off the painful memory. 'But then I didn't give you a choice. I was going into that room declaring my love for you, come hell or high water.'

'I know.' Her lashes fluttered over fresh tears as her lips quivered into the smallest of smiles. 'And I loved you for it. I may not have had the same confidence, but it didn't mean I didn't love you.'

Her declaration warmed his heart, soothed the pain.

'But now what, Freddie? What do we do now?'

'Now…'

He thought about it and felt his gut roll, his skin prickle.

They were at an impasse. Their lives had had no space for them ten years ago; they had even less room for them now.

But they had this. Their week. This was a known entity. No one could get hurt because there was no commitment, no expectation.

Not like there had been all those years ago.

'Now we're here in paradise, no outside world looking in, and I want to make the most of it.'

She blinked up at him, a battle still raging in her eyes, but he was ready to forget again. Forget and live for now.

He bowed his head, but she pressed her palm into his chest.

'Don't you think it's time, though, Freddie?'

'Time?' He frowned.

'Yes, time to fight back.'

'Fight back?' He straightened, his frown deepening.

'Yes.' She wet her lips. 'To put your foot down once and for all with your parents and tell them you have no interest in a marriage of their choosing. Not now, not ever.'

His mouth lifted to one side. 'I've never stopped fighting back, Jas. I fought for you ten years ago and walked out. I've lived in America ever since.'

'That's not fighting, Freddie, that's avoidance, just as this trip with M has been.'

He thought about it. About the conversations with his parents over the years, his desire to keep the peace but also his distance. All to avoid conflict.

'And you won't have the ocean between you soon. You'll be home and you'll have to face it...unless...' she eyed him, her fingers flexing against his chest '...Lady Sara *is* what you want?'

A laugh-cum-scoff erupted. He couldn't help it. There was only one woman he could ever envisage at the head of the aisle, and admitting it out loud wasn't happening. Instead, he told a different truth…more avoidance…but he couldn't risk exposing the truth in his heart.

'Sara's a good woman, intelligent, kind, but Jas, it would be like marrying my mother. And, believe me, Sara knows how I feel, I've never strung her along.'

'It's a shame your parents can't get the same message.'

'They will do,' he said, putting all the determination he felt into his voice as he lowered his hands to her hips and pulled her closer. 'I promise.'

'No more running?'

'No more running.'

'Good.'

'Now can we stop talking about my parents?'

'Why?'

'Because talk of them is ruining all my plans for this waterfall and you and everything I want to do…'

He pressed her body up against his own and kissed her, caught her sweet little sigh with his groan.

'I like the sound of that,' she murmured against his lips, her hands hooking around his neck, her slight frame fitting so perfectly against him and soothing away the painful remnants of old. As for the future…

He deepened the kiss, lifting her as she wrapped her legs around him, and he spun them back under the waterfall, let the pummelling flow pound the back of his head, his neck, his shoulders, anything to beat back the panicked pounding of his heart. The alarm bells ringing so very loud now.

But he wouldn't listen. He couldn't.

He wanted her, for as long as this week would allow, and the pieces of his shattered heart would just have to fall where they may.

He'd survived before. He could survive her again.

CHAPTER TEN

JASMINE LOOKED AT the various outfits strewn across the bed. What did one wear to a couples cooking class when it wasn't all about the cooking but the romance of it?

And, yes, she was trying to tell herself this was heading nowhere, that in four days they would be going their separate ways, but that voice was getting quieter and quieter. Because facing up to their past, talking about it and her reasons for leaving, she felt the glimmer of hope swell.

She wasn't the wallflower she'd once been. The one so fearful of the future, of tearing apart his family, she couldn't see past the bad to keep hold of the good—him.

She lifted the navy palazzo pants she'd pulled out earlier, the linen fabric perfect for the early evening warmth, the colour forgiving enough should she make an absolute mess while trying to impress Freddie with her non-existent cookery skills. She picked up the navy camisole also on the bed and held them together, turning to face the mirror that filled one wall. Practical and subtly sexy. Perfect.

She eyed her hair, beachy waves kinking up her strands even though she'd showered since their kayaking. If she was honest, she liked it. It softened her cheekbones and jawline, made her cheeks look rosy and fuller, and her eyes bigger, greener.

And it's just the sun and sea doing all that, not the man who's put the spring back in your step.

Her lips flickered into a smile, her mind replaying their conversation at the waterfall. He'd said he couldn't hate her, and his eyes had very definitely shone. It had to be more than just desire, pure sex, surely?

The vibration of her phone from beneath the pile of

clothes brought an end to her confusing thoughts and she tossed her outfit onto the bed to dig it out.

It was M.

Or, more specifically, Madison Morgan, the owner of M.

In all the excitement, she'd forgotten this call would be coming. The call to check in on their 'date' and she certainly hadn't prepared herself for it. She considered letting it ring out because, seriously, what could she say other than the truth.

But it hardly felt fair to avoid a conversation with the woman whose team had worked so hard to match her and Freddie together in the first place.

Maybe Madison had already spoken to Freddie, in which case she already knew that they had history and Jasmine wouldn't need to be the one to break the news. But what was to say Freddie would admit to it? Not that he was a liar, but it was hardly straightforward.

She forced a smile, even though Madison couldn't see her. 'Hello?'

'Jasmine, hi! I'm so glad I've caught you!'

'Hey, Madison, you've actually just caught me between activities.' Her cheeks bloomed with colour. Why did 'activities' sound so much like a euphemism?

For the same reason your body overheats at the mere mention of Freddie!

'Ah, fabulous, what is it you have this evening? In fact, I have it all here...ah, cookery!'

'Yes.' She toyed with the hem of the slip she was wearing, her mind wandering ahead to cooking up close with Freddie. 'Couples cooking the creole way.'

'From what I know, it's a lot of seafood, curry and fruit.'

She laughed. 'That sounds about right.'

'And are you liking the Seychelles?'

'I love it here.' Which was the honest truth, but Jasmine

had a feeling she'd love being anywhere as long as her match remained the same. 'It truly is paradise.'

'Ah, I'm so glad. You actually have your match to thank for the location.'

'I do?' She frowned, surprise making her voice soft.

'Yes. Usually when I ask the question, with men especially, what location they think of when I say the word "romance", they often give a vague response, or think about it for a bit. But Freddie came straight out with it so we knew that just had to be the location. And it certainly fitted your requirement for somewhere hot, did it not?'

She couldn't find her voice as the hope she was trying to keep contained completely ran away with her.

'Jasmine, are you still there?'

'Yes. Yes. Sorry, I was distracted.' Distracted by the fact that Freddie had chosen the Seychelles. Distracted by the fact that romance plus holiday still meant the Seychelles for him. Did that in itself mean more? That the Freddie who had loved her wasn't too far beneath the surface, despite the passage of time and their history?

And yet he could have been here with someone else entirely if M hadn't chosen her.

A timely reminder to put hope back where it belonged. Shut tight in a sealed box.

'And was he right?'

She could hear the hope in Madison's voice too, could picture her brown eyes all soft and warm, just like they'd been in her initial interview when she'd asked Jasmine what she was looking for in her perfect man.

And what had she been looking for? Freddie, all Freddie. He'd been her perfect man ten years ago, and he was still as perfect now, even more so with a maturity, a measured control that could only come with age and experience.

'Ooh, I wish I'd video-called, all this silence is hard to cope with.'

Jasmine gave a small laugh. 'Sorry, no, it's…it's perfect.'

'As *romantic* as Freddie hoped?'

Was it? From what Freddie had told her, he hadn't been hoping for romance at all when he'd embarked on this little adventure—another reason to keep hope packed away.

But without hope she felt bereft, and she wouldn't ruin the last few days walking around with fear hot on her tail.

'It *is* romantic.' She thrust positivity into her voice and tried to feel it too. 'Very romantic!'

'That's wonderful, I'm sure Freddie will agree, then.'

'You've not spoken to him yet?'

'No, I did try him first but there was no answer.'

'I imagine he's in the shower, getting ready.'

Or had he ignored the call? Was he, like she had been, worried about what to say?

'Is that right?' There was a smile—or was it a smug smirk?—in Madison's voice. 'Always a positive sign when the client knows what their date is up to.'

Jasmine's laugh was more of a scoff as nerves got the better of her. 'We've not long been back from kayaking and I've been getting ready myself.'

'Well, it's good that I've caught you on your own. I do like to talk to my clients individually if possible. You wouldn't believe how hard that can be sometimes.' Madison gave a soft laugh and Jasmine could just imagine why it was so hard, or was that her insatiable appetite for Freddie getting in the way again?

'So-o-o,' Madison cooed, 'how's it going?'

Jasmine bit her lip. How *was* it going? 'It's…it's interesting.'

'Good interesting, bad interesting?'

'Good, definitely good.' Or at least she hoped it was.

'Are you going to expand on "interesting"?'

Jasmine laughed at Madison's eager persistence. She liked the woman a lot. She was easy to talk to and had the amazing ability to coax things out of her that Jasmine hadn't even been aware of thinking or feeling before. Rather like Sadie and Izzy, she was like the best friend you always wanted, or the big sister you wish you had. It felt like she had your back and cared passionately, when in reality she was a very expensive and very successful matchmaker.

Though there was no reason she couldn't be all of the above…

'Am I only getting a laugh?'

'It's complicated,' she said, flustered.

'Ooh, three days in and it's already complicated. Should I start planning the wedding outfit now?'

As if. Jasmine's laugh was well and truly high, her mind as delirious as her body as she pictured it. Freddie at the head of the aisle, her walking down it…and the severe and disapproving Highgroves, if they even attended at all. And there the scene shattered into a million pieces.

'So, it's a good kind of interesting *and* complicated. You know, I say this about all my clients, but you two in particular gave me such a good feeling, a definite match made in heaven.'

Jasmine plopped down onto the bed, her sigh wistful and wishful in one. She caught sight of herself in the mirror, the silly little smile that played about her lips, her eyes that glistened. 'I wish.'

And she'd really just said that out loud…

'Why does that sound like a hopeless "I wish"?' Madison asked, her frown evident in her voice.

'Like I said, it's complicated.' She took a breath and let it out swiftly. 'Freddie and I have history.'

'What?'

'Yes, we know each other. In fact, we grew up together. My mother was the housekeeper of his family home.'

'You're kidding!' Jasmine had to hold the phone away

from her ear. 'But neither of you mentioned one another in your dating history, unless of course you never...'

'Well, I think that's because we both tried—' *and failed* '—to forget.'

Maybe the odds would be more in their favour now if they hadn't had that history to share. What would it be like, meeting Freddie afresh?

Silly question. She'd have fallen just as swiftly, especially without the first-hand knowledge of his family to put her off.

'To forget? So...it didn't work out...well, of course it didn't work out or else you wouldn't be here now, but...you know...goodness, this is a bit awkward. You just couldn't write this.'

Madison's flurry of words had Jasmine feeling a strange sense of guilt. They'd truly landed her in a pickle, not intentionally, but still, she felt bad and she wanted to reassure her that it wasn't M's system messing up. No, that was all down to her and Freddie.

'Don't worry, it's not your fault and if I'm honest, your system did call it right. Freddie is as much my ideal man now as he was back then.'

'But—but you parted ways?'

'When we were eighteen, I actually... I called off our engagement.'

'No way!'

'Yes way. We were young, it was too much too soon, and it was tricky, with his parents and me being the housekeeper's daughter—it was hardly an ideal match in their eyes, not when they had their sights set on a high society bride.'

'I see.'

'And my mother wasn't best pleased, as you can imagine. They were her employers at the end of the day.'

'And her employers didn't think her daughter was good enough. Oh, no!'

'Precisely.'

'But, oh, my!' Madison exclaimed. 'You were star-crossed lovers! You were meant to be, but were separated by opposing forces. That's so incredibly romantic, tragic but romantic.'

Jasmine laughed with a frown. 'I guess you could put it like that.'

'And here we are now—' she could hear the budding excitement in Madison's voice '—with a chance for you to rewrite your paths, make it work and put all that behind you.'

'I'd like to think so.'

Maybe it was the loss of her mum, the realisation that life was too short, the realisation that what she felt for him had stood the test of time...she didn't know. But those reasons for ending it when she had been eighteen held no weight now and had no bearing on their future either. Yes, changes would need to be made, the kind of changes she hadn't been willing to make for Tim, but for Freddie, for the two of them...

But what was to say Freddie would feel the same? Even if he could trust her with his heart again, would he want to make space in his life for her?

'You're still worried about how his parents will receive you?'

'No. Not really.' And she wasn't. She wasn't the insecure teen she'd once been and she believed that, whatever happened, Freddie had already broken away and found a way to maintain his ties to them. A relationship with her would do no more damage than had already been done, but... 'I'm not even sure Freddie will give us another chance to get to that hurdle.'

'How so?'

'He seems determined to go it alone.'

'What? Life? That's not the impression he gave us.'

Oh, dear, she'd put her foot in it. 'I mean, I don't think he knows how to share his life with someone else.'

She wasn't sure that sounded any better either, but she was trying to be honest.

'Then you just have to show him how good it can be.'

'Oh, I'm trying.'

'Have you been honest with him, told him that you want to try and make a go of it?'

'Not outright. We've dealt with the past, though, and that's something. As for the future...'

Freddie seemed so focused on keeping this week as just that—a week. But she wanted more, so much more.

'Well, there you go, you just need to be honest with him and good things will happen!'

She wished she could share Madison's confidence.

'We've brought you together for a reason, Jasmine, a very good reason, I'm sure of it.'

'I hope you're right.'

'I'm always right when it comes to love.'

She gave a shaky laugh and heard Madison let go of another dreamy sigh. 'I can't believe it. In all the days of M this is most definitely a first.'

'It does feel rather unbelievable.'

'Like a wish coming true.'

'Yes.' Jasmine had certainly wished for a fairy godmother to wave a magic wand back then, and now she had Freddie back in her life again she wished above all else to keep him there.

'Second chance romances have always been a favourite of mine.'

Jasmine smiled. 'Mine too.'

'Well, I'd best let you get on with living your real-life fairy tale with Freddie. This has made my year and it's only July.'

Jasmine grinned, buoyed up by Madison's optimism. 'We're not quite hitched yet, you know.'

'Ah, give it time and I'll be adding a second chance romance to my repertoire. It doesn't get any better than that…'

Jasmine was still smiling as she hung up the phone and busied herself getting ready.

Madison was right, there was only one way to find out if this was going to work and that was to be honest with Freddie, to lay her cards on the table and hope for the best.

Sooner rather than later.

CHAPTER ELEVEN

COOKING WITH JASMINE was an experience.

Her ability to burn something no sooner than she looked at it was quite special. But it was her continuous laughter and those dancing green eyes that were getting to him.

She'd been late arriving at the outdoor cooking pavilion because Madison had caught up with her. A call he'd not been as confident as her to take. He didn't want to pick apart how he felt or lay out their history to an outsider, and he certainly didn't want to lie.

Madison Morgan had a good heart, her business was quite clearly her passion, so it was bad enough that he'd strung the agency along to keep his parents at bay, but to speak to her now when he was struggling to keep a handle on how he felt…

'Don't you like it?' Jasmine frowned at him from across the candlelit table, calling his attention to the fact that he'd barely touched the dish they'd cooked together, and the way she was looking at him suggested she'd been watching him for far too long.

'Sorry, I zoned out.'

'A penny for them?'

His laugh was tight as he shook his head. 'You don't want to know.'

'You'd be surprised.'

He smiled at her and dropped his eyes to the dish, loaded up his fork. 'I think it's nice. What about you?'

He gestured to her plate, aware that they were very much alone again, and she'd chosen to time her question with their first dose of privacy since the cookery lesson had begun. It felt like the opening to something much deeper than talk over the food and he wasn't ready for it.

'Yes, it's tasty. I have to admit I'm glad we made the grilled fish and *satini*. I really didn't fancy the flying bat dish.'

His laugh was much easier now. '*Les Roussettes* certainly gives it a better ring.'

'Until you realise what it means! And I'm surprised you didn't know. You aced languages at school.'

'In my defence, it's not often you discuss fruit bats in class.'

'True.' She grinned, her eyes turning skywards just as the said *roussettes* swept overhead. 'Although now I feel bad, insulting them when they're flying above us right now.'

'Er… I think they'd actually be *relieved* we don't want to eat them.'

She smiled, but steadily the humour dissipated in her expression, her brows easing together, the curve to her lips turning down.

Definitely a conversation brewing, and definitely not one that he wanted. They'd done enough talking at the waterfall.

He threw his focus into eating, though tasting was proving impossible with the uneasy churn in his gut. By the time they'd devoured dessert, he was more than ready to cut off the discussion with more of what he knew how to give and enjoy—pleasure.

He stood and held out his hand. 'Shall we?'

She blinked up at him, those big green eyes working a magic that went far deeper than he was willing to allow.

She slipped her hand inside his. 'I was hoping we could take a walk…on the beach?'

'Walking wasn't quite what I had in mind.'

She laughed, the sound joyous after the strained quiet, her playful nudge in his side with her elbow all the more so. 'Freddie!'

'What? I'm here on a beautiful island, with a beautiful woman. I think it's completely understandable that I might want to do something other than walk.'

'Well, tough. We're walking.'

*And talking...*he reluctantly acknowledged. Though it was silence that accompanied their stroll along the subtly lit trail down to the beach. Glass-dome-covered candles were being used to ensure the sense of romance was never far away. M truly had chosen well with this resort.

And M was the reason he knew this conversation was brewing now.

The sounds of nocturnal wildlife filled the silence, the incessant chatter taking the edge off the silence stretching between them.

'And they say New York is the city that never sleeps...' He was making conversation—*safe* conversation. 'This place seems to have a constant on switch too.'

She smiled up at the stars as she released his hand and hooked her arm through his, drawing him closer. 'I like it, though; it's comforting to know you're not the only one awake when you can't sleep.'

'Do you often find yourself feeling that way?' There was just something in the way she'd said it...

'What way?'

'Awake and...' He shrugged. 'Feeling alone?'

There was that word again: alone. But it beat lonely... even though he knew he meant it in the same way. The same way she'd meant it when she'd said it to him that first night at dinner...

'Sometimes. Nature certainly beats the sounds of the city, and though you get the odd cat cry or shrill fox call, this is definitely more soothing.'

He nodded as he tried to ignore the way his chest ached. The idea of her lying awake in an empty bed, feeling that way. The idea that he could be beside her too swift to follow. No. Just no.

But the image nagged at him anyway. As did the uneasy realisation that he'd let her believe countless women had shared his bed over the years, when the truth was very different.

'You know when I told you…' He cleared his throat '…when I implied that I rarely slept alone, it wasn't quite true…'

'No?'

She looked up at him and he could sense the smile on her lips, not that he dared look as he explained, 'The truth is I hardly have time for even that. More often than not it's more trouble than it's worth.'

'It's only trouble if it's the wrong person.'

He risked a glimpse, saw so much shining back in her gaze and looked away just as swiftly.

'Perhaps.' *She's right and you know she's right*, came the nagging inner voice.

'It seems to me we both need to get a better work-life balance. We should find a way to make time for—for finding the right person.'

He didn't miss her hesitation and he knew what she wasn't saying. That they'd found the right person, they just needed to find the time to carve out a future together.

'I thought you had as much interest in finding love as I did?'

He tried to inject a joviality to his tone, make it into a tease, but it fell flat.

'I've had time to think since then, to reconsider what it is I want from life, and talking to Madison kind of helped put it into perspective for me.'

He tried not to tense up, but he knew his arm locked in hers as his step faltered just a little.

'Did you— Did she manage to get hold of you? She said

she tried to reach you before she called me, but there was no answer.'

He swallowed, kept his eyes fixed on the waves crashing in the distance rather than on her upturned face. The sea was rougher tonight and it matched his mood. The tumultuous chaos of what this was, what it could be, and the fact he wanted to run and stay in one.

'No. She rang, but…'

He let his silence do the rest, and she lowered her gaze, leaned her head into him. 'I know. It's a difficult conversation to navigate.'

'Did you tell her everything?'

She snuck a look up at him and still he couldn't look at her. 'Yes. Well, I had to, really. I was always a rubbish liar and let's face it, M outdid themselves matching us together.'

'That's true.'

'I only gave her the high-level details, enough for her to understand what went wrong. She called us…'

Her voice trailed off and he frowned down at her. 'She called us what?'

Her smile was small, a hint of colour in her cheeks just visible in the moonlight. 'Star-crossed lovers.'

His chuckle was tight. 'Quite the contemporary Romeo and Juliet.'

'Well, not entirely as our families weren't sworn enemies.'

'No…'

'It came down to social standing.'

'It was as much an issue for your mother as it was mine.' He didn't know why he felt the need to even out the blame, but he did. And still he felt guilty as she nodded her acceptance of it.

'Ultimately, I guess it was.'

They reached the end of the path, the white sand

stretched out before them, the moonlight reflecting off the water as the waves continued to crash into the night.

'I meant what I said, Jas. No more avoiding. I will set my parents straight. I know I'm hurting our relationship more by not dealing with it.'

She turned to give him a small smile, and he hooked his hands around her waist, looked into her eyes.

'The thing is, deep down I know they'll stand by me. That they might be annoyed, disappointed even, but ultimately I'm still their son…'

'They'll still love you,' she said softly.

'Yes.'

Her brow creased, her eyes lowering to his chest. 'It makes me wonder…'

'Wonder what?'

She met his gaze, quiet for a beat. 'Whether we could make it work now… Whether we could try and—'

'Don't, Jas…' The tension coiled back through him exponentially. 'Let's not ruin what we have now with talk of an impossible future.'

'Why is it impossible? You've already said you're going to make a stand against your parents so there's no reason we can't take control of our own destinies, write our own future. Together.'

'Is that what Madison said to you?'

She shrugged softly. 'She may have said something like that, but these are my thoughts, my words. We are stronger now, wiser. We can make this work if we both want it enough.'

'Why is now any different to how it was back then? My family are still the same, the circles they move in, that I will move in…'

'But we're not the same.'

He shook his head, looked to the heavens as though they would throw him an answer that would end this torture.

Because it *was* torture to be handed everything he had ever wanted and not be able to take it.

'We have less time now than we ever had. You and Tim broke up because your work came first. I've been there too. We don't have time for ourselves, let alone others.'

'We can make time.'

'It's not that simple, and you know it. I have the charity, I have the company and I have a future back in Scotland—an estate, a title, responsibilities that I have to take on.'

'Together we can—'

'Jas, stop it. *Please.*'

'Why? What is it you're so afraid of?'

'History repeating itself! Don't you see, Jas, we do this, we commit and it falls apart…' He couldn't even breathe for the pain of it, and he gripped her shoulders, dropped his forehead to hers as he sought the strength he needed. 'You wouldn't risk me hating you ten years ago, and I won't risk you hating me now.'

'I could nev—'

He pressed his thumb to her lips, stared down into her eyes. 'Please, Jas. Don't throw my words back at me.'

She went very still and he wanted to take it all back, the hurt he knew he was inflicting, but he couldn't. He wouldn't give her the hope he'd once foolishly possessed, but he would take the strength she'd once possessed to walk away.

He eased his thumb from her lips, cupped her face in his hands. 'We agreed a week, no harm, no foul…no pain.'

'But don't you at least want to try?' She raised her hands to his hair, her fingers gently caressing. 'Don't you want to take the opportunity M has given us to take a chance on us now? Madison reckons—'

'Madison reckons!' He started, anger sparking that she would ask him to take a chance on them when she hadn't been willing to all those years ago. It didn't matter that the anger was irrational, unfair even, sparked by panic, fear—

he just needed this conversation over. The dizzying mess with hope at its heart. Hope that Madison, that Jasmine were right. The kind of hope that had the power to crush him all over again. 'Madison is a romantic, an idealist, and it's in her interest to see us work out. I would take what she says with a pinch of salt.'

Her fingers stilled in his hair. 'That's a bit harsh.'

'Harsh was what you were back then!'

Her sudden pallor gutted him, her paleness so much worse for the light of the moon as her hands fell away.

'I'm sorry— I didn't— I don't...'

There were no words in the face of her pain and he hated himself for hurting her, but he hated their past and the confusion more.

The heavy night air surrounded them, the insects and the waves punctuating the strained silence, but there was nothing he could say, nothing he could do.

She pulled away from him, slipped off her sandals and walked down to where the waves were rolling in.

'Your trousers will get wet. Be careful!'

She didn't seem to hear him, just carried on going until she was walking in the shallows, her whole demeanour defeated, broken, and it was killing him.

She looked so beautiful—beautiful and broken.

He'd never wanted to hold her in his arms more and felt her so off limits.

He walked towards her. 'Red?'

She paused and turned to him, her eyes dark and glittering.

'We have this time now,' he tried softly, 'let's not take it away with the past.'

Her smile lifted to one side. 'You're the one letting the past intervene.'

'No, I'm keeping it real. I'm giving the past the nod it

deserves and the future… I'm protecting us both, just as you did back then.'

She looked out over the ocean. 'You and I have a different version of what the past deserves, Freddie.'

He closed the distance between them, desperate to reconnect, to feel the calm only she could provide. And he knew how messed up that was.

'Let us have the now, please, I beg of you.' He reached out to touch her chin, gently encouraging her to look at him. 'Please understand, I can't go through that pain again, Red, I can't.'

Who are you really trying to convince? Yourself or her?

'But I promise you this right now, I want you and nobody else. Just you. For the time we're here, I will treasure you, I will care for you, I will worship the ground you walk on.'

'And afterwards?' she whispered.

He felt his heart shatter and reformed it with ice. 'Afterwards we go our separate ways, just like before.'

'But…but you'll be in Edinburgh. *I'll* be in Edinburgh.'

'It's a big city, nothing to say we need see each other again.'

He would never be as weak as he'd once been. He couldn't. As for the future, there was no avoiding it. He would be the Laird of Highgrove, and with all the responsibility, the demands on his time, he wouldn't treat her to the scraps that were left over when work was done, and the estate was tended to. He wouldn't be his father.

She shuddered before him and he wrapped his arms around her.

'You're cold.' Though he sensed it wasn't the coolness of the sea or the late hour that had made her so. 'We should head back.'

They retraced their steps, his arm around her, holding her close, but he felt as distant from her as he had been these last ten years.

When they reached the fork in the path, the one that led to his quarters or hers, she turned to look at him and he tugged her towards him, tugged her and struggled to keep his heart in its icy grip.

It's okay to want her now and let her go later...

He only wished he felt the assurance all the way through his once bitten heart that seemed determined to warm, to care, to dream.

'I should probably stay in my room tonight.' She tried to pull away.

'No.' It was out before he could stop it, his arms coming around her as he forced himself to ask, 'Unless that's what you really want?'

'No, Freddie.' She shook her head, her eyes awash with tears, and a lump formed in his throat, making it difficult to breathe, to swallow. 'I want to stay with you.'

'Then come with me,' he managed to say.

'How can you ask that after all you said?'

'Because I never said I wanted this to end now. I want this time with you, Jas. I want this time to forget all else but you.'

He could see the fight in her, could see it and feared it, and so he kissed her. It was a dirty trick. It was cruel to use their mutual desire to keep her. But it was crueller still to torture themselves by separating sooner than their time on the island allowed.

She froze for a split second, her mouth unmoving under his, and then she was kissing him back, her entire body melting into him.

'Please, Red...' He brushed the words against her lips.

She nodded, a murmured acceptance, and he pulled her into his side, kissed the top of her head as relief coursed through him.

They headed towards his room in step together.

'So, since you know the M itinerary off by heart, what

do they have in store for us tomorrow?' Her question was soft, quiet, and he knew she was seeking a light distraction from the heavy echo of their fallout.

'Sailing… We're taking a trip out to Praslin Island.'

'Oh, sailing. That should be fun.'

Fun.

Exactly what this week should be about, and he needed to get better at keeping her focused on that.

She sank deeper into him and he relished it, her willingness to give herself over to the force still pulling them together.

He only wished the force was more powerful than that which had torn them apart. But the pain, the belief that she would run from the force that was his family, his heritage was still there, stronger than ever.

Because above all, he was a Highgrove, and he couldn't ever shake that off.

CHAPTER TWELVE

SAILING WAS NOT FUN!

In fact, Jasmine would go as far as to say it was the very opposite of fun and actually torture.

And she had no idea what she'd done to deserve it, but if she didn't get back on land soon, she feared breakfast would be making a reappearance, not to mention their lovingly prepared dishes the night before.

And thinking about that really wasn't helping…

'Hey.' Freddie's voice was soft in her ear, but not soft enough for her over-sensitised body and she flinched away, even more when his hand touched her back. 'Sorry.'

She sensed him ease back but couldn't risk a peek, she was too busy trying to breathe steadily and slowly, just like they had been advised, but it wasn't working. The catamaran lurched as the waves buffeted it again and she gripped the handrail tightly.

'I don't remember you ever being seasick.'

'I don't ever remember being on a boat that rocked like it was about to capsize before.'

Ooh, too many words. And breathe.

She heard Freddie laugh. The low sound was no longer sexy. Not in the slightest. If she was capable of it, she'd show him just what she thought of his laugh, but that last stream of words had cost her dearly.

'It's hardly going to capsize, Red. It's a gentle rocking motion at worst. Like the kind you'd use to send a baby off to sleep.'

'Less of the rocking,' she said through gritted teeth.

'Try tricking your body into believing you're on land, and that everything is a figment of your imagination.'

She moaned into her fist.

'You only *feel* sick because your inner ear is sending different signals from those that your eyes are sending.'

'Signals?' she blurted. She really couldn't care less about signals, and what they were or weren't doing.

'That's right, different signals than those your eyes are sending. It causes your body to get confused, so try telling it something different.'

'Something different.' She could hardly believe what he was suggesting, let alone do it.

Like it's that simple.

He merely smiled, his blue eyes vibrant and… *Hang on.*

'Are you laughing at me?'

'No.' His face fell, his body straightening.

'You are!' His eyes were definitely dancing…or was it just the effect of the waves being reflected back—? *Oh, no, the waves!*

She buried her head back in her arms.

'I'm trying to distract you.'

'It's not helping, Freddie.'

'It's a shame, it really is beautiful out here.'

Oh, she knew it was beautiful all right, she'd seen enough of it. Before the nausea, stomach cramps and vom— No, she hadn't vomited, not yet, but she wasn't sure how far off that was. And she really didn't want to vomit.

'Ooh, there's a turtle.'

'What?' Her head shot up, her eyes eagerly scanning the clear water.

'*See.* Distracting you.'

'Freddie!' She punched him in the chest, reassuming her position as her stomach cramped. She was going to kick him if he carried on being this helpful.

'Maybe a little sip of water.'

She groaned.

'A ginger ale?'

'No.' She pursed her lips, not that he could see now her head was once more buried in her arms. She must look positively grey, or was it green?

Whoa! The boat lurched again, sending her rocking back and her head up.

'How long?' she blurted.

'How long, what?'

She made a noise with her mouth. Surely it was obvious. 'How long until we get to land?'

'An hour maybe.'

And then they'd have to board the boat again to get back…

She groaned audibly and he must have sensed the direction of her thoughts as he said, 'The captain reckons it won't be quite as bad this afternoon for the return leg to Rosalie.'

Phew. At least that was something, and she murmured her gratitude to the floor.

'You want to hear something sweet?'

He didn't wait for her to reply, which was good because she wasn't planning on saying another word.

'Rosalie Island got its name from a French naval officer. He explored it back in the late seventeen-hundreds and named it after his wife. Quite a gift. Not that he ever came back to see it, or his wife for that matter…'

'He didn't see his wife again. Or she didn't get to see the island?'

'She didn't get to see it.'

'Oh.'

Freddie carried on, his smooth chatter flowing over her, and she found it became less of an annoyance and more of a lulling murmur, his little titbits of information giving her something to focus on other than the rolling of her stomach. He didn't touch her again, he'd learned his lesson there, but he stayed beside her, his attention very much on her when he should have been enjoying the view.

* * *

Over an hour later, her toes curling into soft, warm sand, she managed a meek smile. Land at last. 'Thank you.'

He grinned at her, his sunglasses hiding his eyes. 'For being annoying?'

'I'm sorry. You weren't annoying, I just...' She grimaced, her hand gripping her stomach. 'I've never been seasick before. I didn't know it was a thing for me, or how awful it could be.'

'It's fine, it's not your fault.' He frowned at her hand gesture and looked to where their guide for the day was waiting patiently in the shade of a thatched shack and chatting with new arrivals from another boat. 'Are you sure you're up for this trek?'

She followed his line of sight, felt the heat of the day beating down on her beneath her cap and the truth was she didn't feel it. She felt like she was still on the boat, rocking with the sea, and gritted her teeth as she swallowed down the sudden moisture in her mouth.

'Tell you what,' he said, 'why don't I see if we can rest here for a bit?'

She frowned at him. 'I don't want to waste their time.'

'It's okay, I'm sure they won't mind.'

'But they might be busy later.'

'And if they *are* busy...' he pushed his sunglasses back and the compassion in his vibrant blue eyes made her belly flutter rather than roll '...we'll make the most of Praslin's shoreline. It's beautiful here.'

'It's as beautiful as Rosalie and we're staying there,' she murmured, unconvinced. She didn't want to spoil this for him too. 'When will you get chance to see the wildlife here again and the Vallée de Mai Nature Reserve?'

He cupped her cheek, the move so soft and surprising it stole her breath. 'Stop fretting and sit down before you fall down.'

'Am I swaying?'

His smile lifted to one side. 'Just a little. And if the sea doesn't improve, I'll see if I can get us a flight back to Rosalie. There's a small runway here.'

'No, Freddie, I'm sure I'll be fine after a short rest and I don't want to be a pain.'

'You're being a pain by refusing my suggestions.' He softened his words with another grin. 'Now sit.'

She watched him go, guilt, gratitude and some other emotion too close to the love she was trying hard to suppress rising up within her. She didn't want to ruin this trip for him. But then she hadn't anticipated feeling like this. Here she was in new surroundings, feeling like she'd been tossed off a vicious fairground ride without the candy floss and the hot dogs to fuel it.

And that thought really didn't help.

She took Freddie's advice and dropped onto the sand, sucked in a deep breath and blew it out slowly, her eyes going to the unmoving horizon and feeling marginally better for it. She just needed the ground beneath her to stop moving and all would be well. A few more deep breaths and—

Her phone buzzed from the depths of her straw bag. She frowned and reached inside to pull it out. It was Sadie in their group chat.

Where's our update? Waiting (im)patiently… x

She smiled at the screen in spite of the continued rocking and the knowledge that soon the trip would be over and if Freddie didn't change his mind, they would be going their separate ways.

She tapped in her reply.

Paradise is just that. Paradise x

Sadie's response was instant.

Never mind paradise, what's he like? Xxx

He's…

She stopped typing.

What could she say? She could hardly reveal it was Freddie. She'd considered messaging them the very first night, but every scenario of her offloading the truth resulted in a barrage of questions and very likely phone calls too and she didn't want the chaos of it. Not now when time wasn't on their side.

She also wasn't ready to face their potential wrath. Though they would mean well, their anger stemming from their love for her, they really weren't going to take the news lightly. Part of the whole M thing was about putting Freddie behind her and instead it had done the total opposite.

It had been enough of a shock dealing with it herself. Telling them and dealing with their reactions too…

No, that discussion could wait for her return to Edinburgh. Until then she would make the most of this. Paradise and Freddie.

…perfect x

She sent it. It was the truth after all.

Izzy replied first.

How exciting! M made good on their promise then? xxx

Sadie came next, in true Sadie fashion.

You'd hope so when they charge all those zeroes! But when we're talking perfect, how perfect? Like the full Mr Perfect package—eight-pack ripped, drop-dead gorgeous and a brain? Cos he needs a brain to be with you, Ms Clever Clogs! Mwah!

She laughed at her friend's bluntness and instantly regretted it. Her body really wasn't ready for laughter.

Dragging in a breath, she looked over her shoulder to where her Mr Perfect was now chatting animatedly to their tour guide. He was wearing a white V-neck T-shirt and navy board shorts today, the outfit simple, but on him… even with the churning sensation still underway, her body pulsed with heat. He definitely was her Mr Perfect.

Their tour guide was frowning and nodding at whatever Freddie was saying and her ears burned. He was no doubt telling him how sick she felt, how she hadn't been able to cope with the crossing and was now ruining the day for all of them.

Well, no, he wouldn't be saying that last bit, that was all her as she blamed herself.

Slipping her hand beneath her cap, she rubbed at her forehead and wished the sensation away, but it was no good. She couldn't force her body to toe the line and behave, no matter how much she wanted it to.

Her phone buzzed and she squinted at the screen, Sadie's message blared back at her.

Well???

She pursed her lips and typed.

Yes, he has a brain! And, yes, he has a body you would approve of. He is perfect for me xx

She grimaced. A bit too honest, perhaps… But it was just what her friends would want to hear.

Sadie replied.

Oh, man, I'm so jealous.

Then Izzy.

You change your men as often as you change your underwear, Sadie, you don't get to be jealous!

Sadie again:

Do not.

Izzy:

Do so.

And now it was her friends sending her dizzy. She groaned and dropped back onto the sand, not caring that her hair was still wet from the waves hitting the catamaran and that the sand would cling to it.

Her phone continued to buzz, and she lifted it against the sun and tapped in a message.

How old are you two again?

Sadie replied.

Not as old as you.

Then Izzy:

You really need to learn to mince your words, S!

Sadie:

That's not how the saying goes, and anyway life's too short. Which is why I'm over the moon you've found your man. So, do we get a name at least?

She bit her bottom lip.

You'll have to wait until I get back.

Sadie:

Which is when?

Izzy:

Give her a break, she doesn't want to think about home already!

Sadie:

Izzy, shh!

She thought it over. By her reckoning, if all went to plan, she would be back in Edinburgh Saturday lunchtime and going home to an empty penthouse…

She replied.

Saturday lunchtime xx

Sadie:

Sunday brunch, then?

An afternoon and night alone with her thoughts? No, thank you. The spasm to her gut wasn't so much the gift of the sea now, and she clutched her hand to it.

'You okay?'

She jumped at Freddie's husky voice so close and angled her head back. He was right behind her, a silhouette against the sun.

She covered her eyes and blinked up at him. 'Just catching up with my friends.'

'I meant your stomach.' He gestured to where she clutched her belly and she wondered how he'd feel if she confessed that he was the cause of that particular gesture.

'Hopefully I will be soon. What did our guide say?'

Her phone vibrated in her hand and she looked at the screen. It was Sadie.

???

Then Izzy:

Give the girl a second at least…

'Sorry I just need to sign off and then I'm all yours.'

She sensed his body pulse over her accidental innuendo, and her cheeks flushed—it beat pale and sickly, though.

She tapped out her reply, trying to concentrate on it while her body flooded with salacious warmth.

Saturday night would be better. If you can?

She dropped in a fingers-crossed emoji and added prayer hands too for good measure.

Sadie:

It's a date! I'll cook!

Izzy:

No, I'll cook, you can bring the wine x

Sadie:

Much better plan.

She smiled, feeling their support across the miles, and signed off.

See you then, loves xxx

She popped her phone back into her bag and made to sit up.

'As you were,' Freddie commanded softly. 'I'll join you.'

'You'll get sand everywhere.'

'Ah, yes, the joy of sand.' He sank down beside her and lay back, his hand reaching to cover hers. It was such a comforting gesture, so natural and easy. It felt like it meant something and no amount of trying to rationalise it away as just a thoughtful gesture between old friends was working.

'This stuff is like talcum powder anyway.' He used his other hand to scoop up a handful and she watched as he let it fall through his fingers.

'And when was the last time you came up close and personal with talc?'

She lifted her gaze to his and her heart gave a little leap. The sun glinted off his dark hair, the tanned glow to his skin making his blue eyes even more vibrant and highlighting the chiselled angle of his cheekbones, his jaw, and every breath she now took captured his scent…

'You'd be surprised. My sister thinks it's very important to thrust uncle duties on me at every opportunity when I visit home.'

She smiled, the idea of seeing him in that role warming her heart all the more. 'How lovely.'

'If you say so. James is two but what he lacks in age he makes up for in noise. He'll make a fine Highgrove.'

'Though he won't be a Highgrove, will he?'

'He is.'

'Oh, I would have thought he'd have his father's name. I shouldn't have assumed in this day and—'

'He does have his father's name,' he interjected, tension bracketing his mouth. 'But he's still a Highgrove without the name.'

'I just— I mean…' Her voice trailed off as she realised she was pressing him into a conversation that could only spell trouble.

'You're talking titles. You're talking about my child. My heir. The heir I won't ever have because I have no intention of marrying.'

She swallowed, the pang in her chest too great. 'Yes.'

He said nothing, his eyes on the sky so very pensive.

'Have you considered what happens to the line if you don't?'

Why was she even pressing him on this? Did she hope he would suddenly turn around to her and say, 'Hey, let's forget the last ten years ever happened and get married like we always planned, have a home, kids, a dog.'

Wasn't going to happen.

But…

His eyes flitted to her briefly. Did he see it all in her face? Was that why he'd looked away again so quickly?

'My sister has another child on the way, and likely another after that. There will be no end of possible heirs if she carries on the way she is.'

He offered her a smile but it left her feeling dead inside, her heart breaking as she thought of Freddie never having a family of his own. Yes, if it couldn't be with her, she didn't want to imagine it being with someone else. But to always be alone, to never have kids when it had been his dream when they had been younger. Had she ruined him so much?

The question that left her was far safer: 'When is she due?'

His brows drew together. 'Hmm?'

'You said your sister has another on the way…'

'Oh, yes.' Another smile softened his brow. 'In a couple of months.'

'Wow, so soon?'

He chuckled. 'Now you sound like my father.'

'Not your mother, though. I bet she's in her element.'

'You've got that right.' He went quiet again, withdrawing into his thoughts, and she watched as his lips quirked with whatever they were.

'They make good grandparents,' he said eventually, his tone sombre. 'Better grandparents than parents in many ways.'

She swallowed the little lump that formed in her throat. 'How so?'

'They're more relaxed. Mum's been trying to get Dad home more over the years and he finally seems to be paying attention. You should see him at Christmas now. He's practically regressed into being the biggest kid of all.'

She covered his hand on top of hers. 'Christmas was always very special at Highgrove.'

The manor would be lit up with decorations, festive colour in every room, the scent too. She'd spend the entire holiday season buzzing around the house with Freddie, trying not to get underfoot but getting involved all the same.

'It had its moments.' He turned to look at her, his smile not quite reaching the wistful look in his eyes. 'We had some good times.'

She nodded. 'We had *lots* of good times.'

So much passed between them in a simple look, so many memories. Her mother would always work late into the night, helping with the parties in the run-up to Christmas, ensuring every need was catered for, so they had been free to do what they'd wanted. Sneak mulled wine, eggnog, mince pies from Maggie, whatever had taken their fancy. All those good years of being friends, and then the one year when they had been more, so much more. Engaged and ostracised in one.

'I didn't go back to Highgrove, not even for Christmas, for a long time afterwards,' Freddie said as he travelled the same road as her. 'It took a lot of persuasion from Ally to get me back there, and even then four years had passed. I'd graduated, started a new life...'

'Really?' She frowned. 'But—but Christmas was such a huge thing for your family. It was so important for you all to be together.'

He looked away, withdrawing from her and she clutched his hand tighter.

'Freddie?'

'I told you, I blamed them. I didn't want to know my parents after they forced you out.'

'They did it because they loved you,' she said quietly. 'It must have broken their hearts to have you gone for so long.'

'What about my heart, Jas?' The force of his words made her flinch as he turned to her. 'And how can you lie there and defend them, after everything they said and did?'

'I'm not.'

'You are.'

'I'm just saying I understand, even if it hurt, even if—'

'Even if it tore us apart.'

Her breath shuddered through her and she looked at the sky.

'Sorry...' he said suddenly, squeezing her fingers. 'I've come to terms with it, but...'

'It still hurts.'

He nodded and she gave him a sad smile as she added, 'It still hurts us both.'

His eyes searched hers, taking in her words, accepting them. 'It's a ten-year-old pain, it makes sense that we can't simply shut it off.'

'I know.' She breathed in deeply as she gazed into the eyes of the man she loved so much, the man she'd missed so much… The man who deserved a family of his own to love and to cherish and with whom to continue on all the wondrous Highgrove traditions.

'It's a shame you're so set against marriage, Freddie, because you'd make a wonderful father.'

It may have come out of left field, in his eyes anyway, but she hadn't been able to keep it trapped inside and it was worth the flicker of emotion in his face, the pulse of his fingers beneath hers. Because for that brief moment she knew she'd opened his eyes to it and the joy of possibility.

But then he shook his head, his expression morphing into one of incredulity. 'So I can adopt the same parenting technique my father did for all those years? No, thank you.'

'Technique?' she frowned. 'What do you mean?'

'Absent parenting.' His eyes were on the sky again. 'I often thought the only reason he'd had a child was to produce an heir, someone to pass everything on to. When I was younger he was never around, when I was older all he wanted to discuss was the estate, the business…'

'But he loves you, Freddie.'

He shrugged it off. 'Either I was invisible or I was an asset. He only had Ally to keep Mum happy, to keep her occupied, give her less free time to call on his.'

'I'm sure that's not—'

'Hey, it's okay, Red.' He turned to her. 'I'm over it and, like I say, things are different now. Dad's improving with age, just like a fine wine…'

He was trying to make light of it, but she wasn't having it. 'Freddie, don't joke!'

'I'm not. I'm being serious. Being a grandparent has changed him.'

She stared at him, struggling to find the words.

'And he taught me my most important lesson.'

'Which is?'

'That I make a great uncle. A father...not so much.'

She didn't stop staring at him, her heart caught in a desperate spiral. 'Do you honestly think that because your father was an absent parent, you would be too?'

'Why wouldn't I? I'm just as busy, I'll be more so when I take on the estate, the title. I'll be stepping into his shoes and then some.'

'But you've also learned from his mistakes.'

'I've learnt to avoid them...and before you say it, this isn't the kind of avoidance that needs rectifying, Jas.'

'Of course it is, Freddie! This is worse than not standing up to your parents over the years.' He went to reply, but she wasn't done. 'Having a family of your own, being the good father I *know* you would be...you can't not do that!'

His eyes narrowed but he said nothing, and she could see the doubt, the sadness, the disbelief that he could be something different, something better.

'You're nothing like your father, Freddie... Okay, you look a little like him, and sometimes you can definitely be as brooding and pig-headed,' she teased, and saw the glimmer of a sparkle in his eyes. 'But your heart is your biggest asset. Yes, I love your brains...' *stay clear of the L word*, came the warning but she pressed on anyway '...and your intelligence. You don't look half bad either.'

She rolled onto her side, forcing back the sudden wave of seasickness and the rocking of the entire world as she rested her hand over his heart. 'But when you love, you love with the whole of you. You could never be like your father was, because it's not in you to be that way.'

He held her gaze, quiet, contemplative, and she let her eyes tell him what was in her heart, how she meant every word. Meant it and wanted it…for them.

Baby steps. That's what this was. Baby steps into doing what Madison had advised and getting him to see how good it could be if he opened his eyes to it. To an 'us'.

The problem was that her own heart was opening up right along with it and if she couldn't convince him, if this week truly was to be it…

She shut the thought down and lowered her head to his chest, curled into his side. She had to try, though…

'It's a shame you're so set against marriage, Freddie, because you'd make a wonderful father.'

Her words echoed through him long after their rest on the beach, but the jeering inner laughter that had brushed off her statement as crazy was gradually softening. Hours later, as they trekked through the rainforest and he was supposed to be focusing on what they were seeing, he could feel the change underway inside. The change tugging him back to how he'd once been, the future so bright and filled with promise. The promise of exactly that: a wife, kids, a home in Scotland.

And not just any wife—Jasmine.

It would be so easy to follow that path again, to let her wrap him up in her warmth, her light, her…love.

But then what?

His parents' expectations hadn't changed, the view of their peers hadn't changed. He'd be dragging her back into their elitist world where they would as readily snub her now as they had back then. Could their relationship truly survive it? Survive and flourish? With children *and* all the demands on their time from their respective businesses, his charity, the estate? He could feel his heart racing away with him, and not in a good way.

But if Jasmine was willing to face it, to risk it…

You're getting all fanciful, came the warning. *You haven't had a relationship that lasted more than a month in ten years, why would now be any different?*

Because it was her. It was Jasmine. And she'd made him remember how good it felt to be with someone, the right someone.

But what if it wasn't? What if this only worked now because they were away from all the obstacles that stopped them from having a life together before? What if they risked it now and…?

'Oh, my goodness, Freddie!' Her giddy call cut through his thoughts and he looked at her in the distance, her cheeks all bright again and jutting into her sunglasses as she grinned at him.

For the briefest moment he just treasured the colour being back in her cheeks, her body free of the tension that had held her taut on the boat. He'd wanted so badly to take away her discomfort, he'd wanted to be able to do something, anything…and it was just seasickness, nothing life threatening, but he'd felt so helpless in his desperation.

As helpless as he was in controlling the way he felt around her. The way he felt *for* her.

Day four of seven and she had his world turned upside down. All over again.

He quashed the anxious churn in his gut and grinned at her, grateful that his sunglasses would hide the rest.

'You have to see these, Freddie!'

He picked his way through the dense rainforest to join her and Michel, their guide.

'Welcome to the star of our tour!' Michel chuckled up at him. He was a small man with a big personality. 'This is the *coco de mer*—the coconut of the sea.'

'Look at them, Freddie! Just look!' Jasmine gestured to the ground. 'They look like giant…well, you know…'

She made a gesture like she was massaging a long, curved cylinder—she couldn't mean… He eyed the thick phallic object on the ground, with its small, yellow star-like flowers dotted around it and his grin widened. Oh, yes, she did.

'That is the catkin of the male tree,' Michel explained.

Jasmine gave a little giggle. 'It would be the male, wouldn't it?'

'And *you* would make that remark,' Freddie teased, high on her playfulness as their tour guide laughed heartily.

'Can you blame me? Look at what the female tree produces, it looks like a giant bottom!' She squeezed her fingers together like they held invisible sponges, as if he needed reminding of what one looked like, and then bent to lift a hefty wooden-looking thing off the ground. 'Goodness! It weighs a ton!'

'Yes, the nut or seed of the female tree can actually weigh up to twenty kilograms, if not more,' Michel informed them.

She turned and presented it to Freddie. 'See!'

His cheeks ached with his continued grin. It did indeed look like a very round bottom.

'And you turn it around and it has hair, just *there*!' Jasmine really was suppressing her giggles now and he felt light inside, caught up in her happy aura, her healthy glow, the boat all but forgotten along with his worries of moments before.

'The nut can grow to be as big as half a metre and they come out of the husks you see there.' Michel pointed up to the palms towering above them and the bulbous green orbs hanging there. 'It is the largest seed in the plant kingdom and is very rare, found only in the Seychelles, on the islands of Praslin and Curieuse.'

'Impressive!' She passed it to Freddie. 'Here, cop a feel.'

His laugh burst out of him as he shook his head at her and did just as she asked. 'Very smooth.'

She laughed more.

'You're such a kid.'

'Takes one to know one.' She winked at him and bent to put it back on the ground, ensuring he got an extended view of another bottom entirely and one that he definitely did want to feel. Not that he would in front of their guide. But later...definitely later.

'Because of the unusual qualities to both,' Michel continued, 'many a legend has been told about these trees.'

'Oh, yes...' she sent Freddie a look '...we can imagine.'

'For example, it is believed that at night, when storms rage, the trees come together in a passionate embrace.'

She clasped her hands to her chest. 'How romantic!'

'Indeed. But as they are shy, legend also has it that should you catch them at it, you will go blind or quite possibly die.'

'Well, that's depressing!' she blurted, her pout dramatic.

Freddie chuckled. He wasn't sure what was more entertaining, Jasmine's reaction—which he really, really did want to kiss off her face—or the tale itself. Either way, he knew he had to capture this moment.

He stepped back, pulled his phone from the pocket of his shorts.

'I assume they're not too shy to have a photo taken?' he said to Michel.

'Ah, of course, but let me get one of you together instead?'

Jasmine's smile faltered on her lips. Her thoughts were probably mirroring his own. Getting a photo of her had been risky enough, a permanent memory for him to take with him when this was all over, but a photo of them together...

He offered the phone to Michel, who took it from him

and waved them closer together. 'Closer, a bit more. Do you want to pick up the catkin and the nut?'

Jasmine let out a giggle, her mood lifting as easily as that. 'Get the catkin, Freddie! I'll do the bottom!'

He bent and picked it up. It was impossible not to hold it in a way that *wasn't* suggestive, and Jasmine's body quivered with her continued laughter as she clutched the nut to her front.

He shook his head at her, hooked his arm around her waist to pull her close, inhaled her scent, her giddiness… looked at the camera.

'Say coconut of the sea!' Michel ordered, and they performed for the camera, Freddie's grin very easy when he had his arm around a laughing Jasmine.

It felt so right. So perfect.

And now he would have the photo to remind him of this moment, again and again and again.

Michel handed the phone back to him, his grin turning mischievous, his wink definitely so. 'It is also said that the meat of the nut has powerful aphrodisiac qualities.'

Jasmine leaned in closer. 'Fancy that, Freddie.'

He shook his head again. He didn't need an aphrodisiac when Jasmine was around. He was tuned in, turned on and more alive than he'd felt in years.

Ten, to be exact.

And soon it would be over once more. Unless…

Should he listen to her? Could they give it a shot? A real shot. Take it slowly, day by day. They didn't have to test their relationship at the outset with all that it meant to be a Highgrove. There was time to adjust to the idea, for his family to adjust too, before throwing the responsibilities and social pressures of being a Highgrove into the mix. He could stay in New York a little longer, they could commute, date, see the world. Long-distance relationships worked all the time…didn't they?

He tightened his arm around her, kissed her head, his heart pressing him to agree. 'Let's see what else the Vallée de Mai has to offer before you get any more excited…'

'Moi?' She turned to pout up at him, her nut jutting against his catkin. 'You forget how well I can read you, Freddie.'

She gifted him another wink before placing the nut back on the ground and taking off after Michel, leaving Freddie, his catkin and his racing thoughts hanging.

CHAPTER THIRTEEN

JASMINE LET OUT a squeal of delight and squeezed her legs tighter around Freddie's waist as he swirled her reclining body around in the sea, his grin as bright as the sun.

'I could get used to this,' she said as she relaxed into the move and let him take the lead.

'You and me both.' He tugged her up against his chest and she wrapped her arms around him, kissing him with all the pleasure his words had triggered.

It was day five. They barely had any time left. There would be no getting used to anything if she couldn't change his mind.

He ran his hands through her hair, held her close as he broke the kiss to stare down into her eyes.

'What?' she said, sensing something coming, seeing it swim in his breathtaking blue eyes and spasm in his jaw.

He pressed his forehead to hers, squeezed his eyes shut with a small shake of his head before opening them again. 'Nothing.'

She raised her brows, toying with the damp hair at his nape. 'You could have fooled me.'

'I was treasuring the moment, treasuring you in this teasing slip of a red bikini.' He rolled his body against hers suggestively, but she knew he was trying to distract her from the true nature of his thoughts. 'Is that a crime?'

'No.' She kissed him sweetly. 'I'm treasuring it too. I wish it didn't have to end.'

'All good things have to come to an end, Jas. That's life and why it needs to be treasured now.'

'But this...' She caught her lip in her teeth, searched his eyes that seemed to tell her so much and yet nothing at all.

She needed to be brave. She needed to be honest and confident and strong. All the things she wished she'd been ten years ago. He may not want to get all serious right now, but she did. 'This doesn't have to end.'

She felt the tension seeping into his body. 'Reality has other ideas.'

'You mean your family do,' she said softly.

'Ten years hasn't changed anything, Jas. They still expect a high society bride.'

'But you don't want that.'

He wet his lips, hesitant. Was it a chink in his armour? Was she slowly getting through to him? 'No, I don't.'

'But...?' she pressed, knowing the risk she was taking, that she could be destroying the moment, and potentially the rest of the stay too if she called it wrong. But she wouldn't be afraid. Not this time.

'If life was simple, I wouldn't hesitate to go after the future you seem so sure is possible, but don't you want more? You deserve better than to be surrounded by a family like mine.'

She laughed to hide the sea of emotion inside her. 'I deserve better, and yet I'm the one deemed to be lacking.'

'You know what I mean.'

'I do, Freddie, but I'm not interested in running away. Not any more.'

'You say that like you've forgotten how it was...' He suddenly looked grey in the sun. His blue eyes were pale and haunted, his arms wrapping around her, holding her close. 'Do you not remember how they were? What they said? And the people that witnessed it, your mother included?'

Her lashes fluttered as the memory chilled her heart. 'Of course I remember.'

'I'm sorry, I don't want to inflict any more pain, Jas.' He gritted his teeth, his throat bobbing as his arms flexed around her.

'Don't apologise.' She cupped his face, speared his eyes with her own as she stressed, 'It's all in the past. What I care about is the future, Freddie. The future we could have if we choose it.'

She reached up to press a kiss to his lips, a moment's connection before she dropped back.

'Don't you see, Freddie, we've spent the last ten years filling our days, our nights too, trying to find contentment.'

'And failed.'

'Yes.'

'Because something was always missing.'

She nodded. 'We didn't have each other.'

His smile was small, but they were finishing each other's sentences, which had to be a good sign. It had to mean he was feeling the same way…

'Don't you want to at least try?'

He took a deep breath, his eyes not once leaving hers. 'I'd like to think we could try, but there are so many factors to consider.'

'Like your family?'

'Eventually, yes. But I was thinking more of our work, my charity, our crazy schedules.'

'Isn't the perk of getting to the heights we have that we get to ease off a little now and bring in more people to help, share the load? My mother tried to tell me the same, even in the early days when Work Made Simple was just taking off, Tim too, but my app was my passion then…'

'And now?'

She gave a small laugh. 'You never used to be such a compliment seeker!'

'Not the words I want to hear, Red…' He bowed his head, kissed her deeply, so deeply she almost lost sight of the magnitude of where their conversation was heading.

She pushed him away. 'You're my passion, Freddie. Happy?'

'Very.' His grin took her breath away, but the tension was far too quick to follow. 'How do you feel about a long-distance relationship?'

She frowned. 'But I'm in Edinburgh, and so will you—'

He was shaking his head, killing off her words.

'No. If we do this, I'll delay my return, give us time to date, to do all the things we never had the money, the freedom, to do before. Have a relationship away from the pressures of Highgrove. Give us time to see where this goes on our terms.'

'But you said they needed you to come home, your father, the estate, Rupert...'

'They've waited this long, they can wait a little longer.'

Her frown deepened, hope and relief warring with what was expected of him, what was needed of him in Edinburgh, of his sister, his nephew... Was she coming between them again?

'But—'

'I'm not talking for ever, Red, just until we're ready.'

Was he right? Did they need to take this time now before facing the pressures that had broken them so long ago?

But how would they know when they were ready? She couldn't imagine feeling any more ready than she did right now.

'Hey, don't look so pensive! I thought you'd be pleased, happy. I don't want to be all egotistical about it, but I'd even go as far as to say overjoyed...' He spun her in the water, eased her body up against him until her eyes were at the same level as his. 'What say you, Red?'

Happiness had her chest blooming so much she thought it would burst. 'I am happy, so happy.'

She kissed him, wrapped her arms around his neck tightly, scarcely daring to believe and believing all the same. Pushing out the worry with the strength to follow his lead this time.

'This calls for a drink to celebrate,' he said against her lips.

'*Another* toast?'

He laughed. 'Yes!'

'Come on.' He released her, taking hold of her hand as he turned away.

But she held still. 'I'll follow you in a second.'

'Okay.' He eyed her speculatively. 'Though you are starting to look rather prune-like so I wouldn't leave it too long.'

'Freddie!' She thrust water at him, her laugh high. High on their conversation, on the future, on him, all him.

But the truth was that she needed a moment. Her heart was drumming a crazy beat, her insides alive with a thousand flutters, and she needed to catch her breath. Clear her thoughts.

He chuckled. 'Suit yourself, but don't be too long. I have plans for today and all of them involve you, champagne and whatever creole delights Monique can have delivered to our room.'

'You're insatiable!'

'So are you, my love…'

My love. Her racing heart pulsed.

'Just another of the many reasons we're our perfect match.'

He winked and turned away. Leaving her floating on air rather than water. She watched him wade back towards the deck that reached out over the sea, the rich timber platform creating a seamless connection between their bedroom quarters and the water, and sucked in the deepest of breaths. She wanted to cry out to the heavens in joy, dance on the spot, somersault, do all manner of crazy things to ease the chaos inside her.

But it wasn't chaos, it was a fullness. A rich warmth where there'd once been a chill, an emptiness. A Freddie-shaped hole.

She gave a little squeal, unable to keep it all contained, and turned to dive beneath the surface of the water, enjoying the rush of it cooling off her flushed face. She and Freddie. Freddie and her. It was happening.

She surfaced and rolled onto her back, floating in the water that was so very calm today. Much better than yesterday morning when they'd taken the trip out to Praslin. The memory of it made her smile, even as she touched a hand to her stomach, grateful that the sensation was long gone. But Freddie had been so desperate to look after her, to make her feel better, because he loved her. He hadn't said it yet, but then neither had she. They hadn't needed to. It was there in their words, their faces, as obvious as it had ever been.

Something nudged her foot, and she flinched away, looking to see what it was.

Wow!

Now, *that* was a turtle!

Not one from Freddie's imaginary spiel to keep her distracted on the boat, but a real, bona fide hawksbill, its brightly coloured, intricately patterned shell so beautiful as it glided through the water around her. It wasn't scared of her or wary. It was such a pleasure to watch. The only thing that could make the moment more perfect would be if Freddie were by her side.

She looked towards the shore, trying to seek him out and gesture to him. She frowned, shaded her eyes from the sun as she searched the deck, the room… There he was, in the bedroom. Her frown deepened.

He was pacing, his phone to his ear as he raked his hand through his hair and clutched the back of his head.

She forgot the turtle, forgot the beautiful water.

Something was wrong.

Something was very wrong.

'No. It's fine,' he told his sister firmly. 'I'll be there as soon as I can.'

'Freddie?'

He turned to see Jasmine behind him, the lurch inside his chest so forceful that he had to press the phone to his ear to avoid dropping it altogether. Her green eyes were drawn with concern, her knuckles white where she gripped her fluffy cream towel around her.

He tried to give a reassuring smile, but it was stiff, fraught with the news his sister had just shared. Fraught with the realisation that their time together was over sooner than planned. More than that, they were over. What an idiot he'd been to think they could have time to build a relationship on their terms, under their control, cushioned from the destructive forces of his family, their peers, the demands on his time.

'I'll call you as soon as I have an ETA, Ally.'

He hung up and strode to the bed, tossing the phone down on it and trying to quash the rolling of his gut, the hammering of his heart, his mind awash with what was happening back home and what it meant.

He sensed rather than heard Jasmine move, her fingers soft as they came to rest on his shoulder.

'What's happened?' Her voice was so quiet and all he wanted to do, all he ever wanted to do, was pull her into his arms and hold her close. He didn't want to leave. He didn't want to go it alone. Not any more.

But this… He wasn't ready, *they* weren't ready. But he had no choice. The very reason he had to go was the very reason he couldn't take her with him. His family. His father. They needed him. Not in a year or two's time. Now.

'Freddie?' she whispered, her body gently coming up

against his back, comforting him when he didn't deserve to take comfort from her. Not when he knew what he was about to do would crush her. That off the back of their very recent conversation he was about to take it all back.

He turned, tried to prepare himself for seeing her this close, and still his breath left him, his arms wrapping around her and holding her close as he sucked in a stabilising breath. And another.

Again, not fair. Not fair to take strength from her presence when…

'I have to go. My father— My father's had a stroke.'

'Oh, Freddie!' Her head shot up, her green eyes piercing his tortured soul. How could it be that the one woman he wanted to get him through this was the one he couldn't have by his side? 'I'm so sorry. Is he…is he okay?'

'I don't know. He's stable but…' He released her, ran his hands through his hair, panic rising. 'They're running tests and I need to be there.'

'Of course you do.' She wrapped her arms around her middle, her eyes blazing with her compassion, her concern. 'What can I do?'

'Nothing.' She flinched and he cursed his abruptness, thrust his hands back through his hair. 'I'm going to make some calls. See what flights I can sort.'

'Let me do that.'

'No, it's fine. My PA will take care of most it.'

'Then tell me what else I can do. Anything?'

He shook his head. What he wanted he wouldn't—*couldn't*—ask for.

'There's nothing. Just— I'm sorry.'

'Why are you apologising?'

He looked her straight in the eye, forced the words out. 'For leaving.'

She shook her head. 'You don't need to apologise for that, you need to get home.'

'I don't just mean… I don't— I can't…'

'Freddie?' She frowned up at him. 'You can't…?'

'This changes things, Jas, don't you see?' His head was a jumbled mess, his words too.

'Things? What things?'

'There's no time any more, no time for us before I return to Highgrove.'

'No. But that's okay. I can still come with you. You shouldn't go through this alone. I wouldn't come to the hospital, not with… I wouldn't want to cause distress, but I could be in Edinburgh for you.'

She stepped towards him, and he reached out on impulse, his hands soft on her hips. She was offering him everything in that second and the selfish part of him, the part that had longed for her all this time, the part that had been elated on the plans forming not thirty minutes ago, wanted to say yes.

Say yes, and never look back. But he couldn't. He couldn't see a way to that, not now.

'I can't ask that of you.'

'Of course you can,' she whispered.

She was so small, so petite, and he was transported back ten years. To the same small frame, facing a room full of his parents' nearest and dearest, the laughter in their eyes, the sympathy in some, the scorn in others. No. Never again.

'No, Jas. You should stay and enjoy the rest of your holiday. You work hard, you're supposed to play harder, right?'

He forced a smile, tried to act like his whole world wasn't falling in.

'Don't, Freddie. Don't act like this is all okay, because it's not okay. We were making a commitment to one another… We were making plans.'

'Plans that can no longer happen.'

'So we'll make new plans. We'll work out another path to keep us together.'

Her words teased at his shattering heart, tugged at his chest, and he had to stop them, stop her, stop it.

He pressed a kiss to her lips, a long, desperate kiss to get enough, enough to see him through, and she let him take, her body turning into liquid in his hands...and maybe, just maybe... No!

He thrust her away, tried to ignore the way her body trembled beneath his fingers, the way she shook her head at him, the way her dazed eyes glistened with realisation. This was goodbye. It was over.

'You've had a shock, Freddie, a huge shock, you're not thinking clearly.'

'I'm thinking well enough to know I can't do it. I can't deal with you, us, Dad, my family, all of it!' He'd crashed to earth the second his sister had given him the news. The brutal reality of life hitting him smack in the face and laughing at the very idea he could have had a future on his own terms. 'We were foolish to see this as some fantastical second chance when the reality is so very different.'

'It doesn't have to be all that different, not if we don't want it to be.'

He hesitated, staring into those dizzying green eyes and wishing so hard he could believe it. But he'd gone it alone for so many years and alone he could keep control of his life, his heart. He couldn't inflict pain, neither could he suffer it.

And yet here they both were swimming in it. Pain.

Not even a week in and this was where they were. How would it be weeks, months, a year down the line?

He couldn't listen, couldn't even look at her. He needed this over and he needed to be back in Scotland. At his father's bedside. The man had always been a towering strength, a force to be reckoned with, now he lay vulnerable, weak…

'I'm sorry.' He turned away from her, shutting it all out, something he'd become a master of over the years, and snatched up his phone, dialling his PA. 'Please go, Jas. Let me deal with this. I'll come and find you once I have my flight sorted.'

He sensed her step towards him and stilled, his entire body rigid as he anticipated her touch… But nothing came.

She padded from the room as stealthily as she'd made her way into his heart again and he clenched his eyes shut, forced down the rising tide within him.

Focus on Dad, on your family who need you.

The rest can come later, much later…when she's no longer within reach.

CHAPTER FOURTEEN

JASMINE POURED THE wine as Sadie and Izzy debated the complicated state of her love life. Now that they'd got over the shock of M choosing Freddie as her perfect match, they were rapidly debating her next move.

Like it was some complicated game of chess. Not a star-crossed love affair that had survived the test of years and come back all the stronger for it. All the stronger but with no hope of a future.

Because if there had been, Freddie would have wanted her by his side in his hour of need. If she'd had the option of having him by her side when she'd lost Mum, she would have grabbed hold with both hands.

'You know, I still can't believe it was Freddie Highgrove,' Izzy murmured into her freshly filled glass.

'It's all very romantic.' Sadie swooned dramatically as she flopped back onto the living room floor, her glass safely resting on the coffee table. 'Very fated.'

'Yes, we've done the whole fated thing to death already,' Jasmine grumbled. 'It doesn't make me feel any better.'

'Well, of course not.' Sadie shot up onto her elbows to stare at Jasmine perched on the edge of her teal sofa. 'You're in love and broken-hearted all over again! It's ridiculous.'

'I'm so glad the state of my heart is something to ridicule.'

'I wasn't ridiculing it.'

'You just said it was ridiculous.'

'Yes, well, it is,' she blustered. 'He should have taken you with him.'

'Yes, he should have,' Izzy added softly, from the other end of the sofa. 'But...not many people would react to the news he'd just been given in a sane, rational way. He was clearly out of his mind with worry, and to have your very new, very uncertain relationship on top… It's kind of understandable.'

'Yeah, yeah, I get it.' Sadie nodded vigorously. 'And I hate to say it after all these years and us telling you to forget him, Jas, but I feel sorry for him. And you. It's quite obvious he's hopelessly in love with you.'

'Is it?' Jasmine took up her glass and threw back too big a sip. She couldn't help it. Her friends were a bad influence and as for Freddie…it had been days, days and not a word. Not that they'd exchanged numbers, but she knew Freddie could reach her if he really wanted to. M would make sure of that. 'I don't know how you can think that, not when I'm struggling to believe it.'

'Don't be ridiculous.'

She gave Sadie a hard stare.

'Okay, no more ridiculous. Help me out, Iz!'

'From what you've told us, I have to say I'm with Sadie. I think he loves you and he's protecting you, protecting both of you from the past repeating itself.'

'Exactly!' Sadie declared.

'But we dealt with all that, we were making plans—'

'Plans that kept things in your control,' Izzy said softly. 'Gave you time together before facing such a huge hurdle.'

'He basically panicked, Jas, surely you can see that?'

'I thought so too, at the time, but he's not reached out, not even the briefest of messages.'

'He has a lot on his plate.'

She grimaced. She knew that too and now she felt even worse for questioning it.

'And it's not like you've messaged him.'

'No, but I wanted to give him the space he so obviously wanted.'

'Well, he's had his space!' Sadie blustered. 'Time to close in.'

'Hey, easy, Sades…' Izzy waved their excitable friend down. 'The thing is he's so clearly used to going it alone and keeping a tight lid on his life. The whole talk of planning, taking things slowly, putting off the inevitable showdown with his family and facing his aristocratic world that treated you like…well, crap. And then life comes along and turns all those plans for a future on their head. I get why he walked away from you—he was protecting you from a future so out of his control it scared him.'

'But I don't need his protection, I want us to face it together.'

'Maybe part of him feels that the old Jasmine is still in there deep down, the one that did run in the face of his parents all those years ago,' Sadie supplied, trying to be helpful, but it only frustrated her more.

'I told you, we dealt with all that. And he knows I'm different now, he knows I'm stronger, better equipped to deal with it.' She cursed in her desperation. 'I'm a successful businesswoman, able to stand up in front of thousands and fight for what I believe in, so why would he doubt my ability to stand and fight for us now?'

'Because the risk is far greater.' Izzy gave a hapless shrug.

'Absolutely.' Sadie nodded. 'If he was to believe in you now, and you broke his heart, or worse, if he believed in you and his parents, their world broke you all over again when you are, as you say, a strong, successful, independent businesswoman…'

Her stomach lurched as her friends' meaning hit home. They were right, there was so much more to this. So much more for him to fret over, to worry about, to doubt. Even if he had put their past to bed.

'It's true, honey, think about it,' Izzy urged softly.

Jasmine's brain was racing.

After the initial shock of his leaving the Seychelles, she'd gone over and over everything. Revisiting every conversation, every look. Questioning whether she'd imagined the love shining back at her, the desire to be together, the happiness. Was there a part of him that didn't want to let her in? To share his life? Was it an excuse to end it?

No, she couldn't believe it of him. He was hurting and acting on impulse, pushing her out and doing what he was used to, shouldering it alone. And this in itself was a test, a test she had to win. To prove that this time she was staying. She wouldn't run like she once had, she would stay by his side, where she wanted to be and where she should be. 'I need to show him we're stronger together.'

'Ooh, fighting talk,' Sadie cooed. 'I like it!'

'Only...what if he won't give me the chance?'

Izzy frowned. 'Why does he need to give you the chance?'

'Since when do you wait for an opportunity to come your way? You need to take the bull by the horns,' Sadie said, doing an impression of doing just that with her fists.

'Yes.' Izzy grinned. 'Take the courage to his doorstep.'

She frowned at both of them, deciding the second bottle of wine was clearly a mistake.

'You need to go to Highgrove, silly!' they both said in unison.

'To the manor?'

'Yes!'

'But...they're going through so much at the moment. To turn up when his father is in hospital and potentially stir things up...'

'To be frank...' Sadie said, sweeping up her glass and necking a gulp '...the way they treated you all those years ago, they don't deserve such thought now.'

Izzy waved Sadie down yet again. 'I get what you're saying, but you have the contact details for their new housekeeper, don't you?'

'Yes, she was friends with Mum and is one of my clients now.'

'Then contact her,' Izzy said. 'Find out the lie of the land and then make a call on it. But it seems to me the only way to prove your love for him and have him return it is to go to Highgrove Manor and declare it, just like he did ten years ago.'

'Only this time it's you outing the pair of you, fighting for you,' Sadie added.

'And what if it's the last thing he wants me to do? What if I'm wrong and he doesn't love me?'

'Is it really going to hurt more than it does now?' Izzy said softly.

Nothing could hurt more, but at least she still had the uncertainty, the teeny-tiny glimmer of hope. If she went there and he rejected her…

'You're no chicken, Jas!' Sadie shot up and plonked herself between them on the sofa, slapping Jasmine's back. 'And it's high time you stood up to those Highgroves and stood up for your heart too.'

'You've really got nothing to lose, honey. Sadie's right on this one.'

'And *I* really need to get a phone and record you saying that,' Sadie said, and Izzy shoved her, their laughter filling the room and fading out just as quickly. Their focus returned to her as they grinned with absolute encouragement.

'You can do this,' they both assured her.

Could she? Did she really have it in her?

But then, wasn't that exactly what she was trying to prove? That their love was worth the bumpy road that lay ahead, regardless of how difficult it might be.

'Thank you, dear.' Freddie's mum gently patted his arm as she took the gin and tonic from him and sipped at it. 'I'm so glad to have you home, it's been very reassuring for me and your father.'

'Where else would I be?'

Ally looked at him over the water she had opted for in her present condition. 'Yes, where else indeed.'

He gave her a warning look, but her eyes danced in the light of the study fire, her own pleasure at his return very evident, her amusement over his predicament all the more so. He had told her too much, but then his sister had always been adept at reading him and asking the right kind of questions.

'It will be good to have your father home tomorrow,' his mother continued, unaware of the siblings' silent exchange. 'He won't appreciate the changes that need to be made but together we can convince him.'

'Of course.'

'You will stay for a bit longer, won't you, Frederick?'

'Yes, do stay.' It was Ally's way of saying 'I'm not done with you yet,' though he could hardly see what else she hoped to glean. He'd made it clear to her he was a mess and the only solution, the only thing he wanted above all else, was Jasmine. By his side. And he'd made a complete hash of that.

Would she even let him near her again? Would she forgive him for walking away?

'Frederick?'

He looked at his mother's imploring gaze and scoured his brain for the question he was supposed to be answering. Was he staying? 'Yes, of course I will.'

She smiled at him, her back ramrod straight, her posture perfect, even when she wasn't on show and it was just her children with her. He took up his whisky and strode to the fire, leaned his elbow on the mantel as he stared down into the flames. It had been over a week since he'd left her.

Not just left her but left her without any hope. And all

because of what? He didn't want to inflict pain on her further down the road. Well, newsflash, they were already in pain, a pain he couldn't imagine getting any worse, and he knew the only thing that would take it away was to have her by his side. To give her—no, to give *them*—a chance.

A chance at the future they'd always wanted. It might be a decade too late but in so many ways they were better prepared for it now. He just wished he'd come to that conclusion before he'd walked away from her and left all that was good in his life back in paradise—*their* paradise.

He threw back his whisky, grimacing over the burn of the alcohol and his mistake.

'What is it, brother?'

He shot Ally another look. She knew well enough what was wrong and she'd already made her thoughts clear. That he was a damn fool. A fool for letting Jas go, a fool for giving up the one true happiness he'd ever known.

'*Alison*, really. It's been a tough week for all of us, I hardly think the question necessary.'

'Sorry, Mother, but we know father is going to be fine. It was a timely warning and one that will see him listening to our advice at last and taking it easy. We've been on him for years and even Dr McGivern was starting to get blue faced.'

'Yes,' she agreed. 'In that sense it will be a blessing. He certainly needs to retire sooner rather than later.'

'It should be easy enough to convince him of that,' Freddie said. 'Now that I'm moving back to Edinburgh permanently.'

Both women choked on their drinks.

'You are?' Ally said, her eyes wide.

'I have a few things I need to tie up Stateside but, yes, I expect to make Edinburgh my home again in the coming months.'

'Well, your father will be most relieved,' his mother

rushed out, colour warming her cheeks as her eyes misted over. 'Though he won't appreciate his stroke being the deciding factor.'

'It wasn't. It's been on my mind for a while.'

She narrowed her gaze on him. 'You never said anything.'

'Well, I have now.' He winced at how defensive he sounded but he'd barely slept in a week and it was starting to show. And he missed *her*, really missed her.

'Maybe if you'd said something sooner, this—'

'Mum.' Ally's eyes snapped to her, cutting off the blame that was so obviously coming.

'Yes, well,' his mother backtracked, her voice rising a little as she wriggled in her seat. 'It will make a wonderful change, having you home again.'

'It really will,' Ally said, smiling at him now, her eyes full of compassion and understanding and…hope. Did she know his thoughts? That he was this close to fighting for the woman he'd fought and failed to keep before?

The ancient doorbell rang through the house, its sound jarring and unexpected.

His mother frowned. 'Who can that be? It's a bit late for unexpected visitors.'

Grateful for the distraction, he headed to the door. 'I'll go and check.'

'No need, Stevens will get it.'

'I'll go anyway. The last thing you need is visitors at this late hour. I'll send them on their way.'

'Very good, dear.'

CHAPTER FIFTEEN

SHE WAS ABOUT to reach for the bell again when she saw a shadow approach through the small bevelled windowpanes that made up the top half of the heavy wooden door. Her heart fluttered into her throat and she clutched her chest, seeking comfort from the locket hidden beneath the layers of clothing.

Maybe she should have left it until morning. It was getting late in the day and she knew they'd been to the hospital that afternoon, as they had done every afternoon since the Laird had been admitted. She also knew he was doing well or else she wouldn't be here now. But…

She was nervous.

The long approach to the house had given her too much time to think and agonise over her decision, while reacquainting herself with her childhood and her times with Freddie. Scaling the walls that guarded the main house, climbing the trees that lined the winding driveway, sailing on the loch, building a den and enjoying a stolen tin of Maggie's shortbread, and hiding out in the guest house hidden in the hills…

So many happy memories.

But the trees arching over the driveway had never felt more oppressive as she'd driven beneath them. The house in its vast, austere beauty had loomed dark and grey, looking ever more formidable as she'd approached. Even the rolling amethyst hills surrounding it, the pink hue of the setting sun reflecting off the Highgrove loch and the sight of the deer grazing beside it had done nothing to ease her nerves.

Nothing could penetrate the chill in her heart as she'd climbed the broad stone steps, remembering the night she had run down them, unseeing of the ground, the ice as the tears had rolled freely…

But that was then, and this was now. And she wasn't running scared.

She sucked in a breath as the door began to open, raised her chin as her lips parted, ready to explain herself to the member of staff answering, and…gasped.

'Freddie!'

'Jasmine?'

He looked as stunned as she felt. He scrubbed his face, blinked and blinked again. 'It's really you. What are you…?'

He widened his blue eyes at her, their bloodshot state making her want to cry as her hand wavered between them and she fought the urge to reach for him. He'd aged in a week, lines marring his brow, stubble darkening his jaw, dark smudges beneath his eyes and his skin so very pale against the white of his shirt, the black of his suit. Had she got it wrong? Was his father worse?

Finally, she found her voice. 'Freddie, I'm sorry. I had to see how you were, how your father was.'

He looked back over his shoulder into the darkened hallway beyond, stepped forward and pulled the door to leave a narrow gap.

'He's fine, doing much better already. But you…' His words trailed off as he cupped her face, his thumbs trembling as they swept across her cheekbones. 'After all I said, all I did…'

She covered his hands with hers. 'I had to come, Freddie.'

He shook his head, his lips curving into a smile that was all the more powerful for its sorrow. 'I can't believe you're really here.'

'Well, believe it.' She wet her lips, searched his gaze as she admitted, 'Wherever you are is where I belong.'

He closed his eyes, said her name very quietly.

'I'm here to prove to you that we're stronger together, that you don't need to protect us, to protect me. I no longer need you to be our voice. I love you, Freddie, and I want the world to know it.'

She used his decade-old declaration to bring her point home, but as he opened his eyes, all she saw was anguish and pain, his head shake seeming to reject it all. He opened his mouth and she wanted to cover her ears to whatever was about to come, but instead he drew her body against his. Held her tight.

'I missed you, Red.'

She sank into him, her arms wrapping around him as a sob rose up within her. 'I missed you too. I missed you for ten years, I missed you for a week and, still, I couldn't say which one was worse.'

He pressed a long kiss to her hair, his deep breath an audible rasp above her, but no words came. She pulled back, just enough to look up into his eyes.

'Please, give us a second chance, Freddie. We deserve it, don't we?'

He kissed her, his lips soft and urgent at the same time and she allowed herself the pleasure of it, the joy of being in his arms again, of feeling like she had come home, at last.

But she wasn't. This was Highgrove Manor. And he still hadn't verbally given her his love, his agreement, hope…

She dropped back. 'Freddie, pl—'

'Freddie?' The door shifted open. 'Who is—? *Jasmine?*'

Their heads snapped to a gaping Ally in the doorway, her wide eyes the colour of Freddie's, her sleek black ponytail swinging as she looked from one to the other and back again. And then she started to smile.

'Alison! What's going on?' Their mother appeared alongside her, her voice as grand as the pearls and deep blue trouser suit she wore, her greying hair fixed perfectly into the same tight chignon she had always favoured. 'Jasmine? Jasmine *Walker*? What the devil...?'

She half expected Freddie to jump away or straighten, do anything to lessen their embrace, but his arm tightened around her. 'Jasmine and—'

'I can explain,' Jasmine said over him. It was her turn to do the talking. Or at least she thought it was, but where did she start? She'd recited so many versions of this tale in her head and they all evaded her now.

'You'd better come on in,' his mother said, her eyes both hard and confused, before turning away to march down the hall, muttering something about her son's long-awaited return to Edinburgh making much more sense now.

Ally gave her an encouraging smile, her hand reaching out to gently squeeze Jasmine's arm as her other rested over her very pronounced bump. She looked every bit the elegant aristocrat in the navy woollen dress she wore, but her smile had always made Jasmine feel welcome, accepted. 'It's so good to see you, honey.'

And then she was hurrying off in her mother's wake.

Jasmine moved to go after her, but Freddie held her still. 'No, we're not doing this. Mum,' he called after her. 'I'm going to talk to Jasmine in private and we will—'

'*No*, Freddie.' Jasmine pressed her palm to his chest and gave him a hard stare. 'There are things I need to say and it's important I say them in front of everyone.'

She could do this. She *would* do it. For them.

'You'd best get the girl a drink, Frederick.'

'I love you, Freddie...wherever you are is where I belong...'

His heart beat faster, Jasmine's words repeating over and over in his mind, warming his chest that had been chilled for days. But was she crazy?

After everything that had happened within these four walls, she wanted to come back here and declare it…

The answer was a resounding yes. Everything about her showed determination: striding ahead of him through the hall; entering the room before him; stopping in front of the fire to face the sofa and armchairs either side, one already occupied by his mother.

No hiding, no cowering, only the slightest nip to her lip that told him she was battling nerves. Her freed hair was a mass of colour as the fire danced at her rear, her thick cream jumper swallowing her up, her legs all the more slender in beige leggings and black riding boots. Even with her back straight, her chin raised, she looked petite, but far from vulnerable and never more beautiful to his Red-starved eyes.

He wanted to pull her back into him, whisk her away, kiss her until nothing else and no one else existed.

'Frederick!' His eyes shot to his mother. 'A drink!'

'I'll sort it,' Ally said smoothly, quick to move. 'Why don't you take a seat, Jasmine?'

Ally offered her a space on the sofa and Jasmine gave her a smile and sat, folding her hands in her lap as she gave him—*him*—a reassuring smile.

'What can I get you?' his sister asked her.

'Whatever you're having is fine.'

'Oh, no, you don't want what I'm having.' She rested her hand over the curve of her belly. 'I'm on the water.'

'Water's fine.'

'Okay.' Though his sister clearly thought something much stronger would be wise. 'Ice, lemon?'

Jasmine smiled at her. 'Just as it comes. Thank you.'

Ally disappeared and Freddie found himself back at the fire, his forearm resting on the mantel, trying to give the impression that all was fine, but he knew his eyes told another story. He looked from his mother to Jasmine, hardly daring to believe that this was happening. That she was here.

But this was Red. *His* Red. She embodied everything he'd loved as a teen and she'd grown into a woman with all the confidence and strength he'd tried to thrust on her before she'd been ready.

And on top of that she was smiling at him, *she* was giving *him* the strength.

The corners of his mouth twitched, the beginnings of a smile he hadn't given in days, and, satisfied, she cleared her throat softly and looked at his mother.

'I hope you don't mind me turning up so unexpectedly…'

He looked at his mother too, the wasp she was chewing putting up a good fight.

'It must be very important.'

'It is, Lady Highgrove, it really is.' She glanced at him and then she sat straighter, angling her body towards his mother.

'First, can I just say I'm so glad to hear that the Laird is recovering well. I was very sorry to learn of his stroke.'

'Thank you. Your concern is appreciated.'

Jasmine gave her a small smile, her eyes sparkling with compassion as she planted her palms on her thighs. She breathed in deep, letting it out slowly. 'I don't want to beat around the bush, Lady Highgrove, so forgive me if I get straight to the point.'

His mother's eyes widened marginally but Freddie's eyes narrowed on his dear sweet firecracker with her blazing red hair and her bright green eyes, cheeks as pink as a rose, lips as sweet as candy. His heart swelled with both love and pride.

She didn't need him to do anything but watch.

She didn't *want* him to do anything.

And it was a pretty good job too, because right now he

was the one that was weak, utterly immobilised by her. Hanging on her next move, her next word, all her.

'No forgiveness necessary. Please, continue.'

'I am in love with your son,' Jasmine blurted, and his heart leapt with her confession, his smile twitching to life again as she pressed her lips together and bit the inside of them.

His mother gave no reaction at all as Jasmine leaned closer. 'Truth is, I've never stopped loving him. I've loved him for almost all of my life and, frankly, if that's not a good enough reason for me to be worthy of him, then let this be another. I *know* I can make him happy. I will love him, care for him and be there for him. I have no need of your family name, your wealth, your social status—'

He was torn between watching his love declare her feelings for him so passionately and watching his mother's face slowly change. The flickering emotions sweeping across her features were hard to judge, but he knew one thing, she wasn't immune.

'I am my own woman, with my own substantial fortune, and I can stand my ground. I don't need a man to secure my place in this world, but I do need Freddie to make me feel complete. I am lost without him, Lady Highgrove. And if he will have me then I promise to spend my life loving him and doing right by him, in sickness and in health, till death do us part.'

The room fell silent, the pounding of his heart very loud in his ears as he realised that, whatever happened now, nothing would get in the way of them. Nothing.

'Right, what have I missed?' Ally returned, her eyes flitting between all three of them and taking in the weighted silence.

And then he was moving, as fast as his stride would permit. He took Jasmine's hand and pulled her up into his arms.

'If I will have you? Are you crazy?' His words were

muffled against her neck as he buried himself there. 'It's me that should be asking that of you after I left you like I did. I'm sorry, so sorry.'

'Stop apologising, Freddie! I want to be with you. I want to marry you. I want to have kids with you. I don't want to waste a second more when we've wasted so many already.'

'I wouldn't say it was wasted, dear.'

They jerked away from one another just enough to eye his mother, who looked as close to tears as she'd been the day he'd returned from the Seychelles.

Ally was still, so still he almost forgot she was there.

'It seems to me you've grown into a fine, independent woman, and you've made something of yourself.'

Everyone frowned, save for his mother whose lips had the hint of a…*smile.*

'It wasn't that we doubted your love for one another all those years ago. You were just too young, too young and too foolish, and too fuelled by hormones. Youngsters just have no patience in this day and age.'

Ally swallowed something that sounded a lot like a surprised laugh.

'I won't pretend that we didn't want more for you, Freddie. It was always the way that we would expect a high society marriage.' She waved a hand through the air like she was discussing something as simple as the weather. 'After all, an arranged marriage never did us any harm and look at your sister too, the picture of health and happiness. But you, you were always one for doing your own thing. From the moment you could walk right up until the day you upped and left for Harvard. Your father and I worried we'd lost you for good.'

He shook his head. 'If you were so worried that you'd lost me, why keep pushing me into a marriage I didn't want?'

'You can hardly expect us to be happy with your bachelor status. Life is hard, Freddie, you need someone to share it with. And you can't blame us for trying to find you a suitable match, it's expected of us to do so. It's the topic of conversation at virtually every function.'

Her eyes lowered to Jasmine, a faraway look creeping into her blue eyes that were so like her son's. 'We never banked on you coming back, though.'

He sensed Jasmine swallow, felt her arms twitch around him as she said, 'There's a bit of a tale to that.'

'Yes, Alison has said as much.'

'She has?' He looked at Ally, who gave an awkward smile.

'I haven't said *that* much, just that M waved her magic wand and brought you back together.'

'And you didn't say anything to me?' he asked his mother.

'I figured you'd say something in your own time, *if* there was something worth telling.'

'I see…' But did he?

'You have to admit, it is kind of like fate,' Ally said wistfully.

'Trust you to believe in fate, little sis,' he murmured, distracted by his thoughts, still trying to gauge his mother's reaction and the battle ahead. If there was to be a battle…

'Your sister makes a very good point. Even you have to admit, dear, that of all the men and all the women M had access to, bringing you both together was nothing short of a miracle.'

Jasmine and Freddie stared at her, their disbelief growing.

'What?' She gave a short laugh, her cheeks colouring beneath her flawless make-up. 'Is it so hard to believe that I can think fate played a hand? I can be quite a romantic… when I want to be.'

Hard to believe? Try impossible.

'Yes, well,' she rallied into the stunned silence. 'Your father is less so. Best to leave him to me.'

And still no one moved.

'Right, Alison, give the girl her drink and let's go and see what Maggie can rustle up for supper. It seems we have a guest for the night. I assume you will stay, Jasmine.'

'I— What?' She dipped in his arms as though her knees had buckled, and he tightened his hold around her.

'That would be lovely,' he said, giving Jasmine the strength that she'd already expended. It was his turn to step up.

'Yes. Thank you, Lady Highgrove.'

'Annie, please.'

Jasmine swallowed. 'Annie.'

His mother paused at the door, turning back to smile at them both, her eyes resting on Jasmine.

'Your mother was always very proud of you, dear, and quite rightly so. Tonight you shine so brightly that your light is sure to have reached her in the heavens.'

The door closed softly behind her and slowly they turned towards one another. His hands reached into Jasmine's hair as their gazes locked and he witnessed her love for her late mother, for him, for what was to come glistening back at him.

'I love you, Red,' he whispered into that look. 'I've always loved you, and only you. Will you marry me?'

Tears welled in her brilliant green eyes. 'I will Freddie, I will.'

'And I will of course do that again properly, with the ring.'

She clutched his face in her hands, her smile breathtaking. 'I don't need the ring, Freddie, I just need you.'

'Don't let my mother hear you say that because she's going to want me to use Granny's ring this t—'

His words were cut off by her kiss, her passion, her love… The love of his one and only Red.

EPILOGUE

One year later

NERVOUSLY, JASMINE BIT into her lip as Freddie tugged her away from the doors that led into the manor's great hall. The noise from the other side ebbed and flowed with music and chatter, the clinking of glasses, the sound of laughter. The evening reception was in full swing. Friends, relatives and staff had all gathered to celebrate their wedding.

'Are you sure we should just sneak off?'

Freddie chuckled and pulled her into his chest. 'It's tradition.'

'Making our secret getaway?'

'Yes. And as I have the jet on standby, it would be rude to keep the pilot waiting.'

She shook her head with a laugh, the loose curls framing her face brushing against her cheeks. He looked so handsome, so impressive in full Highland dress, the kilt giving him an edge she could definitely get used to. As for his hair, it was longer, not quite as foppish as it had once been, but the perfect length for her to run her hands through and she did it now. Gazing up at him with all the love she felt inside. 'Since when have you worried about keeping people waiting?'

'Since I was left waiting ten years for you to come to your senses!'

'*Me* come to *my* senses?'

He chuckled deeper, pressed a kiss to her affronted mouth. 'You *and* my parents.'

'Are my ears burning?'

His father emerged from his study, his face as severe as

the day he'd caught her stealing Maggie's shortbread and Jasmine smiled at him, her heart softening. Behind that severe look were eyes that now danced like his son's. Yes, grandparenthood had changed him, but even in the last year she'd witnessed him change further. Whether it was the health scare, the change in his lifestyle or seeing his son so happy, she wasn't sure, and ultimately it didn't matter.

She walked up to him and touched a kiss to his cheek. 'I'll leave you to sort out your son. I just need to speak to Annie before we go.'

She moved to leave, and Freddie caught her up, tugging her back. 'Not yet you don't.' He pressed a kiss to her lips. 'Now you may go, but don't be long.'

She laughed. 'I wonder if marriage will teach you patience.'

'Hey, I waited ten years, remember…' he called after her, and she grinned as she pushed open the doors to the hall and scanned the guests.

So many smiles, so much happiness. The room itself glowed in the light of the chandeliers and the candelabras that ran along the panelled walls, illuminating the paintings and tapestries and hunting regalia from yesteryear.

She spied Annie in the corner, chatting animatedly with a glowing Madison Morgan, their talented matchmaker, or fairy godmother as Ally liked to call her…

She joined them with a smile. 'Ladies, Freddie is quite insistent that we sneak away, but I couldn't go without saying goodbye, Annie. Thank you so much for all you've done to make today so very special.'

She pulled her mother-in-law into an embrace, which was readily returned.

'You're very welcome, dear.' She pressed a kiss to her cheek. 'Yet again you have done your mother proud, and Alan and I couldn't be happier. It is us that should be thanking you for giving us Highgroves a second chance.'

The wedge in her throat swelled with every word and as Jasmine leaned back, she saw that Annie too was close to tears. They squeezed one another's arms and she managed a whispered. 'Thank you.'

Then she turned to Madison. 'And thank you too. Without your magic we wouldn't be here now.'

'I'm not so sure…' Madison smiled at her, her warm brown eyes all knowing. 'I think one way or another you were destined to meet again. I just made it happen sooner rather than later.'

Jasmine gave a soft laugh and pulled her into a hug. 'Whatever the case, thank you.'

'You're very welcome. I hope you have a fabulous honeymoon. Has he given away the destination yet?'

'He doesn't need to, there's only one place for us.'

'Ah, of course!' She gave a knowing wink. 'Back to Rosalie.'

'Ooh, you'd better go, dear, your husband is on the prowl and I wouldn't put it past my son to throw you over his shoulder and carry you off.'

She turned to see Freddie stalking towards her, his intent clear in his mischievous grin. She picked up her skirts and dashed towards him.

Yes, she was running, but this time she was taking him with her.

'I'm rea—'

Her words became a squeal as he swung her up into his arms, cradling her body to his. 'I'm done with waiting, wife.'

'Freddie! You can't carry me out!'

'Oh, believe me, I can. I've waited eleven years for this honeymoon, I'm not waiting a second more.'

'But—'

He kissed away her words and she clung to him as the

room of people fell away, leaving just her and Freddie and their love that had stood the test of time.

When he eased his lips from hers, she was breathless and flustered and very much in need of the cold outdoors.

'That was rather foolish of me,' he muttered, rapidly striding for the exit.

'Was it? I rather liked it.'

'I rather liked it too…too much.'

She frowned up at him. How could one like a kiss too much?

'Never mind going into battle without undergarments beneath your kilt…' he continued. 'Try kissing your wife a little too deeply in front of an audience…'

She covered her mouth with her hand, tears of laughter and happiness spiking. 'If it makes you feel better, I do love a true Scotsman.'

He clutched her tighter, his grin swiftly returning. 'You'd better.'

'Always, Freddie. Always.'

* * * * *

AWAKENED BY THE CEO'S KISS

THERESE BEHARRIE

MILLS & BOON

To my incredible family.

The love I have for you keeps me hopeful.

Thank you for reminding me of the world's beauty.

CHAPTER ONE

For the second time in his life Tyler Murphy was staring at the most beautiful woman he had ever seen.

The first time had been five years ago, at a coffee shop around the corner from the hospital. He had been visiting his sister, who'd just given birth to his nephew, and he had been dealing with some…stuff. Mainly the fact that his mother, who had passed away months before that, wouldn't get to meet her first grandchild. The woman who had prized family so much wouldn't get to see hers expand.

He'd needed some space from the hospital. And there had been Brooke. Standing at the counter, staring at the menu with a dazed look on her face.

He thought about that day a lot. The days after, too—that week they'd spent together. The sadness that had lurked in her eyes even when she was smiling. How often she would trail off when she spoke, as if she had forgotten what she was saying. She would always beam at him after, especially if he prompted her, and he'd put it down as one of her quirks.

Those memories were all he had of her. Her first name—only her first name—and his memories. It hadn't mattered then. He had known she was the type of person who picked up litter when she saw it on the street. Who allowed elderly people ahead of her in a queue. She hoped for a world where people were kinder, less self-centred. She didn't like intolerance, and she had told him about the times she'd stepped in when she'd witnessed it.

But her name and his memories hadn't been enough for him to find her. He'd discovered that at the end of the week when she'd disappeared. They hadn't shared any information about where they lived, who their families were. They hadn't even exchanged contact details. It was as if they'd purposely avoided it. As if *she* had purposely avoided it.

He might have thought it dramatic if he hadn't been staring at her now, waiting for her to recognise him.

He got nothing.

'You're not Tia Murphy,' she said, her voice a frustratingly adorable lilt of confusion.

'No, I'm Tyler Murphy.' *Which you already know. But I guess if we're playing this game...* 'I'll be helping you out for the next—'

He didn't get the chance to continue. Brooke let out a cry as her body bumped against the door. Seconds later, the door opened wider. He didn't catch what flew past them, but he knew it was some kind of animal.

'No!' she shouted. 'Mochi, you come back here *right now*!'

She ran down the three steps that led to the front lawn, before bolting towards what Tyler could now see was a dog. He didn't think she'd expected to chase after a dog. Or maybe she had; he wasn't proficient in what kind of clothes people who required housekeepers wore.

Sure, technically, he could be one of those people, but his mother would have killed him. If he'd got a housekeeper now, she'd probably become undead for the sole purpose of killing him.

And, since he wasn't 'one of those people,' for all he knew Brooke's silky nightgown and flip-flops were standard attire.

Watching her running after a dog in that outfit lightened some of the tension he felt, but it couldn't eradicate it completely. In fact, it complicated things. In the days they'd spent together, he hadn't once seen this much of her. Now he could add the strength of her arms, the width of her thighs, to what he'd been missing.

Get it together, Murphy.

Brooke was now his boss. Indirectly, since he was standing in for his sister. But still... He needed to keep things professional. The situation was precarious enough without the added complication of him knowing Brooke.

Except... Was she pretending that week hadn't happened? Or did she not remember it? He did, because he had never been so attracted to anyone. Not any of the women he'd dated, though there had only been a few over the years. None of them stood out. But he'd thought he and Brooke had shared something. If not physically, emotionally. They had been *friends*.

And she didn't remember that?

Was he so out of touch that he'd made up their connection?

He exhaled. Now was not the time to dwell on the past. Especially when the present was providing enough distraction.

The dog was having the time of its life. It was a collie cross of some kind, with glossy black fur and brown and white paws. It barked at the woman frequently, as if taunting her. It was probably taunting her because it barked every time she paused to take a breath. When she started chasing it again, it zoomed past her, literally running circles around her.

He wanted to be the better person and help her. And he would. But he'd watch for a while longer before he did. It wasn't something he was proud of, but it did offer him a measure of satisfaction. As did the steam he was sure he could see coming from her head.

He walked down the steps, put his fingers in his mouth and whistled.

'Mochi,' he called, lowering to his haunches. 'Come on over here. Introduce yourself.'

In no time at all the dog was in front of him, wagging its tail enthusiastically as it licked Tyler's face and smelled his clothing.

'How did you do that?' Brooke demanded, walking over to him. 'I've had him for two weeks and never—*never*—has calling him worked.'

'You need to call with authority,' Tyler replied absently, smiling when the dog lay on his back for a belly rub. 'Dogs need to know who the alpha of their pack is. If they think they can take advantage of you, they will.'

'Ah,' she said, nodding.

Tyler picked the dog up and tucked him under his arm.

'Well, thank you so much… Tyler, you said your name was?'

'Yes.'

'Thank you, Tyler.' She took the dog from him. 'Let's go inside so you can explain why you're here and not Tia. Don't worry,' she added casually, 'I'll be sure to remember my *authority* during our conversation.'

Tyler opened his mouth to reply, but she hadn't waited for one. Good thing. He had no real answer, and if he came up with something on the fly he'd surely put his foot in it again.

'I assume the fact that you share a surname with the person who's supposed to be here is significant,' she said, when they were both inside the house.

She closed the door and put down the dog, which immediately went to Tyler. He didn't dare look at it.

'Explain.'

She folded her arms, appearing oblivious to the fact that the movement might, in someone with less self-control, draw attention to her chest. The way her nightgown formed a V at her cleavage, creating soft semi-circles of flesh, might, again, in someone with less self-control, cause desire to shoot straight to a part of the body inappropriate for a professional setting.

That someone was obviously not him. He had plenty of self-control. Exemplified by how he was focusing on her face, not her cleavage. Focusing on those brown eyes that wore fury and command as though they were cloaks. On the perfectly formed eyebrows, dark like the hair pulled into a bun at the top of her head, highlighting sharp, almost regal cheekbones. On the full lashes that made her the perfect model for mascara, though he knew she hadn't used any. On the plump pink lips that were currently in a thin line, like a disapproving teacher.

He had never, not once in his life, had a teacher fantasy, but he was beginning to see the appeal.

Had he implied that this woman had no authority? No—he'd *said* it. Foolishly, considering she held his sister's employment in her hands. Stupidly, considering she wore only nightwear and somehow still had an aura of power coming off her as if it was a particularly potent brand of perfume.

He was already enthralled, already aroused, and they'd spent all of fifteen minutes together. How the hell was he going to get through a month?

Distance. Right, yes. Distance and professionalism. Two characteristics he generally displayed without much effort.

He cleared his throat. 'Tia Murphy is my sister. Unfortunately, she won't be able to fulfil this commitment due to unforeseen circumstances.'

'The agency sent you instead?'

He hesitated. 'No.'

'Care to elaborate?'

'They…they don't know.'

'So you're telling me I have a random man in my house who hasn't been verified by the agency I've already paid?'

Mochi whined at his feet, as if in warning.

'That's not how I would phrase it...' Tyler said carefully.

'How *would* you phrase it?' Her voice was dangerously cool. 'I'm very interested in knowing. I could do with a concise explanation, too, since I have to leave for work in—' She broke off as her eyes fluttered to the clock on the wall behind him. 'Crap. I leave in fifteen minutes.' She narrowed her eyes. 'Should I trust a random man in my home while I change?'

'We've been alone for a while, and I've been perfectly respectable. Plus, your dog trusts me.'

She studied him. Didn't at all seemed convinced. She looked at Mochi. 'Make sure he doesn't steal anything,' she instructed, before walking up the stairs without a further word.

He looked at the dog. 'I'm not sure she likes me.'

Mochi only tilted his head.

This was a confusing situation on multiple levels. For one, Brooke Jansen hadn't expected to be dressed as though she were preparing for a boudoir photo shoot when she met her temporary housekeeper for the first time. But Mochi had woken her up and refused to leave her alone until she gave him something.

What he'd wanted, she didn't know. She'd barely managed her morning routine before he'd started barking. Sharp, piercing barks that demanded attention. Then the doorbell had rang, and Mochi had escaped. She wouldn't be surprised if he'd been planning it since he'd woken her up.

The second thing was the man she'd found on her doorstep. She had been...surprised. It wasn't that she thought he couldn't be a housekeeper. Her brain had just taken a moment to reconcile his sheer physical size with what the job required. He looked more suited to doing something that required strength. Like carrying heavy items from one place to another.

For a brief moment she considered how many tasks she could find that would allow him to do that. And would allow her to watch.

Very quickly after that thought she gathered her wits. After chiding them for their inappropriate behaviour, she realised he wasn't meant to be here.

Which brought her to a third confusing aspect: *he wasn't meant to be here.*

That was something she needed to sort out. Honestly, she was annoyed. She had hired a housekeeper to help her since her focus was almost entirely on work these days. She didn't need a housekeeper to add to her problems. Especially a sexy housekeeper.

Sexy? She had entertained, however briefly, the idea of watching him work, but *sexy*?

What was going on? She hadn't cared about any of that since Kian had died. She wasn't even sure she cared now.

Except she might care. Why else was she wearing a top that made her breasts look appealing under a stylish blazer, with jeans that did impressive things for her butt? And why was she now slipping on a pair of heels, putting on more accessories than she had in months, doing elaborate make-up? Her hair was due for a wash, so the best she could do was put it back into the bun, forcing any stray pieces into place with gel.

But that was *all* she was doing.

The bare minimum, really.

Ignoring any thoughts to the contrary, she made her way downstairs. The smell of coffee hit her first, before she realised Tyler wasn't in the hall where she'd left him. She hadn't really expected him to stay there. Though the fact that she was surprised he wasn't there now proved otherwise.

Her eyes swept over the house. Nothing seemed out of place, which was a positive. She wouldn't have been impressed with herself if she'd let a criminal into her home. Less so if she'd been attracted to the criminal.

Not that she was attracted to him. She could objectively notice a man's attractiveness without being attracted to him.

Her thoughts stalled when she saw Tyler in the kitchen though. Her heart skipped and time… Well, it did what time always did. It moved on. So slowly that she could hear every tick of the clock, as if it were trying to tell her something.

But that couldn't possibly be. What would it have to tell her? And why was that question more important than all the others she had? About Tyler looking as if he belonged in her kitchen as much as he did carrying very heavy things from one place to the next.

'I made coffee. It's in a takeaway cup.' He nodded his head to the kitchen table. 'With a toasted cheese sandwich you can have for breakfast.' He studied her. 'I assume you haven't had breakfast?'

A restless sensation slithered up her spine, sliding its hands over her shoulders and settling over her heart. She didn't know how much of it was surprise and how much of it was concern. She hadn't had someone take care of her this way in the longest time. Her brother was a constant presence in her life, and he would have, certainly, if she let him. But she rarely did. Accepting the dog he'd given her because he was worried about her had been a concession because she knew that. Now there was a stranger doing things for her. Was she supposed to accept it?

'You're overthinking things,' he told her, his tone curt. 'I'm here to do a job. This is part of it.'

'Except this isn't your job, is it? You're standing in for your sister.'

'She and I have the same skills.'

'But you haven't been vetted by the agency. For all I know you're a master criminal, preparing to rob me of everything I own.'

He snorted. 'Your imagination is something.'

She opened her mouth to reply, but he continued before she could.

'My name is Tyler Murphy. Look me up. I own an online education company. We provide courses aimed at older students, accredited by the government. There are multiple articles about me, including a detailed personal history, all of which should address your concerns about me being a master criminal. Among other things,' he added coolly.

She had no idea what he meant by that.

Eyeing him suspiciously, she took out her phone and typed in his name. Everything he said was truc.

'This doesn't make what you and your sister are doing okay.'

'Believe me, if there was another choice we wouldn't be doing it.'

Oddly, she believed him. She didn't approve, but she understood. She would have stood in for her brother in a heartbeat if he'd needed her—although she doubted she would be able to do Dom's job as a police officer.

'Fine. I won't tell the agency, but obviously you're on probation.'

'Obviously,' he said blandly.

She lifted her brows. 'Since you have your own company, you might not know how to interact with an employer. Generally you don't sass them. Nor do you imply that they don't have authority in their own homes, with their own pets.'

He had the grace to wince. 'I'm sorry about that. I realised it was a mistake as soon as I said it.'

'No, you realised it was a mistake as soon as I pointed it out.'

She hadn't fully appreciated his face until that moment, when his mouth curved into an almost-smile. It softened his eyes, edging the colour from brown into green in a startlingly contrary way. Or perhaps it wasn't a softening, but a sparkle. An acknowledgement of sass and truth that was delightful on the hard angles of his face. It cast a light on his stormy features—on the dark brows and lashes, the tight pursing of his lips—and she wasn't sure she liked it.

Liar, said an inner voice.

Mind your business, she mentally replied.

She couldn't say much more than that.

'You're right.'

'I know,' she said primly, before looking down at Mochi. He was sitting calmly on the floor between them, panting blissfully with his legs crossed. 'You're a show-off, Mochi.'

'Why do you say that?' Tyler asked.

His eyes were sparkling with vague amusement now. Something prickled in her body.

She cleared her throat. 'He's very well behaved around people, but as soon as you leave he'll do what he did outside.'

'Play?'

'Yeah, if you mean it in a play *me* kind of way.'

'I didn't, but I guess that works.'

He smiled now. A full smile. An easy smile. The kind of smile that made her think of summer and driving through the city. With the sun streaming through the windows, heating her face, her arms, her legs. She could almost hear the music through the speakers.Could almost feel Kian's fingers twined through hers—

Her heart stopped.

For a few seconds, her heart just stopped.

Because she'd looked at one man, this man in front of

her, and thought about her dead husband. And that didn't feel right. It felt complicated. She didn't even want to think it through.

His smile disappeared.

'Tia's briefed me on what you require,' he said formally.

She wondered at the change. There was no possible way he could know what she had been thinking.

'I understand what my responsibilities will be in the coming weeks. And I am good with dogs. As you can see.'

He lowered his hand to his side. Mochi immediately stood, placing his head directly beneath Tyler's fingers.

Brooke tilted her head. 'Neat trick.'

'It's not a trick, Ms Jansen.' He gave her a cocky smile.

Why did the man have so many variations of his smile? And why did they all have a familiar shimmer of awareness going through her?

'I need time to think through this situation,' she said, though she hadn't been prepared to say it. 'I'll let you know if you can come back.'

'You're not hiring me?' he asked, indignation a hoarse undertone in his voice.

'Not yet, Mr Murphy.' She picked up her coffee and the sandwich and nodded her head towards the door. 'Now, do you mind? I'm already late for work.'

CHAPTER TWO

'How did it go?'

Tyler pressed the phone to his ear with his shoulder, deliberating on how he should answer. He could tell the truth: the woman Tia had asked him to work for was the same woman he'd formed a friendship with five years ago. He thought about her often, especially when he was considering dating, and those thoughts usually put him off dating. After all, how was he meant to establish a connection like that with someone else?

Of course today, he'd discovered that connection was one-sided. It had kept him from asking Brooke why she was ignoring him. If he really had been the only one to experience their connection, it would be embarrassing to demand that she address their past. He had his pride, damn it. And he was nursing his wounds now, using the sting to establish boundaries that would keep him from doing something stupid.

Like beg her to remember him and their week together.

Wasn't it as special as I thought? he'd probably ask. *Didn't we share something?*

But that would only lead to more stupidity, as it had today. When he'd insulted Brooke, treated her coolly, and jeopardised Tia's job. Tia was more important than his hurt feelings. He couldn't allow those feelings to motivate his behaviour again. He would have to ignore the past, just as Brooke was doing.

No, he couldn't tell Tia any of that. So he lied.

'It went great.'

'Yeah?'

The relief embedded in that word made him glad he lied. She was under a lot of pressure. The least he could do was reassure her.

Until she finds out you're lying and she loses her job at the agency.

That wouldn't be ideal. Especially when she was desperately trying to *keep* her job, hence him filling in for her in the first place.

'I've already used all my leave, Ty. If I tell them I need to take care of Nyle again, they'll fire me. And you know I need this job,' she'd said when she'd asked for his help.

'Yeah, I know,' he'd replied, 'because you won't let me help you.'

'Financially,' she'd emphasised. 'But I do know of another way you can help me…'

How could he have said no then?

Plus, his job allowed him to work remotely. Hell, his company was independent enough that he could take a couple of weeks' leave. Which was likely why he was getting so restless professionally. In its current state, it no longer provided a challenge. Expansion, on the other hand—

As he had been doing for the last month, he stopped the thought in its tracks. There was no point in indulging it. He wouldn't be taking the opportunity. It didn't matter that it was an incredible opportunity that had seemingly come out of the blue.

He had been at a function at one of the universities his company was partnered with when he'd been approached by the CEO of a company similar to his own. Apparently, he'd heard about what Learn It, Tyler's company, was doing in South Africa, and wanted a merger since he was doing the same in the UK.

Tyler had imagined the possibilities—and he *would* only imagine the possibilities.

There was no way he would leave Tia and Nyle to fend for themselves. They were family, and his mother had taught him he should never abandon family. Drilled it into him, really, after his father had left.

It was ironic that his father's departure had been because of a business opportunity, too. Tyler could almost understand it now. Could see the temptation of it. Except *he* loved his family more than he loved ambition or success. He wouldn't leave for either of them.

'How's Nyle doing?' he asked, mentally shifting gears.

'He still has a fever, but he doesn't feel bad enough to stop complaining about the rash.' Tia exhaled. 'He had the vaccine… I don't understand why he still got chickenpox.'

'It's common enough.' Tyler had done a lot of research to confirm that. 'And it'll be less severe because he was vaccinated.' He paused. 'Tia, you did your best. Stuff like this happens.'

'I know. I know.'

She would still be hard on herself, though. She had been for the last five years. As if being hard on herself would somehow make up for the fact that her boyfriend had left without so much as a word before she'd even found out she was pregnant. When she had found out, she'd done everything she could to find him. She'd even asked Tyler to hire a private investigator.

The investigator had found him pretty quickly. He'd been living six hours away, with his wife and three kids.

Tia hadn't known a thing about any of it, but she'd admonished herself as if she'd made the choice to get involved with him deliberately. She'd informed him she was pregnant, got the confirmation she hadn't really needed that he didn't want anything to do with her, and prepared to become a single parent.

Tyler liked to think Tia had him, but the truth was she barely asked him for anything. When she did ask him, it was because she had no other option. It was her pride—their mother had raised them with an abundance of it—though heaven only knew why that pride included him. They were family.

But this wasn't about him; it was about Tia. He needed to respect that.

Sharp barking interrupted his thoughts.

'What is…? Ty, did you take in another foster dog?'

He didn't appreciate the accusation. So, again, he found himself lying. 'No.'

'I can hear a dog barking.'

'It's the TV.'

'You're a terrible liar.'

Not about everything.

'You say that like it's a bad thing.'

'You need to stop taking in stray dogs,' Tia replied. 'You're getting a reputation.'

'Again—you say it like it's a bad thing.'

'I say it like a woman who knows there are liars and con people in the world. If someone ever wanted to set you up, they'd just need to use a dog and—'

'No one is going to set me up using a dog.'

'You don't know.'

'I do. Besides,' he continued, hoping to distract from her concern, 'this one was curled up on the side of the road. I couldn't leave her there.'

Tia muttered something that sounded suspiciously like, *'How come you keep finding dogs, but not a woman to bring home?'*

'What was that?'

'I hope your tetanus shot is up to date,' she said.

'Since you ask me that every time, you already know the answer. Now, do I need to bring anything over for you and Nyle?'

It took some cajoling, but eventually Tia agreed to have him bring over some groceries. But only if he left them at the front door since he'd only recently got his chickenpox vaccine. An oversight by their mother which, considering she had already passed away when they'd discovered it, they would never know the reason for.

The only reason they knew now was because Tia had insisted they check their vaccine status. She'd only cared about hers so she could be prepared, but since Tyler had at first offered to look after Nyle while she worked, she'd insisted he check, too. It was one of the few times Tia's micro-parenting had worked out.

'Want to come with me?' he asked his new dog.

He'd temporarily named her June until the owner came forward, but he suspected it would be while. He'd put up fliers at the local vet clinics and in the area he'd found her since she didn't have a chip.

June's tail wagged so fast he thought she might sprain it.

'Okay, okay, let's go.'

He left her in the car when he went to get Tia's groceries, but decided to take her for a walk once the shopping was done. The store wasn't far from Tia's place, so he left his car in the car park. Twenty minutes later, the goods had been delivered and he was on his way back.

Then he saw his new maybe-boss.

'Mochi, I swear if you don't stop pulling, I'm going to—'

Brooke broke off as she passed a couple walking their own dog. Neither of them seemed as annoyed as she was. But then, their miniature fluff ball of a dog seemed nowhere near as passionate as Mochi, who was pulling at the leash so hard it felt as though he wanted to win a race.

Brooke half-ran, half-stumbled to keep up. She was about to give Mochi another talking-to—because that was truly working *so* well—when someone spoke.

'Are you walking Mochi or is Mochi walking you?'

Her mouth was dry long before she met his eyes. When she did, she felt a small jolt. It was recognition, but a deeper kind than what meeting him a few hours ago should have brought. She brushed it off. It was probably because he was attractive. And, contrary to what she had told herself that morning, she *was* attracted to him. To the faint smirk that she so badly wanted to flick off his face. To the slight folds between his eyebrows that made his face look stormy once again.

What was she supposed to do with all this information?

'Tyler.'

She stopped, struggling to keep Mochi back when he, too, recognised Tyler. Tyler looked more thrilled to see the dog than he did her. Not that she cared, of course.

He had his own dog with him. It was mixed breed, and sat patiently at his side, staring at the scene as if it had never once in its life misbehaved.

'What are you doing here?' he asked, dropping to give Mochi some love. Mochi allowed it for all of ten seconds before moving to sniff Tyler's dog.

'Is this area reserved for people who aren't me?'

He gave her a dark look as he straightened. 'It's a little far from home.'

It was, but this was where her brother had told her the SPCA had picked Mochi up when they'd got news about a stray dog in the park. Brooke thought the area might comfort him. She wasn't sure about that, but it did seem to excite him.

She told none of this to Tyler, especially since it was fairly self-evident why she was there, apart from it being far from home. The park was large and surrounded by trees.

There was a path for those who wanted to walk, and in the middle, a play area with some benches. It was a pretty standard park in a Cape Town suburb, and it was a great place to walk a dog.

She didn't know why she was resisting telling Tyler the truth. None of it was incriminating. But the thought of sharing it with him felt intimate in a way she couldn't explain.

She shrugged. 'Mochi likes it here.'

'How exactly did you figure that out?'

Oh, she'd walked into that one.

Instead of answering, she deflected. 'Who's your friend?' She gestured to the dog beside him.

'This is… Well, I'm not sure.'

'You're not sure?' she repeated slowly.

'She's a stray. Or she might be. Again, I'm not sure.'

She found his uncertainty strangely refreshing.

'I found her on the side of the road. She doesn't have a chip, so she might be a stray, but she was in good condition. Well-fed, clean, and she seems trained.'

'So let me get this straight: you picked up a stray dog…' *Of course* a man who looked like him would be partial to picking up stray dogs. Why would the universe make things easy? 'And it's the perfect dog?'

'Well, I didn't say…' He looked down, smiled.

It was a fond smile this time. A gooey smile. Urgh, she hated his range.

'Yeah, she's pretty perfect,' he said.

'Of course she is.'

'What does that mean?'

'Nothing.'

'Please, tell me.' It sounded strangely demanding.

'It means… Well, you finding a perfect stray dog seems consistent with what I know about you.'

'What you know about me?' he repeated, his voice hard. Too hard.

'I'm sorry, that was inappropriate. I shouldn't have implied...' She trailed off when she saw his frown. 'Look, we've spent less than an hour together and yet somehow we've ended up on each other's bad sides.'

'Less than an hour, huh?' he asked, a wry twist to his mouth. 'Is that just today, or are you speaking about for ever?'

'I... I don't know what you mean.'

'Of course you don't.'

She stared at him. At this confusing man who inspired more emotion in her than anyone else had in years. Since Kian had died, she'd rarely felt anything but ambivalence towards men.

To be fair, that was pretty much how she felt about everything since she'd become a widow. The years after the car accident that had taken her husband's lifc—and a limited part of her memory—were a blur of neither high nor low emotions. She had moved on from it. As much as she could, considering what she'd lost.

She didn't mind losing the memories so much. The doctors had told her it was trauma, physical and emotional. She'd been in an accident; she'd lost her husband. In light of that, the days between his death and funeral wasn't all that much to lose. She remembered only parts of them. Flashes of emotion or scenes. But for the most part, it was lost to her.

Whenever she wanted to mourn it, she would remember that she'd lost her husband. She'd mourn something bigger then.

'I shouldn't have said that,' he said. 'I apologise.'

'I don't quite know what you're apologising for,' she replied after a beat, 'but I'd rather we move on from it. Especially if you're going to work for me.'

'I'm going to work for you?'

His smile was brighter than she'd seen it. She took a step back, as if she were afraid she would burn.

Oh, you're afraid, all right.

'Yes,' she said curtly. Damn her thoughts. Damn her emotions. 'Don't screw it up.'

He was still grinning when she walked away.

CHAPTER THREE

TYLER COULDN'T FAULT his sister for being too proud to accept help when he had some of that pride, too.

Some? a voice in his head scoffed.

Fine. He had a healthy amount of pride.

It had been the reason he'd got into a fight over a girl when he was at school. He hadn't been able to let go his rival's flirting with his girlfriend, even though he'd known his mother would kill him for it. And it was why he didn't have a relationship with his father. The man had abandoned his family for a *job*. It hadn't started out that way, of course, but what did that matter when that was how it ended?

Today, his pride was the reason he had taken a more… formal approach to his first full day of work at Brooke's.

'Oh.' Her eyes widened when she opened the door, scanning him as if she were a metal detector at the airport. 'You're…um…' She heaved out a breath. 'I shouldn't, as your employer, comment on your attire. Or should I? Honestly, I've never had a housekeeper before, and it feels a bit more personal than… No, you know what? I should keep this professional.'

She stopped rambling when she saw the way he was looking at her. He couldn't have said which way that was. He was reluctantly charmed, even if he did now see the flaw in his plan—and his pride.

'A suit is hardly the most sensible attire for a housekeeping position, Mr Murphy.'

Her spine had straightened; her tone was clipped. It charmed him even more. Perhaps because it was clear he had some effect on her. He hadn't worn a suit for that reason. He'd just wanted to make a good impression since he hadn't been on his best behaviour the day before. Witnessing that effect now made the embarrassment worth it.

Because *of course* a suit wasn't the best outfit to wear for a housekeeping position. He must have known that on some level because he had a change of clothing with him.

Maybe he *had* worn the suit to see how it would affect her. And if he had, he couldn't call his pride healthy. It wasn't healthy to figure out if a woman he'd met five years ago was affected by him when she was pretending she didn't remember him. It was stubborn. Idiotic. Childish.

More so when he was this pleased at her response.

'I wanted to show you I'm serious about being here,' he said.

'Do you have a change of clothing?'

'I do.'

She lifted chin. 'Well, then. I suppose that's good.'

He didn't give in to the smile at the reluctant comment. Only walked in when she opened the door wider and said, 'Come inside.'

He shrugged off his jacket and turned to ask if she had a coat rack. He found her staring at him. 'Is everything okay?' he asked.

'Yes. Of course.' Her face flushed. 'I was just wondering what you were thinking.'

'I've already told you.'

'I think you're lying.'

'Why would I do that?'

'Because this job involves cleaning and making sure my dog doesn't destroy the house. It hardly requires a suit.'

'You don't think people who clean deserve to take pride in their appearance by wearing something like this?'

Her mouth opened for a solid few seconds before she replied. 'That's not what I said. Or meant.'

'Isn't it?'

'Of course not. I meant…' She trailed off. Started again. 'When you start a job, you dress for the job. The time to impress is during the first meeting. Or the interview.'

'I believe the time to impress is every day you show up.'

She studied him. Took in the curve of his mouth that he could no longer keep in. Rolled her eyes. 'I can't believe that you run a company of one hundred and fifty people with your level of maturity.'

His brows lifted. 'Been looking me up?'

She didn't reply to that. 'I'll walk you through what I need you to do today.'

He followed her, though this time he hid his smile. He wasn't that big an idiot.

She showed him where everything was, explaining what she wanted quickly and concisely. It was a good thing his mother hadn't coddled him. She'd raised both him and Tia to have the necessary skills to survive. He knew how to clean, how to cook, how to do laundry. When he was growing up, he'd cleaned his room every day, the house once a week. He'd alternated with Tia on cooking, except on the days his mother hadn't had to work, which hadn't been all that often. As for laundry… His mother had flat-out refused to wash a teenage boy's dirty clothes.

'You good with everything?' she asked when she was done.

'Yeah. I'm good. Where's Mochi?'

She brushed a strand of hair from her face. It was in a long, sleek ponytail at the base of her skull, with a few pieces falling around her face. It went perfectly with the outfit she wore. A floral dress that flared at her hips in a whimsical way that still managed to look professional.

He wanted to take her hand and ask her to spin around. He wanted to hear her laugh breathlessly as she did so, embarrassed that he'd asked, but still wanting to please him.

He hated himself for it. For the fact that *he* wanted to please *her* because she made his heart thud and she clearly didn't feel the same way.

'He's with my brother for the day,' she answered, not meeting his eyes.

'Did something happen?'

'No. I… My brother has dogs. And a kid. And I think Mochi's happier there than he is here, so I thought… It's your first day. I thought I wouldn't let him bother you.'

'He's not a bother,' he said automatically. Then paused. 'You don't think Mochi is happy here?'

'It's not that he isn't happy here…but he's happier elsewhere.' She lifted her hands in an awkward little gesture. 'I think maybe he's happier with someone else.'

'So you don't think he's happy here *or* happy with you?'

'When you say it like that it makes me sound like I'm delusional.' She gave a self-conscious laugh.

'Brooke,' he said slowly, 'I'm not sure why you think your dog doesn't like you, but—'

'Besides the obvious behaviour problems?'

'Behaviour problems are a result of many things, and training helps with almost all of those things. But honestly, it sounds like you don't think he likes *you*. As in, you as a person?'

The vulnerability on her face reminded him of the day they'd met. Of the days after. It was an expression that would come and go in between smiles and laughs. Sometimes those smiles and laughs had been hard-won, but that had made them seem worth more.

He'd been naïve. That much was clear, based on how

badly he'd misinterpreted their 'connection.' But now he could see that his naivety went deeper than he'd initially thought. He'd never once attributed Brooke's vulnerability to self-doubt. No—not self-doubt. Something deeper. Something more complicated.

What was it? And why did he want to know so badly?

'I have good instincts, Tyler. And I trust them.' She exhaled and smoothed the front of her dress down. 'Anyway. I'll see you after work. Or I won't.'

She walked to the kitchen and came back with a set of keys.

'You can use this to get in and out. When I'm not here in the morning, I'll leave a list of the things I need done on the kitchen counter. And that's it. Any questions?'

'No, thanks. I'm good.'

'Great. Then I guess I'll see you when I see you.'

With a curve of her mouth that he could hardly call a smile, she grabbed her things from a small table at the base of the staircase and left him alone. He stared after her for a while, then began his new job.

He started in the kitchen on the ground floor. It was a large, modern room, with light coming in from windows on one side and a glass door on the other. The door led to an outside area that was neatly decorated, with a large pot plant surrounded by two chairs. He went to wipe down the outside furniture, but completely forgot that task when he turned to his left.

It was a garden. A *gigantic* garden. With trees and flowers and a little pond all in one space.

When his business had started doing well, he'd bought himself a house. He'd actually wanted to buy one for his mother, but she'd refused. They'd fought about it for months, and in the end he'd bought the house he'd wanted to buy her for himself, so at least she'd get to experience it.

But buying something this extravagant hadn't even occurred to him.

He should have expected it. Brooke's house was in a notoriously wealthy neighbourhood in Cape Town. The house itself was enormous, and from what he'd seen on the inside, it had earned its place in the area.

But this… This was more than simply expensive. It was art.

There was a patio edged by wooden pillars. Between the pillars were three comfortable-looking couches with red cushioning surrounding a small round table. The table held a candle and some fresh flowers that had clearly been taken from the garden.

White stones led from the patio to a larger outdoor area and through trees in an S-shaped path that eventually looped around and led back. At regular steps of the path was a larger slab of stone to walk on. In the middle of the garden was the pond, with water lilies and actual, real-life fish causing the surface to ripple.

For the first time he noticed the bridge that went from one side of the pond to the other. As he walked the area, he saw that some of the larger trees had benches beneath them. One of them had a swing. And by the end of his exploration, he was wondering what the hell Brooke did to be able to afford this kind of artistry.

When he eventually went back to the kitchen to clean, he tried to use the task to distract himself from that question. But the problem with cleaning was that it gave him time to think. It always had; it was part of the reason he liked it so much. The fact that it was giving him that time now though, when he distinctly did not want it, felt like a betrayal.

So as he cleaned the white marble countertops and backsplashes, did the dishes, polished the wooden cupboards, his mind kept spinning on that question. The same thing happened as he washed the windows and the glass door, cleaned the oven and the microwave, vacuumed and mopped the floors.

He was tired of thinking by the time he moved to the dining room, where the most beautiful wooden dining table he'd ever seen sat on a beige carpet in front of a rustic fireplace.

And on the mantel of that fireplace was a picture of Brooke in the arms of a man.

She was wearing a wedding dress.

CHAPTER FOUR

WHEN BROOKE GOT to Dom's that evening, Mochi wagged his tail, which her brother said meant he liked her.

'You sound like Tyler,' she said, rolling her eyes.

'Tyler?' Dom asked. 'Who's that?'

'Oh…um…' She cursed her skin when it started going warm. 'He's my new housekeeper.'

Dom stared at her. 'Okay, I have a lot of questions.'

'I imagine you do,' she replied dryly. 'You might as well ask them. I know you won't stop bugging me until I answer.'

He didn't even bother pretending it wouldn't happen. 'Why do you need a housekeeper?'

'I don't have a spouse to help me, like you have Sierra.'

He gave her a look. 'That's not going to work on me.'

'It almost did though. Just a little.'

He ignored her. 'How about the real answer?'

She sighed. 'You know how crazy things are at work. They'll be that way until the app launches, which is only in a month's time. When I come home after a long day, I can't deal with a messy house. Before I decided to hire Tyler there were dishes in the sink from the weekend. It was Thursday,' she said, dropping her voice, disgusted with herself. 'So, yeah, I called an agency and I got them to send someone to help me.'

Dom took all that in his stride. Or she'd have thought so if she hadn't known him. Since she'd spent many years studying his expressions—and the last five in particular learning what his *My sister's husband is dead so I need to worry about her a million times more* expressions were—she knew he was still concerned.

There hadn't been one day in the year after Kian had died that Dom hadn't worn that concerned expression. In the years after, his expression had vacillated between concern and pretence. She had mostly come out of her depression by then, and he hadn't wanted her to notice his concern and worry. So he'd pretended.

'Dom, it's fine. *I'm* fine.'

'Yeah. Yeah, I know.' He shoved his hands into his pockets. 'So, tell me about this Tyler.'

She shrugged. 'He's a housekeeper.'

'He...?'

She narrowed her eyes. 'Don't be a jerk.'

'I didn't say anything.'

'You didn't have to.'

He smirked. 'So...what? He's been lecturing you on Mochi?'

'He might have witnessed some behavioural things. And I might have expressed some feelings about it.'

'Like the fact that you think your dog adjusting to his new home means he doesn't love you?'

'I did not say that.' *Not in so many words.*

He studied her. 'Okay, sure.' He paused. 'You're okay with this guy?'

'Yeah. I mean, he works for an agency. They vet the people they send out thoroughly. It's the safest way to do this.'

She chose not to tell him Tyler didn't actually work for the agency. Good thing, too, since Dom didn't even seem convinced by the version she had told him. She understood he was worried about her. Understood he'd got Mochi for her because he was worried.

He didn't want her to be alone. As if being alone was some kind of problem that needed to be fixed.

She had thought that, too, in the beginning. Because then being alone had meant she'd had time to think about all the things she and Kian had done. Soon, that progressed to all the things she and Kian had never got to do. Like that trip to Japan he'd always wanted to take. Or building the house they'd always imagined together.

She'd done some of those things as a way to celebrate their union after he was gone. Or had it been a way to grieve? She'd certainly done enough of both during the experiences.

The house had perhaps been the hardest. Still was. Because every day she made tea in the kitchen they'd once dreamed about. She ate at the table they'd been saving to buy in a dining room they'd dreamed of having. She slept in the bedroom they'd designed together and she did it alone. All of it so alone.

The garden was the worst part. Or the best.

But she didn't want to go there right now.

It didn't stop the feeling, the memories, from following her into her home. She resented it, because although it was hard, it was still home. Her comfort. A place for her to relax and dream and reminisce about the past.

But she was used to the ebbs and flow of grief, even years after Kian's death. Perhaps because it was years after death.

When she and Mochi got home, she found Tyler packing containers into the fridge.

Mochi's reaction was somewhere between a yelp and a bark, his excitement apparently too much to contain in a simple response. He ran to Tyler. Brooke was about to tell him not to jump, but Tyler lifted a hand and Mochi skidded to a halt in front of him, almost on his hind legs. But he remained firmly on the ground.

And this is why I don't think he likes me.

She almost said the words out loud, but she didn't want to deal with another conversation about her feelings regarding her dog.

'What are you still doing here?' she asked instead, kicking off her heels—good heavens, how was she still in them?—and throwing her handbag onto the counter. Usually, she discarded both at the front door, but she'd wanted to let Mochi out as soon as possible so he could expend some of his energy in the garden.

'I got caught up making dinner,' he replied, his eyes searching her face as if he could see something worthwhile on it. 'I'll be out of your hair in a couple of minutes.'

'No,' she said quickly. Too quickly for her own liking. 'No, I didn't mean it like that. I just...' She sighed. 'It's been a long day.'

His expression was unreadable. 'Why don't you sit and I'll heat up some food for you?'

'No.'

That answer was as quick as the first. Discomfort turned in her stomach. But feeling the way she felt... She couldn't let this man take care of her in her home.

'Okay,' he said.

'Would you...do you want to go out and get something to eat with me though?' she asked, surprising herself. Because apparently she could let this man comfort her *outside* her home.

'No,' she said, 'please don't answer that. It was inappropriate. I shouldn't have asked. I absolutely don't expect you to have dinner with me. I also don't want you to think that I don't appreciate what you've cooked for me. I'll eat it, I promise. I... I wanted to get out. Which I know sounds weird, since I only got in now, but...'

She trailed off when she realised she was making it worse. She sucked in her bottom lip, then fought for a smile.

'I'm sorry about that, Tyler. Please, feel free to go home. I will see you tomorrow.'

Which she knew was a lie; she would be avoiding him for as long as she possibly could.

'Yes,' he said.

She blinked. 'I'm sorry?'

'Yes. Let's go and get some dinner.'

'But what about the food you made?'

He shrugged. 'It'll keep.'

She thought about it. Well, no, she didn't. She actively didn't think about it. Because she hadn't realised until she'd walked through the front door that she didn't want to be alone. Today, being alone *was* a problem she needed to fix. And if she'd realised that before she'd come home, she would have stayed at Dom's for dinner. Distracted herself.

'You know you don't have to do this, right?' she asked quietly.

His lips curved into a small smile that soothed something inside her. It had the faint sound of alarms going off in her head. But since she wasn't listening to anything going on inside her head, it didn't matter.

'I know,' he said. 'Why don't you take a shower and change, and I'll finish up here?'

She nodded and went upstairs. Her house was all wood and cream, in the design she and Kian had agreed on after the countless vision boards she had forced him to make with her. She adored it, and would have even if Kian hadn't agreed to the design, too. It made going into her bedroom with its soft plush carpet and muted colours more comforting than disarming.

What *was* disarming though, was showering when Tyler was in her house. She put it down to the fact that usually she had her house to herself. She wasn't used to anyone being around. It was as simple as that.

But she was naked, and she couldn't deny that her body

was feeling much more than simple. She could see the way her nipples were reacting, her skin turning to gooseflesh, her body aching in places that hadn't ached in literally years.

She turned the water cold so she could blame the reaction of her body on that, and not him. The man who worked for her. The man she hadn't known for more than two days—didn't know anything about, really. The man she'd asked out to dinner.

What am I doing?

She dressed quickly, not answering herself, and went downstairs. Tyler was waiting for her in the living room.

'I put Mochi outside with some food and fresh water.'

'Thank you.' And when that felt awkward, she added, 'Are you sure you want to wear that?' She gestured to the jeans and T-shirt he'd changed into from his suit. 'I happen to know you have a different outfit that would be—'

'Brooke,' he interrupted, his voice gentle but firm. 'Let's go eat.'

And somehow, despite her nerves, she laughed.

It wasn't crossing the line. He was doing what she'd asked. It contravened the distance he'd been determined to put between them, but what should he have done? Said no when she'd looked so…so…*vulnerable*?

He was beginning to realise that look was a trigger. It took him back five years to when he'd thought he was making a new friend. To when he'd thought that their friendship would someday develop into something more.

He had known at the end of the week, when they'd shared that kiss and she'd all but run from him, that he had been wrong. So why was he acting as though this was the first time he'd discovered he'd read more into things than he should have? Why was he still trying to find reasons for what had happened?

Like the fact that apparently, she had been married. Or was married. But people who were married lived together, didn't they? Unless their relationship was on the rocks, like his parents' relationship had been before they'd got divorced.

When his father had left to work in Dubai for two years, it had been for the sake of the family. That was what he'd told them. Until two years had become three, then five, and then the end of a marriage.

Back then, his mother had slowly removed all the pictures of his father from the house. His belongings had followed. Based on that experience, Tyler didn't think Brooke would have a picture of her ex-husband on her fireplace mantel. Except he hadn't seen any other signs of a man in her home…

He exhaled. He needed to let it go. All of it. The constant memories of the past. The comparisons. The questions he would get no answers to.

If he was going to survive working for Brooke, he needed boundaries. She had set them by not acknowledging the past, and he'd already decided it wasn't worth it not to respect that. For his sake and Tia's.

Now, he had to set boundaries within himself, too. To remember that everything that had happened was in the past and that he needed to leave it there.

Which he would.

After tonight.

'I know this is pretty far to go for dinner,' Brooke said when they met in the car park. She had taken the lead, with him following her—he tried not to read too much into that—and she'd driven to the beach.

It was a beautiful night for it. The sky was lit with the moon and the stars, as if it were a painting of a perfect night rather than the real thing. The weather was cool, but not cold enough that they needed covering—a welcome reprieve from the heat of the day.

The street was busy, cars and taxis full of people taking advantage of the summer night. From the promenade came the sound of laughter and chattering, of a kind of carefree-ness he envied. And beyond the promenade was the beach.

He could only see as far as the night sky allowed, but that was okay. He could hear it. The gentle crash of the ocean, which he knew wouldn't sound so gentle if he went any closer. He could smell the salt in the air, feel the moisture in the breeze when it caressed his face.

'If I'd thought about it, I would have come here, too,' he said.

She took a deep breath. 'I needed it, you know? The ocean and the sound of happiness.'

They lingered, those words, when he didn't reply. But he couldn't manage to. He was caught in the contradiction of her. The way her mouth curved but her eyes glittered with sadness. The relaxed set of her shoulders but the tight way she clasped her handbag.

Despite himself, he remembered the curious mixture of hope and defeat she'd carried with her before, five years ago. It had fascinated him then, too.

He shook it off. 'I'm glad we came.'

She turned to face him, a soft smile eclipsing the confusing emotions on her face. 'That's kind.'

'Don't get used to it,' he said gruffly, when her smile set off an explosion of happy butterflies in his stomach.

His response only had her smile widening.

He braced himself, then said, 'What do you want to eat?'

'Oh, I don't know.' She looked around at the street, lined with restaurants. 'Should we walk until we find something that appeals to us?'

He nodded and let her lead the way. She chatted casually as they went, pointing out restaurants that looked good or making suggestions. He liked the sound of her voice. She spoke in a unique pattern of rising and falling, as if her words were dancing to some tune only she had the pleasure of hearing. It sounded easier now, as if the tension she'd shown before was slowly escaping from her body like air from a balloon.

It felt as though the tension in him had eased, too.

He shook his head. Did he need to make an appointment with his psychologist? Surely this type of thinking meant he was teetering close to emotional instability?

'What?' she asked.

He looked for Brooke, but she wasn't next to him. She'd stopped walking.

He turned back. 'What?'

'That's what I asked you.'

'Okay. Why did you ask it?'

'You were shaking your head, but I wasn't saying anything.'

'You saw that?'

It was out of his mouth before he could stop it. He'd thought he was too old to blush, but apparently his skin felt differently. It wasn't a light *Oh, this is embarrassing* blush either. It was an honest to goodness, *I've spent too much time in the sun* flush.

He cleared his throat. 'I was...thinking.'

She bit her lip, but they both knew she was resisting a smile. 'I would love to ask you what about, but luckily for you I've already crossed too many lines today. I'll let you have your secrets.'

'Thank goodness,' he said on an exhalation. Again, he felt his cheeks heat. His filter seemed to have broken. An annoying development considering he needed it now more than ever. 'What I mean to say is, I don't have any secrets.'

She was no longer resisting the smile now; those lips she'd coated in a whimsical pink were curving in amusement. Heat curved inside him, too. A dangerous heat that was much too close to his heart.

'How about this place?' she asked, pointing to the restaurant next to them.

'Sure.'

'You didn't even look at it.'

'I'm trying to redirect your attention, and this seemed like a good way to do it.'

She laughed. The sound shot through the air, piercing his chest, turning heat into fire.

'Well, then, let's hope you like it.'

The server seated them at the front of the restaurant, where the doors had been pushed back to the walls, allowing access to both see and hear the ocean. When the woman handed him a menu, he saw that the place specialised in grilled food, which was fortunate. He wasn't sure he could handle anything fancy right now. A good old steak would probably anchor him. Turn his fanciful thoughts and feelings back into parts of himself—*logical* parts of himself—that he could recognise.

Brooke ordered a glass of wine, he ordered a beer, and while they waited she said, 'Again, I'm really sorry I asked you to come to dinner.'

'Why?'

'Well, it's not appropriate.'

'Employees and employers can be friends.'

'Can they?' she asked softly. 'I'm not entirely sure.'

'Is this the first time you've been someone's boss?' he asked.

'No. I…um… I work for a software development company. I'm a lead engineer, so I have a couple of people reporting to me.'

'You're in IT?'

'Yeah.' She tilted her head. 'Why's that surprising to you?'

'It's not.'

A smile played on her lips. 'It very clearly is, Tyler. Is it because I'm a woman?'

'No,' he said quickly. 'Of course not. I believe women can do anything. If I didn't—which, again, I very much do—my sister and mother would have killed me.'

'They sound like the kind of people I would like.'

His mouth lifted, thinking of it. 'I think they'd like you, too.'

'Yeah? Tell me about them.'

He waited until the server had set their drinks down and they'd placed their dinner orders—steak for both of them—and when she left, Tyler said, 'My mom was a force of nature. She had a couple of jobs. She worked for a call centre during the day and cleaned hotel rooms at night.'

'So housekeeping's in the family?'

'Not sure I'd say that.' He took a moment to figure out how much he wanted to reveal. A lot, as it turned out. 'Tia became a housekeeper after she found out she was pregnant. Things weren't great with the father already, but then she found out he was married.'

Her lips parted, though she didn't respond immediately. 'No wonder you're protective.'

'I'm not… How did you…?'

'Please,' she said, ignoring his splutters. 'You're filling in for her when it's obviously something outside of your area of expertise. I don't mean that you're not doing a good job,' she added quickly. 'I mean because of your actual job. Unless, of course, I'm naïve in believing that you're not a serial killer who's really good at covering your tracks.'

'I'm not a serial killer.' His voice was pained. 'How would I cover my tracks? By creating a full profile of myself online? Establishing an entire business to support that profile?'

'I said you were really good.'

'Brooke, I'm not a criminal.'

'Hmm.'

She reached for her wine and took a deep gulp. She believed him, but Dom's doubts had trickled into her head, forcing her to make sure. Well, it wasn't only Dom's doubts. It was her own. What did she know about this man beyond what he'd told her? Beyond what she'd seen online?

Sure, a man with his online presence and apparent success probably didn't need to trick her into letting him work for her. But how else could she explain the pull she felt towards him? As if they'd shared a past life together, It was giving her the oddest sense of déjà vu.

Surely that was a clue to his ability to manipulate? Manipulation was an important tool for criminals. Never mind that there hadn't been one moment when she'd actually *felt* manipulated.

Apart from that annoying pull, of course.

'Look,' he said after a while. 'I know you have no reason to trust me, but I'm not lying to you. Yes, I am protective of my sister. She's a single mother, and currently her kid is sick with the chicken pox. I can't look after him, which had been our Plan A, because I've only just got the vaccine and—'

'*What?* Why only now?' she demanded, outraged.

His lips twitched. 'Long story, but I have it now.' He got serious again. 'The point is, Tia has no more leave and she can't afford to lose her job with the agency. She won't let me help her financially,' he said, frustration deepening his voice, 'so this is the only way I *could* help.'

Brooke didn't reply. What could she say? *I believe you, but I need to make sure because I'm attracted to you and I thought I'd lost that part of myself after my husband died.*

It would be selfish. And he obviously was not. The passion when he'd spoken about his family made that clear. He would do anything for them—even step in to do a job with a boss who wouldn't stop interrogating him.

'Would you like to call my sister and check with her?' he asked.

'Yes,' she said, before she could stop herself.

She should have stopped herself.

She didn't want to speak with his sister because she wanted verification, but because she wanted to know more about their relationship. Still, she held out her hand.

'I'd like to speak with her.'

He winced. 'She's going to kill me for this. She'll think I'm risking her job.'

Her hand didn't budge. 'I'll assure her you're doing the opposite. And if that doesn't do it, I'll go to your funeral and pay my respects.'

With an exaggerated sigh—as if he hadn't been the one to suggest it—he tapped his phone screen before handing it to her. Since there weren't many people around them, she put the call on speaker.

'Ty? Where are you? I've been messaging you for ever.'

'Hi, Tia. This is Brooke Jansen. I believe you're supposed to be working for me this month?'

'Ms Jansen?' Tia squeaked. 'Are you…? Hold on…' Tia said, suspicion creeping into her voice. 'Did my brother hire you to trick me?'

'Why would I do that, T?' Tyler inserted.

'Oh, you're there? Lovely,' Tia said, in a tone that indicated she did not find it lovely at all. 'Ms Jansen, I know you have a million reasons to report this to the agency, but I assure you I had no choice. I absolutely wouldn't have done this if Nyle had had anything but the chicken pox.'

'Tia,' Brooke said slowly, 'your brother has explained the situation to me. I… I understand.' She caught Tyler's look of relief, but refused to respond to it. 'I'm just calling to make sure he's not a criminal. Can you verify?'

'Oh. Well, yeah. He's a dork who runs an online education company.' There was a short pause. 'Wait—you do really believe us? I mean, we could have coordinated this. I work for the agency, send my brother in as a replacement, he establishes some form of trust and if you begin to suspect something, he has you call me to verify his story.'

'Tia,' Tyler moaned, rubbing a hand on his forehead. 'What is *wrong* with you?'

'Hey, I'm just looking out for her. She seems like a nice lady.'

'Thank you,' Brooke said, suppressing a laugh. 'I do believe you. And, while I think going behind the agency's back has some moral problems, you've both dealt with this as ethically as you could. Besides,' she added wryly, 'I'm pretty sure that if you two were a criminal duo, one of you would have ratted the other out by now. Or you'd both be in prison.'

'Definitely a possibility,' Tia said.

At the same time Tyler said, 'Probably.'

'Not to mention that my brother is a police officer,' Brooke continued conversationally. 'So if this *is* a ruse, you'll soon be ending your reign of terror.'

A nervous laugh came through the speaker.

Brooke grinned as she met Tyler's eyes. But he didn't smile back. Just gazed at her with a sincerity and gratitude that made his brown eyes look deeper, more soulful. She hadn't spent much time looking into his eyes—she had some sense of self-preservation—but she wouldn't have said that it was possible. There was enough soul and depth there without any emotion strengthening it. And when emotion did strengthen it…

She exhaled. 'Thank you, Tia. I hope your child feels better soon.'

'Thank you, Ms Jansen—'

'Brooke, please.'

'Thank you, Brooke. I… I appreciate this more than you know.'

After she ended the call, there was a long silence. It wasn't an easy silence either. In fact, she was fairly certain it was filled with cement and steel and everything hard and unyielding. And it sat at the empty seat at their table as if it had been invited to dinner.

Eventually, Tyler cleared his throat. 'Thank you.'

'Don't mention it.'

'I don't mean that casually.' His fingers clenched around his glass of beer. 'Tia's the strongest person I know, but she's stubborn. Proud. We both are.' He swallowed. 'I think if this hadn't worked out she'd have never let me help her again. Not out of stubbornness, but out of fear.'

Brooke understood that better than most.

After Kian had died, she'd felt helpless and so unlike herself. But she'd worked for a company that had thought three weeks' leave was adequate to get her back to who she used to be.

She had trusted those people. Thought they would know that the person she used to be no longer existed.

They hadn't.

When she'd no longer been able to work at the capacity she—and they—were used to, they'd pushed her out. It hadn't been that hard a push; it hadn't needed to be. She had already been perched at the end of a cliff, ready to leave behind everything from the life she'd had with Kian, including her job. She'd only realised afterwards, when she'd been able to work through some of her emotions about the situation, that she'd felt betrayed.

She'd taken a completely different approach when she'd started working for her current company. She didn't trust them, and only saw them for who they were: colleagues and employers. Fear kept her from opening up even a tiny bit in case taking the chance and doing so would leave her in the same position she'd been in at her last company.

So she nodded and said, 'Don't mention it.'

Something in her tone must have told him how much she meant that because he obeyed.

CHAPTER FIVE

'ARE YOU GOING back to your car?' Tyler asked when they'd finished dinner and she'd paid for their meal. She had insisted and, since things hadn't moved away from the confusing and frankly absurd level of awkwardness between them, he'd agreed.

'No, actually. I think I want to take a walk on the beach.'

'I'll come with you.'

'Oh, you don't have to. I would like some time alone, actually.'

'It's after ten p.m.'

Surprised, she glanced at her watch. 'Where did the time go?'

'It's been a long day.'

She curled her fingers over the rim of her bag. 'I should probably get home then.'

He studied her. 'How much do you want to walk on the beach?'

'I don't, really.'

'Brooke.' He waited until she looked at him. 'How much?'

It was a while before she said, 'A lot.'

'Then let's go. You can walk ahead,' he added. 'You'll get your alone time.'

'Well, no. Insisting on that now makes me feel like I'm a terrible person when you're being chivalrous.'

He smiled. 'You can still walk ahead.'

She didn't refuse his offer this time, though she stayed relatively close to him as they crossed the road to the beach. It was much quieter now, only the hardcore night owls strolling down the promenade, making their way to different parts of town where things were livelier.

He took off his shoes when they got there, and he was done before her. Mainly because his shoes didn't have any complicated straps.

'Do you need help?' he asked when she struggled to keep her balance and still couldn't take her shoe off.

'It's fine.'

As she said it, she lost her balance.

Her hands flailed out, trying to find something to steady her. Being the gentleman he was, he became that something.

'This is what I get for being stubborn,' she said, peering up at him.

Because, of course, he hadn't simply offered her a hand when he'd seen her fall. He'd stepped forward, offering his entire body to stabilise her.

He'd done so without thinking. Truly—it had been instinct. Now he wondered where that instinct came from. Did he really want to help her, or had his body simply wanted to feel hers? He hadn't ever got the chance. Not during that week five years ago. Not until that kiss. And even then, it had only been a meeting of their lips before it ended.

Now here he was holding her. And she was pressed against his chest, as if she were glued there.

She didn't move. At least not her body. Her face was an explosion of movement. Her eyelashes fluttered up at him. Her lips parted. Air, warm and smelling faintly of the mint she'd eaten after dinner, touched his skin. She breathed in deeply, sharply, and exhaled again, hitting him with the warmth of that air again, forcing him to wonder about her taste.

Their kiss hadn't allowed him to sweep his tongue into her mouth and truly *taste* her. Now, she would almost certainly taste like mint. But what about beneath that? His gut told him it would be something sweet, with the slightest hint of a kick.

Except it wasn't his gut. It came from parts of him he hadn't cared about much in the years since he'd met Brooke. Not because he hadn't felt anything for anyone, but because those feelings had seemed inconsequential. Nothing had come close to the spark he'd felt light up his body when his eyes had met Brooke's and lingered.

And this? This felt even better than that spark. Holding her in his arms, feeling her body against his, wondering about something as simple as kissing her.

But nothing about this was simple.

That knowledge had him gently straightening Brooke, ensuring that she had her balance, and taking a step back.

'Thank you,' she said after a moment, her voice shaky.

'Don't mention it.'

It was the same thing she'd said in the restaurant, about the situation with his sister. He'd known she meant it. Now, he hoped she knew he meant it, too.

'Do you mind if I take off your shoes for you?'

'If I say no, that would make me a fool, wouldn't it?' she teased.

Teased. As if she hadn't felt her world shift only seconds ago, as he had. But he could pretend to be unaffected, too.

'Are you a fool?' he asked mildly.

'I'm sure the answer to that changes in each situation, but for this one? No.'

He was smiling as he lowered himself to the ground to take off her shoes. He wasn't sure why. It seemed his emotions were on a cross-country ride, going from panic and desire to amusement and calm in too little time for him to process.

Though the strap of one shoe was already undone, she hadn't managed to actually take off the shoe. He did that, then started on the next.

Seconds into the task, she leaned closer to him, resting her hand on his shoulder. Before that, he had been able to pretend that her proximity wasn't affecting him. He couldn't any more. He felt electrocuted, and he was grateful for the dark so she couldn't see his hands shaking.

Desire covered his skin as if it were in the breeze that passed them. But he refused its call. Refused to allow himself to feel as though he were a teenage boy unable to handle his hormones.

When he straightened and she smiled and thanked him, he felt very much like that teenage boy. Zero to one hundred in a matter of seconds, and then all the way back again.

'Are you okay?' she asked, frowning.

'Yeah,' he said, his voice hoarse. He cleared his throat. 'Yes. Why?'

'You seem…strange.'

'That hardly seems like the kind of thing you should say to someone who's helped you.'

'That's probably true. Although we've already established that I'm not good at saying what I'm supposed to say when I'm supposed to say it.'

'What do you mean?'

'I asked you to come out for dinner with me even though you work for me.'

'I thought we'd already settled that?'

'We have,' she agreed. 'I'm just pointing out that there are some flaws in my being.'

He laughed softly, though he wasn't sure why.

'But now that the truth's out am I really your boss?' she asked. 'Technically, your sister's my employee.'

'Does that mean I don't have to do the job then?'

'Huh,' she said. 'Good point. We should probably still work within the confines of an employer/employee relationship.'

He was certain she didn't mean that in the way he took it, but he couldn't help but agree. It was best if they stayed as boss and employee. Sure, she was right: it wasn't the traditional relationship. But for the sake of his sanity, he would cling to it.

'Sounds good to me,' he replied.

'I thought it might.'

Her words hung in the air between them as they walked in silence.

There were no more impromptu dinner requests, no more inappropriate comments, and certainly no more touching after that night. Brooke made sure of it.

Except she did it in the only way she knew how: she avoided being at home.

She left before Tyler arrived and came back late enough that if he was still there, she would warn him about working too hard. Fortunately, she had enough work to warrant the long hours. Her latest project was going well, but she still had a lot to do before the app launched in three weeks. So Brooke kept busy.

Still, she couldn't get Tyler out of her mind. Mainly because he kept doing stuff for her that made her think about him.

A few nights after their dinner, she came home to a note.

Walked Mochi today. Twice. He's the kind of dog who needs it. Might be useful to know for the future. Tyler

She was relieved. At first. But when she thought about it, she felt only guilt. Because she was Mochi's owner; he was *her* responsibility. And it wasn't because she needed to work that she was neglecting him. She was doing it because she didn't want to see Tyler.

So the next day she took Mochi for a walk before she left for work and left Tyler a note of her own.

Walked Mochi before I went to work. I can do it again later, so you don't have to. He's not your responsibility.
Brooke

She was already at work when she thought back to the note and wondered if it sounded defensive. And as soon as that occurred to her, she couldn't get it out of her head. More than once, one of her employees checked to see if she was okay.

She did not appreciate it. Nor did she appreciate Tyler's note when she got home.

Walked Mochi this evening so you don't have to. Also put a lasagne in the fridge. You can freeze the rest when you're done.
Tyler

PS I'm here to help you with your responsibilities. That's exactly what you're paying me—well, Tia—to do.

She was so annoyed that she almost refused to eat the food. But she had nothing ready-made in the fridge, and calling out to get food would take too long. She was hungry, and cooking wasn't an option—when was it ever?—so she dished up a portion of the lasagne.

It was the best thing she'd eaten.

Damn it.

'Why does he keep doing this?' she asked Mochi as she lifted a forkful of lasagne from her second helping. 'I don't want him to be nice. I would honestly prefer him to be a complete and utter jerk who isn't competent at his job.'

And he was more than competent; her house was in a better state than she could ever make it herself.

'Hell, I'll take the aloof and distant guy he was when we met. Except even then he was thoughtful. He made me food that very first night! And now he makes the best lasagne in the world! The cheek!'

Mochi tilted his head, as if to say, *I don't see the problem here.*

'Is this why you like him? Because he's nice?'

Mochi didn't answer.

'Well, it won't work on me.'

She finished her meal, washed the dishes, then went to the garden to play catch with Mochi for a little while before bed.

As it usually did, the garden calmed her. It was the first thing she had done in the house. The space had been the reason she'd bought it after all.

When they'd started dating, Kian had told her they would get married someday. It had been a ridiculous thing to say at the start of a relationship, but they'd been young and he'd been her first boyfriend. And sure, the fact that her parents had met and fallen in love almost instantly had had some effect on her. They were the happiest couple she knew—of course it would affect her. So she hadn't run away, as her instinct now would be, from a silly man and his silly romantic proclamation.

For her birthday that year, Kian had given her a framed landscape design.

'For our home,' he'd said, 'when we're married.'

He had still been studying back then, but his talent had been evident. He'd died before the world could truly take advantage of that talent, which had made his gift so much more meaningful. She was one of the few people who had an original Kian Jansen design. It would have seemed almost rude not to follow through.

It had taken years after his death, but she'd done it, and she was proud.

Though it might not be the best garden for a dog, she thought, as she accidentally threw the ball into the pond and Mochi jumped in after it.

He brought the ball back to her with a wagging tail and a drenched body.

She heaved out a sigh. 'We probably need to sort you out now, don't we?'

She left him outside when she went to fetch his leash. She was about to go back out when the doorbell rang. Wondering who it could be, so late, she peeked through the eyehole and saw Tyler.

It took her a couple of minutes—and another ring of the bell—to answer.

'Tyler?' she said, acting surprised. She probably wouldn't win any awards for it. 'What are you doing here? It's almost nine p.m.'

'I left my wallet here.'

He shoved his hands into his pockets. The movement made his muscles ripple. Not that she noticed.

'Can I get it?'

'Sure.' She opened the door wider.

'Thanks.' A second later, he asked, 'Where's Mochi?'

'Outside,' she said with a sigh. 'There was an accident.'

'Are you okay?'

'Yeah, we're fine. We were playing and I threw the ball in the pond and he went to get it. So…' she lifted the leash '…we're going to have a bath before bed.'

'That sounds like an exciting way to end a long day of work.'

She snorted. 'Exactly!'

'I can help,' he said. She noticed the words came tentatively. 'If you want.'

'Oh, no. It's fine. I mean, I was just going to bring him into the bathroom...'

'Wet?'

She hadn't thought about that. 'Well, I don't know if I can do it in the garden. A couple of the outside lights aren't working and I forgot to buy bulbs to replace them—'

'And you didn't think to ask your housekeeper?'

She paused. 'That does sound like something I should have done, doesn't it?'

He watched her for a moment, then said, 'Brooke, you hired me because you needed help. So why don't you want me to help you?'

Because I've been thinking about the way you held me on the beach every day since. Because I can remember the heat of your touch, the strength of your body. Because you're the kind of man who helps his sister out but does it in the least dishonest way possible. Because you helped me take off my shoes, even when I was too stubborn to ask you at first. Because you walked with me on the beach after, and you walked my dog, and all of it feels like asking you to help would be more intimate than I can stand right now.

'I'm not used to help,' she said honestly, because she was still processing all the other stuff—she hadn't expected her brain to be quite so honest at this time of night—and she didn't particularly want to process it.

'You hired me.'

'Because I need help. Which, yes, I know makes me seem stupid for not asking for it, but...but it's a habit, okay? I had to learn how to rely on myself and now it's a habit. I didn't have to for the longest time. First, my parents did everything for me. Then Kian. And when he died, I—'

She broke off at the expression on his face. Replayed everything she said. When she realised she'd spoken about Kian, her face heated.

It wasn't because she was embarrassed to talk about him. It was more that she hadn't realised she *had* talked about him. And sharing his name or her experiences before and after his death, didn't feel like something she should be sharing with Tyler. Again, it felt too intimate.

'Kian?' Tyler prodded softly.

Of course he did.

And what other choice did she have but to tell him?

'My husband. He died five years ago.'

Tyler's mind spun with this new information. He hadn't thought he would hear anything like it from Brooke. She had closed up on him since that day at the beach. Not that she had been an open book that night, but she had been easier than this. He had known it even though he hadn't seen her since the beach. And it was part of the reason he'd doubled back this evening.

Oh, he'd definitely forgotten his wallet. But he could have easily collected it the next day. When he convinced himself to go round at nine p.m., he wondered if his subconscious hadn't been the thing to make him leave his wallet behind. He wanted to check on her, make sure she was okay. Perhaps see whether she was still as affected by their night at the beach as he was.

Her notes seemed to indicate otherwise, but it was entirely possible that she was deflecting her feelings—or that he was grasping at literally anything to make the fact that he couldn't stop thinking about her, his possibly married boss, less alarming.

But she wasn't married. She was a widow. Had been for five years. Which might have made his pining a little less creepy if it hadn't caused other questions about the time they'd spent together five years ago.

Had she been married then? Had her husband already passed away? If so, how long before they'd met? And did that change anything?

He couldn't answer those questions without speaking to her, but since she seemed determined to forget that they'd even met before, he couldn't exactly ask her.

Unless he should.

Should he?

No. He was leaving the past behind him. Boundaries and all that.

With a shallow breath, he said, 'I'm incredibly sorry to hear that.'

She lifted her shoulders, a gesture meant to indicate that it wasn't a big deal but one that only succeeded in telling him it was a very big deal.

'It's been five years. I'm okay with it for the most part.'

'But it lingers, doesn't it?'

She looked at him, blinked. And with that blink, something cleared in her vision. 'You've lost someone, too.'

It wasn't a question, but he replied. 'My mother.'

'I'm sorry,' she murmured. 'When you spoke about her the other night…' She trailed off, as if she'd just realised he'd spoken about his mother in the past tense. 'I should have realised.'

Three sharp barks came from the garden.

Brooke winced. 'Clearly he'd like us to have this conversation some other time.'

Since it would give him the break he needed to gather his thoughts, Tyler nodded. 'Do you have a bucket or something to wash him in?'

'I do. It's in the garage. Should we bring him inside? The light out there is bad.'

'I'm sure we can manage between the two of us.'

She nodded. 'Let's do it.'

She gave him instructions on where she kept the dog shampoo and an old towel. Minutes later, Tyler was running water into the bucket in the downstairs bathroom. When it was done, he carried it outside, to where Mochi and Brooke were waiting.

Brooke was murmuring comfort to the dog as he laid his head on her knee. It hit Tyler in an entirely unexpected way. Not only the intimacy of the moment, but the desire for it to be...permanent. Because of it, water splashed over the rim of the bucket before he could put it down.

'That's what you get for showing off,' she said tartly, but she smiled before uncurling her legs and standing.

What was it about this woman that he couldn't stop himself from being drawn to her? He wanted to know things about her he shouldn't want to know. Like the way she'd become independent after years of not being. How had that affected her? Was that the reason she couldn't see how deeply her dog loved her? Was that why she berated herself for not having the boundaries she thought she should have with him?

But why did he care about any of it? She had a husband. She'd *had* a husband when they'd met or she had just lost her husband. Either way, the situation was a minefield he shouldn't want to navigate.

He knew all about relationship minefields. His parents' relationship... Tia's relationship with Nyle's father... They'd both shown him how complicated things could be. And they hadn't had the added factor of a dead spouse who might have been alive when they'd first met.

'You okay?' she asked, studying him now as she held Mochi while he shampooed the dog.

'Why wouldn't I be?' He offered her a smile that he was certain wouldn't reassure her. He was right.

'You're awfully quiet. Did I bruise your ego earlier?' she teased.

Damn if his heart didn't skip at the easiness. At the longing for it to be easy, only easy, between them.

'My ego is fine.'

'Your feelings then.' Her tone shifted to something more serious. 'You're upset that I was making fun. I didn't mean—'

'I'm fine, Brooke,' he interrupted curtly, and immediately regretted it.

Hurt skipped across her face, but it was gone so quickly. 'Of course.'

They washed Mochi in silence for the next few moments. The dog whined softly, though he didn't try to move. Tyler wondered if that meant he wasn't whining at being bathed, but at the tension between the humans who were bathing him.

When they were done, Brooke said, 'I can take it from here.'

'What?'

'I have the leash and his brush, and it won't take any longer or be any easier with you around.' She winced, as if she regretted the phrasing, but she didn't correct herself. 'You can get your wallet and go. I'm sure you have other places to be.'

'Brooke—'

'I can do this by myself, Tyler,' she said, more sternly now.

What could he say to that?

He nodded, stood up, grimacing at the sight of his own clothing that was wet in patches now. But he didn't say anything. Only dusted his feet off as best he could, grabbed his wallet and went to his car.

Once there, he hit the edge of the steering wheel. 'Idiot!'

Because he was and he deserved to hear it. Any progress they'd made tonight—and he felt as if they'd made some—had been completely and utterly ruined because he couldn't get out of his own head.

It was probably for the best that she'd kicked him out. There was no telling how much more damage he would have done if he'd stayed.

CHAPTER SIX

BROOKE SUCCESSFULLY PUSHED Tyler out of her head until Friday.

She was quite proud of herself, honestly. She hadn't thought about him, or the way she could almost still feel his skin on hers from that night on the beach, or the way he wanted to help her and then didn't. Or maybe he did, but there was something that had kept him from being comfortable that night with Mochi.

She didn't have much experience, but she couldn't imagine knowing that she was a widow made things easy. Not that it was some thing to be made easy when there was nothing going on between them. It wasn't like they were starting a relationship and he was freaked out by the fact that she had once been married and the only reason she wasn't now was because her husband had died.

But, since she wasn't thinking about it, it didn't matter anyway. And that was why she was almost okay when she walked into her kitchen that morning to find him sitting at the counter with his laptop open.

'Morning,' she said, going to the coffee machine.

He'd already made it, which wasn't a thoughtful thing she needed to get mushy about. It was his *job*. He was doing his job, not thinking about her.

It was the same thing every time he made her food.

Bought her groceries.

Discovered what her favourite scent was and put candles in her study and her bathroom.

Fluffed her pillows and made them smell like that same scent.

Left notes when he'd walked Mochi.

All of it was his job.

All of it.

She gulped down her coffee, not even caring that it burnt her throat.

'Rough night?' he asked, watching her.

Determination alone couldn't stop her from blushing, so she just said, 'Yeah. We've been testing an app that's launching soon. There have been some bugs, but nothing hectic. I can't imagine that'll continue, so I'm trying to prepare myself.' The blush got deeper when she realised he probably hadn't wanted to know any of that. 'Everything okay with you?'

She was looking at him properly now, so she could see the faint shadows under his eyes.

'Of course.'

'You said that a little too quickly.'

He offered her a wry smile. And instantly she knew she would no longer be able to resist thinking about him. Because of that smile.

His eyes softened, the skin around them crinkled as his cheeks lifted. The curve of his mouth thinned his lips, though that didn't lessen the seductive quality of them one bit. Hell, if anything, it made her want to lean in and—

She froze. She found him attractive, yes, but that attraction had never taken a detour into fantasy. She wasn't sure how she should feel about it.

But worrying about that was for another time. Now was for worrying about something else: those shadows under his eyes.

'You're more perceptive than most people,' he said.

'Maybe. Doesn't change the fact that you said it too quickly.'

He exhaled, as if in defeat. She would have enjoyed it more if he hadn't looked so… Well, defeated.

'What is it, Tyler?' she asked, her heart picking up on his tension and beating faster than she liked. 'Please, for heaven's sake, don't keep me in suspense.'

He sighed, but he answered. 'My company… has been offered an opportunity to expand.'

'Okay?'

'From a company in the UK,' he continued after a beat. 'It would mean… Well, it would mean that I'd have to live there for a while, and I can't do that.'

'Why not?'

'I'm the only family Tia and Nyle have. I can't abandon them.'

She opened her mouth to point out that it wouldn't be abandoning them, but the conflict in his eyes stopped her. A simple observation wouldn't do him any good when he was in this state. Especially since him even using the word 'abandon' meant he must have had some baggage.

Instead, she said, 'So what's with the sad eyes on your laptop now?'

'The company is trying to tempt me.'

She searched his face. 'And it's working.'

'No,' he answered, though it hadn't been a question. 'No, it's not.'

'Tyler—'

'Does my attending one of their events over here tonight sound like a good idea? Maybe,' he said, as if she hadn't spoken. 'I'd learn more about the company, the people I'd potentially be working with. I could engage with them on my ideas about how the expansion would work…'

If he hadn't seemed so torn up about it, she would have told him to stop drooling.

'But,' he went on, 'that would only be relevant *if* I were interested.'

'Which you are.'

'No.'

She waited to see if there was more, then said, 'Tyler, you're interested. There's nothing wrong with that. You haven't betrayed anyone by being interested.' When he didn't say anything, she prodded. 'That's it, right? You think you're betraying your family?'

'I think…' It was a while before he finished the sentence. 'Yeah, I do. Being interested is the first step towards doing something, isn't it?'

It was a rhetorical question, but somehow she felt as though she needed to answer. Perhaps because it resonated with her, and unknowingly, it pointed out one of her own issues. She was interested in Tyler. And, yes, that did feel as though she was moving towards betraying Kian.

She didn't need her therapist to tell her that it was a normal part of moving forward. They'd spoken about it plenty of times with regard to other areas of her life. Her work, her home. Even her family. Whenever her life changed or evolved she felt guilty because it was changing and evolving away from the life she'd shared with Kian.

At the same time she felt as if she had to move forward. She owed it to him.

But did she owe it to him to move on with *this* part of her life?

'It's complicated,' she answered softly.

'Yes.' He paused. 'I haven't told my sister.'

'Okay.'

'I told myself I would mention it in passing,' he said. 'So that I could get her opinion on it. I was hoping…'

When he didn't finish, she finished for him. 'That she'd give you the permission you feel you need from her to do something you really want to do.'

He opened his mouth—to argue, she thought, seeing his body tense. But he deflated quickly. 'Yes.'

'And you haven't told her because…?'

'Because I'm a coward.'

'That doesn't sound fair,' she chided.

He gave her a sad look. A defeated look. It crashed into her heart as if it were a car going too fast on a highway. And, just like that car, she had apparently lost control, too, because she found herself saying, 'What if I went with you?'

His eyes widened. That was his only reaction. He didn't respond verbally, didn't move a muscle beyond that. And when, after at least a million minutes of silence, he still didn't reply, Brooke set her half-full mug on the counter and wiped her palms—sweaty now—on her trousers.

'Well, that's all the time I have this morning,' she said, knowing she sounded like a talk show host. 'I guess I'll see you around.'

But probably not.

Then she basically sprinted from the kitchen. The scene of her death.

Fortunately, when she got to work there was an urgent issue that kept her from thinking about anything that had happened that morning. But by lunchtime things had quietened and mortification filled her.

'Why did I think that would be a good idea?' she asked out loud, squeezing her stress ball with its smiley face for all it was worth. 'I'm not ready for it to be a date, but that's what I offered, right? Or was I offering something a friend would do? Except we're not friends, so now it's…' She trailed off. 'Now it's confusing. For both of us.'

She sighed. Blamed it on his expression. That look of hopelessness and frustration and defeat. She wanted to get his smile back. It was somehow imprinted on her brain, regardless of how much she wanted it not to be. Especially when she could barely remember Kian's face these days…

Most of the time, she understood. This was what happened. Those vivid memories of every detail of his face, his body, had faded over time. She remembered the general things about Kian, and that was what was most important.

He had been handsome in such a traditional sense of the word that when she'd been with him, she'd often tell him how annoying it was. He had been strong, but not in any way dictated by the gym. His strength had come from the time he'd spent outdoors. Hiking or running or carrying things when he was messing around in a garden. And he had been kind. So kind that some days she had marvelled at him. Tried to be more like him. And, really, those *were* the most important things.

But it smarted, just a little, that she could remember everything about Tyler. The light in his eyes when he smiled at her unexpectedly; the curve of his lips that courted his cheeks; the scar he had next to his right eye that was hardly noticeable to someone who wasn't determined to notice everything about him.

He wasn't traditionally handsome. No, his features were too rugged, too sharp for that. But there was something about the way they came together. Or maybe it was the way he carried himself. With a confidence that told her he didn't care about being handsome. With the easiness of not caring.

It was clear he cared about other stuff though. His family was important to him. There was obviously more to the situation than she knew, but she could understand his concerns about going overseas. She couldn't imagine leaving the only family she had or having them leave her. If she had to choose between that and moving forward with her life? That decision wouldn't be easy.

A glance at the clock told her lunchtime was over and she got back to work. But no matter how hard she tried,

Tyler crept into her consciousness. She was immensely relieved when she got home that evening and discovered she was alone.

But when she walked into the kitchen, she found a note on the fridge.

I'd like to take you up on your offer. Please. You'll find what you need in your bedroom. I'll be over at seven.
T

'This is a joke, right?' she asked the empty room.

For a full five seconds she expected an answer. Someone to jump out of the closet and say, *How did you figure it out?* and then she wouldn't have to go to her bedroom and find out what he thought she needed.

She looked at the clock. It was almost six. She had an hour to figure out what to wear, to do her hair, her make-up. And she hadn't done anything of the sort in years. An hour was not what she would have given herself to rediscover those skills.

'Okay. Okay,' she said because apparently today, speaking out loud was the only thing keeping her from panicking. 'One thing at a time.'

She got Mochi's food ready, went out to feed him, then refilled his water and gave him some belly rubs with the promise of a long morning walk. Then she went to her bedroom.

There was a gold dress hanging on her cupboard.

Something strange happened to her breathing. She inhaled sharply, exhaled, then exhaled again, as if somehow she had more than enough air in her lungs. Slowly she moved forward, touched the material. It was silk…smooth. It felt like luxury. She dropped it, worried that she would damage it somehow by simply touching it.

On the floor beneath the dress was a shoe box. She almost didn't open it, afraid of what extravagance she would find there. But she dropped down, opened the lid. She was more prepared this time, but it still felt like an out-of-body experience. The shoes were gold perfection, their straps covered with shiny stones that she traced and immediately loved.

She straightened, shook her head. She couldn't malfunction right now, no matter how much she wanted to. She needed to get her hair done, which would likely take most of her time. And then she needed to figure out make-up; she couldn't remember what the appropriate style was.

With a deep breath, she started preparing.

CHAPTER SEVEN

He was holding his breath. It was a stupid thing to do, considering he needed air to survive. But as he rang Brooke's doorbell—it would have felt like an invasion to walk in—he held his breath.

Tyler wished he had dealt with the situation differently that morning. When she'd offered, he wished he hadn't frozen. Why hadn't he accepted her kindness then? It would have made it less awkward, especially when she was doing something for him.

But, no—he *had* frozen. He had frozen because he'd wanted to say yes so quickly he'd been afraid of what it might tell her if he did. He also hadn't expected it. He'd been so in his own mind, berating himself for not being honest with Tia, for wanting things he couldn't have, for admitting all that to a woman he felt so complicatedly about, that her offer had come out of left field. By the time his mouth had caught up, she'd been out the house.

The least he could do then was get her attire sorted so things were as easy for her as possible. Hopefully it would help so she wouldn't regret her decision.

Although he was fairly certain it was too late for that.

The door opened before he could think on it for too long. And then he wasn't thinking at all.

'I think it might be a size too small,' Brooke said, instead of greeting him.

That was fine with him. Because the fact that she'd said it meant he could look at her without it seeming as if he was ogling.

Though he absolutely was.

The dress was sleeveless, revealing firm brown arms. One strap was thin, widening into gold material that clung to her breast in a teardrop shape, while the other strap was thicker, falling into loose fabric that covered the rest of her chest and then cinched in at the waist. From there, the dress flowed to the ground, sweeping over shoes that looked beautiful on her feet.

'You look incredible.' Quickly he realised she might not be comfortable with the dress. 'I'm sorry. I should have checked with you.'

'No, no, it's okay.'

Her fingers tightened around the clutch purse he'd bought. Gold as well, though simpler than the dress.

'I was just worried that this area—' she made a circle above her chest '—would be distracting.' She changed the subject abruptly. 'I didn't realise this event would be so formal.'

'It's a cocktail party. Hence the suit and the dress.'

'You…um…you look nice too.'

'Thank you.' He paused. 'Do you feel uncomfortable?'

She shifted. 'Not about the dress.' She winced. 'I didn't mean that the way it sounded.'

'It's okay,' he said. 'I get it. I feel it, too. The only reason I got dressed and decided to go through with this is because you offered to come with me. I'm not… I'm still not sure I want to do this.'

She reached out to take his hand. 'You want to do this.'

His throat felt odd for a moment, but he swallowed and the moment passed. 'Thank you. Thank you for coming tonight.'

'Don't mention it.'

She dropped his hand, curved her fingers around her ear as though there was hair there. But she had sleeked her hair back, curled her edges in a fascinating pattern over her forehead. The rest of it fell in a long, straight ponytail down her back.

It made her face stand out all the more, though he had no idea how that was possible. She already had the most striking features he'd encountered. But without any hair framing her face he could see the smoothness of her brown skin, the little dots on her cheeks, the full, plump lips, the dark, thick lashes. All of those features were more prominent because she'd put on make-up. Black encircled her eyes, a light pink touched her cheeks, a deep red coloured her lips.

Her breasts weren't the distraction he was worried about; *she* was. By simply being at his side. Of course it didn't help that she looked like a goddess on a day designated to celebrate her greatness. He was willing to bet she'd distract everyone in the room tonight.

That might not be such a bad thing. He might not feel as much pressure about being there if she did.

'Is it strange that I'm nervous?' she asked, stepping out of the house and locking up behind her. 'I'm only the plus one.'

You could never only be the plus one, he wanted to say. Thank heavens he stopped himself. 'Maybe you're feeding off my nerves,' he said instead.

He held out his hand, offering her support if she wanted it. Her eyes dropped, lingered, then she took it.

'It'll be fine,' she said, to both of them.

He swore he heard her voice shake, but he couldn't be sure.

He didn't react at the contact as he helped her down the stairs to his car. But holding her hand felt as though he was holding something precious. He couldn't drop it, no matter what.

He opened the passenger door before going to the driver's side and getting in himself.

'What should I know?' she asked as he drove down the short path from her house to her gate. 'About this event?'

He told her what he knew about the company and its possible areas of expansion. When that led to questions about his own work, he answered them. Explained how his mother hadn't been able to study when she was younger because she hadn't been given the opportunity to do so. And how when the opportunity had come—when her family life and financial position had finally aligned to allow it—his father left.

'She was essentially a single parent,' he said, trying to keep the emotion out of his voice. 'And her dreams got delayed even longer.'

'Why did your father leave?' Brooke asked softly.

He hesitated. It wasn't because the information was a secret, but because sharing it with her felt… It felt like crossing a line again. One of his own lines this time. One of those boundaries he'd told himself he had to keep when he'd started working for her.

But then, almost as soon as he'd set them those lines had become blurred. He knew it simply because the distance he'd planned to treat her with had slowly but surely disappeared. He couldn't be cool with her, despite their history. Despite the fact that that history was apparently more complicated than he'd originally thought.

They were edging into new territory, and he had no idea how to handle it.

In this case she saved him from deciding as she said, 'Since your thinking is steaming up the car—which, as I say it, sounds like a dangerous way of phrasing it—I'll change the subject.' She pivoted, exactly as she said she would. 'So, you're basically saying that you started your company to provide online learning specifically geared towards people of an older generation, who have a lot on their plates, because you were thinking of your mother?'

'Yes,' he answered, both relieved and oddly disappointed. 'I had been looking into different programmes for her to follow when I realised that with her schedule, she wouldn't be able to fit much in. I thought I'd try to design something bespoke for her, and as I was doing that, I thought it might actually work for more people than her.'

He took the turn-off for the highway, saw Table Mountain in the distance. If he didn't take this opportunity—and he wouldn't—at least he would still have this. His home. His memories.

The beauty of Cape Town was so inextricably linked with those memories that he'd never give it up. He couldn't. Not when Tia still needed him. Not when his mother wouldn't have wanted him to. She had made so many sacrifices for them. For their happiness. To ensure that they still felt like a unit, a family, after his father left. She would be ashamed of him for even considering taking the same path as his father.

'There you go, thinking again.'

He exhaled. 'I'm sorry. It—*this*—is harder than I thought it would be.'

'What is?'

'Thinking about what I want. Tia and I weren't raised that way. We were raised to think about family. My father left and it was the three of us and... Well, we had to be there for one another.'

'You can still be there for your family if you do this, Tyler,' she pointed out. 'You're not disappearing off the ends of the earth. You're taking an opportunity that will—what? Require you to spend some time in a different country? That's not abandoning by any means.'

'My father took an opportunity that required him to spend some time in a different country,' he said quietly. 'A job in Dubai. He was doing okay here, but he wanted us to be more comfortable, he said. So he left.' He took a steadying breath. 'A two-year contract turned into a permanent situation. He started a brand-new life without us and we had to accept it.'

'I'm sorry,' she murmured, the words heavy despite her soft tone.

Silence followed, and he realised he was supposed to fill it. He shrugged. 'Now you know why this isn't simple.'

'Yeah.' There was a long pause again. 'I get it. I mean, I know how hard it is to move forward when something in your past keeps pulling you back.' She gave a light snort. 'Even saying it that way sounds bad. Like my dead husband is a hindrance of some kind.' She exhaled. 'Sorry. That was morbid.'

'No,' he said, taking her hand. 'It was honest.'

She nodded, looking out of the window. 'Anyway, my point is that I do get it. I feel the guilt and the betrayal and the resentment, too. It sounds like yours is directed at your father, which is fair. Mine… Mine is directed at me. Because how can I be angry at someone for dying?'

She shook her head. Opened her mouth. Before she could utter the apology he was sure she intended, he squeezed her hand.

'Don't,' he told her. 'Don't feel bad for sharing. That's how you feel and it's honest. There's no shame in that.'

'I… Thank you.'

He nodded. Let the silence linger until he pulled into a parking space and said, 'I guess I'll be doing this for both of us. Taking a small step forward.'

She blinked, but her lips slowly curved into a smile. 'I like that. I like that very much.'

* * *

Brooke walked out of the elevator slowly, appropriately impressed by what she saw.

There was the mountain, of course. The layout had been angled so that most of the room faced it, but she was more enamoured by the view of the city.

It was busy, as to be expected on a Friday night. The sound of traffic fluttered up, occasionally interrupted by the sound of human beings living: laughing and talking and an infrequent shriek. It reminded her of that night at the beach, multiplied by a thousand.

Because that was what the centre of Cape Town was. The sound of life times a thousand. That was what she loved about it.

The venue was beautiful. The rooftop was lit with classy light bulbs, strung across the space as though they were stars. She looked to see how they were being held up, but the poles weren't obvious. The bar was on one side, and a dessert station was next to it, but apparently the main course would be plated.

'It's an odd decision to have dessert there,' she said, tilting her head as she stared at a chocolate fountain. 'What about people who have no self-control? Or who prefer to have dessert before dinner?'

'Where do you fall?' Tyler asked, grabbing two flutes of champagne and handing her one.

'Why do I have to choose?'

She smiled. When he smiled back, she realised it wasn't her smartest decision. Because he had an effect on her. The entire package of him in that suit, its black lines skimming his impressive shoulders, the shirt beneath it clinging to a chest she wished she knew more about it. And when he smiled, with that crinkling of his eyes…

She felt as if she was the only person in the world.

She had no right to feel that way. Especially when they'd

just spoken about how difficult it was to move on. Because she knew it, she downed her flute of champagne, wishing she could be as light as one of those bubbles. Floating away into the night sky, avoiding all her desires.

'We should probably speak to people, right?' she asked.

'Right.' He took her empty glass, replaced it with a full one as if it didn't concern him at all that hers was empty when he'd barely touched his. 'Let's go find some people.'

People loved him. Of course they did. He was easy and charming and he smiled. A lot. And not in a creepy way, but in a way that made people feel comfortable. The British company was clearly courting him. Each conversation was a pitch hidden in mundane observation. She could sense their respect in all of it. She wondered if he realised how much they wanted him.

He introduced her as his 'friend,' which didn't feel like the right description. But then, she didn't know what the right description would be. If they weren't friends, and they weren't in a relationship, what was left? Employer and employee? And since neither of them wanted to explain *that* situation, friend seemed like the safest bet.

For dinner, they were seated at a long table in the middle of the room, with the CEO of the company that was courting Tyler and a few more executives. It wasn't as bad as she expected, making conversation with strangers. She hadn't done it in a long time, but that didn't mean she couldn't do it.

The knowledge subtly nudged something inside her. It took her a moment to realise it was her confidence. She hadn't been avoiding social situations because she didn't have the skills to navigate them. She'd been doing it because she hadn't been ready to face them. And now… Well, now she thought that maybe she was.

At the end of the dinner, music began to play and some people moved to the dance floor. Others went to the bar.

She went to get dessert.

'You've been waiting all evening for this, haven't you?' Tyler asked when she told him.

'Why would you say that?' she asked innocently, but winked. 'Should I get you anything?'

His lips had parted and he was staring at her. For a short moment, she thought he might be having some kind of medical episode.

'Tyler…?'

'Sorry.' He blinked. 'Get me whatever you're getting.'

'I'm not sure you can eat all I'm getting.'

He smiled, but still seemed distracted. 'Try me.'

'If you insist.'

She grabbed a tray and began putting two of everything that appealed to her on a plate. She was reaching for an eclair when someone started speaking.

'You're Brooke, right? You're here with Tyler?'

'What?'

She turned, found herself staring at a woman with long dark hair. Brooke hadn't spoken to her yet that evening; she was the spouse of one of the executives who had been sitting some distance away from them.

'You're Tyler Murphy's wife?'

She opened her mouth, exhaled a little, then managed a smile. 'No. We're…we're friends.'

'Oh. I'm sorry. You both…' She shook her head, a blush lighting her cheeks.

She hadn't said it to get a reaction, Brooke realised. She'd genuinely thought Brooke and Tyler were married.

'We both what?'

'I've already made this more uncomfortable than it needed to be. I shouldn't have assumed.'

'I'd like to know,' Brooke said softly, though she was almost certain she didn't.

'You both look…close.' She lifted a shoulder. 'Like you

have a secret no one else is privy to. That's how people used to describe me and my husband. But I've clearly made a mistake.' She offered a tentative smile. 'Friends can have that, too.'

Except she and Tyler weren't really friends.

She was right; she hadn't wanted the answer at all.

CHAPTER EIGHT

SINCE BROOKE HAD come back with their dessert, she'd been acting strangely.

Of course, it could have been a reaction to the way he'd malfunctioned when she'd winked at him. His body had simply gone haywire. It had taken one teasing wink, re-imagined in an entirely different context—something much more intimate than a formal function—and suddenly he'd been hotter than the evening called for and immensely glad his lower body was obscured by a table.

But it couldn't be that. Brooke hadn't seemed to notice the moment, and he didn't want to project when the reason for her behaviour could be entirely different.

A slow song began to play. More people moved to the dance floor, and he thought he might have a chance to figure it out.

'Would you like to dance?'

Brooke's hand paused as it brought a spoonful of chocolate mousse to her mouth. 'Now?'

'After that bite, if you'd like.'

She blushed, but despite that, her hand hovered, as if she were deciding what the best course of action might be. He started to hide his smile—but what was the point? So he watched her, enjoyed her, and felt yet another shift in their relationship.

'Don't judge me,' she told him. 'You offered.'

She ate the spoonful of mousse, swallowed, then drank from her glass of water. A second later, she stood, regal as ever, and smiled. 'Thank you for asking.'

'I should thank you for accepting,' he replied, taking her hand and leading her to the dance floor.

In movements that should have been too smooth for him to have done it, he brought her into his arms and began to sway.

'I was certain you were going to say no,' he said.

'Why?'

He'd wanted this, hadn't he? A moment to speak with her and find out why she had been acting strangely these last few minutes. But now that he had the opportunity...he didn't want to take it. He didn't want to hear whatever it was because it was sure to upset her, and she wasn't upset now.

Or was she?

Now that he was paying attention, he could feel the tension in her body. It was slight, but clear. She held herself away from him. Not enough to make it seem weird as they danced, but enough to make it obvious that she wanted distance. But it didn't seem as if she was doing it for *him*. It seemed as if...as if she was doing it for someone else.

'Did someone say something to you?'

The tension in her body became much clearer. Her stiffening very much directed towards him now.

'What do you mean?'

Her voice was too high, too false for him to buy the act.

'Brooke,' he said softly. 'You don't have to pretend. You can tell me.'

The music swelled, their bodies shifted, and he wished he could focus on the conversation instead of her proximity.

Her scent filled his nostrils, more exotic than the one she usually wore, but somehow still entirely her. The heat coming from her body felt as if it had permeated his skin, settling in his body in a way that wasn't normal, but didn't feel foreign. One of her hands was in his, her other rested on his shoulder, and despite the distance between them he was thrilled she was so close.

The last time had been at the beach, and that had been an accident. This was intentional. She'd consented. It was a heady sensation, that knowledge. It didn't make sense at all, and yet he felt it.

'Someone said we looked...'

She trailed off. Her hand tightened in his. He didn't think she noticed.

'Close. As if we were...married.'

It took him a moment. 'They asked if we were married?'

'Assumed, actually.'

If she hadn't been in his arms, he would have sworn. 'I'm sorry, Brooke. I thought I'd made it clear to people that we aren't together.'

She met his eyes. There was a faint sheen in them. Not tears, but emotion. Powerful emotion that made him feel foolish for not anticipating this. The assumption and her reaction.

'Why are you apologising?' she asked. 'You *have* made it clear. Not once have you said that you and I are together.'

'I should have protected you from—'

'What?' she interrupted. 'The logical assumptions people might make in this kind of situation?'

'Yes,' he said desperately. 'Maybe I shouldn't have brought you here. I wouldn't have if I'd known it would cause you pain.'

'It hasn't caused me pain.'

'What?'

'I'm not upset that someone assumed we were in a relationship.'

She said the words as if they were simple. They were not. Not to him.

'I was more upset that when she realised her mistake,

she said we must be close because we're friends. We're not,' she said softly. 'You're my employee.'

'Not really though,' he replied, because he couldn't help it.

'I'm paying you, which I'm certain means we're not friends.'

'That money is going to my sister, Brooke.' Since he already had no self-control, he let go of her hand to brush her chin with his thumb. 'So try again. Think of another reason why you and I can't be...' he hesitated '...friends.'

If she noticed his hesitation she didn't show it. She only stared up at him, her gaze open and disarming.

'The power dynamics—'

'What power dynamics? I. Don't. Work. For. You.'

She exhaled. 'Why are you making this so complicated?'

'I thought I was simplifying it.'

'No.' She shook her head.

He dropped his hand from her face, but only so he could take hers again.

'No, Tyler. Nothing about this is simple.'

'Because of your husband?'

She made a strangled noise, but didn't deny it.

'Okay,' he said. 'We can work with that.'

'We?'

'Relationships generally work that way.'

'You are trying to kill me tonight,' she muttered.

He chuckled. 'Friendships are relationships, too.'

'And, of course, you and I will only ever be friends.'

His heart did a little twirl in his chest. Because if she was saying that, she clearly believed that whatever was happening between them wouldn't stop at friendship.

He didn't understand why he felt happy about it. She was right: this situation *was* complicated. He managed to remind himself of that whenever he needed to. Except now, apparently.

But this was Brooke. The woman who had stayed in his mind for five years after one week together. This was Brooke, the most beautiful woman he'd ever seen. She was kind and generous, and not only to people who knew her. She'd allowed him to continue working in her home because she understood Tia's position. She had been wonderful with all these people tonight, even when they'd asked questions that had made her feel uncomfortable.

'I'm okay with friendship,' he said, meeting her eyes. Because he would be okay with having anything—*anything*—with her. And wasn't that dangerous, too?

She studied him, then sighed and closed the distance between them. She put her head on his chest. 'Of course you are,' she said, so softly she probably thought he hadn't heard her. 'You're much too perfect not to be.'

He wasn't sure if that was a slight or a compliment. From her, he would take either.

He wasn't perfect. Brooke was certain about that. But the words had left her mouth when really, she'd meant to say *of course* he would be okay with friendship. He would try to understand her complicated emotions, not push her, and be content with what she could offer.

It stayed with her long after they said goodbye that night. And it kept her awake. That was okay though. It meant she was up to do an early walk with Mochi, as she'd promised him. As she got ready, she decided he deserved more than a simple walk. She would give him scenery.

Except she hadn't done it before because she wasn't entirely sure she could handle Mochi in unfamiliar terrains. What if he got too excited? What if he saw another dog and ran off and she lost him?

The thought sent an uncomfortable wave of despair through her. As if sensing it, Mochi whined at her feet.

'Yeah, buddy,' she said, lowering her hand to give him belly rubs. 'I know.'

He barked.

She was pretty sure he hadn't really said anything with that bark, but she frowned. 'No, that wouldn't be appropriate,' she said.

He barked again.

'Mochi, we can't just ask him if he wants to go with us. He probably has plans.'

Mochi didn't make a sound then, only gave her a pitying glance that had her heaving a sigh and reaching for her phone. She assumed the number the agency had given her was Tia's, so she messaged her, asking for Tyler's number.

She got it almost immediately, with no questions or judgement. Which somehow, in itself, felt like a judgement. Because of course she didn't *need* Tyler with her. She could have asked Dom. He would have readily agreed. But then she'd have had to talk about things she didn't want to talk about.

He would almost certainly have mentioned the man working for her—it was in his nature as a police officer—and she would almost certainly have given a suspicious answer, or done something equally mortifying like blush, and he would have known something was up.

And the minute Dom knew, Sierra, his wife, would know. And then her mom would know, and her dad, and it would become a thing when it wasn't a thing. It might never be a thing.

Tyler, with all his complications, was better than facing that.

It took her a long time to figure out what to type. In the end, she just put:

Do you want to come with me and Mochi for a walk? Brooke.

Seconds later, he replied.

June and I will be there in twenty minutes.

She stared at the message, wondered if she'd made a bad decision. If she had, it was clearly becoming a pattern. She had done the same thing the previous night. Spoken before she could really think it through. Which meant she needed to spur herself into action before she could think at all.

She pulled on some comfortable clothing, went downstairs to put on coffee. Mochi hadn't eaten that morning, and she wouldn't feed him until they were done with the walk so there was no chance of an accident in the car. But she gave him water, grabbed a granola bar and was eating it when the doorbell rang.

'You know you have a key, right?' she asked as she opened it.

He smiled. Damn him and his smiles. It was as if he knew how much they affected her. It didn't help that he looked as amazing in casual wear as he had in the suit he'd worn the night before.

No, that wasn't true. He looked great now, but he'd looked amazing last night.

It was entirely possible that she was conflating that observation with the way he'd made her feel. Dancing with him had been an *experience.* And now he was smiling at her as if he wanted her to remember the feel of his hand on her waist. Or the way he'd brushed his thumb over her chin…

'I won't use the key unless it's for work.'

'I appreciate that.' She looked down and found June, staring up at her adoringly. She lowered. 'Hey, girl. How are you?'

The dog immediately pushed her snout into Brooke's hands, before leaning against her for more rubs. Brooke laughed even as she fell over.

'June,' Tyler said in quiet command.

'No, no, it's okay. I understand.' She gave June a cuddle. 'You're just excited to see a new friend, huh? You can probably smell Mochi, too.'

'Where is he?'

'Out back.' She took the hand Tyler offered to help her up. 'Should we get them together?'

'Yeah,' he said, even though he was still staring at her and hadn't let go.

'Tyler?'

'Yeah?'

'You're staring,' she pointed out, even though saying it made her blush.

'Sorry.'

He sounded sheepish. She sucked in her bottom lip to keep herself from smiling. She could do nothing about the warmth fizzing in her stomach though, like the champagne they'd drunk the night before.

'Can I take her out back?' he asked.

'Sure,' she said, letting them both in. 'Do you want some coffee?'

'I'd love some.'

'I can put them in to-go cups. I've accumulated some over the years.'

'Yeah, sure.' He started walking towards the back door, but turned before he could open it. 'Is that something we have to talk about? Why you've accumulated to-go coffee cups over the years?'

'No.' The tone sounded too bright even to her. 'Why would we need to talk about that?'

He chuckled, walked out, and then the barking started and she could no longer hear his voice.

'That,' she said under her breath, 'is a problem.'

The fact that she wanted to hear his voice, that she felt as if she'd lost something because she couldn't… She couldn't feel that way. She knew it, although the reasons for it now seemed hazier.

What had changed that she was suddenly giving it, *him*, space in her head? Had it been that moment at dinner when she'd spoken to his sister? Or afterwards, at the beach, when he'd held her and she'd no longer been able to deny that there was a spark between them? And if things hadn't changed then, they certainly had the night he'd helped her wash Mochi. Or even last night, when he'd asked her to be his friend.

The truth was that all of those things had contributed to the change, and she knew it. A better question was *how* had things changed? Yes, she'd offered to accompany him to his business function and called him to join her when she took her dog for a walk. But she still felt… Not uneasy, but not entirely comfortable either.

Some of that might be because she was trying to figure out something completely new. Friendship or something more, it didn't matter. She hadn't forged either since Kian's death. And that 'something more' part made things messier.

She had been moving her life forward. She *had*. But this was different from moving house or getting a new job. This was…personal.

'Well, they're fast friends.'

She whirled around, spilling the hot coffee she'd been pouring into a cup over her wrist. She dealt with the situation swiftly, setting down both the coffee and the cup and going to the sink.

Tyler met her there, all concern and care. 'I shouldn't have scared you like that,' he said, taking her hand and putting it under cool running water.

'It's fine.'

But it wasn't. Because she was quite sure the burning she felt in her wrist wasn't because of the coffee.

'Do you scare easily?' he asked.

'Not usually.'

'So just when I'm here?' He offered her a wry smile.

'No. *No,*' she emphasised with a shake of her head. 'I was thinking about something. I got distracted, that's all. It has very little to do with you.'

He made a sound that made her think he knew it had a lot to do with him, but he didn't correct her. Instead he turned off the water and disappeared to find the first-aid box. As she waited, she inspected her wrist. It was red, a little sensitive, but nothing some aloe gel couldn't fix.

The lingering tingles from him touching her, however, were harder to shake off. Especially when he returned and gently smoothed the gel over the offending area.

She couldn't help but watch him as he did it. He was frowning, his eyes focused on her wrist, his lips lightly pursed. Even with an expression of concentration he was good-looking. His features were so rough that his concern almost seemed out of place. Except it wasn't. He wore his concern for those he cared about as if it were a second skin. In fact, nothing about his personality coincided with his looks.

A big, muscular, dangerous-looking man like him might easily have had a big, muscular, dangerous personality. But he was charming. Kind. Generous. He was thoughtful and good with dogs and everything about him made her…

She blinked when her eyes began to fill up. She must have made a sound because he glanced up and immediately removed his hands.

'Did I hurt you?'

'No.' But then she realised he was giving her an out and she should take it. 'I mean, yes. Not you, just it. It's painful.'

And it was—but not her wrist. This. Moving forward. It was painful, and that was why it was so messy.

'Brooke,' he said, moving his hands completely away from her wrist now and cupping her face. 'What's wrong?'

'Nothing.'

'Tell that to your eyes.'

He brushed away a tear she hadn't realised was falling. She bit her bottom lip. This wasn't supposed to be happening. None of this was supposed to be happening. She just wanted to take her dog for a walk, for heaven's sake. She didn't need to be punished for that.

Punished?

She didn't know where that word had come from, and she didn't have a chance to think about it when he was so close. He smelled like an early-morning breeze and man, a wholly Tyler smell that was part of what made all this so difficult.

'It's a walk with a friend, Brooke. Nothing more.'

'I know. I know.'

'Good. Okay.'

But then he leaned his forehead against hers, something so intimate that she closed her eyes, trying to gain some measure of control over her emotions.

'It isn't any more than that, okay.'

She opened her eyes. 'You already said that.'

'I know.' He pulled away with a small smile. 'I thought we could both do with the reminder.'

CHAPTER NINE

THE SUN WAS barely in the sky when they got to the park Brooke had suggested, but the air was already starting to warm.

'I don't think we'll be able to stay for long,' Brooke murmured, getting out of the car before helping Mochi out.

'No,' Tyler agreed. 'We should have about an hour under the trees.' He tightened his grip on June's leash. 'This was a good choice.'

'Thank you.' She smiled brightly. 'I did some research.'

'You haven't actually brought Mochi here before?'

'No.' She gave the dog an absent pat on the head. 'We haven't done many outings beyond our usual walk. I...' She trailed off, adjusting her cap. 'This is going to sound like a confession, and I guess it kind of is, but I swear I didn't only invite you because of that. I could have asked my brother—' She broke off.

One of his favourite things about Brooke was when she got carried away. She realised it too late, and by then, he had all the information he could possibly want about a situation.

'I'm afraid Mochi will see something or someone that interests him and he'll run off and I won't be able to control him.'

It took a second, then he caught up. 'So you asked me along because you thought I'd be able to control him better?'

She quirked a brow. 'You have a way with him. It must be all that *authority.*'

He chuckled and they began to walk. It was a gorgeous day despite the heat, and the place she had chosen really was beautiful. A large sign designated the trail, with trees rising high and curling over the path. A silver railing kept the explosion of nature on the right at bay, and the green of it made everything seem cool as it surrounded a stream that ran alongside the trail. The water wasn't deep—if he had to guess, he thought it would probably reach his knee—and it was clear, affording them a good view of the pebbles, large and small, that sat beneath the surface.

Further down would be a river, he knew, but he didn't think they'd get there. Not if they wanted to keep the dogs and themselves from overheating.

'Mochi needs to fit into your life, not the other way around,' he told her.

'I know that,' she said. 'But my life before would never have entailed walking park trails, so it's all about balance.'

'It wouldn't?' He set an easy pace, which seemed to work for all four of them. 'What would it have entailed?'

'Before Mochi?' she asked.

He nodded.

She thought about it for a long time, stopping for Mochi to smell a branch that had fallen from one of the trees. 'Mostly work, I guess. Occasionally, on a Saturday, I'd go to one of the food markets and get some things to eat for the weekend.'

'Mochi could do that with you.'

'Yeah, but what happens if he sees a little kid and gets excited?' she asked. 'I'd be banned for life.'

'So we need to work on you controlling him.' He stopped. As he did so, June sat down, looking up at him for guidance. 'Like this.'

Brooke looked down at June, then back at him. 'How

could you have possibly taught her that already? You haven't even had her for that long. And she's a stray.'

'Dogs learn pretty quickly, especially if you're consistent. This is pretty basic, really. Get him to walk with you, to stop with you. That foundation will help you to control him more when he's around other dogs and people.' He eyed Mochi, who was, to his credit, walking well. 'This is already pretty different to the way he was walking when we bumped into you a couple of weeks ago.'

'I think the two walks a day are helping with his energy,' she admitted sheepishly. 'I feel silly for not realising he needed it before.'

'Don't feel silly,' Tyler said. 'Just figure out what he needs. Do some research on his breed.'

'He's mixed.'

'Well, he looks part collie to me, and that breed is notoriously energetic. Two walks are the bare minimum.' At her stricken look, he laughed. 'You play with him in the garden, don't you?'

'Yes.'

'Well, that's another way for him to get out his energy. And the good news is he's a smart dog. He'll learn pretty quickly. Here—let's swap and I'll show you.'

He took Mochi from her and started with basic sit and stand commands. He'd brought treats for June, and Mochi was greedy, so it didn't take him long to learn. And then they walked.

As he did all this, Tyler talked it through with Brooke. After a little while, he had her take Mochi. That required slightly more work.

'You're asking him to sit, not telling him.'

'If someone just *told* me to sit, I wouldn't feel very good about that,' she argued. 'But if they *asked* me, I would welcome it.'

'Brooke,' he said, mustering all his patience while simultaneously fighting a smile, 'he's a dog. He doesn't want to be asked. He wants to be told and to be rewarded for doing what he's told. You're his Alpha.'

She narrowed her eyes. 'Again with this Alpha business?'

He didn't fight the smile. 'It's nature.'

'Sure,' she replied darkly. 'Most things in the male understanding of the world seem to be based on "nature."'

'I'm pretty sure the right answer here is for me to apologise for all of mankind.'

'Apology accepted,' she said primly, but she offered him a small smile.

She put more authority into her tone after that. When it worked, she gave him a dark look, as if to say *Don't you dare say I told you so.* He lifted his hand in surrender. He didn't have to say it. The fact that he was grinning like a stupid person told her as much.

He preferred this to what had happened that morning. When her vulnerability had been so raw it hurt his heart as if it were nails on a chalkboard. Things seemed to switch effortlessly between easy and hard with them. If he were inclined to, he might say that was part of what made it special between them. But he wasn't inclined to. Because her reaction that morning had reminded him of the stakes.

Oh, he'd been intent on charming her. The night before, when she'd been in his arms, once again displaying that vulnerability, he'd promised her they would be friends. He'd believed it would be a foundation between them for something else. Something bigger. But there were too many factors at play.

He'd left that function the night before even more confused about what he wanted to do. Well, no. He knew what he *wanted* to do. He was just conflicted about it. He couldn't leave Tia and Nyle. No matter how much Brooke assured him it wouldn't be abandonment, he didn't believe it. Perhaps because it wasn't her assurance he needed—it was Tia's. And getting it would involve telling Tia about the business opportunity, which he wasn't ready to do.

While he was dealing with all that he *couldn't* lay a foundation for anything more than friendship with Brooke. Not only because he couldn't offer her the certainty she deserved, but because if he left he would be leaving her, too. How could he do that to her? He wasn't his father; he wouldn't leave the people he cared about.

He'd told her once that employees and employers could be friends, and he believed that. Now he wished he didn't. Now he wished he'd left his desire for her locked behind the pretence of professionalism. Now he wished he didn't have any past with her complicating things.

They reached a break in the path and made their way to a bench in a small, open grassy area. He was thankful for the reprieve from walking. Maybe because he was hoping it would give him one from his thoughts, too.

'This is probably a good place to turn around,' Brooke said as she lowered to give the dogs water. 'After a break.'

'You need a break?' He forced himself to tease her. 'I could do this for ever.'

She stuck out her tongue, before taking off her cap and drinking some water herself. A bead escaped the bottle, trailing over her chin, down her neck, before disappearing into her cleavage. He'd done his utmost not to notice that cleavage when he'd got to her house that morning. In truth, it was perfectly respectable. Except he couldn't look at her and respond in a perfectly respectable way.

He remembered too clearly the gentle swell of her breasts in that gold dress, the material hugging her curves, the colour seemingly designed for her skin.

He couldn't only blame it on that though. Everything about her made his body react. She could be wearing a black bin bag and face paint and he'd still be dying to hold her in his arms, caress her. So the tight top meant to support her breasts as she walked would inevitably distract him.

He wanted to follow the trail of that water with his tongue. He didn't care that her skin had a light sheen of sweat. She would taste of salt and Brooke and he couldn't think of anything he wanted more.

He exhaled sharply, pulled his own water from his backpack and drank like a dying man. He felt as if he *were* dying. How else could he describe his response when he had only just thought about all the reasons he needed to have boundaries with her? When he'd been doing so from the beginning of their reunion?

'Uh-oh,' Brooke said softly.

His head turned. She was looking at his face, so it was unlikely she was noticing his body's reaction. Good. He wouldn't be able to explain that after he'd assured her they were only friends.

'What?' he said, once he'd got his thinking under control.

'You're having a Brooke moment.'

'What does that mean?'

'Well, it's good that you ask because it could mean a number of things. The one I'm currently thinking about has nothing to do with the patriarchy—' she gave him a small smile '—but with getting lost in your own head.'

'I'm not—' He broke off with a sigh. 'I am. I thought about something and it unravelled quickly.'

'That's how it happens, I'm afraid.' She patted his hand. 'One moment you're thinking about how cute a guy is, the next you're remembering your deceased husband and wondering if he'd be okay with you thinking about how cute another guy is.'

'Is that what happened this morning?'

'Oh, no,' she said, shaking her head with a laugh. 'I'm not falling for that.'

He stared, but she didn't elaborate. For a minute he deliberated about whether he should push, but her expression told him it wasn't a good idea.

'You're really not going answer that?' he asked.

'Nope.'

'At least confirm that I'm the cute guy?'

'You're not,' she said. 'I was talking about the guy who helped take my groceries to the car the other day. He even called me "ma'am," which made me feel old, but also made me feel kind of fancy.'

She twisted her shoulder in an endearing way and he smiled. How could he not be delighted by her? She drew him in—no, locked him in, really—and he was so enamoured that he'd handed her the key.

'You should stop doing this,' he said. He meant to tease, but his tone was serious.

'What?'

'Being so…so *you*.'

She studied him. 'I would be offended if it weren't for that look on your face. It's telling me that you're actually complimenting me.'

'Yeah.' His hand lifted to twirl the ends of her hair around his finger. He stopped when he realised what he was doing. 'Sorry. I—'

He didn't finish, and she reached up and caught his hand. 'You know what I think would solve a lot of this tension? If we kissed.'

'You… Excuse me?'

'Get it out of the way. Out of our systems, you know?' She barrelled on. 'If we both want it, of course. If not, I'll gladly never speak of—'

He was kissing her before she could finish.

CHAPTER TEN

GETTING DESIRE OUT of their systems might have been one of the reasons they were kissing, but Brooke knew there was more to it. For both of them. Though she was sure their reasons were different.

For her, it was the tension. It danced between them. Sometimes to a slow and lingering beat, almost harmless in its laziness; other times the beat was sharp and passionate, demanding to be heeded. Today, both those beats had played in her.

And then there was this.

An utterly irresistible rhythm that neither of them could ignore.

It didn't seem to matter that she'd thought of a long list of reasons as to why kissing him was a bad idea. All of them were very much still valid, but she thought some of her problem lay in curiosity. What would it be like to kiss him? To kiss any man, really?

Though even as she thought it she knew that was a lie. It wasn't her curiosity to kiss *any* man that was causing her internal conflict. It was her curiosity to kiss *Tyler*. To find out if she was ready to move on with him.

So now they were kissing.

A nice, simple way of sorting through her feelings.

How she was only figuring out that was a lie now, as she was kissing him, was anyone's guess.

It was an overload of sensations. The gentle press of his lips against hers…the way he dropped her hand to cup her face… Their lips moved tentatively against one another. Testing, tasting, teasing. If somehow they'd been transported to the stream beside them, submerged in water, she wouldn't have been surprised. Every single movement felt as slow and deliberate as if they were under water. Every breath she took felt hard-won, her lungs no longer working as they normally did.

But they seemed to be adjusting to this new reality. To being under water. Hell, she might be turning into a mermaid. If so, he would definitely be the prince she sacrificed her voice for. It was a choice she would gladly make if it meant she could keep kissing him.

Of course, when she was rational again, she would protest against the idea of sacrificing anything for the sake of a kiss. But he had just swept his tongue into her mouth and heat was curling in her belly and she was ready to do whatever she needed to do to keep these sensations coming.

Even if it meant losing her sanity.

A part of her was aware of what was happening. It was because of that overload of sensation. With the lick of his tongue, it was as if something inside her began to inflate, more and more, until she was certain she was floating up into the sky. It wasn't a bad thing. At least, it didn't feel that way right now. It felt like a gift. The way his hand moved down from her face to her neck, over her collarbone, down her arm… The way it moved to her hip, lingered on her waist, settled on her ribs.

Higher, she thought. But the bottom of her breast was already touching his hand and she thought she might lose her mind. She could only imagine what would happen if he actually touched her skin, stroked her like she wanted him to.

The heat in her belly would boil, overflow, trail a pathway down to her core. For the moment that ache between her legs was a pulsing need. It was as if her body had separated her desire into the heat in her stomach and the pulsing between her thighs. Probably to save her. Because the moment those things converged, she would lose herself completely. And if she did that she would do something insane. Like straddle him, placing his desire against hers and checking whether, together, they could sate their appetite for one another.

The thought was as good as a bucket of ice over her. She pulled back, leaning away until she was at the edge of the bench. Tyler did the same at his end. Both of them stared. With a trembling hand, she traced her lips. Why did they suddenly feel like the scene of a crime? As if they'd done something illegal and were waiting to be caught?

Mochi tugged at his leash, reminding Brooke that he was still there. She looked down, amazed that she had managed to keep hold of him when her world had completely and utterly changed.

'Yeah,' she said softy. 'Yeah, let's go.'

She stood, her legs feeling weak and unstable beneath her.

'Brooke,' Tyler said.

When she turned, she found him standing behind her.

'Are you okay?'

'Sure.' She offered him a smile that she was sure wasn't very convincing. 'Are you?'

'Yes. Except I feel like you're lying to me.'

He lifted a hand and curled it around her ear, as if she had hair there. But she'd tied her hair up that morning, and she knew what he was doing was more to touch her than anything else.

She resisted the urge to close her eyes, to sigh. Instead, she moved back. Gently. It didn't matter how she'd done it though, she realised as a flash of hurt crossed his face. His reaction would have been the same regardless.

'I'm not lying.'

'Brooke—'

'Tyler,' she replied deliberately. The look of expectation on his face didn't change. She sighed. 'Give me time, okay? I need...a moment.'

'So you're not okay?'

'Are *you*?' she challenged. 'Because you pressing me now feels like an excuse to not face your own feelings about what happened.'

June whined, and Tyler gave her an absentminded rub on the head. 'Maybe we both need time.'

'Yes,' she agreed.

Not waiting for him to say anything further, she began to walk.

By the time they reached the car they were both sweaty messes. At some point during their walk, the sun had got much hotter. They'd had to stop to give the dogs water often, and it had taken longer to get back than it had to get to the grassy area.

'You can drive,' Brooke said, throwing him the keys. 'I'm not sure I'm capable of that yet.'

His smile was crooked and a little reserved. She understood. Hell, she deserved it. She had pushed him away, quite deliberately, and now she was pretending it hadn't happened.

But some time during the walk back her fear had melted into something else. Guilt, mostly. She could have reacted better about the kiss. She should have. Except her legs had been shaking, along with some other choice parts of her body, and she hadn't been able to deal with that *and* force herself to have a logical conversation.

But that wasn't his fault. Well, her emotional reaction wasn't his fault. The physical reaction... Her entire body clenched at the memory, as if somehow tightening her muscles would prevent the sensations from gripping her.

Without thought, she looked at Tyler. Part of her wanted to check whether he was experiencing these aftershocks, too. Apparently not. He seemed perfectly calm, his face holding a serene expression despite the turmoil of what had happened before their walk back. Despite the slight sheen on his face and his body from the exertion of their walk.

She tried not to pay attention to the sweat that was still periodically rolling down her back and in between her breasts.

'What's wrong?' he asked.

She frowned. 'Nothing. Why?'

'You're looking at me and fanning yourself.'

She looked down. Saw that she had, indeed, been lifting her top as if she were fanning herself. It was all perfectly innocent, and yet it looked incredibly incriminating.

'I was thinking that you look all cool and calm while I'm sweating buckets. The fanning was a thoughtless response.'

'Hmm.'

She rolled her eyes at the disbelieving sound, but couldn't help the tickle of a smile at her mouth. Because she could understand what he was thinking. If the roles had been reversed, she would have thought the exact same thing.

'I work out a lot,' was his next comment.

'I figured.' The flick of his gaze made her realise what she was saying. She didn't bother hiding her reaction. 'You look like you do.'

'How do I look?'

'Not falling for that.'

He gave a soft chuckle. 'Looks aren't exactly a good criteria for working out, but if we're going to use them, I'd say you work out a lot, too.'

She refused to blush. 'You're trying to make me say something weird again, which is entirely possible, yes, but I'm not going to fall for it.'

'It was a compliment.'

'You know as well as I do that I do not "work out a lot."'

'How would I know that?'

'One, I work too much for "a lot." Two, that gold dress didn't hide much.'

'It didn't, did it?' He gave her a sly look. 'It's almost as if someone bought it with that very thing in mind.'

She laughed because he was teasing, and because she preferred this to the silence of their walk. It was unfair of her. How could she want him to be like this when she didn't like where it led? Teasing led to flirting—hell, they might already be flirting now—and flirting led to touches, to kisses.

With the way that man kissed, it would lead to other things that she was in no way prepared for.

But then, she would have thought she wasn't prepared for Tyler *at all* a few weeks ago. She'd been ready to get out there, to move on then, but thinking about it and doing it were entirely different.

Her plan had involved arranging drinks with friends she hadn't seen in while. Or going to a bar by herself. Anything that would have moved her personal life forward *slowly.*

The plan certainly wouldn't have looked like this. This fast and almost inevitable progression of whatever was happening between her and Tyler, as if they'd forged some kind of a foundation long before.

Even with Kian, when she had been young and nothing in her life had cautioned her against falling, the pace had been slower. They'd been friends first, then they'd started dating. Weeks later had come the first kiss. It had been months later before anything more happened.

If she could ask whoever was in charge of controlling these things some questions, she would ask what that meant. Did the fact that she had fallen for her husband in slow and subtle ways mean what she was feeling for Tyler now was dangerous? Her relationship with Kian had been the most significant thing in her life—surely anything that didn't feel like that meant it wasn't worth pursuing?

But what about that feeling of inevitability? Because with Kian she had felt very much in control. With Tyler… she did not. That felt significant, too.

It was what scared the hell out of her.

'Brooke?'

She looked at him.

'We're here.'

They were indeed in front of her house.

'Right.'

This was her chance to escape. To put some distance between them so she could think about what had happened last night, this morning. She could give herself a chance to catch up with 'the inevitability'—if that was what she was going to call it.

So heaven only knew why she said, 'Do you want to come inside for breakfast?'

The invitation came as a surprise. More surprising was the fact that she offered him a shower, clean clothing—he tried not to think about the fact that it might have been her husband's—and the spare bedroom on the ground floor to change.

He appreciated all of it. He wanted a chance to speak to her about what had happened. If breakfast didn't give him that chance, at the very least it would help him reassure her that she had nothing to worry about.

Which was a lie since he was worried himself. He was trying not to think about the reasons for that.

Priorities. Your family. Your job. And those two seem interchangeable since you're considering leaving your only family for a job.

He wasn't succeeding very well, clearly. But it did serve

as a reminder that he had enough problems; he didn't need to add Brooke to the list.

Yet here he was, getting ready to take a shower in the en suite bathroom in her spare bedroom.

He put the water on, let it heat while he went to grab clothes from the bedroom. And paused when he saw Brooke there.

They stared at one another for a moment. Him because he hadn't expected her to be there, let alone with a handful of toiletries. Her, probably because he'd already stripped down to his underwear.

'I am so sorry,' she said, whirling around.

In the process, one of the bottles in her hand went flying against the opposite wall.

'I heard the shower, and I thought you were already in it. I was just going to leave these things here because I didn't want you not to have deodorant or lotion. I did not expect to find you almost naked. I am so sorry. I am so, *so* sorry.'

He was grinning by the end of it, though he probably should be feeling a little more compassion for her situation.

'It's okay,' he said easily, refusing the temptation to tease her. 'I appreciate you bringing me all that stuff. It's almost like being in a hotel.'

'Except in a hotel, you get privacy.' She nearly turned back, but stopped herself before she could. 'If you go in the shower, I'll leave these things on the bed, okay?'

'Okay.'

He was still smiling when he went into the shower, aware of the fact that she had completely swept all thoughts of priorities out of his mind. It should have been bad. It *was* bad. But she forced him to live in the present. Not in the general *now*, but in the very moment that was happening.

When was the last time he'd ever had that? When he was younger, probably—except he couldn't pinpoint any moment when that had been true.

Even before his father had left, he'd been concerned about the tremors of unhappiness he'd felt between his parents. He hadn't understood what it truly meant, but he'd known his mother didn't smile as much with his father as she did when she was with Tyler and Tia.

After his father had left he'd been worried about his mother, his sister. Their future had been financially ominous, along with their precarious emotional state after being abandoned by the man who should have taken care of them.

As an adult, he was focused on making himself successful. If he did that, he could take care of his mother and sister's financial fears. Although they would barely let him, which was another concern. It felt as if the past was haunting them. They were both too accustomed to working hard, to not relying on anyone but themselves. They were afraid that relying on anyone, even him, would make them vulnerable again.

So, no, he hadn't lived in the present for a very long time. No wonder Brooke appealed to him so much.

He made quick work of the shower, then used all the toiletries with a grin he knew was stupid before he got dressed.

Brooke was in the kitchen, freshly showered herself, preparing eggs in a bowl.

'Hey,' he said.

'Hey,' she replied, giving him a small smile. Her hands stilled. 'Once again, I want to apologise for—'

'There's nothing to apologise for,' he interrupted firmly. 'It wasn't like you were intentionally hoping to catch me in my underwear.'

'No,' she said, very quickly. 'Not at all.'

If she hadn't been so tense, he would have asked her why. But he could read the room.

'I didn't think so.' He changed the subject before she could get caught up on the details. 'How can I help?'

There was a pause, but then she gave him instructions

to help her with the French toast, bacon, scrambled eggs and fruit she was preparing.

'Are you sure that's enough?' he teased, getting the bread.

'Isn't it? I would usually only eat one of the above, but I figured you'd be pretty hungry.'

'Should I be offended by that?'

'You work out a lot,' she said with a wink. 'You probably need the sustenance.'

They worked in tandem, easily helping one another out. Tyler noticed that she was avoiding touching him. Hell, she was actively trying not to be in his space at all. She seemed to be doing it without thinking, shifting when he shifted, moving when he moved, as if she had some radar when he was in her space and adjusted accordingly.

It took him a moment, but he realised he had an internal radar when it came to her, too. Attraction. When she came close to him, the heat from her body sank into him until every part of him was saturated. If it wasn't the heat, it was the awareness, skidding over his skin, causing every hair on his body to stand on end.

If she felt that, too, then she was simply avoiding those physical feelings. And he couldn't be upset about that. One, because she was clearly responding out of instinct. Two, because she felt it. Something. Anything… Of course he knew that she did. She'd instigated that kiss; she'd responded during that kiss.

He took a deep sip from his water, remembering that response. The little moan she'd given when their tongues had touched; her shudder when he'd skimmed her skin; her exhalation when his fingers had sunk into the flesh at her hips…

Another gulp of water reminded him that now wasn't the time to think about it. Now he wanted to make her feel better that it had happened—and that certainly wouldn't be the case if he started responding physically to the memory of it.

'I'm sure I've told you this before, but you're really good in the kitchen,' she said.

'My mom forced both me and Tia to be,' he replied, grateful for the reprieve from his thoughts. 'The household chores were a team effort. We'd rotate cooking and cleaning between the three of us after my father left.'

She was waiting to flip the last of the French toast, so she had the opportunity to study him. He felt her gaze pierce through him, even though he was standing so she couldn't see his face.

'You guys really were a unit,' she said.

'Yeah.'

'It must have been hard when your mom died.'

'It was.' He paused, letting the wave of grief roll over him. He didn't try to hide it. Out of all the people in the world, he was certain she would understand. 'She had a heart attack in her sleep. I found her one morning.'

'*You* found her?'

'Rather me than Tia,' he said, hearing the compassion in her voice. 'I could handle it better than she could.'

'Yeah?' she asked. 'Is that something she's said to you, or is that your perception of the situation?'

He frowned. 'Does it matter?'

'I guess not,' she said thoughtfully. 'But my gut tells me that it's the latter, and that it's the same reason you haven't told her about your business opportunity. You think she can't handle it. And where has that thinking brought you, exactly?'

CHAPTER ELEVEN

'OH!' BROOKE EXCLAIMED as soon as she said the words. 'That was much more personal than I intended on getting.'

'You think?'

At the dry note in Tyler's voice, she winced. She placed the final slice of French toast on a plate and turned to face him. His expression didn't look upset, more pensive.

She slid the plate over to him. 'Truce?'

His gaze flickered down. 'You're offering me an entire plate of French toast to make up for saying something that might be true?'

'Only if it works,' she replied. She waited a beat. 'Might be true, huh?'

She couldn't describe the look he gave her as a glare, but it wasn't entirely a positive one.

She pushed the plate closer to him.

He narrowed his eyes, but she could see the faintest twitch at his lips.

'You can't bribe me with food.'

'I'm not bribing you,' she said truthfully. 'I'm comforting you.'

'I don't need to be comforted.'

'Well, in that case…'

She reached out to take the plate back, but he snatched it up into the air. It was so unexpected that she gave a startled laugh, before lifting her hands in surrender.

'Fair is fair.'

Seconds later he set the plate down next to the eggs and bacon he'd already fried. She'd meant it when she'd told him he was good in the kitchen. Much more efficient than she was. But she had managed to put the coffee on before he'd come out of the shower, and…

Her brain paused for a moment as she remembered walking into the spare room when she'd thought he was in the shower. She'd only seen him for a few seconds, but it had been enough to make an impact. She knew he worked out, knew he was built, but the man had muscles in places she wasn't sure should have muscles.

She had never found that kind of build attractive before—she preferred tall and lean—but apparently she'd been waiting for Tyler.

And really, that should make her ashamed of her superficiality. Oddly enough, she didn't feel bad at all.

'Coffee?' she asked, hoping he wouldn't somehow pick up on the lust in her voice.

'It's too hot for that.'

She turned. 'Too hot for coffee? A life-giving liquid?'

He smirked. For some reason it made her think about how he looked in his underwear again. She shoved the thought out of her mind.

'I know it's unbelievable. Do you have something colder? Juice?'

'Of course.'

She got the juice out, poured him some, then suggested they eat outside. After they'd put all the food on the table and settled in under the veranda, silence stretched over them. It was the kind of silence that came after a hard day of work: quiet, content, comfortable. Almost as peaceful as their dogs laying beneath one of the trees in the garden, exhausted from their morning activities.

She hadn't thought that, after what had happened between them that morning, they'd be able to share something like this. It made her think of the inevitability between them, and tension rolled in her stomach.

It was so unknown, all of this, and she couldn't comprehend it. There were times when she felt that she must. That she would suffer if she couldn't figure it all out. But at other times, when she didn't think about it, only allowed herself to *be*, it didn't matter at all.

She released a breath, striving for the latter. If only to make it through their breakfast together.

'When my dad left I did assume a lot of responsibility at home.'

She turned, not nearly as surprised that he'd broken the silence as she might have been if she weren't so aware of him. He'd obviously been thinking about what she'd said in the kitchen. His contemplative expression, his silence, the stiff way he held his body, told her as much.

So she didn't interrupt, only let him work it out.

'Now I'm wondering if that happened because my mom and Tia needed me, or because I decided they needed me.'

She tilted her head. 'Could it be both?'

He blinked. 'Yeah, I guess.'

She gave him a moment. Or maybe she was giving herself a moment to decide whether she wanted to say what she was thinking.

'Just say it,' he said, a smile playing at his lips as he studied her.

'Only if I get immunity?'

He lifted his eyes to the sky, but nodded.

'I don't think it's a bad thing, caring for your family. Especially during something as traumatic as abandonment. But… How can you think what you want to do is the same as what your father did?'

'He took a job in a different country.'

'And that is literally the only thing this situation and

his have in common.' She paused. 'Unless you plan on not coming back? On leaving Tia and her son to fend for themselves?' She waited for it to settle. 'I don't know the details of what happened,' she added gently, 'but it sounds like that's what your father did, and that's what you want to avoid.'

There was a long, drawn-out silence. Eventually, Tyler said, 'He said he was leaving to make our lives better. But they weren't better when he left. Mom was more stressed. He sent money, but she didn't want to use it. It took me a long time to realise it was because she didn't want to give him a reason to stay away.' He scratched the arm of his chair. 'They weren't happy when he was here, but I think… I think she wanted to work on it. And his response was to leave. Things got bad financially, and she had to start using the money, and that…' He shifted his hands, his grip tightening on his chair. 'It made her unhappy. I think she felt like she was conceding something by taking it. Her pride and her marriage.'

'So you're saying that you're not worried about Tia financially,' she said slowly, trying to put all the parts together, 'but emotionally? That if she needs you, you won't be there, and that'll make her unhappy?'

'No…' he said, but he looked doubtful. He sighed. 'I'm worried about her financially *and* emotionally. I don't want her to get to the place my mom was in before she accepted help. While I'm here, at least I can monitor the situation.'

'Or control it?'

'Help her,' he corrected with a wry twist of his mouth. 'Like step in for a job when she needs me to.'

'Have you had to do that before, or is it just this once?'

He didn't answer. But then, he didn't have to; she already knew what he'd say.

'Basically, you're putting your life on pause because of

a potential situation that might or might not arise if you leave?'

'It's not that easy.'

'No, it's not,' she agreed. 'And it sounds like the only way you'll figure it out is if you talk with her. She might feel the same way about you, Tyler.' At his confused look, she elaborated. 'She wants *you* to be happy and secure in the same way you want *her* to be happy and secure, I'm sure. Give her a chance to let that happen.'

When he didn't look convinced, she leaned over and rested a hand on his. 'There's nothing wrong with wanting a life where you're important, too.'

His eyes were soft, emotion shimmering through them like a rainbow after a day of rain. Slowly, he tipped over their hands so that his lay on top of hers. It should have been a warning for what he said next. She was fairly certain it was—she had simply ignored it. So when he said his next words she wasn't prepared.

'Is that something I could say to you, too?'

Her response was to open her mouth, stare at him, and eventually say, 'No.'

Tyler didn't reply immediately. Hell, he probably shouldn't have said anything in the first place. But she'd spoken so firmly, so kindly about his situation, completely unaware of how her words applied to her own situation.

He tilted his head. 'You don't think you've been living for someone else these last few years?'

She pulled a face. 'It's not the same thing.'

'Why not?'

'He's not here,' she said, spreading her hands out in front of her. 'How can I be living for him when he's not even here?'

It was such a raw question that he didn't speak. He didn't want to push her, certainly not when, again, some of his intentions were selfish. He wanted her to know that it was okay for her to move on. It didn't have to be with him—*liar*, an inner voice taunted—but moving forward with her life wouldn't be tainting her husband's memory in any way.

Spending that week with me before or after his death though...

He frowned. He'd been successfully ignoring the fact that they had a history together just as she was. Oh, it slipped into his mind here and there, but for the most part he kept to his earlier resolve. This was yet another reason why. If he started thinking about it, he would have an endless number of questions as to why she wasn't addressing it.

Did she not remember it? That seemed impossible, considering what was happening between them now. So why was she still pretending it hadn't happened? The only reason that made sense was if she had been married at that time. And if not married, a freshly grieving widow. If that was the case, she must have been using him. If *either* option was the case, she had been using him.

Their kiss back then must have popped the bubble they were in, bringing her back to the real world. Making her realise what she was doing.

But that didn't seem like the Brooke he knew now. The woman who wouldn't fully utilise the person she had hired to help her in her home, for heaven's sake. Why would she use a stranger to help her forget about her husband?

Except she was reticent about her husband.

He could put it down to grief, but that was an easy solution. A simple one that didn't feel right…

Why did he suddenly feel like ignoring their past was no longer an option?

'I don't like this,' she said. 'I don't like it that you can see things I can't when you barely know anything about the situation.'

'So tell me,' he said quietly. Selfishly. Because now he wanted to know what things had been like with her husband so he could figure out where he'd fitted into the situation.

But she didn't reply, not for a long time, and he thought she might not answer. And if that were the case, he couldn't stay. He'd need to keep to his boundaries then, or at least get some space where he could figure out why he was feeling so out of sorts.

That feeling might easily have come from what he'd revealed—to her and to himself. Mostly to her. Because now, she knew more about him than he could ever hope to know about her. Unless she decided to share. Which, considering she still hadn't responded, was unlikely.

Then she spoke.

'It was a car accident.'

When she looked at him, her eyes reminded him of the ocean during a storm.

'We were driving home from the birthday party of one of Kian's friends and someone ran a red light...' She trailed off, her fingers curling into her skirt. 'His condition was critical since we were hit on his side. Mine wasn't. I barely had any injuries.'

'You were...you were in the car?'

She nodded. 'He spent about a week in the hospital after that, and his heart kept failing. It put his body under so much strain, so I signed a DNR. He...' She cleared her throat. 'He died a couple of hours later.'

'Brooke, I'm...' Speechless. He was speechless. 'I'm sorry.'

'Thanks.'

When she sat back, he realised for the first time that she had moved forward, to the edge of her seat, at some point during the conversation. He wanted to lean over and take her hand, as she had done for him earlier, but since she had been the one to pull away it felt like crossing a line she had drawn.

'The trauma took a long time to work through,' she said, as if there hadn't been a pause after she'd last spoken. 'I had a concussion, which wasn't bad compared to Kian. I lost some of my memories, but he lost...' She met his eyes. 'He lost his life.'

Again, he was reminded of the ocean during a storm. Of the thrashing of waves against rocks, a violence that was evident but seemingly caused no damage and left no scars. What had happened to Brooke had affected her deeply, even though she seemed fine now. But just because no one witnessed how the waves eroded those rocks over time didn't mean the damage wasn't there.

The metaphor tangled his brain into a web for a long time. So long he didn't realise what she'd said until she was already standing, putting the plates together.

'Wait—did you say you lost some of your memories?'

She didn't look at him. 'Yeah.'

'As in...amnesia?'

'Selective,' she confirmed. 'Parts of the accident and some of the time after. A lot of what I've told you my brother told me.'

'You don't remember it? Any of it?'

'I remember bits and pieces. But most of the events surrounding the accident and the week or so after I don't remember. The doctors said it was a result of the physical and emotional trauma of the accident and then losing Kian.' She pulled the plates against her body. 'So, Tyler, if I'm not living for myself, it's because I had a husband who didn't get to live at all. Living for him doesn't feel like a choice now, does it?'

She didn't wait for a reply, moving into the house. He didn't follow her. His mind was too busy spinning. He was afraid that if he did follow her, he would push past the line she'd set. He might be selfish, but he wasn't a complete jerk. Besides, he had a good idea of where all the questions he had would lead.

He'd met Brooke outside the hospital. It must have either been during the week her husband had been in hospital, or after he'd died. And if that was the case, she *didn't* remember any of the time they'd spent together. Not because it didn't mean anything to her, but because she had amnesia.

She didn't remember him because she couldn't.

He would have to tell her...wouldn't he?

Why did that seem like the nuclear option all of a sudden?

CHAPTER TWELVE

BROOKE HADN'T SEEN Tyler in over a week. Not since they'd had that fairly explosive conversation during breakfast. That might not be the right description considering they hadn't exactly had an argument, but it had felt emotionally explosive. And the carnage hadn't only been memories she'd managed to keep at bay for a long time, but apparently their fledgling friendship.

If only she'd known that all she had to do to stop their relationship from progressing faster than she liked was to tell him about her dead husband.

'What?' Dom said now, looking up from a plate of food stacked ridiculously high.

'What?' she replied.

'You laughed.'

Brooke pulled her face. 'I did not.'

'You did,' Sierra said, giving her a sympathetic look.

'I did *not*,' she said, although at this point she was fairly certain she had. She looked at her nephew. 'Did I, Marcus?'

Her nephew nodded solemnly.

She sighed. 'Only four years old and already turning against his aunt.'

But she winked at him, and he offered her a bright smile. She snorted when she saw the potato in his mouth, then sobered quickly when his mother reprimanded him.

'So, are you going to tell us?' Dom asked.

'No.'

Dom paused before he took a bite of his own potato. 'No?'

'No.'

'You're acting weird.' He lowered his fork. 'Come to think of it, you've been acting weird since you arrived.'

'It's seeing your new haircut,' she replied, even as a ripple of unease went through her. 'That fade is not a good look for you.'

Her brother looked as if he wanted to swear at her, but his eyes settled on his son and he merely said, 'You're lying.'

'I am,' she agreed. 'Which should tell you how unwilling I am to talk about whatever it is making me act weird.'

They stared at one another. Brooke held his gaze because she knew that if she didn't, it would look as if she was hiding something. She wasn't. Yes, there was the small matter of wanting to move on with her life, but there was nothing wrong with that. Right? Wasn't that what she'd told Tyler? That wanting a life where she was important, too, wasn't a bad thing?

Except it had been easier to tell him that than to believe it herself. She didn't know how to feel about moving on sometimes. Especially in this circumstance. Was it because things with her and Tyler were different from how things with her and Kian had been? Or was it because she felt as if she was betraying her husband by wanting someone else? Was it guilt because the only reason she *could* want someone else was because her husband had died?

She should make an appointment with her therapist, but she already knew what he would say. It was probably all of it.

They'd already established that she wanted to live her life for Kian. To move forward because he couldn't. For the most part she was succeeding. She was doing well at work, her relationship with her family was strong. It was really only moving on romantically that was the problem.

And knowing that didn't change anything one bit.

'Brooke—'

'Sierra,' Brooke said, ignoring her brother and whatever that placating tone of voice was about to bring, 'how's work going?'

Sierra's eyes shifted between Dom and Brooke, but she answered Brooke's question, as if realising it would be safer than whatever Dom had been about to ask. The conversation moved from there to Brooke's work, and the fact that she was nearing the end of a project pretty soon.

'Another week, maybe a few more days, and we'll be done.'

'Days before deadline, too,' Dom said, and there was pride in his voice even though this was the first time he'd spoken since she'd brushed him off.

'Yep. Hopefully that'll mean the launch will go smoothly.'

'Do you still want me to come with you?'

'Oh.'

She'd forgotten she'd told Dom she wanted him to come. It had felt like a significant event, one she didn't want to deal with alone. But between when she'd asked him and now she hadn't thought about it again.

She warned her brain not to point out any helpful reasons as to why.

'Yeah, I'd love that,' she said.

'You sure?' Sierra teased. 'You hesitated for a bit. Is there someone else you'd rather take?'

It was teasing. Simple teasing. And if she'd brushed it off, called it ridiculous, they would have laughed and moved on.

Except she didn't.

She opened her mouth. Closed it. Like a fish at the water's surface, eating its food. Only she wasn't doing something sensible like eating or, say, defending herself. She was revealing something she'd rather not have anyone know. Not now, when it was messy and complicated. Maybe not ever.

And then—*then*—she did the next worst thing. She blushed. A blood rushing to her face, heat exploding in her cheeks blush.

'Oh...' Sierra said slowly, her mouth forming the letter, too. 'Oh, Brooke. I'm so, so sorry.'

Brooke looked at Sierra. Sympathised. At least she would have if she hadn't been the one in the line of fire. Because the reason Sierra was apologising wasn't because she'd teased Brooke, but because of the reaction such a revelation was going to elicit from Dom.

'She's right?' Dom asked, his gaze intense. 'There's someone in your life?'

She took a second to reply, aware that her physical reaction had already revealed a lot.

'I have many people in my life,' she said slowly.

'Brooke,' her brother said with a patience she knew he didn't feel, 'do you have someone *romantic* in your life?'

'Well, considering how you treat Sierra, I think you're romantic. Does that—?'

'Brooke.'

It was a bark now. She winced.

'There might be someone. But honestly,' she rushed to say, not allowing him to interrupt, 'it's nothing.'

'Who is he?'

'Who said it was a he?'

'Brooke.'

'Dom,' she deadpanned. 'You realise I am thirty years old? An adult?' She spelled it out for him. 'I do not have to justify my actions or my decisions to you. I am not a kid, nor am I a suspect you can interrogate simply because you want to.'

The silence that followed was long and tense. Brooke stared at Dom; Dom stared right back.

When it dipped into ridiculous territory, Sierra spoke. 'Hey, Marcus, we're just about done here. How about you and I take dessert…?' She trailed off, as if realising she hadn't exactly thought it through, then said, 'Literally anywhere other than here!'

Marcus eyed Brooke and Dom, but silently slipped off his chair and followed his mom into another room.

As soon as they'd left, Dom leaned forward. 'That's unfair and you know it.'

'Maybe,' said Brooke, 'but so is making me feel like I'm doing something irresponsible.'

'I never once said—' He broke off at the look she gave him. 'All right, fine. I might be giving off that vibe. But it's not because I don't trust you to make good decisions for yourself.'

'Really? Because it sure sounds like it.'

'I don't trust other people,' he said. 'And I know you're about to tell me that's a cliché, but it's literally my job to be suspicious. Is it so wrong for me to be protective of my sister? My sister who's lost too much in her life and deserves happiness?'

Her heart softened, which she knew had been his intention, and she narrowed her eyes. 'I know what you're doing.'

He gave her a twist of a smile. 'Is it working?'

'You know it is.'

His smile widened. There was a slight pause before he said, 'Are you happy?'

She sat back in her chair. 'What does it mean that I don't know how to answer that?'

'You should be happy,' he replied carefully. 'But I think it'll be hard for you to figure out because you don't know what that means any more. At least not when it comes to romance.'

She blinked. 'That's surprisingly astute, Dom.'

'I've been married for ten years.'

'I thought most of that success was Sierra's doing.' But she smiled at him before she sobered. 'It's true.' She paused. 'I don't know. I don't know if what I'm feeling is what I'm supposed to be feeling. It feels like too much, too soon.'

'The relationship? Or the fact that it's happening at all?'

'It's been five years,' she answered, though it wasn't really an answer. At least, not a truthful answer.

The truth was that sometimes it felt like either one of those. Sometimes both—sometimes neither. But she couldn't tell her brother that. She would sound unstable. She *felt* unstable.

'I want it to feel normal,' she admitted. 'I want it to be easy and normal and… I don't know… I don't want to feel like I'm coming into this relationship with some kind of internal deficit. That's how I feel right now.'

'Like your grief is a deficit?'

'Baggage,' she said with a nod. 'Why would anyone want that?'

Dom took a while to answer. 'Everyone has baggage. This guy—or whatever this person's gender,' he added, 'will have it, too. Sure, it might not be grief, but it'll be something. No baggage is equal in a relationship, but that's probably what makes it equal.'

'That makes no sense,' she teased.

'Yeah, I know.'

'It's still pretty wise, though.'

'I know that, too.'

She laughed.

They sat in silence again, but it was easy this time. It made her nostalgic for the days when they were growing up. They would fight as though they had everything to lose, even when the fight was over something idiotic like the remote control. An hour or so later they'd be sitting together on the couch, watching a show and arguing without heat over something as idiotic as the topic of their original fight.

'There's no such thing as normal,' Dom said gently.

He reached out to take her hand, and the comfort of having her big brother holding her hand soothed the uncertainty in her heart.

'We pretend like there is, but there isn't. There's only what works for us. So if this person works for you, B, that's enough. You don't have to have all the answers now.'

She smiled at him, thanked him, and then went to tell Sierra it was safe for her and Marcus to come back to the kitchen. Brooke and Dom made a special effort to show Marcus they were getting along, so he knew that their tiff had been a simple one.

'It's time you got him a sibling,' she told Dom when she left. 'He needs to know that family fights aren't the end of the world.'

'Your wish is our command.'

'That's a weird— Wait,' she said, when she took in his smile. 'Sierra's pregnant? You're having another kid?'

'In seven more months, yeah.'

She squealed, jumped into her brother's arms, and then went back inside to tell her sister-in-law that she was excited and would be there for her no matter what.

The happiness of the news followed her as she drove home. It coated her thoughts, so that they felt happy even though she was still thinking about what Dom had said.

Did Tyler work for her? There were certainly moments. Those moments happened when they were together. It was the distance between them that was filled with uncertainty.

But that wasn't what stayed with her the most. What struck her the most was Dom saying she didn't have to have all the answers now. Under normal circumstances, she would have agreed. Except with Tyler it felt as if there was an element of urgency. A time limit if he was leaving.

And he wanted to leave, so the fact that he would seemed almost inevitable.

If distance was what caused uncertainty, there was no hope for a long-distance relationship.

So yeah, she did kind of feel that she needed to figure out all the answers now.

When she got home, she found Tyler sitting on her front step.

'I didn't mean *right* now. Like at this moment,' she muttered under her breath as she got out of the car. 'What are you doing here? No—wait,' she said as she stopped in front of him. 'That was rude. Hello, Tyler. What brings you here?'

He gave her a half-smile she didn't feel was completely sincere.

'Was that better?' she asked.

'Six out of ten.'

'A pass.' She wanted to smile at him, but his expression didn't encourage that. 'So, are you going to tell me?'

'I... Do you mind if we go somewhere?'

'Somewhere?'

'There's a vineyard a little way from here.'

'Wine? Are you trying to soften me up?'

'Would it work if I was?'

He was teasing, but something in his voice made him sound serious. And curious.

She angled her head. 'Yeah. Sure. Should I drive with you? Or...?'

'You can drive with me.'

'Lead the way.'

He did. And, after the slightest moment of hesitation, she followed.

Tyler knew she was picking up on how strangely he was acting. He wasn't particularly proud of it, but a sense of inevitability had woven a spell over him. A dark, disruptive spell that wouldn't allow him to continue his life without having this conversation with her.

He'd spent a week going over it in his head. Did he tell her the truth? That they'd met before or shortly after her husband's death? It would be a hell of a thing for her to find out, and that was part of why he needed to figure out whether he should tell her. How would she respond? Would it bring anything good?

But he couldn't sit on the information. The only reason he had before was because he'd thought she had chosen not to acknowledge their shared past. Hell, at this point, he didn't even know if he could call it 'shared.' Could he still think that it happened to both of them if she didn't remember it? And what did he tell her about it?

It had been a week of dinners and friendship, including going to the vineyard he was taking her to now—a sneaky attempt at jogging her memory, especially because he knew it was pointless.

If she was going to remember their time together, it would have happened already. He didn't understand the science behind memory loss, despite the hours of research he'd done, but from what Brooke had told him it was her trauma. Which meant it was designed to protect her. Not much could change that. He didn't want anything to change that.

So maybe the reason he was taking her to this place was more for him. To assure himself that something *had* happened between them.

It was all so messy.

'What's wrong?' Brooke asked as he took the curved road leading to the vineyard.

It was one of many vineyards in the area, with fields of green and gold stretching out for metres and metres around them. On another day, he would have taken the time to enjoy the view. The way the sun hit the leaves, casting light, making the colours seem as if they were glowing.

The mountains in the distance, all curves and angles of darkness balancing the expanse of green.

It was one of his favourite drives, especially as they got closer to the vineyard, when trees reached over the road, shadowing the cars beneath them. When a burst of sun trickled through the gaps of the leaves, or through the stretches without trees, or when the fields and mountains were once again unobscured.

But he couldn't enjoy it today. Only he didn't want her to know that.

'Why would you think anything's wrong?' he asked.

He glanced over to see her arch her brow, as if to say, *Which example would you like? The one where you show up at my house unannounced after a week of no communication? Or the one where you ask to take me to a vineyard without telling me why? Or your general current broodiness?*

As a gift to both of them, she merely said, 'You were shaking your head.'

'I was…thinking.' He stuck his tongue into his cheek, ashamed of how inadequate that was.

'Okay.'

He looked at her again, but she was looking out of the window, so he couldn't see her expression. He didn't need to see it to know she was giving him an out. She had been since the moment she'd got home. She hadn't questioned him too much, wasn't pushing him when it was clear that he didn't want to talk about something.

It wouldn't last, so for now, he enjoyed it. Or, since enjoyment wasn't something he could feel at this moment, with tension skittering over his skin like a ghost, he accepted it.

The rest of the drive was quiet, and when he pulled into the car park he got out, waited for her to join him, and then took the short stone path to the front of the restaurant. He helped her up the steps.

When she gasped, he gave her some space to enjoy the view. He hadn't intended for it to be this way, but the sun was lowering beneath the fields in the distance, and the patio they were standing on allowed them a perfect view of it.

It was breathtaking, truly, but his attention was on Brooke. The sun made her look like an ethereal being who had come down from heaven to give him an impossible task. He would have readily accepted it, he knew.

How could he resist that golden-brown skin, shimmering like the grains of sand at a beach? Or the pink of her cheeks, her lips, a hue he had only ever seen on the most tempting of fruit? Or her eyes, the brown lighter than ever under the sun, that looked as though she were ready to give away every secret? Or perhaps as though she could keep such secrets. The deepest, darkest kind. The sweetest kind.

He didn't realise he was closing the distance between them until he had. When he was there, his hand lifted. She shifted just as a breeze floated over them, mingling her scent with the spicy sweet smell of the wine, with the grounded smell of the earth around them. Her shift wasn't to move away. Even though her eyes traced the movement of his hand as he tucked some strands of her hair behind her ear, she didn't move away.

She leaned in.

It undid him in ways he couldn't explain, hadn't expected, and his head was dipping to hers before he could talk himself out of it. She met him halfway, her lips soft and ready, as though made for his kiss.

The kiss was neither firm nor gentle; not intense nor easy. It was simply a kiss. An acknowledgement of their attraction and of the *more* that haunted each of them.

He cupped her face. Opened his mouth. Swept his tongue

inside to taste her. It was a taste that would mark him for ever. An exaggeration, perhaps, though his senses didn't seem to think so. It reminded him of the sun during early spring, of cold water after a hot summer's day, of a fire during the frigid cold.

Her touch was both foreign and familiar. Even now, with her fingers hesitantly touching his torso. And seconds later, when they curled into his shirt, bringing him closer to her with a strength he didn't resist.

His body was aware of her every motion, as if she were tracing his skin with a block of ice. Desire sent pulses to every pleasure-point in his body, and he shifted, sliding his arms around her waist, pulling her closer so that when they parted, no one would see the evidence of what she did to him.

Then he realised that he was allowing her to feel what she did to him. He angled himself, trying to give her space. His body complained. So did she. And with that came another shift of her body, moving the softness of her against the hardness of him.

He was terribly aware of her breasts pressing against his chest. His fingers ached to trace them. His eyes wanted to feast on them. To memorise their colour and shape and curve, every mark on her skin. And when he was done looking he wanted to taste. Run his tongue over every point. Lick the marks to celebrate their uniqueness.

And when he was done there he would move on to the rest of her body. To her waist that sloped over hips that were plush and ready for lifting. She would wrap her legs around him and give him better access to her heat. He would finally give the hardness between his legs what it was asking for. What it was demanding.

'Whoa,' she breathed as she pulled away.

For a second he wondered if she had some idea of what

he'd been thinking. If she was scandalised or agreeing to what he wanted to do to her.

Then she said, 'That was a…a hell of a kiss.'

She exhaled, the air rushing through her lips and touching his face. It did nothing to ease his arousal. Only heightened it, reminding him of what she tasted like.

He took his own steadying breath. A couple more. Eventually, he said, 'Yeah.'

Her tongue slid to the corner of her mouth. There was an amused look on her face. 'I've rendered you speechless. I quite like that power.'

'By now you should already know you have it.'

'No,' she disagreed. 'By now I know that no matter what I say, you'll always have the perfect response. It'll be charming and very annoying and I'll still feel a part of me…' She trailed off, the teasing tone of her voice disappearing. 'Soften,' she finished.

If his body had been all in with that kiss, now it was his heart's chance. Her words sank into it like rain into fertile soil. It was too early to tell what would grow from that soil, if anything. Because the moment he told her the truth, it would yank out the root, and any hope that something beautiful and full of life would come from it would be gone.

'I have to tell you something,' he said, stepping away from her. Leaving the heat and the desire in that little space where they'd kissed.

Her eyes became unreadable, and she stepped out of the space, too. He spent a moment too long staring at it, wondering if what they'd left there was simpler or more complicated than what they were about to enter into.

'What?' she asked carefully.

With a fortifying breath, he said, 'We've met before.'

CHAPTER THIRTEEN

BROOKE COULD TELL by the tone of his voice that he wasn't talking about a random meeting. She couldn't remember it. And, although it was true she didn't remember many men from the time when she was with Kian, she was certain she would have remembered Tyler. He was striking to look at, and she would have at least made that distant connection, even when she was in a relationship.

A ripple of unease went through her body, rolling over her skin much as the breeze did.

'Okay, so, you've brought me to a vineyard with a beautiful view and a stunning restaurant—' she assumed it was stunning since she hadn't really taken a good look inside the building and doubted she would now '—to tell me… what? We've met once before?'

'It wasn't just once.'

She felt the impact of those words physically.

'We know—*knew*—one another.'

'I… I don't understand.' He opened his mouth to explain, but she held up a hand. 'And if I'm going to understand, I think I'm going to need wine. Which, I assume, is at least part of why you brought me here?'

His expression was sombre as he nodded, gesturing for her to walk in front of him.

It was hard for her to imagine that this was the same man who'd kissed her so thoroughly only a few minutes ago. She had thrown caution to the wind—hell, she'd been swept away by that wind—and kissed him in public because the look he had given her had been so damn intimate. And trusting. She couldn't forget that. It had triggered something inside her. He trusted her and, yes, she trusted him.

So, she'd kissed him. Let him touch her soul with the lick of his tongue and the caress of his fingers.

Now she felt as though she were about to lose it all.

The thought distracted her from really noticing the restaurant, though she knew it was gorgeous. The wall facing the vineyard was made from glass and metal panels, the space above it decorated in an intricate white pattern. But all she could do when they were seated in a secluded section of the room was stare at the menu.

She chose a wine with a high alcohol content. Didn't speak until that wine was brought for her approval. In truth, she didn't taste it. But she pretended to, so that the waiter would leave.

When he was gone, she drank the entire glass. With a nod, she told Tyler, 'I'm ready.'

He had been silent since they'd left the balcony. The crinkle around his eyes, the purse of his lips, told her it was nerves. An echo of the same thing danced in her chest, her stomach. She soothed it with deep breaths, in and out, and tried to focus on that and not on the signs of Tyler's nerves.

It was about fifty per cent effective, and then, when he began to talk, it stopped working entirely.

'We met on the tenth of July five years ago. I was at the hospital to see my sister. She had just given birth to her son. And I needed…' He shook his head. 'Well, I found you in the coffee shop around the corner when I went to get something to drink.'

The tenth of July… That was the day she'd signed Kian's DNR. She knew that. The accident had happened on the evening of the second, Kian had been in the hospital until he'd died on the tenth, the funeral had been on the seventeenth.

Her first real memories of that time started at some point after that.

Tyler was waiting, as if he'd known that she would need time to get it all straight in her head. The fact that he had given her dates supported that.

Nausea welled, and suddenly she wished she hadn't drunk the wine at all.

'What...what happened?' she asked hoarsely.

'You looked like you'd had a rough evening. I thought I could help with that.' He shrugged, as if the logic of that seemed shaky to him now. 'I asked you if you wanted to have your coffee at my table and you agreed.'

'We had *coffee*?'

'Yes.'

'The night Kian died I had *coffee* with a *stranger*?'

Again, it felt as if the news had physically hit her.

She sat back, tried to remember what Dom had told her about that night. He'd wanted to take her home, but she hadn't been ready to leave. She'd insisted on staying. She'd wanted space. And because her family was so supportive, so understanding, they'd given it to her.

She had always assumed she had gone home. Mourned and grieved like everyone had expected her to. But no. Apparently, she had gone out for coffee.

'I'm sorry,' said Tyler.

Her eyes flickered up. 'You didn't know about any of it.'

'You believe me?'

'Why would you lie about this, Tyler?' She asked the question with a hopeless kind of despair. It would have troubled her at another time, but for the moment it was appropriate. 'Apart from the fairly obvious fact that we've known one another for over a month now and you haven't mentioned any of this before.'

He winced. 'I thought you weren't mentioning it intentionally. I was about to work for you. You seemed to be all about boundaries, so I was, too. I didn't want to push for the sake of Tia's job, but also because I thought—' He broke off with a sharp exhalation. 'I thought wrong, clearly.'

'Knowing what you know about me now,' she said slowly, 'like the fact that I can't keep a secret to save my life, you thought I wouldn't mention going out for coffee with you?' She snorted, though she knew it was an ugly thing to do. 'Did we not have a good time? Did I give you some kind of sign that I'd pretend it had never happened if we ever met again?'

Colour entered his face. It was a charming red, something that belonged among fields of flowers, and she would have found it charming if it hadn't been so alarming. It was an indication that she was missing something—which, yes, obviously—and something significant.

'What?' She almost hissed. 'What happened? Oh, no, ' she said, rearing back. 'Did I…? Did we…?'

'No! Well, we didn't… We didn't sleep together.'

'But something else happened?'

A curt nod. 'We kissed.'

Good heavens.

She reached for her wine glass before realising it hadn't been refilled. Desperately, she looked around for the server. Didn't see him. Unhelpfully, her mind told her that she had just regretted drinking the first glass of wine. A second would likely have similar consequences. And yet she still desperately wanted to drink. To fill the sudden void that came with the knowledge that she had kissed someone the night her husband had died.

What kind of person did that make her? Certainly not the one she had always thought she was. Not the woman who had, for the last five years, been living a pious life of offering to her deceased husband.

She hadn't thought about it that way, of course. But now it seemed obvious that she had been. Only she hadn't realised it was in atonement for her sins.

'Right,' she said after a moment, taking a deep breath. 'You and I kissed. Okay. Sure. That's fine. I mean, I'd only been single—and I use that term really lightly, because *wow* it messes with my brain—for literal hours.'

Again, colour appeared on his skin. It wasn't embarrassment though. She knew it deep in her gut—a feeling that had nebulous implications now she knew they had some sort of history together. No, it was distress. He didn't want to tell her any of this.

If she hadn't trusted him, she would have thought that was why he'd waited so long before he'd said anything. But there was still something inside her that *did* trust him, despite this earthquake to the foundations she'd thought they'd built. And the same gut feeling told her that the distress wasn't for himself either, but for her. He didn't want to upset her.

'What?' she asked flatly. 'Please, tell me. I don't think… I think these little bursts of shock are worse than you laying it all out for me. So just…just tell me.'

He nodded. 'The kiss didn't happen the night your husband died. It was a week after. We saw one another every day for dinner in the days leading up to…it. For that whole week.' Though he looked uncomfortable, he didn't shift. 'We'd look up places the day before and meet there the next evening. We didn't have each other's numbers. We knew one another's names, but that was the only personal information we shared. Mostly we spoke about random but meaningful things. Or we made the kind of ridiculous observations that you'd only feel comfortable making with a stranger.'

He paused. She wasn't sure if it was to take a breath or to give her a moment to process. If it were the latter, she should tell him not to bother. She currently only had the mental space to receive information. Understanding that information, emotionally or mentally, would require energy and a presence of mind that she didn't have.

So she waited. And when it became clear that she wasn't going to speak—it seemed he *had* been waiting for her to process—he continued.

'It was a good week. For me,' he clarified. 'I thought for you, too. Especially when we...' the slightest hesitation '...kissed. Hell, that's why the kiss happened. But then you disappeared. I didn't see you again until a month ago. And I thought—'

'You thought I hadn't felt what you felt,' she said, seeing it now. 'You thought I was ignoring everything that had happened between us because I didn't feel the same way. That's why you didn't say anything.'

He sucked in his bottom lip, but nodded. 'And then last week, when you told me you had amnesia, I realised... I realised it wasn't a choice.'

'And that it had nothing to do with you or your ego.' Abruptly, she pushed her chair back. His eyes widened, but she was walking away before he could say anything. Before her mind could catch up with what her body was doing.

'Brooke!'

He called after her, but she didn't respond. Only kept walking. Likely because some part of her knew that he would have to stay behind, sort out the bill. It wouldn't give her hours—in hindsight, she should have come with her own car—but it would give her enough time to figure out how her lungs worked again.

She rushed down the stairs, clutching at the railing when she almost fell on the last two steps, then walked towards the vineyard, metres from the building. When she reached the entrance, she ran. Not her smartest idea, considering she was wearing a white dress and sandals. But she didn't care about calling herself smart when she was only trying to survive the onslaught of feelings Tyler's words had awoken in her.

She'd described it as an earthquake before, but that had been in terms of them. That wasn't the only thing his revelation had affected. It was an earthquake for all the emotions she'd thought she'd worked through since Kian's death. If she looked at them now, it seemed she had merely been stacking them neatly, and now, with this earthquake, they were falling over. Coming to crush her, really, like an avalanche rushing down a hill. And, like any person on that hill, she had no hope of dodging it, only delaying it.

She could only delay it for so long.

She dropped to her knees, not caring that dirt caked the material of her dress. The only thing she cared about was the fact that she was far enough away from the restaurant that no one would see her unless they were standing on the balcony. And if her own actions on that balcony were anything to go by, whoever stood there now wouldn't be paying attention to a sobbing woman crouching in the dirt.

Sobbing? She lifted her hand and realised that there were, indeed, tears coming down her face. But her lungs were working again, which surely was a good sign. So what if her breathing wasn't optimal? So what if that rush of in-out, in-out meant panic and anxiety and not normal, functioning human organs?

'Brooke.'

She groaned, sitting back on the ground and bringing her knees up so she could hide her face in between them.

'Do you…do you want me to go?'

'What would make you think that? The fact that I literally ran away from you? Or the fact that I'm crying in the middle of a field of grapes?'

She said all those words between inhalations and exhalations of air, between splutters and hiccups, and all from between her knees. So when she felt Tyler sit down next to her, she thought she might not have delivered the words as concisely and as sharply as she'd intended to.

'I figure whatever you're saying means yes, you'd like me to go.'

Perhaps she *had* delivered the words that way.

'And I will,' he continued, 'as soon as I'm sure you won't get killed out here in the middle of nowhere.'

'Killed?' she repeated, lifting her head. 'Really?'

He shrugged, but his eyes were soft. 'I wanted to say as soon as I'm sure you're okay, but I didn't think you'd be receptive to that.'

'But I'd be receptive to the prospect of murder?'

'You're not crying any more.'

She did a mental check, and of course, he was right. She sucked in her lips and rested her chin on her knees. Then she turned her head and rested her cheek there instead. It was more comfortable. It also had the added benefit of allowing her not to look at Tyler.

To his credit, he didn't bother her. Apart from with his presence, which always had some kind of an effect on her. That attraction, the electricity… She hated it now. Hated the overwhelming awareness that he was here and Kian was not.

She shut her eyes, but the thought had already brought more tears. Silent, thankfully. In fact, it was much less dramatic than running into a field and sobbing. But her hysteria had hidden the deepest factor in all of this. The thing that had caused the drama, ironically.

The betrayal. Because heaven—and likely Kian—knew that she had betrayed him.

And she couldn't remember it.

She wanted to call her psychologist and ask whether that made it better or worse. Maybe it was the reason for her memory loss. That kind of betrayal would have been deeply traumatic to her, especially if her husband had just died.

She could already hear her psychologist's voice, pointing out how she had had both physical and emotional trauma, and that both of those things were already adequate explanations. But how did that account for her actions after Kian's death? Hadn't she remembered the accident and everything else then? Dom had told her she'd handled everything in a daze, but she'd handled it.

Someone who didn't remember her husband, who didn't know what she was doing, wouldn't have done that.

Did that mean she'd remembered Kian but started dating a stranger? Had it been some kind of grieving process?

Even the idea of it was abhorrent to her. She hadn't dated in five years as part of her grieving process. Falling for someone immediately after Kian's death didn't seem likely.

So what had happened?

Slowly, she turned her head to Tyler. He wasn't looking at her. He was affording her as much privacy as he could, apparently. He must have sensed that she was looking at him though, because he turned then, holding her eyes.

And even in that moment, even in her turmoil, she felt it. A gentle tug in the pit of her belly, a fluttering in the region of her heart. It was awareness, and attraction, but neither felt dirty nor shameful, though in the circumstances, both should have.

Maybe this was it. This was the reason she had agreed to have coffee with him. There was a pull between them that defied logic and circumstance. Something that had nothing to do with choice or agency. Something inevitable.

She wanted to ask him questions, to find out the nature of the relationship that had led to that kiss. But all she could do was shut her eyes and press them into her knees.

Because she had just realised she was in love with him, and it was a hell of a time for that.

* * *

'You're not supposed to be here. Nyle is still sick and—'

'Tia,' Tyler interrupted.

He didn't intend it to come out as a plea, but he couldn't think of any other intention when he actually heard his own tone of voice.

Leaning into it, he added, 'Please.'

Tia's eyes swept over his face, then she stepped outside. 'Nyle's sleeping at the moment, but I'm not sure how long that'll last. He's feeling better, and apparently I've gone back to having a ninja in training in my house.'

'A ninja in training?' His mouth curved, despite the rawness that had had him driving to his sister's house after dropping Brooke at home. 'Your words or his?'

'His,' she replied dryly. 'Once we get through this, I'll have to talk to him about putting limitations on his dreams. He could be a ninja, not just one in training.'

'At least he's being realistic.'

'He's five. I'm not sure that's the lesson I want to teach the kid.'

'That's why you're such a great mom.'

Her eyes narrowed a fraction. 'Your face looks like you've witnessed a murder *and* you're complimenting me? Something must be wrong.'

He didn't bother to answer, only sank down in front of the door. It meant he was sitting directly on the pathway that led to the door from the garage.

Tia lived in the house their mother had bought once the divorce from their father had been finalised. She hadn't paid off the mortgage before her death, but Tyler had taken care of that, and when Nyle had arrived, he'd signed his share of the house over for his nephew to inherit when he was old enough. It had been the only help Tia had accepted, and he was fairly certain the only reason she had was because she had still been grieving their mother.

He could remember the days when he'd come out the house to see his mother struggling with groceries. She would never call for him, and he would always ask why she hadn't. Her answer would be a look. A look said, *I can do this by myself.* And, sure, she could—but she hadn't had to. That had been his mother's greatest flaw, and it was one Tia seemed to have inherited.

He hadn't though. When he'd dropped Brooke off and she'd left the car with only a murmur of thanks, he'd known he needed someone. And the only person he had was Tia.

That was why he couldn't leave. Certainly not for the other side of the world. But he couldn't handle thinking about that now. He'd deal with it later. Right now, he was panicking about something entirely different.

'Let me guess,' Tia said, lowering herself down next to him. 'This is about our boss.'

His head whipped towards her. 'How did you know? Also—*our*?'

'Technically, she's my boss, but in reality she's yours. Besides, she texted me to ask for your number. Did you not think I'd put two and two together?'

'You *were* suspiciously quiet about that.'

'I was dealing with a sick kid.'

'When has that ever stopped you?'

'Maybe I knew that you'd pitch up at my door, desperate for my guidance.'

She wasn't being entirely snarky—although with Tia, that was always a factor. There was also a sincerity that made him wonder what she'd seen to make her respond this way.

'Am I that bad at relationships?' he asked.

'I don't know,' she answered honestly. 'That's why I expected you to come to me. Not because I'm in any way an expert at relationships, as you well know, but because...' She looked out at the road in front of them where a couple of kids were kicking a ball back and forth. 'When you need advice, you ask. It's one of the things I admire most about you.'

He didn't give himself time to enjoy his surprise. 'Go on.'

She stuck her tongue out. 'If you had any real friends, you'd probably go to them—'

'Ah, *there* it is. I knew the compliments wouldn't last.'

'But the people you call friends are mostly colleagues and you wouldn't go to any of them about something you consider personal.'

She wasn't wrong.

'And since Mom has died, that leaves me. So, how can I help?'

'After everything you've just said, I shouldn't want your help.'

'But you need it.'

He sighed. He did need it. So he told her everything, from the moment he'd seen Brooke in that coffee shop. He didn't stop until he reached today. He left out anything physical—he didn't need his little sister knowing about that—as well as Brooke crying in the middle of the vineyard.

He wasn't sure why, but that felt as if it were a secret. His or hers, he didn't know. But it felt precious that he'd seen her so raw, so vulnerable, and he couldn't bear the idea of sharing that moment with anyone else.

It didn't even matter that seeing her had broken his heart. Had made him want to build a wall around her so she never had to face anything that would upset her so much again. Even him. He considered it a privilege that she'd been so open with him and he wouldn't do anything to betray that trust.

So he merely ended by telling Tia that Brooke had been upset. That he had been, too, and that was why he was there.

'I'm sorry,' Tia said, curling her fingers around his. 'I'm sorry you're sad and I'm sorry that this relationship is so complicated. You don't deserve it.'

'Don't I?' he asked bitterly.

'You don't. You helped Mom take care of us. You took care of me. You still help me and Nyle.' She squeezed his hand. 'You deserve only good things, Tyler. You've spent a lifetime earning good karma.'

Maybe I've cancelled it out these last few months. By wanting to expand my business and to leave you and Nyle to fend for yourselves. I want it more every time I think of it. Despite knowing what Dad did. Despite not wanting to put myself first like he did, I'm still considering it.

It would have been so easy to say it. To finally be honest. But, coward that he was, he didn't. He only squeezed her hand back and allowed himself to lie, telling himself it was because he was focusing on one disaster at a time.

'It doesn't matter,' he said. 'This job will be over in a week and it won't be a problem any more.'

'Won't it?' Tia asked lightly. 'Since when does running away from your problems make them any easier to deal with? I'm asking that sincerely,' she added, 'because I've been running for five years, yet I still think about the lying piece of crap that gave me the most beautiful gift in the world.'

He softened. 'It's *because* he gave you that gift.'

'No,' she denied. 'It's because there's still a part of me that loves him. And you don't have to say it. I know I'm an idiot.'

'I've spent five years comparing anyone I was even remotely interested in to a woman I didn't see again after she literally ran away from our kiss. I'm the last person to judge.'

They fell into silence. He didn't know what Tia was thinking about, but he was thinking about all the mistakes he'd made since he'd been reunited with Brooke. If he'd maintained a professional relationship with her…if he'd been honest with her upfront…if he'd asked her why she'd run after their kiss…

There had been so many opportunities to alter where they had ended up now, only he had been too in love to take them.

He should be surprised by that revelation, but he wasn't. The feeling had been there for longer than he'd realised. He'd been like a frog in heating water, not realising he was being boiled until it was too late to escape. But even if he had realised it, he wasn't certain he would have escaped. He had enjoyed that heating water too much, just like he'd enjoyed the falling.

Spending time with Brooke. Getting to know her mind, her humour, her heart. He wouldn't have sacrificed that even to save himself from the inevitable heartbreak. Because it would be inevitable. They had no future. They couldn't when their past together was an obstacle between them. When her past would keep her from moving forward.

He didn't resent it. It was a part of her life and he didn't want her to ignore it for the sake of his comfort. Especially not when he had his own past to consider. His own obstacles.

What would happen if he left South Africa? If by some miracle he actually went to London and worked towards his dreams? Would he leave Brooke behind? Would he leave a woman he loved behind? How could he claim to be better than his father if he did that?

'What do you want, Tyler?' Tia asked, interrupting his thoughts. 'In an ideal world, what would you want?'

'Her,' he answered honestly, despite all the reasons he'd told himself he couldn't have her. 'I'd want a life with her. She's smart and funny. Sweet.' He smiled, thinking about her and Mochi. 'She has a dog she thinks hates her because she can't give him the love he deserves, even though it's clear he adores her and she gives him more love than she knows. She works hard. She has this special project she's working on and she loves her job. And...' He trailed off, his mind finally catching up to his mouth. 'But I can't have her.'

'Because she doesn't feel the same way?'

'Because we have too many obstacles in the way of being happy together.'

His sister was quiet for a while. 'Seems to me that if you feel the way you do, and she feels that way, too, the biggest obstacle is already out of the way. The first and most logical step now would be to figure out if she thinks *you're* smart and funny and sweet and all those other things. Doubtful, but you've got to try.'

She bumped his shoulder to show she was teasing. He already knew that. What he couldn't fathom was why her advice made him feel better. Even if Brooke did feel the same way, he'd just told himself why it didn't matter. So why did it feel so urgent to know?

'You're a lot smarter than I give you credit for, do you know that?' he told Tia.

'I do,' she said with a smirk, but sobered quickly. 'You can't make decisions when you don't know the facts. She can't figure out if she wants to be with you if you don't tell her that you want to be with her.'

'You're right.' And Tia deserved to know all the facts, too. He took a huge breath. 'T, that's not the only thing I want to talk about...'

And finally, after months of stalling, he told his sister the truth.

CHAPTER FOURTEEN

'YOU'RE ACTING WEIRD,' Dom pointed out unhelpfully.

'It's the launch of my app,' Brooke snapped. 'What's normal in these circumstances?'

'Not snapping at your brother for making a simple observation.'

She didn't reply, but stuck out her tongue. The action held the same tone as whatever she might have told him anyway.

Thankfully, he didn't respond, verbally or physically. It was as if, for once in his life, Dom knew she didn't need his snide comments.

She was highly strung, without a doubt. She had been since that conversation with Tyler. She'd been going back and forth about what it meant and how she felt in every spare moment she had.

Those moments had been rare, fortunately, because the final week before the launch of the app had been busy. And tonight, they would officially go live.

As was the custom for her company, they'd planned a black-tie event to watch the clock tick down and celebrate the exact moment. Dom had pitched up in his tuxedo when she'd asked him to, which had also annoyed her for some inexplicable reason. Even though he'd picked Mochi up earlier, to stay with him and Sierra for the night.

But none of that meant she was acting weird, regardless of what he'd said.

The doorbell rang. She looked at the clock. 'That can't be the driver yet. There's still thirty minutes before the car's meant to arrive.'

'And yet you asked me to be here thirty minutes ago,' Dom muttered.

'I didn't want to risk being late.'

He merely grunted, which was an appropriate response to her lie. She hadn't only wanted to avoid being late. She'd wanted to celebrate with her brother. Yet the unopened bottle of very expensive champagne she'd bought at the start of the process still stood in her refrigerator, untouched.

She couldn't bring herself to celebrate. It didn't feel right when there was so much that felt wrong in her life.

For example, the fact that you don't really want Dom here, but Tyler.

Irritably, she stomped over to the front door and yanked it open.

And stared.

She might have been ashamed if Tyler hadn't been staring at her, too.

She thought it might both have come from shock, although their reasons might be different. For her, it was simply his presence. Had she somehow manifested him? She didn't even care, too distracted by a strong wave of pleasure that hit her at seeing him again.

His expression was sombre, those beautiful lines of his face arranged in a serious expression she wasn't used to seeing. But he was still heartachingly handsome. He wore a simple shirt and jeans, and her fingers itched to touch him. It felt like such a long time ago that they'd shared those kisses, but she remembered them so vividly.

And all of it felt like a terrible irony considering she couldn't remember the time he claimed they'd spent together.

No, not claimed—the time they *had* spent together.

She was pretty certain it had happened. There was no benefit to him in lying about it. And it made sense, though it had taken her long to admit it. It explained how she'd felt such a bond with him only shortly after they'd met. All those times when things had felt familiar between them. Why she'd asked him out to dinner even though he worked for her. Why she trusted him when she hadn't trusted anyone outside of her family in years.

There was something inside her that did remember him. And even if that hadn't been true, she felt something for him now. She loved him. These last weeks had been enough for her to know that. So even if something she couldn't remember had created that pull, she'd acted on it. *She* had. And she had done so *now*. And that was significant, wasn't it?

If only all of it didn't feel so wrapped up in emotion that wouldn't allow her to accept it.

She blinked, realising she'd been lost in thought. But he didn't seem to mind. He was still staring at her.

'Surely this dress isn't that gobsmacking?' she commented dryly.

'It's pretty damn gobsmacking.' He tilted his head, lifting his eyes to hers. 'Is that how one should use that word?'

'If "one" refers to me, then, yes, because that's how I just used the word.'

His lips twitched before that sombre expression took over again. 'You're clearly on your way somewhere…' He trailed off in a way that made it clear he wanted to know where.

'The app launch.'

'That's tonight?' He was rolling his eyes before he finished. 'Of course it's tonight. Tia's contract to work for you ended today.'

A punch landed in her gut. She steeled herself so it

wouldn't cause her to stagger back. She'd forgotten that today was the last day of her contract with the housekeeping agency. She'd forgotten that today would be the last day he'd be working for her.

It was silly to feel disappointed since for pretty much half of the time, she hadn't seen him. But she'd known he was there. She'd known he was cooking for her and cleaning for her.

She would have been ashamed of taking pleasure in that knowledge, but it wasn't because she was on some kind of power trip. She just felt more secure with him doing those things for her. It was a form of caring she was no longer used to, even if she was paying for it.

She wasn't sure if that made her pathetic or not.

'Why are you here?' she asked softly.

He swallowed. 'I'll come back.'

'No, Tyler,' she said, before he could turn away. 'Just… say it.'

He stared at her for a long time. She wished she knew whether that meant he would answer her. Whether he would tell her the reason he'd shown up at her door now, on the final day of his contract.

Just when she thought he might, Dom called out from the lounge.

'Everything okay, B?'

She looked over her shoulder, saw him walking towards her. 'Yes,' she said primly.

She turned to Tyler. His expression had gone from sombre to unreadable. She tilted her head. Wondered at the reason for it. Then she realised how it looked. Dom in his tux, her in a dress, the night of the launch.

'Tyler, this is Dom,' she said, shifting so that Dom could stand next to her. 'My brother.'

Tyler's eyes flitted to hers. Relief mixed with something

else, something she couldn't quite identify, but looked fierce and passionate, rested there.

Seconds later, before she could even try to name it, Tyler shook it off and held out a hand. 'Nice to meet you, Dom.'

Dom studied the hand, but didn't wait too long before he took it. 'Tyler,' he acknowledged. 'The housekeeper, right?' He paused. 'And also the man my sister is seeing.'

'Dom,' she warned.

Tyler merely gave Dom a steady look. 'I'm not sure either one of us would classify it that way, but a version of that is certainly true.'

'It is?' she asked, surprise more than anything taking control of her tongue. 'I mean, it is,' she confirmed, nodding to Dom.

Dom gave her the look he saved for when she was being stupid. She couldn't even call him out on it. She had just done something stupid. She'd doubted the qualification the man she loved tried to provide for their relationship out loud, and then she'd tried to cover it up.

She was a mess.

'You should be the one going with her this evening,' said Dom.

Her attention snapped to her brother. 'No,' she said, in another warning. 'Don't get involved.'

'You want him with you, Brooke,' Dom said casually, as if she'd already offered the information to the world and he wasn't sharing a secret she didn't want anyone to know—let alone her brother and the object of what could only be described as an obsession. 'You should take him.'

'Dom, can I speak to you privately for a moment?' she asked through her teeth. 'Tyler, you can wait inside.'

Without waiting to see how he responded to her command, she grabbed her brother's arm and marched him to the kitchen.

'What are you doing?' she snapped. 'You need to have my back, not make things more complicated.'

'Am I wrong?'

'You—' She cut herself off before she admitted something she wasn't ready to admit. 'It doesn't matter.'

'Except it does, B,' he said, stepping closer and brushing a hand over her hair. Her styled hair.

She swatted at his hand. He ignored her.

'I was wondering why you were acting so strange, but when he showed up it made sense. And then you introduced him to me, not the other way around. You were more concerned about him thinking we were a couple than you were about my opinion. That means something.'

'I don't...'

'You don't have to.'

Dom's words were gentle and he was right, despite the fact that she hadn't even finished her sentence.

'I keep telling you this. You don't have to have all the answers right at the beginning. It's okay to work your way through it.'

It seemed pointless now to tell Dom that she did have to have the answers. She couldn't risk everything she would risk for the *chance* of something.

'I don't think I can ask him to go with me,' she said honestly, because it was the only answer she could give. 'It's short notice, and he doesn't have a tux, and—'

Dom was walking out before she could stop him.

'You and I are about the same size, aren't we?' Dom asked Tyler.

'Dom—'

'I think so,' Tyler replied, interrupting what would have been her protest.

'Cool. Do you want to wear this so you can go with my sister tonight?' Dom didn't wait for an answer. 'We can change in the spare bedroom.'

'Brooke,' Tyler said. 'Do you want me to go with you?'

Dom grunted. It was in approval, she knew, because she had long since learnt the nuances of his grunts.

Tyler looked faintly alarmed, but his eyes were still on her, as if her answer was more important than her brother's faintly threatening sounds.

'Do you want to go with me?' she asked.

Dom's snort made her glare at him. But then Tyler answered, and she forgot Dom was even in the room.

'Very much so.'

Her lips parted and she nodded, hoping he'd understand that she was saying she did, indeed, want him with her. And it seemed he did. He gestured to Dom, who thankfully didn't comment, and they were both gone a second later.

She paced the room, trying not to worry about the fact that her brother was alone with Tyler. Or vice versa, for that matter. She hadn't told Dom about her and Tyler's past together. Wouldn't tell him—she was too ashamed.

But should she really be ashamed of what she couldn't remember? *Yes*, her brain answered for her. Because not remembering it didn't change the fact that she had done it.

She hadn't ever particularly cared that she suffered from amnesia. She didn't want to remember what had been the most traumatic time in her life. What she *could* remember wasn't easy or pleasant, so she had never begrudged her mind for trying to protect itself and her.

Now, though… She wished she could remember what it had been like. What had been going through her mind? What had she felt during those dinners together? Had she made Tyler believe she wanted him to kiss her? Had she initiated the kiss?

She didn't have answers to many of those questions, but there were some Tyler could offer her. And she didn't think it was wrong of her to want them. She simply hadn't asked for them before because that would have entailed talking to Tyler, which would have required seeing him.

But she was seeing him now. She could ask those questions and maybe get some closure. Except that implied the conclusion of whatever was happening between her and Tyler, and that felt oddly painful.

Even though she didn't know what to do about her feelings for him.

Even though she knew he might be leaving.

Even though their past and their future seemed so misaligned.

The doorbell rang, and this time she knew it was the car. She told the driver they'd be there in a second, got all her things ready, then waited for Tyler at the door.

She caught her breath a little when he came out of the spare bedroom. The tux fitted him perfectly, though it looked entirely different on him than it had on Dom.

Perhaps because she didn't feel as if the air around Dom was electric. Magnetic, with an answering magnet inside her, demanding that she go to Tyler. Curl herself around him or against him, she wasn't fussy.

She took a breath to steady herself. 'You look nice.'

'Thanks,' he said.

'Funny, you didn't tell me that when I wore it,' said her brother.

'It would have been weird if I had,' she told Dom with a shrewd look. 'Are you ready to go?' she asked Tyler.

'If you are.'

They walked to the car.

Brooke tried to ignore the wave Dom gave them as they drove off. But he was doing it so damn happily, as if he were proud of himself for setting this up.

'Why do I feel like a kid being waved off to prom?' Tyler asked.

Brooke snorted. 'That's exactly what I was thinking.

Well, not exactly. Also I doubt he would ever wave off his own kid that happily. Dom's more the scowling parent type, if that makes sense.'

'Since I used to have one, it does.'

'Your mom?'

'Dad.'

He curled his fingers, but Brooke didn't think he noticed.

'He wasn't the approving kind. Not initially, anyway. And his disapproval was more directed towards Tia than me.'

'So he was a misogynist?' she said, trying to lighten the mood. Although, in hindsight, insulting his father probably wasn't the way to do it.

But Tyler agreed easily. 'Pretty much. Although I guess I can understand it. She was always more vulnerable than me.'

'Because she was a girl?'

'Because she's Tia.' He paused. 'I know you haven't met her, but she's fierce. Except it's all mostly on the outside, for the sake of the world. Deep down, she's…sensitive.'

Something about the way he said it made Brooke search his expression. Pain tightened the skin around his eyes, his mouth. She wasn't sure how she knew that it was pain, but she did.

'You told her about London,' she guessed.

His head whipped towards her. 'How did you know?'

'I'm not sure,' she answered honestly. 'A gut feeling?'

His eyes softened. Something softened inside her as well. She was certain that something was her heart, but acknowledging it felt as though she was approving of it when really, she desperately wanted her heart to behave. Things were too uncertain for it not to.

'How did she take it?' she asked, trying to distract herself and her organs.

He exhaled. 'About as well as you would expect.'

'Ah… So she didn't care that you're considering leaving, only that you waited so long to talk to her about it because you believed she wouldn't support you. Because you were using her as an excuse to avoid facing the real issue, which is your feelings about yourself and your father.'

He stared at her. 'Is this your gut again?'

She shrugged. 'I've made some deductions during our time together.'

'No kidding.' He shook his head. 'I guess I could have handled this entire thing better.'

'We all usually think that, looking back.'

'It's strange, isn't it? We can psych ourselves up about something. Make it worse than it is when in reality, it's simple.'

She angled a look at him. 'Why do I feel as though you're not only talking about your sister?'

'I'm not sure,' he said easily, though the expression on his face told her she was right.

When he shifted the conversation back to his sister, it seemed to prove that he was deflecting.

'Tia did care that I wanted to leave. Not as much as I thought she would—I blame my ego for that—but in a normal way. A healthy way,' he added, almost as an afterthought.

'In the same way you care that you're thinking of leaving?' she asked. 'Because you'll miss her and your nephew.'

'Yes.' He paused. 'As for the other stuff… We didn't get to that. *I* didn't get to that.' Another pause. 'But you're right. This is about my dad, and my not wanting to be like him.'

The sadness in his voice had her reaching for his hand. 'You're not like him, Tyler. Deep down, you know that. And not only because I've told you so a million times. You know it deep in your gut.' Her hand tightened. 'You're scared, and that's okay. It's okay to be scared. But you have control of this. *You* do—not your father.'

She waited to see if he would respond. When he didn't, she pushed on, needing him to believe her.

'You chose to tell your sister and get her opinion on the situation. She might need some time, but she wants you to be happy so she'll choose to support you. Once you're in London, you can manage your time. You can keep in touch with your family. Arrange visits for Tia and Nyle. And you can come back,' she pointed out softly. 'Whenever you like. To visit, to keep in touch. You can make Cape Town your base again once you've set everything up. All of that is in your control, Tyler. Don't allow anything to make you think otherwise.'

He didn't reply for a long time, and she watched him. It felt as though she was watching the sun rise over the darkest hills. The shadows on his face faded, his shoulders loosened. She swore she could see the muscles in the rest of his body ease, too. And when he looked at her, his face brighter than she'd seen in a long time, she felt that sun shining on her. Warming the coldest parts inside her, shining light on the feelings she'd shoved into the crevices of her heart, her mind.

She loved this man, who cared so deeply for his family. Who took his responsibilities seriously. Who didn't push her for answers she didn't have or ask her for things she couldn't give.

A deep, crushing sadness moved over the light, even though she desperately tried to clutch it in her hands. Desperately tried to keep the darkness from creeping into her soul. What was the point of sadness when she couldn't pinpoint the root of it? When she couldn't express why she felt the way she did? When she only knew the sadness was different from the precious feelings she had for Tyler?

'You've simplified things I've been complicating for a long time,' he commented.

His words felt as warm as the hand still in hers. 'Only if it works.'

'I… I need time to think it through. But I think… I think I can see that there's no danger of me becoming like my father when we're different people. Our priorities are different.' He ran his tongue over his teeth. 'I want to know that Tia's on board with any decision I make. I want us to make it as a family. There never was that with him. He decided and we had to accept that. I think that's what hurt my mom the most.'

'And he doesn't even know what he lost because of that decision,' she said. 'That's his punishment. A life without knowing who you and Tia have become. A life without knowing his grandchild. It was in his control to make decisions that would have changed that, but he didn't.' She shook her head. 'There's no danger of you becoming like him at all, Tyler. At the very core of it, you're too good a man to allow that.'

'You're too good a man to allow that.'

The words carved themselves into his mind the moment she said them. Not because he believed them, but because she'd said them.

Brooke thought he was a good man. And even if that wasn't true—though he'd like to believe it was—the very fact that she thought it made him want to be a good man. He would do anything and everything he could to become the man she thought he was.

It helped, of course, that she had pointed out his power in the situation. He had been so focused on his issues with his father that he hadn't recognised that power. But now he could see the possibilities. The *choices.* This didn't have to be permanent. This didn't have to take him away from his family. He would talk to Tia and Nyle as often as he could. He'd visit them, or they'd visit him. This opportunity wouldn't mean the end of their family.

If only he had come to that conclusion before hurting his sister.

She was disappointed that he hadn't trusted her, she'd said.

'Didn't you think I'd want this for you? Did you really believe I would keep you from doing something that excites you because of my fears?'

But she was still afraid—he had seen it. He couldn't blame her when that was the curse of what their father had done to them. Only Tia didn't shy away from making tough decisions because of it, like he had. She faced them. Even if she had said she needed some time before she could talk to him without wanting to kick him for being so stupid.

Despite that, he was cautiously hopeful for the future. Until he thought about Brooke, about where his leaving would leave *them*.

He hadn't known what to expect when he'd shown up at her door. Did he want to tell her he loved her? Tell her about what had happened with Tia? Ask her how she was feeling about everything?

It was likely a combination of all three. There was an urgency to it, too, since after today there would be no more chances to 'accidentally' bump into her. There would only be intentional meetings from here on out. Which was why he was here, accompanying her at the launch party.

She looked beautiful. Her green dress was loose, but skilfully arranged over her body, showing peeks of her breasts at its neckline, of her right leg through the slit. She blended in with her surroundings here at the venue, where green vines draped around wooden arches and high, steady mountains rose all around them.

They'd driven quite a distance to get there, but Brooke's

company had once been situated close by, and it was still their tradition to hold launch events here.

He could see the appeal. They'd driven up a winding road to get to the top of a hill, and the restaurant overlooked the Stellenbosch area, giving magnificent views of the mountains surrounding them. It was secluded and private, felt expensive and high class, and he understood now why he'd had to wear the tuxedo.

Although merely standing next to Brooke demanded that he be dressed equally formally. He wanted to say equally stunningly, but he didn't think that was possible.

Her hair had been swept back, much as it had been that night at his business event, but this time, it was parted in the middle. Somehow it gave greater prominence to her face. It seemed sharper, more distinct this evening. He didn't know if that was because she'd put on make-up or because his mind was marking every single feature.

This night felt significant, though it was too early to tell why.

He exhaled.

'I thought I was the one who was meant to be nervous,' Brooke said mildly at his side.

'I'm not nervous,' he said automatically.

She merely lifted an eyebrow. He felt as if someone had thrown a piece of him into hot oil.

No, an inner voice told him. *You cannot muddle things with desire now.*

'*Are* you nervous?' he asked, shifting direction. 'You don't seem like it.'

'She's never nervous,' one of Brooke's co-workers said, stopping in front of them. It was an older woman he'd been introduced to earlier—as Brooke's 'friend'—but he couldn't recall her name now.

'Nonsense, Sharon,' Brooke said, waving the words off.

She winked at him. It took him a second to realise she'd

used the woman's name for his sake. He offered her a grateful smile.

'I am nervous,' she continued, directing her answer to Sharon. 'I just try not to show it. My team doesn't need their manager pacing about.'

'See what I mean?' Sharon said with a smile. 'This is pretty much how she is at every launch of hers.'

'This is only the third.'

'In five years. That's more than many others in your position.'

'Sharon,' Brooke said, waving a hand. A blush reddened her cheeks. 'Stop!'

'And that's another winning characteristic: humility. If she weren't so damn efficient, I'd probably fire her for it.'

Sharon smiled and left them alone.

Both he and Brooke stared after her for a moment, then Tyler turned to her. 'That's your boss?'

'Yeah.' She frowned. 'I'm pretty sure I told you that.'

'That's not the point. The point is that she clearly thinks you're amazing. You shouldn't be humble. You should be basking in her praise.'

The colour flooding Brooke's face was like a flower blooming on a spring day. Innocent, pure, beautiful. His lips were curving before he could stop them.

'What?' Brooke asked defensively. 'Why are you smiling at me like that?'

'You're cute when you're embarrassed.'

'I am not embarrassed.' But the red deepened.

He was full-out grinning now. 'Why are you embarrassed by praise?'

'I'm just doing my job, Tyler.'

'Sounds like you're doing it pretty damn well.'

'Isn't that how you're meant to work?' she demanded. 'You're not supposed to be mediocre. I know you don't believe that, so why are you making me feel bad?'

'Am I? I thought I was giving you a compliment.'

'I…well…okay.' She took a breath. 'Thank you.'

He bit his lip to keep himself from smiling again. People were looking at them, and he didn't want them to think he was deranged. He knew it was curiosity, and he'd bet anything that Brooke didn't usually bring people to her launch parties.

Besides family, he corrected, thinking about Dom. And about what Dom told him when they'd been changing.

'The fact that she wants you with her tonight means something. Don't mess that up.'

A warning and a revelation in one. And that was why he wasn't going to talk to her about anything other than the launch.

'I'm glad you asked me to come tonight,' he said softly. Because he couldn't resist it, he reached out and ran the hair falling over her shoulder between his fingers. 'I get to see you in a different light.'

'Do you…?' She stopped and looked away from him, but seconds later looked back.

Determination glinted in her eyes. Damn if that didn't make him love her more.

'Do you like what you get to see?'

'How could I not?'

She smiled, the determination eclipsed by a warmth he was sure he didn't deserve.

The moment didn't last—someone wanted her attention for something—but it stayed with him the entire night.

A night he spent watching her watching those around her.

He'd never felt more content in his life.

CHAPTER FIFTEEN

SHE COULDN'T DESCRIBE how relieved she was that everything had gone smoothly. She might have been acting cool in front of everyone—it hadn't been humility as much as a display of confidence for her team's sake—but she'd been worried. This might be her third project, but it had been the most challenging. It had required all her skill and ingenuity, and that of her team, and she'd been holding her breath pretty much the entire time.

That might have been because of Tyler, too, but she wasn't ready to think about that. As it was, she was already having a hard time with him in the car.

The drive was almost an hour long, and forty minutes had gone by with them chatting idly about the evening. Now they were quiet, which allowed her to focus on other things. Like how, despite the fact that he was wearing her brother's tux, Tyler smelled like himself. A heady, tempting smell that made her want to curl into his side and sniff him.

Sniff him? Good heavens, she was losing her mind.

'When we get back do you want to share some celebratory champagne?' she asked, turning to him and surprising herself.

He looked over, smiled a gentle smile, and said, 'I'd love to.'

How did that turn her to mush?

At least it kept her distracted until they got home.

He waited in the garden while she got the champagne and glasses, but immediately got up to help her as soon as she returned.

'To you,' he said, when he'd poured them each a glass.

'To the team who made it possible.'

'Still not able to take a compliment, huh?' he teased, but he clinked his glass against hers and took a sip.

She didn't answer, drank from her own glass, and enjoyed the way the bubbles felt over her tongue. Then she sighed and kicked off her shoes, putting her feet up on the chair in front of her.

'It's been a long eighteen months,' she said with a sigh.

'You've been working on that project for eighteen months?'

'Yeah. Some days it feels like it was for ever. Some days it feels like it was just a few weeks.' She shook her head. 'I'm glad it's over. We have to monitor for bugs and do updates, of course, but the app itself is out there and I'm relieved.' She looked over at him. 'I imagine this is how you're going to feel once you get things established in London.'

With that, the air between them changed. She hadn't meant it to, but something about the way Tyler held himself made her realise it had. She tried to think about what she'd said, but it had only been an allusion to him leaving. Why would that upset him? There had been no judgement in her tone. She'd been trying to be supportive, for heaven's sake, even though his leaving would break her heart.

Besides, they'd spoken about it before, in the car. He hadn't seemed upset about the situation when they'd been talking about Tia. Which made Brooke think that this was about *her*, which hardly seemed fair.

'I've always wanted to ask why you have such an incredible garden,' he said.

The words came out of nowhere, and Brooke had to take

time to readjust. Tension crept over her. Irrationally, she wondered if that had been his intention all along. Had he known she'd done it for Kian and wanted to give her something to be upset about?

But that wasn't possible. He didn't know about Kian. Unless she'd told him during their time together and she couldn't remember it. He'd said they'd never talked about anything personal. He hadn't known she was married. So maybe not?

'My husband was a landscape designer. We met at college and dated for a while before we got married. When we did, we were too poor to have our dream house. So he drew up this plan for our for ever home one day. I… I didn't ever tell you?' she asked, to be sure. 'About my husband, I mean? When we were…during that week?'

She saw the confusion in his eyes under the garden lights around them—one of which he'd replaced—but it quickly cleared, replaced by understanding.

'No. I didn't know you were married. I didn't know about your husband.'

'Okay.'

'You did nothing wrong,' he added softly, and the words were almost carried away with the night breeze. 'That week…it was friendship, Brooke. We were friends.'

'Except we kissed,' she scoffed. 'And we didn't talk about anything personal. How could that be "friendship"?'

He set his glass down, shifted so his elbows rested on his knees. 'We talked about important things. Things we valued. You knew I cared about my family. I knew you cared about yours, too.' He paused. 'It was clear that something had hurt you, and you were steering clear of that. So I didn't push, and you didn't push me.' He took a breath. 'I was dealing with some stuff back then, too. My nephew was just born and my mother wasn't there to see it. Neither was my father, for that matter.'

There was a lingering silence, but he continued.

'We were friends, Brooke. The kiss was a…a mistake.' He looked at her. 'When we were together it was like the world didn't exist. The world and our responsibilities. That night, it got to us. We had too much wine and the chemistry that had made us get along so well turned into something more. But it stopped before it started and we both… We both knew it was a mistake.'

Something about the way he'd said it made her wonder. 'Did we?' she asked. 'Did *we* both know that?'

He took a moment to reply, but when he did, his voice was steady. 'What do you want me to say, Brooke? That I knew it was a mistake because you pushed me away almost as soon as our lips touched? That you looked distraught and I knew that even though we were both a little tipsy we shouldn't have done it?'

She opened her mouth, but couldn't reply. Not with what she wanted to say, which was that she was relieved she'd responded that way. That she was relieved they'd been drinking and hadn't been thinking like themselves.

She didn't think she had to say it though. Tyler was studying her too intently, seeing too much. He knew her, knew versions of her that even she couldn't remember. She had no doubt he knew what she was thinking.

'If you want to know more about that time, Brooke, you only have to ask,' he offered. 'I'll tell you everything you need to know.'

'Thank you.'

She wished she didn't have to ask any of the questions she had, but they spilled over her lips anyway.

What had she told him? How had she been? Had he thought it strange they weren't talking about their lives? What had he told her? And were things different now? How?

He answered each question thoroughly, patiently. And each answer did make it seem as if they had been friends.

Until those last two questions, at which he paused. Looked at her.

'I think you know the answer to those two questions.'

'Do I?' she asked lightly.

He turned the watch at his wrist. The action was so deliberate that she shifted. Curled her feet under her. Folded her arms.

'Yes, things are different,' he answered. 'I know more about you now than I ever did then. I understand how complicated this is for you.'

'It's complicated for you, too.'

'And that's different, too. It was easy then. We only saw one another for a few hours a day. We met up, ate things we liked, then left and didn't know anything about where the other person was. I had to trust that you were safe. That you had people around you who would keep you safe.'

'And now?'

'Now…' He took a deep breath. 'Now I need to be sure you're safe. I want to be one of the people who keeps you that way.'

She stared. 'Tyler—'

'I know it's complicated,' he said over her interruption. 'I know none of this is fair, and that having this conversation is only going to complicate things even more. But you asked how things are different, and the answer is this. Back then, I was enamoured, sure. I thought you were beautiful, compassionate and smart. But I was okay with being your friend.'

She almost didn't want to ask, but she did it anyway. 'Now you're not?'

He shook his head. 'Now I'm in love with you, Brooke. Your beauty comes from how you look, of course, but it's *because* you're compassionate and you're smart. You work hard, you love hard. And you constantly want to do more.

Now I can't be your friend.' He met her eyes. 'And you don't want to be mine either.'

Her fists clutched at the material of her dress, but because her arms were folded she didn't think Tyler could see it.

In her mind, she was completely fine with him seeing her as cool and aloof, as if she were taking this information steadily and it didn't cause her heart to beat harder than it had in years. In reality, she was tense. She knew Tyler would soon look at her and see someone who was panicking.

And yet he remained steady. He looked at her with the kind of confidence he shouldn't have after declaring his love for her. Unless he was that sure she felt the same way.

'What does it matter?' she asked, not even caring that her question revealed that she did feel the same way. 'I have baggage heavier than I can carry sometimes. And you… you're leaving.'

'But you love me?'

She exhaled, impatient with the question when he already had the answer. 'Yes, Tyler. But what does it matter?'

'What do you mean, what does it matter? It *does* matter,' he insisted. 'If we feel the same way about one another, surely we can work out the rest?'

'How do we work out that I feel guilty about falling for you?' Words spilled out of her mouth now, no filter—which she would no doubt regret. 'I mean, I had been working it out until I realised that I was probably falling for you the week after my husband died. I was working out my grief by starting a "friendship" with you—' she used air quotes '—and how can I make that okay?'

He blinked. Then blinked again as he leaned back in his chair. His expression was unreadable, with none of the passion he'd been speaking with earlier shadowing his face.

'That's how you feel?' he asked.

'Isn't that what happened?' she replied, even though it didn't feel right. None of this did. 'How do I reconcile what I feel for you now with what happened back then?'

'No,' he replied woodenly, 'what you really want to know is how you can reconcile what you feel for me now with what you feel for your husband.'

'No. *No.* I'm ready to move on. Just…not with you.' She closed her eyes. 'I didn't mean it like that. I meant not with what's happened between us.'

'Okay,' he said, straightening. 'If that's what you need to believe.'

'What I need to—?' She broke off, standing now, too. 'Tyler, you're leaving. You're *leaving*.'

'So come with me.'

Her mouth fell open. She shut it quickly, afraid that her heart was beating so voraciously it would jump out given the chance.

When she was finally able to speak again, she didn't recognise her voice. 'I should come with you? Leave my family, my job—everything I've worked for in the last five years?'

'We'll figure it out.'

He seemed unaware of the desperate edge to his tone.

'And what happens when you're done in London, Tyler?' she asked. 'When you want to come back? Do I leave whatever I've built there *again*?' She shook her head before he could answer. 'I built a life around a man before and it didn't work out because of something entirely outside our control. I can't… I can't let go of the stability I've worked so hard for since then. I… I…can't.'

'Even for the sake of us?'

'Are you listening to yourself? Are you listening to *me*?'

He looked as if he were about to answer, but no words came from his mouth. Slowly, she saw him realise what he'd asked, what was happening. He took a step back, then another. Took a deep breath, then another.

'I… I'm sorry. I didn't…' His eyes met hers, the plea in them clear. 'I didn't realise…'

She didn't have anything to say to that. There was too much panic in her brain, in her body, for her to be receptive to an apology. To an explanation.

'I love you,' he said, a long time later.

'And I love you,' she replied. 'But that doesn't change anything.'

She was faintly aware that she was pushing him away. That she was closing herself down to protect herself in any way she could. But when she succeeded and he left, she didn't feel protected at all. She only felt empty.

And, standing in the garden her deceased husband had designed for them, she also felt alone.

CHAPTER SIXTEEN

'YOU'RE STILL MOPING AROUND? It's been three months since you stopped working for Brooke!' Tia said, eyeing Tyler.

Two months, two weeks, four days, to be exact.

Tyler didn't respond with that, though. Instead he glowered at her, before turning his attention to his nephew. Nyle was fascinated by the trains at King's Cross Station, his eyes going wide each time one stopped. Too fascinated to pay attention to the adults in his family.

'He's not going to help you,' Tia commented. 'He's been like this since we got on the train at the airport.'

'Has it only been a month since I left?' he asked blandly. 'I have missed you so.'

She stuck out her tongue and he smiled because, damn it, he *had* missed her. She'd called him a week after he'd finally told her about the expansion opportunity because she was ready to talk. When they had, of course she'd supported him. She'd needed some time to get her head around it, she'd said, but she wanted the best for him.

The remaining weeks he'd spent negotiating his contract with his new business partners, convincing Tia to look after June while he was gone, and then preparing to live in London.

He'd wanted that preparation to include closure with Brooke, but he hadn't known how that could happen. He'd messed up royally, and he had no idea how to fix things.

The realisation had haunted him before and after he'd left. She hadn't contacted him; he hadn't contacted her. The best thing for both of them to do was to accept things were over.

Except he hadn't been able to do that in the last five years—when he hadn't even been in love with her. It sure as hell wasn't going to be easy now that he was. Especially when he knew he had pushed her too hard, too fast. He *knew* it. He had panicked, had thought being together was better than being apart, and he hadn't realised how much it would scare her.

When he had realised, it had been too late. He'd realised he was forcing her to make a decision she didn't want to make for *his* sake. His fear had pushed him into his father's territory. He had stopped before he'd put a flag into the land and declared it his own, but he was horrified. And so was she.

So, yeah, he had no idea how to fix that.

'Are you going to keep moping, or can we get going?' asked Tia.

Tyler didn't bother answering, but he made a concerted effort to let go of his melancholy. It was his constant companion. When he was lucky he could forget it, but those moments never lasted for long. Not when he wanted to talk to Brooke about the opportunity of his lifetime. Not when he saw the vibrancy of London, noticed its moods, enjoyed its people and wanted to share it with her.

But for his sister and nephew he would try harder.

He thought he was doing well until his sister heaved a sigh during dinner and said, 'Maybe you should come back home.'

'What?'

'Come home and fix things with Brooke.' She helped Nyle with his food, the restaurant's signature pizza. 'You're clearly not going to be happy until you do, and what's the point of even being here if you're not happy?'

'I *am* happy,' he said stubbornly. 'Besides, you don't know what happened between me and Brooke.'

'I know enough.'

'How?'

'You're not together.'

It was a simple answer he had no comeback for.

'Plus, she's miserable, too, so clearly whatever happened isn't what either of you—'

'Wait—what? How do you know that?'

'Oh, didn't I tell you?' she said smugly. 'Brooke called the agency with a glowing recommendation of my work and asked if I could work for her permanently.'

He stared at her. The only thing that came to his mind was, 'I thought they only dealt with temporary jobs?'

'They do, which is why they said no. But then she called me directly, made me an offer I couldn't refuse, and now we're here.' She stole an olive off Nyle's pizza and popped it into her mouth.

'And you're only telling me this now?' he asked slowly. 'How long have you been working for her?'

'A couple of weeks.'

'Again—you're only telling me this *now*?'

'I thought it would have more impact if I told you in person.' Her eyes sparkled at him.

'There's a lot about this that bothers me...'

'And we'll get to all of it, I'm sure.'

'But the foremost question I have right now is *why*?' he continued, as if she hadn't interrupted him.

'It's a good opportunity. And it comes with insane benefits, like the fact that she's letting me bring Nyle to her house after school and will give me as many sick days as I need. Also, she's told me that June can come over to play with Mochi whenever I want. I almost asked her to look after June while we were over here, but I thought that might be too awkward. We left June with a friend.'

He closed his eyes, letting the information run through his brain. 'You've had good opportunities before,' he said slowly, and opened his eyes. 'And if I'd known you wanted something like this I would have—'

'No,' she interrupted. 'I didn't want to work for my brother. Nor for any of his rich acquaintances who see the help as being beneath them.'

'You don't even *know* Brooke!' he exclaimed. 'How do you know she's not like them?'

'Because you wouldn't have fallen in love with her if she was.'

He hadn't told her that, but of course she knew. He sighed in answer, hoping the tension would rush out of him like air from a balloon. But no. He was still curling his fingers under the table, his shoulders still felt as if there were boulders on them, and he was still actively trying not to frown, so as not to upset his nephew.

'I also would have quit if she was terrible,' Tia continued, oblivious to his turmoil—or perhaps not caring.

'And you would have lost your job with the agency in the process.'

'I would have found another. And this way, I can spy for you.'

He resisted for all of ten seconds. 'In what way?'

'I've already told you she's miserable.'

'That's it?'

'What more do you want?'

'I don't know,' he answered because he really didn't know what he wanted. It was unlikely that Brooke would tell Tia if she wanted to be with him.

Huh. Maybe he *did* know what he wanted.

'Do you want to tell me what happened?' Tia asked.

'Not really.'

He told her anyway, since she already knew everything that had happened except for the argument that last night.

To her credit, she didn't say anything. Not even when he told her about his stupid request for Brooke to come to London with him. She just listened in between eating and helping Nyle to eat, nodding in encouragement or acknowledgement every now and then.

When he was done, she said, 'I feel partially responsible.'

'Why?' he asked. 'Because you made me hope things would work out when you told me that love would conquer all?'

'I did *not* say that.'

He gave her a look.

'Okay, fine, I said something like that. But I hoped…' She heaved out a sigh. 'I think I made you think you needed to figure it out right at that minute, when really you both needed time. She probably needed more time than you.'

'Yes, I can see that now,' he said dryly.

'So why are you still here?'

'What do you mean?'

'Well, if you're still miserable, I figure you didn't tell her that. She doesn't know that you regret pushing her and that you'll give her as much space as she needs. That you'll be there when she's ready, whenever that might be. Assuming you will be, of course,' she added.

His initial answer was yes . He had spent five years waiting—what was five more? Ten more? But he knew he had to give himself time to think it through.

He gave himself until the night before Tia and Nyle were due to leave, actually. He sat up after they'd gone to bed, trying to think about what it would mean to commit to Brooke in that way.

No matter what angle he came to it from, he reached the same conclusion. He loved her. He wanted to spend his life with her. And, after what he'd said to her that night, he needed to prove that he was serious about it.

So he booked himself on the same flight back to South Africa as his family.

When Tia found him the next morning, she took one look at his face and said, 'Don't get me fired.'

'I can't promise that,' he replied, hope curving his lips into a grin.

It made him feel lighter than he had in a long time. Which turned out to be a good thing, since that feeling of weightlessness helped him duck when Tia threw a pillow at him.

Brooke didn't spend her days missing Tyler. No, sir. She spent them working. Fixing bugs or anticipating them. Helping with other projects. Since she had come out of the first phase of her project, and the second phase required time to figure out how Phase One would affect it, she had free time, too. She spent it wisely. When she got home, she put everything into training Mochi, which was bittersweet.

Every time she succeeded she would hear Tyler's voice in her head telling her she was doing a good job. Every time she failed she'd hear him saying it was because she wasn't being assertive enough. Or she would hear him tell her to keep trying, which she did. Not because he was telling her—even though it was only a mental version of him—but because she knew Mochi needed consistency. That was what the training videos she watched and the books she read said. And, to their credit, it was working.

Mochi seemed happier than he had been in months. He was thriving. He loved having a friend to play with whenever June came to visit. Which was bittersweet as well because it never failed to remind her of Tyler.

Dom had attributed Mochi's behaviour to the fact that Brooke was at home more, that dogs loved having their humans close by. He was probably right. Hell, she thought he might have been right about Mochi all along. The dog seemed quite fond of her now. And she thought that she might have been pushing Mochi away, too, thinking that he didn't like her.

Which made her wonder how much she had sabotaged things with Tyler. Clearly, if she couldn't accept love from a dog, she wouldn't be able to accept it from a human.

It took her a long time to figure out she was scared. Scared of being robbed of that love again. She made an appointment with her therapist to talk it through. It helped, even if he did tell her things she'd already known he would say.

Her biggest takeaway was the fact that it was okay that she needed time. Except it didn't *feel* okay. Not when Tyler hadn't been able to give it to her and she felt as if she'd robbed them both of something beautiful.

Over time though, she stopped blaming herself so much and started blaming him a little more. Why hadn't he realised that she needed time? That everything was happening too fast and the information about their past would make it seem even more like lightning speed? Why hadn't he thought about how losing her husband would affect her ability to be in a relationship?

Because you didn't say any of that to him.

It was an annoying realisation to have when, again, she absolutely did *not* spend time thinking about him.

Mochi started barking, giving her a reason to stop thinking about what she wasn't thinking about.

'Oh, you're hearing Tia, are you?' she asked him, though he'd already sprinted through the trees for the back door.

She could leave it open these days since Mochi spent any time she was in the garden at her side.

It was more comforting than she'd anticipated, the dog's company. As was Tia's. She only saw her new housekeeper in the mornings, and sometimes after work if she came home early. When she did, she got to see Nyle, too. And seeing Tyler's family made her feel as though he wasn't so far away even as it reminded her of his absence.

Sometimes, when she walked into the house and heard people in it, she still thought it was Tyler. And Tia and Nyle's faces held enough of Tyler's features that her heart would stall when she saw them—and then break when she realised they weren't him.

Still, she wouldn't trade it for anything. Not when they were her only connection to him.

She could hardly believe it had been three months. She had felt this emptiness echo inside her for *three months*.

And she'd believed she'd succeeded in not thinking about him. She was a fool.

With an exhalation, she walked back to the house. Her lighter workload meant she didn't have to work the same hours she had during the last project, but she did have to show her face at the office at a reasonable time.

She stopped when she saw Tyler crouched on the patio, rubbing Mochi's belly.

Until the moment he lifted his head and met her eyes, Brooke was pretty sure he was an apparition. Seeing him was just one small step away from hearing his voice, after all. But she wouldn't have been able to conjure up that little jolt of electricity she felt when their gazes locked. Or the way her stomach felt as if it were an eagle, swooping down from the sky.

No, an apparition wouldn't have had that effect.

'Hey,' he said, his voice both familiar and unfamiliar.

She wanted to record it, play it back when this was over, so she never had to feel as if it was unfamiliar again. Only she wasn't sure she wanted her skin to feel so aware at the sound of it every time.

'Hi,' she said.

'You probably want to know what I'm doing here?'

She tilted her head. 'It's definitely one of my questions,' she allowed. 'The others are: what are you doing in South Africa and how did you get into my house?'

'Tia let me in.' He straightened. 'She's aware that it's a violation, but she's trusting that I won't screw this up again and it won't matter.'

Her breath caught, but he didn't notice. Instead, he looked up at the house.

'I think she's somewhere upstairs now, trying to give us privacy while desperately wanting to know what's happening and figuring out if she still has a job.'

Brooke took a second. 'Well, I'm not thrilled she's letting people into my house, but I'll let her off with a warning. I didn't hire her so I could fire her. Even if she has given me this really good reason to.'

'I don't think she thought I was "people,"' he said, with a wry twist of his mouth.

It didn't hide the hurt in his eyes.

She wished she could be immune to it. He had hurt her, too. More than she'd thought possible. Her therapist had told her it was a good sign. That if she hurt more than she'd thought possible, she probably cared more than she'd thought possible, too.

Surprisingly, that didn't make her feel better.

'Can I ask you a question?' he asked softly.

She nodded. Braced herself for it.

'Why did you hire her?'

It was so completely unexpected that she actually answered him. 'She needed a stable job with someone who wasn't going to punish her for trying to be a good mother. Someone who could give her the support she needs financially. Someone other than you, I mean.'

Little lines wove themselves into the skin between his

eyebrows. 'You… You did this for her stability? For my nephew's?'

And maybe because she reminds me of you.

But she only shrugged. 'I did it because we can all use flexible employers. Employers who are understanding of family responsibility. I didn't have that when Kian died, so I thought I'd pay it forward.'

'You didn't have to,' he said slowly.

'I know.'

There was a pause. 'I think you did it for me.'

'I…did…*not*.' It was half-scoff, half-splutter. 'I *did* it,' she emphasised, 'because I knew she could use the help and she wouldn't accept it from you.'

'Yeah, but there are plenty of people out there who could use that kind of help.' He stuffed his hands into his pockets, his eyes intent on hers. 'And there are plenty of people out there who could help her. She *had* a job.'

'Not a very good one.'

'You wanted me to have peace of mind while I was gone,' he continued, ignoring her.

'You're giving yourself too much credit.'

'She didn't tell me until I saw her this past week, you know.'

'What?' she asked. 'Why? I thought she would—' She broke off when she saw his smirk. 'No!' she said again, even though it was kind of pointless.

'I can't tell you how much it means to me,' he said, serious now.

She shook her head. 'Not everything I do is because of you, Tyler.'

'No,' he agreed. 'But some of what you do is because of me. I know that because some of what I do is because of you.' He paused. 'Like taking leave less than a month into my new job so I can tell you in person that I'm sorry.'

She didn't want to hope. Refused to on principle. He had hurt her.

But she had hurt him, too. She could see it in his eyes, in the way he carried himself.

So she stayed where she was, rooted to the spot by a responsibility she didn't feel to anyone but her family.

'I'm sorry, Brooke.' He took a step forward. 'That night… I asked for something I had no right to ask for. I panicked. I thought that if I asked you to go with me, I wouldn't be leaving you behind. Like my dad.' He shifted. 'It wasn't until you told me to listen to you that I realised… Well, I saw I was being like my dad anyway. Forcing you to accept a decision I'd made without considering your perspective.'

She hadn't even thought about why he'd asked her to go with him. She'd been so fixated on the fact that he had. Now, she felt guilty. Because it was so obvious that his reaction had come from fear, too. He loved her, and he didn't want to treat her the way his father had treated the family he'd claimed to love, too.

'Seems I didn't consider your perspective either,' she said softly.

'Because I was pushing you. You barely had your feet steady beneath you after everything I told you about our past. With our feelings for one another.'

'So you *have* thought about my perspective. And I… I've only realised yours now.'

'I might have thought about it, but I almost let my fears ruin…' He trailed off and took a deep breath. 'When I spoke with you that night, I was scared of being like my father. When I realised that, I was scared that I'd already ruined us. That's why I didn't contact you after that night. I thought… I thought you'd hate me.'

'I don't hate you,' she said quickly. 'I could never hate you.'

'But I shouldn't have let my fears keep me from telling you that I was an idiot.'

'No,' she agreed. 'But it gave me time to… I've figured some things out while you've been gone. I clearly still am figuring things out if what you're telling me is still able to surprise me.' She paused. 'I was scared, too. It felt like too much in such a short time because of…because of all the things you've already said.'

'I'll wait,' he said quietly. 'That's what I should have said before. My being in London doesn't have to mean the end of us. It will give me an opportunity to figure out what I want to do. It will give you the space you need to come to terms with us.'

He was desperate. She could see it in his eyes. Hear it in his tone. And she thought it was cute.

'I'll wait until you're ready,' he went on. 'Even if that means waiting after I get back from London, too.'

She pursed her lips. 'I wasn't done. How do you know I want you to wait if you don't know what I was going to say?'

He glanced down at Mochi, as if the dog had the answer. 'Please,' he said, clearing his throat. 'Continue.'

Her lips twitched. 'I was going to say that I might have made *you* feel like there was no waiting time, too. There was only then, in that exact moment. I wasn't ready to accept what was happening then, so what choice did you have?'

'You're giving me an out.'

'No,' she said honestly. 'I'm claiming my responsibility in this. I was panicking. I thought about moving away from everything I've built here and I panicked.'

'I shouldn't have—'

'Tyler,' she said sharply. 'Let me tell you that I'm sorry, too. And don't you dare tell me I have nothing to be sorry for,' she added, when he opened his mouth. 'If I'd told you that I love you, but I needed time to figure out how I could love you in light of…of everything, you would have given me that time, I'm sure.'

'I walked away.'

'And I let you.'

He frowned. 'You're making it very hard for me to grovel.'

'I don't want you to grovel. I want you to tell me that you understand. That you know if we move forward things won't always go smoothly. I want you to promise that when we make mistakes you won't punish yourself so much that you don't talk to me. And that you won't let your fears get in the way of whatever this can be.'

She paused to catch her breath, then went on because she was afraid she wouldn't be able to continue if she stopped.

'Tell me all that, promise me all that, so I can promise you I won't do any of that either. I won't use our mistakes to push you away, nor will I do it because of the intensity of what we feel for one another. I'll keep going to therapy so I can be as mentally healthy as I can be. And if you'd like to do that, too, we can even go together.'

His mouth split into a grin, but he stayed where he was. 'You go to therapy?'

She gave him a look. 'I'm a widow, Tyler. For me, going to therapy is basically like going to the spa.'

'Your sense of humour can be really morbid at times, you know that?'

She laughed. 'I'm a widow. What do you expect?'

'I promise,' he said, the soft smile on his face not dampening his sincerity at all. 'I promise every single thing you said, plus some promises of my own. I won't rush you. And we'll talk—really talk—about what we both need, even if it's hard.'

She stepped closer, clutching at his shirt with her fingers. Oh, he smelled good. And being in his space felt good. Like his proximity, his promises filled the emptiness that had been inside her since he had left that night three months ago.

'I'd like that,' she said.

His arms circled her waist. 'We can go slow.'

'We'll have to,' she said, abandoning his shirt to put her arms around his neck. 'You still have an opportunity to take advantage of in London.'

Concern flickered in his eyes. 'Are you okay with that?'

'I was the one who urged you to pursue it, wasn't I?'

'That was before.'

'Before what?'

He narrowed his eyes. Sank his fingers into her flesh. 'Before this.'

'Yeah, well, I'm coming up on some well-deserved leave, so I could probably join you in London for a while. And after that... We'll figure it out.' She rose onto her toes, bringing their lips to the same level. 'We don't have to have all the answers right now.'

His eyes softened, one of his hands leaving her waist to cup her face. 'No, we don't. Because we love one another and we'll figure it out.'

'We will,' she affirmed softly. 'Although I do have one thing we need to figure out *right now*. Do you know what it is?'

'A kiss. You want me to kiss you.'

'So stop talking and do it already.'

And he did.

* * * * *

MILLS & BOON

Coming next month

SECOND CHANCE TO WEAR HIS RING
Hana Sheik

She laughed lightly then, her eyes sparkling, the hint of gloominess from earlier gone. He wished he didn't have to ruin the peaceful moment. But time was pressing, and they couldn't stand around reminiscing all day. Soon she'd want to return to her office, and he still had his piece to say.

"Amal, what was your doctor's prognosis for the amnesia?" he asked. Saying her name was tripping him up. It sounded too familiar on his tongue. Like coming home. But he was undeserving of the happy relief that welled up in him.

As for this amnesia business—he couldn't shake the absurdity of it.

Her memory loss was perfect for him, and yet terribly painful, too. Perfect in that it saved him from explanations and reliving heartbreak, and painful because he was going through it alone.

She had no recollection of their long-distance conversations about building a future together, let alone his marriage proposal and her hasty rejection.

In her mind, it seemed their long-distance romance had never existed. While he recalled—and replayed, clip by clip—how their friendship had blossomed into…more. Something he'd had no name for until she herself had shyly confessed to liking him romantically.

No, she said she loved me.

And he had asked for time to process it.

Process it he had—and that was when he'd come to her, closing the seven-thousand-mile gap between them with a diamond in one hand and his heart in the other. He'd planned to offer her both—and he had. But she had shocked him with her refusal.

How could she not remember?

Did it matter, though? He knew it didn't alter the situation they were in now, standing and facing off like strangers. He'd do better to focus his energy on what he could change. Like having her consider the options of medical treatment elsewhere.

"The doctor said I could regain my full memory."

She folded her arms over her chest.

"There's also a possibility that I could stay like this forever. The timeline for my recovery is uncertain," she said softly, defeat beating at her words.

"And yet you could seek better medical care and technology elsewhere," he said.

She snapped her bemused gaze to him.

"I know you heard my mother and I speaking," he said.

Amal opened her mouth, closed it, and frowned. Smart of her. No point in wasting time and breath arguing about her eavesdropping. Actually, right then he appreciated it. It saved him from explaining what he'd already told his mother. That he had business in Ethiopia.

"Why not join me? You could visit with a doctor in Addis Ababa, and we could try for a second opinion."

Continue reading

SECOND CHANCE TO WEAR HIS RING

Hana Sheik

Available next month

www.millsandboon.co.uk